To my family and friends

Chapter One

The Lock and Key of England

Summer 1864

'Make haste or we'll miss the event of the year,' Violet called as she tied the ribbons of her bonnet and checked her appearance in the mirror in the hall. She was pleased with what she saw: a slim figure; white-blonde hair scraped back into plaited loops at the nape of her neck; striking blue eyes; well-defined cheekbones and full lips. The only feature she would change if she could was her nose, which she felt was a little too large for her face.

'Oh, do stop admiring yourself,' Eleanor teased as she hurried down the stairs. 'You're so vain.'

'I'm not,' Violet said, feeling hurt. 'I like to look my best, that's all, little sister.' She put the emphasis on 'little', Eleanor being a head shorter than she was. 'What do you know about anything? You're only fifteen.'

'Stop sparring, you two.' Ottilie joined her sisters from the parlour. 'You know how it upsets Mama to see you at each other's throats.'

Violet backed down – she looked up to Ottilie in more ways than one, being a few inches shorter than her. Her elder sister was twenty to her eighteen, her hair was blonde, but darker like honey, and she wished she could be more like her: self-controlled and content with her lot.

'Where is Mama?' Violet picked up her parasol from the hallstand.

'I'm on my way,' she heard her mother say. 'You are overwrought. Perhaps you should remain at home with Eleanor later this evening.'

'And not go to the ball? Oh, Mama!' Violet turned to her mother who was standing on the bottom step of the staircase with a shawl around her slender shoulders and a fashionable straw hat over her silver hair.

'How can I present you to Dover society when you can't go about with the decorum that befits a young lady of your age? You're eighteen.'

'I'm sorry,' Violet said, feeling contrite; she had promised to behave herself.

'Are we all ready?'

'Yes, Mama,' the three sisters said in unison, and they stepped outside into the bright June sunshine.

'I wish you a good day, ladies,' Wilson said, holding the door open. Their butler was an older gentleman in his fifties who had been with the Rayfields for as long as Violet could remember. He was well spoken and always smartly dressed, with his hair oiled and fingernails kept blunt and clean.

Violet glanced up at the house as he closed the door behind them. It was one of ten four-storey yellow brick houses that ran in a terrace between New Bridge and Wellesley Road – everyone who called on them acknowledged that their home in Camden Crescent was one of the best addresses in Dover.

Having put up their parasols, they began to walk in the direction of the seafront, skirting the lawns where a military band was playing next to a crowded marquee. They passed the war memorial dedicated to the soldiers of the 60th Rifles who were lost in the Indian Rebellion, then

crossed the road to reach the sweeping curve of the promenade.

Violet couldn't believe her eyes.

Their town had been invaded by hundreds – no, thousands – of people from all over the kingdom who were
cheering and waving flags as they looked out at the yachts
in Dover Bay. There were other vessels too: skiffs; herring
boats; galleys and pleasure boats.

She hastened on ahead of her mother and sisters, but
Mama soon called her back.

'Violet, what have I said?'

'That I should behave with decorum,' she sighed, but
she didn't think her mother had heard her above the calls
of the street sellers at their stalls, offering bags of shrimp,
pots of winkles, confectionery and ginger beer.

'Buy, buy, buy!'

'Boo'iful whelks – a penny a lot. You'll never taste
better!'

'Strawberries ripe! The best you can find in all of
Kent!'

The Rayfield ladies wended their way through the
crowds, using their parasols to fend off those who were
in their cups, until they reached the shingle and emerged
on to the beach between the rows of sea bathing machines
and herring boats.

Tasting salt on her lips and with the scent of tar, fish
and seaweed in her nostrils, Violet looked towards the sea
where the rowing boat crews – four-oared galleys – were
preparing for their race. The marshals were lining several
boats up at the start, but they were having trouble with
them drifting on the current. As soon as one was deemed
ready, another had to be called back, and it took some
minutes before all the coxes put their hands down, indi-
cating that they were ready.

'That's Mr Noble.' Eleanor pointed towards one of the galleys which had the name 'Mary Ann' painted along her side. 'He rows for Dover Rowing Club.'

'Eleanor, what have I told you about it being rude to point?' Mama said. 'Yes, that's him with the dark hair, I believe, and his cousin is number two.'

Violet couldn't see his face at first, just the black curls tumbling from beneath his cap, and the width of his shoulders as he rested his oar flat on the surface of the water. He was facing the cox, with the rest of the crew dressed in royal blue and white flannel shirts behind him. As if he'd become aware of her watching him, he looked straight at her and smiled, making her heart skip a beat. She had never seen anyone quite so handsome and self-assured.

'Then we must cheer them on,' Eleanor went on, nudging Violet's arm to draw her attention back to their conversation.

'But we have never been introduced,' Ottilie countered.

'They were at the launch of the *Dover Belle* – Uncle Edward shook his hand,' Eleanor said. 'Mr Noble is the son of the master of Pa's ship.'

'The *Dover Belle* belongs to our father and Uncle Edward,' Ottilie said, correcting her. Violet smiled – it wasn't that Ottilie liked to be right. She had to be right. 'William's elder brother is junior engineer.'

'The Nobles are a sea-faring family,' Mama said. 'Your father has known Captain Noble for many years.'

Mr Rayfield had started out as a shipping agent before investing in the railway and buying the *Dover Belle* with Mr Chittenden – whom they called uncle, although he wasn't related to them by blood.

'Come forward,' the *Mary Ann*'s coxswain called out.

There was a bang, making Violet almost jump out of her skin.

'Fraidy cat,' Eleanor laughed. 'It's only the starter.'

As the crews took their first strokes, sending the galleys through the water, Violet spotted the smoking mouth of a miniature cannon which was perched on the pier, and felt rather foolish.

The galleys made progress towards the buoy at Castle jetty, the coxes' heads jerking with every stroke. The *Mary Ann* was in the lead until one of her crew caught a crab in the choppier waves further out.

'Long and strong!'

'Quick through the water!'

The coxes yelled orders and encouragement, and the *Mary Ann* rounded the buoy, gradually catching up then edging ahead and taking up the lead once more.

'Keep the fire!'

'They're winning!' Violet stood on tiptoes for a better view, willing the *Mary Ann* on as the boats set out on a second circuit. Returning towards the finish, the sound of the oars clunking in the rowlocks and the splash at the catch grew louder. The cheering grew louder too as the *Mary Ann* crossed the finish line, winning by half a length.

'They've only gorn and done it,' somebody said from beside her. 'Them Dover boys 'ave taken that race for the second year in a row. There'll be some sore 'eads tomorrer.'

'I 'ope the new Lord Warden's impressed with what 'e's seen so far,' another said.

'Well, I reckon this is the best regatta ever, and Lord Palmerston should be delighted with the show we've put on for 'im. What's next anyway? Ah, the tub race. There, I've answered me own question.'

Violet noticed how Mama looked askance at their neighbours. She wondered what she thought of Mr Noble who was wading towards the beach, holding his arms up and grinning in triumph as the crowd greeted him and the crew – our boys, even though they were all over twenty-one – like heroes.

Was it possible that Pa could be persuaded to introduce Mr Noble to her so she could dance with him at the ball?

The Rayfields stayed on to watch the novelty race where men crewed tin bathtubs, willow coracles and rafts made from logs and leather bags. The winner was the only craft to make it to the finish line, the rest undoubtedly capsizing, taking on water or spinning in circles.

When the splashing, shrieks and laughter had died down, Mama suggested that they return home.

'So soon?' Eleanor said, sounding disappointed.

'It's the fashion to arrive late for a ball, but not so late that it is over by the time one gets there. We're booked to dine at nine with the Chittendens and Mr Brooke.'

'We're going to meet the mysterious Mr Brooke at last,' Violet said.

'There's nothing mysterious about him,' Mama said. 'He's a new acquaintance of your father's, a gentleman with whom he wishes to do business.'

'Will we have to dance with him?' Ottilie asked.

'If he marks your card, then yes, you will dance with him – with good grace.'

'He's more than likely to be married,' Violet said. 'He'll bring his wife.'

'If he doesn't, there's something wrong with him,' Eleanor said. 'He will have pimples or a squint, or both. You know, I don't think I could marry someone who looked in two directions at the same time.'

'This is all speculation. All I know is that Mr Brooke is over thirty, unmarried and a gentleman of substance,' Mama said. 'Come along now.'

They turned and walked back up the beach in the direction of the town which sat in the valley of the River Dour,

6

between the towering chalk cliffs. The fortifications of the Western Heights stood to the west, and Dover Castle to the east.

Pa said that Dover was a place where anyone with a little capital and an ounce of common sense could make their fortune, what with the two railway companies competing to install tracks and tunnels and build new stations, and the extension of Admiralty Pier. Violet assumed that Mr Brooke was hobnobbing with her father, in the hope of being introduced to the men of influence among Dover society.

Having arrived home, Violet retired to the parlour to add the final touches to the train of her gown: a layer of muslin over ivory silk. The butterflies she had embroidered in the latest ombre threads seemed to flutter up from the flowers in a cloud of colour, as she stood up and laid the gown across the back of the chaise.

'It's beautiful,' Eleanor said from behind her. 'All the gentlemen will fall in love with you.'

'Don't be silly. You must wish you were coming with us.'

Eleanor shook her head. 'I'm quite happy to stay at home and read until Mama decides I'm old enough to come out. I'm not interested in dancing and the company of gentlemen.'

'According to Mama, everyone who is anyone in Dover will be there.'

'Which is an even better reason for not going. There'll be the old families, the county set who look down on the Rayfields because our father is a self-made man.'

'That isn't true,' Ottilie said, joining the conversation. 'Pa is a gentleman of good standing. He's almost one of them.'

'I don't expect to meet my future husband at my very first ball. You didn't, did you, Ottilie? Or perhaps you did,' Violet said, noticing how her sister blushed.

'You don't have to marry straight away – you can have intrigues and love affairs,' Ottilie said quickly – rather too quickly, Violet thought with a smile.

'You'll have to settle for a husband one day,' Eleanor insisted. 'Who will he be? Tinker, tailor, soldier, sailor, rich man, poor man, beggar man, thief?'

'Or a shipping agent who organises the passage of cargo from every corner of the Empire, or a baronet or a prince.' Violet giggled. 'Where are you going, Eleanor?'

'Off to the kitchen to fetch cherries, so we can count the stones to foretell your future.'

'Don't bring them anywhere near my dress,' Violet warned. 'The juice will ruin it.'

'All right then – another time,' Eleanor sighed. 'I wish I could write each of you the perfect husband.'

'He mustn't feature in one of your wilder stories,' Ottilie said sternly. 'He must be kind, reliable and handsome.'

'And rich,' Violet contributed.

'To that end, you must dance well to impress,' Eleanor said. 'You can remember the figures of the Lancers Quadrille?'

'I don't think I can,' Violet said, panicking. 'What if I find myself glued to the spot? What if my mind goes blank?'

'Just follow your partner and listen to the master of ceremonies prompting the dancers,' Ottilie said. 'Forward and back, forward again and turn.'

Eleanor offered Violet both hands and they turned a full circle, then another, until they were giddy with laughter.

'You see? It's coming back to you!' Eleanor exclaimed, throwing herself down on one of the overstuffed armchairs to catch her breath while Violet retrieved her gown. She picked off a stray gold thread which had come from one of the tassels on the velvet drapes. When Pa had bought the house about twenty years ago, Mama had furnished the parlour in the French style, but the red, green and gold patterned carpet was fading and some of the buttons on the chairs had fallen off.

'Let's go upstairs and I'll help you finish getting ready,' Eleanor said, getting up again as the gilt and enamel clock on the mantelpiece chimed six.

Holding her gown very carefully, Violet followed her sisters up the two flights of stairs to the bedroom she shared with Ottilie. Eleanor laced her corset up tightly then helped her into her gown and began fastening the hooks and eyes at the back.

'You'll have to breathe in,' she said.

'I am!' Violet gasped.

'Try harder. Oh, I've done it.'

Violet didn't mind that her dress was too tight; according to the magazines Mama read, close-fitting bodices were quite the rage.

'I don't know how you'll be able to dance like that,' Eleanor said. 'You'll fall into a faint by the end of the first set, you mark my words.'

'There will be plenty of gentlemen willing to catch her,' Ottilie said with an air of superiority. She bit her lips to bring colour to them, and Violet did the same. Ottilie borrowed Mama's sapphire pendant to match her pale blue tulle and silk dress, while Violet wore her grandmother's string of sea pearls.

They were ready, and she could hardly wait for the cab – a brougham with an extra pair of foldaway seats – to turn up and whisk them off to their destination.

Dusk was creeping in when they arrived outside the venue in Snargate Street which was chock-a-block with carriages: cabriolets, britzkas and even a clarence. Pa, who was wearing his black dress coat and trousers, waistcoat and patent leather boots, helped Ottilie and Mama down from the cab.

'You look beautiful, my dear daughter,' he said, his eyes filling with pride as he offered Violet his arm.

'And you look very smart,' she said, reserving judgement on his mutton chop side whiskers and moustache, the style he'd adopted from Prince Albert.

He steered her around a steaming pile of horse manure that the street-sweeper hadn't yet had a chance to clear up, and returned to his wife's side.

Ottilie took Violet's hand, and they stepped through the double doors of the theatre into a grand hall lit up by chandeliers, their cut-glass teardrops seeming to drip with opulence.

'Are you wearing the devil's trickery on your faces?' Mama said, catching up with them. 'Violet, you have freckles – what have I said about wearing your bonnets when out in the sun?'

'We never leave the house without them,' Violet said, giving her sister a warning glance on their way to the ladies' dressing room. It was the truth – they just didn't always have them on their heads.

Pa was waiting for them in the reception area.

'How long does it take you ladies to get ready?' he chuckled. 'I have your ball cards and look, both of you have your cards marked for the first three dances.'

Violet's heart leapt. Someone had requested her company, but who was it?

Pa handed her her card. The first dance was taken by Mr Brooke, and she was to dance the second quadrille with Mr John Chittenden, and the third with Uncle Edward. She didn't like the idea of dancing with Uncle Edward – he was old and married, and occasionally over-affectionate in his attentions towards her.

'There are other young men eager to dance,' Pa said as Mr Noble entered the room and acknowledged Mr Rayfield with a nod of his head. His cousin followed behind him.

'Gentlemen, congratulations on your success – your winning the challenge cup is the talk of the town. Allow me to introduce you to my daughters, Miss Rayfield and Miss Violet Rayfield.' He turned to them. 'Mr Noble is the son of the master of the *Dover Belle* and is apprenticed at the Packet Yard, while Mr Lane is in the building trade,' Pa went on, making it clear that Violet and Ottilie were not to consider them as potential suitors.

The young men bowed and Mr Noble flushed as he caught Violet's eye, but to her disappointment, they didn't have a chance to mark their cards because Pa quickly dismissed them, having caught sight of the friends they were meeting for dinner. 'Ah, here they are.' He nodded towards a bust of the Iron Duke, alongside which stood the Chittendens, including Uncle Edward with his dangling side whiskers, salt and pepper beard and drooping moustache that might have looked well on a young dandy, but made a man of his mature years look like a bearer at a funeral. 'Come with me, ladies.'

Mama took Pa's arm, and Violet took Ottilie's and they walked across to greet Mr and Mrs Chittenden, and their son John, a handsome, yet reserved young man a couple of years older than Ottilie.

'What a wonderful evening this is turning out to be. It's your first ever ball, Violet, is it not?' Uncle Edward said.

'Yes, and it's a pleasure to be here,' Violet said stiffly.

'I told your father that you wouldn't want to dance with me, but he insisted that I mark your card even before he'd introduced us.'

11

'Well, we don't want any wallflowers,' Pa said affably.

'Mr Rayfield!' A man – not a gentleman, Violet surmised – pushed into their circle. 'I am looking forward to joining you and the rest of your party for dinner.'

Violet noticed how Mama rolled her eyes in Mrs Chittenden's direction and how Mrs Chittenden smiled ruefully. She was about the same age as Mrs Rayfield, but she cut a far less elegant figure in a deep blue dress with gold stripes which made her look shorter than she really was.

'This is Mr Brooke,' Pa said, shaking his hand. 'Allow me to introduce you to our party. Mr and Mrs Chittenden and their son, John.'

Mr Brooke offered a bow.

'Good evening, sir,' John said. He looked sophisticated in an immaculate black dancing coat and trousers cut from the finest cloth, but Violet couldn't help remembering him as a naughty, smelly little boy who picked up slugs and snails from the park.

Pa turned towards his daughters. 'These are the Misses Rayfield.'

'How marvellously … marvellous it is to meet you,' Mr Brooke said, inclining his head and bowing again.

'This is Miss Rayfield – she is the eldest. Then there's Miss Violet Rayfield,' Pa went on proudly.

Violet exchanged greetings with Mr Brooke, a little disappointed by his age and appearance. He was a short, rather rotund person with a well-trimmed beard and sandy hair falling in waves to his shoulders. A signet ring gleamed from one finger of his left hand.

'Mrs Rayfield, I presume.' He took Mama's hand briefly before releasing it. 'I have heard so much about you from your husband. He is indeed a lucky man.'

'Well, thank you, Mr Brooke,' Mama said.

'It's Arvin. My mother was French – she gave me her father's name.' He smiled disarmingly before turning to address Uncle Edward. 'This is a meeting of great significance to me, as I've heard Mr Rayfield tell that you are one of the most influential men in Dover.'

'You flatter me, sir,' Uncle Edward said sternly, but the ebullient Mr Brooke was not to be suppressed.

'It is an honour to become a friend of Mr Chittenden. By all accounts, you have a great talent for spotting opportunities for investment in the railways and shipping.'

'I hope that Mr Rayfield hasn't been giving away all our secrets,' Uncle Edward said with a hollow laugh.

He seemed ill at ease, Violet observed.

'A man is best described by his occupation. It reveals much about his character. For example, a physician with his knowledge of the art and science of medicine will be of sound mind and robust health, while an engineer will be precise and attend to detail, a man on whom one can rely.'

'I don't believe in your theory,' Uncle Edward said. 'I have met medical men who care more for their fee than their patients, and engineers who produce the shoddiest machinery.'

'There are exceptions to every rule, but this one can be applied in a general way. Let's take Sidney – I mean, Mr Rayfield – as an example.' Mr Brooke touched Pa's shoulder. 'He has had success in many areas – now that could signify that he is capricious, buzzing from one flower to another like a bumblebee, finding success by chance not design, but that isn't right. He is a man of great curiosity, passion and intelligence.'

'What do you think of that analysis, Edward?' Pa beamed at Mr Brooke's compliment while Violet fidgeted, wishing they would stop talking and the dancing would begin.

'I am bound to admit the accuracy of Mr Brooke's judgement of your character in this particular case,' Uncle Edward concluded. 'I've heard that you're in the wine trade.' He emphasised the word 'trade'. 'What does that say about you?'

'That is for my friends to judge,' Mr Brooke said with a deep bow. Violet wondered if his obsequiousness was real or mocking. He was committing a terrible faux pas that he seemed completely unaware of, dressed in a red velvet jacket more suitable for the stage or – God forbid – the circus, than a ball.

'I hear music,' Violet whispered to Ottilie as the band struck up in the next room.

Mr Brooke bowed deeply for a third time.

'Miss Violet, I believe we are partners for the first dance.' He offered her his arm, and taking a deep breath, she took it, glancing at him surreptitiously as he escorted her to the ballroom. He was at least thirty if not older, and not in the slightest bit handsome. The ladies were staring at him, hiding their amusement and ridicule behind their fans.

As the master of ceremonies put the couples into fours, Violet caught sight of Mr Noble with his dark curls pushed back behind his ears. He was standing with his cousin in the crowd, watching her.

How she wished she was dancing with him, not Mr Brooke, she thought, a rush of heat flooding her cheeks when he smiled, not out of sympathy or with the intent of mocking her for her current misfortune, but in a kindly – possibly even admiring – way. Perhaps he would ask her later now that they had been introduced.

'It has been said that I have two left feet, but one cannot be good at everything,' her partner said.

'I believe that's true,' Violet said, suddenly unsure of herself.

As well as wearing clothes that made him look out of place, Mr Brooke danced the quadrille in a ridiculous manner, not gliding smoothly across the floor, but bouncing along on the balls of his feet. She kept her eyes averted and prayed that the dance would soon be over. At least, she didn't make a mistake – it was her partner who was in error, stepping forwards when he should be stepping back, and turning to the right when he should have been turning to the left.

'Oh, my sincere apologies,' and 'Oh la la,' he kept saying, swaying his body and keeping his arms out straight and stiff.

Her first dance was certainly memorable even if it was for all the wrong reasons. As the music came to an end, Mr Brooke held her gloved hand high in the air, and Violet found she was stuck to the floor.

'Mr Brooke,' she said, trying to be discreet. 'You are standing on my dress.'

'I'm what?' They both looked down as they heard something tear. Violet could have cried as she saw the embroidered butterflies on her train ripped and dirty.

'Oh, Miss Rayfield, I beg your pardon. What can I do? There must be something I can do,' he implored. '*Je suis desolé.*'

'It's no matter,' she said, trying not to cry. 'I'll go and see if one of the maids can repair it.'

'I'll come with you to pay for any services rendered – it's the least I can do,' he said, propelling her across the floor and off to the dressing room where he left her to seek assistance.

'This kind of thing happens all the time, miss,' the maid said through a mouthful of pins as she knelt to make a temporary repair. 'It's such a shame, though – I've never seen such delicate embroidery.'

'There is a man outside, trying to look in,' one of the other ladies exclaimed.

'The Frenchman in the red coat?' said another. 'Is he supposed to be here? He isn't dressed for dancing.'

'He's an acquaintance of the Rayfields,' somebody else said.

'Then Mr Rayfield should have a word with him – he has no idea how to act.'

'They must do things differently in France.'

Violet kept her head bowed.

'There! You can hardly see it now.' The maid struggled to her feet. 'I've put a couple of stitches in to hold it together.'

'May I take your name, so I can make sure you receive payment?' Violet enquired.

'It's Miss Devlin, but there's no obligation – the committee are paying me royally to be here tonight.'

'Thank you. I'm most grateful.' On leaving the dressing room, Violet discovered that she'd missed the next two dances and it was time for dinner. The Rayfields took their places at their table and Violet found herself sitting between Uncle Edward and Mr Brooke, and opposite Ottilie, John and Mama.

'Where have you been?' her mother asked.

'I'll explain later,' she said at the same time as Mr Brooke interrupted, 'I put my great big hoof on Miss Violet's dress while dancing.'

'All is well, though,' Violet said quickly, forgiving him for his clumsy mistake.

'You stood me up,' Uncle Edward smiled. 'Never mind. There'll be more dancing later.' And then he turned away to talk to Mama, leaving Violet wondering what on earth she and Mr Brooke could possibly have in common.

'It was an honour to dance with you,' he said.

'How do you find Dover?' she said, unsure how to respond.

'Ah, I'm growing rather fond of the town which people like to call the lock and key of England. Although the castle and forts are rather forbidding, the inhabitants are utterly charming.'

'Will you be staying long?' Violet sipped punch from a crystal glass.

'I hope to remain here for quite some time. The climate isn't as agreeable as that of the South of France and the food is poor, but England is a land of opportunity. That is the case, is it not, Mr Chittenden?'

'What were you saying, Mr Brooke?' Uncle Edward said, looking irritated at having his conversation with Mama interrupted.

'How England is a land of opportunity if you know where to look for it. French wines are more affordable here, thanks to the free trade treaty between our countries and Gladstone's decision to reduce import duties, and now, with the Single Bottle Act, grocers can sell wine for drinking at home.'

'I disagree with those who suggest that increasing the availability of wine will reduce drunkenness,' Uncle Edward said. 'It's dressing up what is a licence to print money for those who are involved in the wine trade as a move towards temperance.'

'You are cynical.' Mr Brooke placed his hand over his glass as one of the waiters offered to pour him some of the claret which Pa had ordered for the occasion.

'Do try it,' Pa said, noticing his reaction. 'I'd value your opinion.'

'No, thank you. I never drink.'

'But you say you are a wine merchant? This is intriguing.' Uncle Edward raised his eyes in astonishment.

'You promote the sale of wine, yet you do not partake. You can't possibly be a prohibitionist. The promotion of abstinence would send you straight down the road to bankruptcy.'

'I believe it is everyone's duty to encourage temperance and civilised behaviour,' John ventured to say.

'While I believe quite the opposite,' Mr Brooke said. 'Let all gentlemen – and ladies too – be merry, but then I would say that because I'm completely immersed in the industry. I've made it my business to become an expert in everything, from the cultivation of the best strains of grape, to the harvesting, fermentation, ageing and bottling. Wine has been my life, my raison d'être for many years.'

'Many years, sir? You make it sound as though you've been in wine for decades, when I would guess that you aren't much over thirty. Though you are certainly older than my son here, who cannot yet raise a full moustache,' Uncle Edward said. 'I'm afraid he won't attract the ladies with that scanty herbage.'

'Mr Chittenden, don't tease him,' his wife said. 'What were you about to say, Mr Brooke?'

'Only that I am over thirty and have devoted my entire adult life to the wine trade.'

'But how can you possibly judge the quality of the wines without imbibing?' Uncle Edward asked.

'I taste and spit,' Mr Brooke said.

Violet heard Ma's tiny gasp of shock and saw Mrs Chittenden wrinkle her delicate nose in disgust.

'One of the tools of my trade is a silver spittoon.'

'Not in front of the ladies,' Pa said in warning.

'I apologise for causing offence – you will find me a straight-talking man,' Mr Brooke said, looking round the table. Violet gazed towards Ottilie to gauge her reaction, but she was making sheep's eyes at John.

Feeling light-headed from the punch, Violet was relieved when the waiters served a light supper of potatoes with ham, tongue and pre-cut chicken that was held together on the plates by ribbons. She ate quietly, listening to the rest of the party making conversation about the weather and mutual friends before returning to their inquisition of Mr Brooke. By the time they had been served trifle and blancmange for dessert, they had ventured on to more personal topics than comparing Paris with London, and the sorry state of the port at Calais compared with that of Dover.

'You are not married, Mr Brooke?' Mama asked.

'Not yet,' he said smoothly, 'but I should like to settle down. As for family, my parents are long dead, God rest their souls. My father traded in wool, and my dear mother –whom I adored for her sense of joy and delight in everything – was a French noblewoman born in the Languedoc. I have but one sister.'

'We should like to meet her one day. She must come to visit us.'

'She is ill, I'm afraid, confined to the chateau with a disfiguring skin condition.'

It was a plot worthy of one of Eleanor's sensationalist novels, Violet thought, feeling sorry for his sister's affliction.

'What do the doctors say?' Mrs Chittenden joined in.

'Alas, it's incurable. I've employed the services of the renowned surgeons and physicians of Paris to no avail.'

'She is not married either then?' Mama said.

'There is no hope of that. Poor Claudette. Her appearance is quite ... repulsive to those who do not know her.'

'What is the chateau like?' Mama asked, moving on to safer ground.

'It's like a palace with many well-appointed rooms, four grey stone towers, and a lake. Behind it are the vineyards – rows of vines as far as the eye can see.'

'I think I'd find a chateau rather draughty,' Mrs Chittenden said.

'It has all the usual domestic conveniences – it isn't a hovel.'

'Oh, I'm sorry. I didn't mean to suggest—'

'I know you didn't, Mrs Chittenden,' he said.

'I think we've finished here.' Pa drained his second glass of claret. 'I have a fancy for a cigar while those who wish to dance do so.'

Violet stood up and walked back to the ballroom with Ottilie, where they sat down with Mama and Mrs Chittenden.

She wondered where all the gentlemen were, but then John made his way over to them.

'Good evening, Miss Violet,' he said. 'May I have the next dance?'

She smiled, grateful not to have been left out.

She danced with John, then Mr Noble requested the pleasure of her company for the next quadrille while John danced with Ottilie. Violet felt as if she was dancing on air as her partner led her on to the floor.

'You look like the cat who's got the cream,' Ottilie whispered as they passed each other.

Mr Noble was very handsome indeed with his square jaw and even teeth, but it was the vigour and intelligence in his striking blue eyes which caught her attention the most.

'I saw you rowing today, Mr Noble,' Violet said.

'William. It's William,' he said.

'Congratulations on your success, William.'

'Thank you.' She fancied he was blushing as he continued, 'It was a team effort. My father, uncle, brother and cousins are all members of Dover Rowing Club.' He smiled. 'There's nothing better than being out on the water.'

'Your father is master of my father's ship, the *Dover Belle*?'

'That's right. He and my brother are at sea at present on a round trip to the Azores, and due back at any time. My mother can hardly wait to see them.'

'It must be hard for her.'

'She misses them, but that's enough of my family. Oh, I don't know what else to say … except that you look very beautiful.'

Violet didn't know how to respond. Perhaps her expression had been one of shock, because he immediately stumbled on, 'I'm sorry. I've been too forward. Without a sister to guide me, I have no idea how to pay a young lady a compliment.'

'There's no need to apologise. I'm flattered …' Her fingers touched the pearls at her throat as she gazed into his eyes. 'Truly I am. I'm as out of my depth as you are, I think. This is my first ball.'

'And it won't be the last, I hope.'

He smiled again, and her heart melted, even though she knew it shouldn't, because although William was a winning rower, he was a lowly apprentice at the Packet Yard, and his family was not of the same social standing as the Rayfields. Even as the band played, and they danced, smoothly and in step as though they had danced together before, Violet knew that her parents would never consider him as a potential suitor for her or her sisters.

Chapter Two

The House in Camden Crescent

One morning, a week after the ball, Violet was in the schoolroom on the top floor of the house in Camden Crescent, where she and her sisters spent much of their time in the company of Miss Whiteway. Even though Ottilie and Violet considered themselves too old to have a governess, Mama insisted that they continue with their education at least until Eleanor turned seventeen.

'It wouldn't be a horror to me to have to make my own living. It has to be more interesting than staying at home to run the house and bring up one's children.' Violet walked to the open window and looked out at the patch of green where the military band were assembled in their scarlet uniforms, their brass trumpets and cymbals glinting in the summer sun, as they played a stirring march. Beyond the lawns and Marine Parade, she scanned the sea and shingle beach, hoping in vain to catch a glimpse of William and the Dover Rowing Club out on the water in their cutters and galleys.

'There is no need for you to go out to work,' Miss Whiteway said. 'Your father is a wealthy man who expects you to become a devoted wife and mother. You may have interests and hobbies to divert you, such as embroidery and growing ferns, but making your own money is out of the question.'

'What if I should go against our father's wishes?' Violet said, vexed.

'Heart's alive! What are you thinking of? A daughter's duty is to obey her father, and then her husband after that in a lifetime of submission,' Miss Whiteway said with irony and a certain amount of satisfaction, perhaps, that she hadn't found herself in that situation. 'My role is to prepare you for the duties you will take on as a woman in society, whether or not I believe it's fair. Despite being ruled by a queen, Her Majesty Victoria who has been placed above all men, the rest of us are still not treated equitably by the Church or the State.' Miss Whiteway sounded very old, yet she was only thirty – Violet and Ottilie had often discussed the fact that she could easily pass for forty-five with her plain clothes and horn-rimmed spectacles. 'Ah well, nothing will change until more women are able to speak out, and men learn to tolerate living with an equal at their fireside.'

Could it be said that Pa treated their mother as his equal? Violet thought back to the discussion she'd heard between her parents a few days before, when Mama had asked him to have her room redecorated. He had begun to argue against it until she had cut him short, telling him she would invite Mr Jones to provide a quote. This had not been a question, but a statement of fact.

'However, in spite of what I said before in recognition of your parents' wishes, it is never a bad thing for a young lady to have something to fall back on. Violet, you have skills you can employ to earn your living.'

'What skills?'

'Embroidery, of course. Your whitework is exceptional.'

'Do you think so?'

'I've always been a little envious of your needlework. It comes so naturally to you. But you are diverting me.

23

Please, sit down and continue with your drawing. It is a fair attempt, but it could do with more colour. Perhaps a wash of watercolour will liven it up.'

Holding up the skirts of her brown day dress, Violet turned away from the window and returned to the waxed pine table where Ottilie was sewing buttons on to a pair of gloves. Eleanor was leaning back in her chair in what Violet considered a theatrical manner, with the back of one hand pressed to her temple and the end of a pencil in her mouth.

Violet took her place and scrutinised her picture, a representation of Mama's white pet cat with a bow around its neck. Its nose was too long, its fur too dark and its eyes too human. There was nothing that could redeem it.

She glanced up, on hearing Miss Whiteway address Eleanor.

'Have you completed your poem?' Violet noticed her heavy brow suddenly furrow. 'Oh no, that will not do. It is too dark, too disturbing to be read aloud – "The Ballad of Whetstone Moor" by Miss Eleanor Rayfield is unsuitable for consumption within the confines of the drawing room. Gentlemen don't want to hear about dying heroines. Strike it out and start again.'

Grudgingly, Eleanor picked up the wooden rule and scored a pencil cross into the offending page.

'I'll be a famous writer one day, you'll see,' she said.

'Then you'll never find a man who wishes to marry you,' Ottilie cut in. 'Men find intelligence in a woman most undesirable.'

'Because it means they might answer back,' Violet said. Her ambitions were changeable and churning like the sea, while all Ottilie wanted was to settle, marry and bear children, and Eleanor to write her stories.

'If you complete the tasks I've set in a timely manner, we can take the air this afternoon,' Miss Whiteway told them.

'Mama has said we must join her at eleven to meet Mr Jones. It's already half past ten,' Violet added, looking at the clock on the mantel.

'Do we have to?' Eleanor sighed. 'I have no interest in paints and wallpapers.'

'Mama has requested our opinion.' Violet suppressed a smile, recalling how she had engineered the arrangement earlier that morning.

'If Mrs Rayfield has expressly requested your company at eleven, then I must bow to it,' Miss Whiteway said. 'This isn't an example of your scheming, is it, Violet?'

'No, Miss Whiteway,' she said sweetly. 'May we be excused?'

'Of course. We'll meet again for luncheon.'

'What luck,' Ottilie said as the three sisters started to walk down the two flights of stairs. 'How did you get Mama to agree to this?'

'With my natural charm and persuasion.' Violet smiled. 'Any excuse to get us out of the schoolroom.'

'I was quite happy doing my writing,' Eleanor complained.

'There'll be plenty of time to do it later in the week,' Violet said, feeling a touch guilty for thwarting her sister's creative urges.

'Studying is duller than dull.' Ottilie's eyes lit up as she flicked through the pile of letters lying on the silver tray on the hall table. She pulled one out and slipped it into her pocket.

'A letter for you? Who sent it?' Violet asked.

'Oh, it's just a note from our cousin Jane.'

'Aren't you going to open it?'

'Not yet. Hurry – we mustn't keep Mama waiting.'

They went into the dining room where their mother, dressed in a navy crinoline with wide sleeves trimmed with ivory silk, was awaiting the decorator's arrival.

'Good morning, my dear daughters. I hope you've been applying yourselves to your studies,' she greeted them with half a smile, as they took their seats at the highly polished mahogany table.

'Yes, Mama,' Ottilie answered for the three of them.

The dining room, which had doors leading out on to the balcony, was in dire need of redecoration. Violet looked up at the five-armed gasolier with its shades of pale blue opalescent glass. It hung from an elaborate plaster rose blackened by the large leaping flames which appeared whenever the gasolier was ignited. The wallpaper above the panelled oak was turning brown and the heavy velvet drapes had seen better days.

'Mr Jones won't be long,' Mama said, but he was at least another ten minutes, during which time Eleanor sat fidgeting, and Violet gazed at the curios Pa kept in the cabinet near the door. There was an alabaster Buddha with a topknot, a sandalwood elephant from India, and a shrunken head from the Amazon which gave her nightmares. The head – about one-fifth the size of a living head – was that of a dark-skinned woman with black hair. Although her expression looked peaceful – her eyes were closed, and her lips had been sewn shut with thick cord – Violet couldn't help wondering if it had been done to keep her from screaming while she was murdered in the depths of the rainforest.

'Ah, I hear voices.' Mrs Rayfield stood up as their maid of all work, who was in the pink of neatness in her uniform, showed a gentleman into the room.

'This is Mr Jones, ma'am,' the maid said, bobbing a curtsey. She had long auburn hair plaited and put up under her cap, and Mama had to tell her to wash her neck sometimes, but she had a good heart. May was twenty-five and had been with the Rayfields for seven years. She was calm, capable, and obliging – and rather put upon for all that.

'Thank you, May. That will be all for now.'

'Yes, ma'am.' The maid pulled the door shut behind her as she returned to the corridor, and all eyes were on Mr Jones. He was a small man with a Roman nose and a wig – at least, Violet guessed it wasn't his own hair – like a brown doormat affixed to his scalp in three or four places with dabs of glue. He wore a green velvet coat and carried a leather portfolio of drawings and a bag of samples.

'Good day, ladies,' he said with a bow. 'I'm very grateful to you for receiving me, Mrs Rayfield. I believe you will be delighted with our plans. I've incorporated your suggestions and ideas for the colour scheme, and added a few thoughts of my own – merely to add the finer details which are currently in vogue in London. As I'm sure you're aware, every house should have a green room. Green is the colour of Nature, and most soothing, entirely suitable for the bedroom and anywhere else in the home where one wishes to find rest and repose.'

'I'm looking forward to seeing how the room will look. I hope you don't mind, but I took the liberty of inviting my daughters to join us as part of their education, not so much to give their opinion, although …' Mama smiled, '… I am content for them to give it if it tallies with mine.'

'You speak wisely, Mrs Rayfield,' he said, looking towards Violet in particular. 'It's essential for a young lady to acquire an interest in decoration for when she moves into her own establishment.'

'Oh, that won't be for a while. They're all too young for marriage – I don't want to lose them just yet.'

'They are a credit to you, Mrs Rayfield.' Mr Jones stared pointedly up at the ceiling. 'I wonder if you would like me to give you an estimate for redecorating this beautiful room, no obligation.'

'That would be most acceptable.'

'If you were to accept my quote today for the bedroom and dining room, and you were pleased with the work undertaken, I'd be very grateful if you'd provide me with a written testimonial.' He unpacked some wallpaper samples from his portfolio.

'There's such a vast range of patterns nowadays that I've had to be selective in what I show you – my firm deals only in papers of the highest quality, not the cheap alternatives which fade almost as one puts them up.' He spread the samples across the table, all opulent colours: reds, blues and greens. Some had scrolled floral patterns which caught Violet's eye. 'Had you thought any more about your choice of hue, Mrs Rayfield?'

'One of my acquaintances has told me that it's aesthetically pleasing to choose either adjacent colours, or those on opposite sides of the colour wheel. I found the discussion confusing to say the least.'

'Ah, the latter is more popular. We call it the creation of harmony by contrast,' Mr Jones said. 'Are you drawn to any particular colour?'

'I'd like this green for both rooms.' Mama touched the paper nearest her.

'It is wonderful, I agree.' Mr Jones smiled gleefully. 'It's extremely popular – in fact, if you wish to have this one, I'll put an order in as soon as possible before the company who makes it runs out of stock.'

'Do you think that's likely, or is this your way of hurrying me into making a decision?' Mama enquired.

'Oh no, it's a genuine concern. There is such a demand for it.'

Mama turned to her daughters. 'Well, I've asked you here to give me your opinions, so what do you think? Eleanor first.'

'I would like the green if it were darker,' Eleanor said quietly.

'Ottilie?'

'The wallpaper you have picked is a most acceptable colour, although blue seems more suitable for a bedroom. You did ask for my view, Mama.'

'Yes, I suppose I did.' Their mother sighed and tipped her head to one side. 'What about you, Violet?'

'I have it on good authority that green is bad for the constitution.'

'Pray, tell me on whose authority?' Mama said, annoyed. 'You've read it in one of those dreadful novels.'

'Miss Whiteway told us about it when we were discussing chemistry. There have been many cases of poisoning in fashionable society recently.'

'Your governess has no business teaching you such terrible and disturbing untruths. Nobody in Dover has been poisoned by the colour green, or I would have heard about it.'

'That's correct, Mrs Rayfield,' Mr Jones agreed.

'She says it's been in the newspapers – there were letters in *The Times* on the subject of arsenic in wallpapers.'

'I will have Scheele's Green – Mr and Mrs Chittenden have it in their dining room and they have always struck me as being in excellent health.'

That's because they usually dine out, Violet wanted to say. The Chittendens were more often to be found dining at the Rayfields' house than their own.

'Really, Violet, your claim is quite outrageous. I'll be having a word with Miss Whiteway about her tales.'

'Everyone in Kent has at least one green room in their house nowadays. I accept that arsenic is a poison if taken by mouth in large doses, but when applied to the walls of the home as paint and wallpaper, it is perfectly safe.

Look at me – I am the very picture of health.' Mr Jones puffed himself up and strutted about like a rooster to demonstrate.

Violet suppressed a giggle, but Ottilie caught her eye, and it turned into a cough. Eleanor patted her on the back as Mr Jones went on, 'If it will ease your minds, I will personally eat a pound of paper to prove it.'

'That isn't necessary. It's clear that it wouldn't be in your interest to go around poisoning your customers,' Mama said, but Mr Jones was determined not to lose her patronage.

'I use only the best quality wallpapers – I can rub it with my fingers.' He demonstrated on the green paper. 'I can even ...' he bent over the table and pressed his mouth to it, leaving the wet imprint of the tip of his tongue when he straightened '... lick it. You see – the colour does not come off.' He licked it again and Violet couldn't contain herself any longer.

'Excuse me,' she said, choking back laughter as she fled the room.

They didn't get to take the air that afternoon because she had displeased their mother, but they were allowed to dine with their parents as was their habit before Mama and Pa retired to the parlour, and the sisters to their rooms.

'The decorator called today,' Mama said when the maid was clearing dessert away.

Violet sat very still, afraid her mother was about to reveal how she had run out of the room, but she merely gave her a glance and continued, 'He's bringing an estimate for the work.'

'We should obtain some comparisons,' Pa said as Violet breathed a sigh of relief. 'When you look after the pennies, the pounds look after themselves.'

'We have money in the bank. We aren't penniless,' Mama went on impatiently, at which Pa nodded. 'Then you will permit me to have the dining room and my bedroom completely redecorated.'

'It seems rather excessive to me. Can't we have somebody in to touch up the paint?'

'Oh no, that won't do. The paper's peeling from the walls, and the damp is getting on my chest. We can't be seen to be letting the place go to rack and ruin. Perhaps we should consider moving to one of the East Cliff Mansions, for example. Mrs Chittenden says there's one coming up for sale.'

'This is our family home. I have no desire to leave it.'

'Then we should look after it, not allow it to fall down around our ears.'

'All right, Patience. You have twisted my arm.' Pa's eyes twinkled with amusement, and Violet smiled to herself, relieved that her father had been taking the rise out of his wife. 'I'll set a budget and you will promise not to trouble me with this again. Suffice to say, business is buoyant, and I have great expectations …'

'But?' Mama said. 'You seem troubled. Is there something wrong?'

'Nothing's wrong,' Pa said.

'I know you too well …'

'I shall tell you then. Much as I have no desire to disturb your peace of mind, the fact is that the *Dover Belle* hasn't arrived back in port as expected, and there's much speculation as to what's happened to her. However, for the moment all we can say is that she didn't arrive when she was due. Seafaring is unpredictable, subject to the vagaries of Nature, and of God's will. She was supposed to have returned from the Azores with her cargo of oranges and lemons last Monday.'

'Perhaps she has run out of steam or lost her sails to the wind,' Mama said.

Violet recalled the story of how the *Dover Belle* had run out of coal towards the end of her maiden voyage, and the previous captain, fearing that he would miss the deadline and that the fruit he was carrying would spoil, had ordered the furniture and crates to be burned instead to move the giant pistons of the steam packet. She had always wondered if Pa had been entirely fair, removing him from his employ for his oversight in carrying too little coal on that occasion, but he said that business was business, and he'd had to make an example of the man.

'She's a good ship, reliable in all weathers – she always makes good time even with the wind and tide against her, which is why it is a little out of the ordinary. She has never turned up this far behind schedule before.'

'Captain Noble is a fine master,' Mama said.

'He's someone on whom we can depend to bring the ship, her cargo and crew safely home, which is why Edward and I gave him his commission. Let's bide our time. I have every expectation that in the next day or two she'll have returned with all hands on board, and I'll be able to sleep easy at night.'

Her poor father was never at ease, Violet reflected, always available for business and any difficulties which arose, such as sodden consignments of tea, rotten fruit, theft and mutinous crew, but a missing ship? That was different, another level of concern, and she recalled William talking of his family and wondered how worried he must be, knowing that the *Dover Belle* was delayed somewhere out on the open sea.

After dinner, the three sisters retired to bed: Eleanor slept in a room across the landing from Ottilie and Violet, but they left the doors open so they could talk without disturbing the rest of the household if they wished. Sometimes, Eleanor would wander in to join them and end up sleeping beneath Violet's coverlet, if Mama didn't come up to chase her out.

Tonight, she perched on the edge of Violet's bed, writing in her notebook while Violet embroidered and Ottilie read her letter by candlelight.

Violet rested her hoop on her lap and threaded her needle with woollen yarn, ready to fill in the outline of a pattern she'd sketched on the linen.

'What does Jane say in her letter?' Eleanor asked.

'Nothing much. She asks how we are, and tells me of how her little dog has had puppies. Eleanor, you should write your own letters, not take vicarious pleasure in hearing about other people's. I expect Jane would like to hear from you.'

'I don't have time to write letters,' Eleanor said.

'I can't believe you're still scribbling,' Violet said.

'I'm in the middle of a story. In your opinion, is death fair retribution for a gentleman who mistreats a young lady?'

'He can hardly be described as a gentleman in such a situation,' Ottilie countered.

'It depends on the context. Look at Uncle Edward – he could be called a gentleman for opening the door for us, but I don't like where he puts his hands when he follows you into the room. What has this man done to offend?' Violet asked.

'He has tricked her, pretending he is without attachment when he is already engaged to be married.'

'Then he's too mean to be the hero of your story,' Ottilie said.

'He is the villain. I think the lady in question's brother will call him out and kill him in a duel. Or is that too much?'

'He has betrayed not one, but two ladies,' Violet pointed out.

'I can't kill him twice,' Eleanor said, her voice light with mischief. 'Although I could prolong his agony.'

'Then that is your answer,' Ottilie said.

'What happens to the ladies he deceived?' Violet asked. 'Won't they both grieve for him?'

'I don't know. I haven't got that far.' Eleanor chewed on the end of her pencil, a bad habit that Miss Whiteway had tried to break by dipping the pencil in bitter aloes before telling her she would die from eating the lead when the first ploy failed.

'I wouldn't grieve – I'd think he'd received his just deserts,' Ottilie said. 'As for the ladies, their fate depends on whether or not the villain's left a stain on their reputation in the eyes of society. If he has, they'll be cast out and doomed to spend the rest of their lives as spinsters.'

'That's a monsterful story, Ottilie. Now I have too much to write about!' Eleanor said. 'I'll set it on a ship sailing the high seas.'

'That seems a little insensitive, considering what Pa was talking about earlier,' Ottilie said.

'The *Dover Belle* ... I wonder if she's been taken over by pirates.'

'Your imagination as always runs wild. The most likely explanation is that she's been becalmed,' Violet said, her thoughts flitting back to William. 'When the winds pick up, they'll soon blow her home.'

'One dance with an apprentice engineer, and you think you know all about steamships,' Ottilie teased.

'Oh, Ottilie,' Violet sighed, 'I danced with Mr Brooke as well. And John. And William's cousin.' She had danced until her feet had ached.

'That Mr Brooke is a most peculiar gentleman, so pre-occupied with trying to impress that he doesn't show his true character,' Ottilie said.

'It's natural for a person to attempt to fit in with company and make themselves agreeable,' Violet said. 'Pa was trying equally hard to impress Mr Brooke. I have to say I felt a little sorry for him – I thought I detected a hint of sadness in his eyes.'

'Perhaps the reason he isn't married is because he's loved and lost,' Eleanor said, before regaling them with increasingly outrageous stories of what might have happened to Mr Brooke during his various affairs of the heart, until Violet didn't know how she would face him if their paths crossed for a second time.

'Go back to your room. Quickly,' she said, hearing footsteps on the stairs. 'It's Mama.'

It was too late. Their mother was upon them, a lantern in her hand.

'Have you any idea what the time is?' she said wearily.

Eleanor shook her head while her sisters remained silent.

'It is past midnight.'

'I'm sorry,' Eleanor said, scurrying away.

Mama's voice softened. 'Goodnight, my dear daughters. Sleep well.'

'Goodnight, Mama,' they said.

Violet leaned across to the bedside table which stood between the two beds and blew out the candle. The flame expired, leaving the scent of smoke curling through the air.

Chapter Three

Scheele's Green

Three more weeks passed and there was no definite news of the *Dover Belle*, only reports that she had left the port of Ponta Delgada on 31 May in fair weather with her cargo and several passengers. She had twelve hundred miles to cover en route to England, and Pa had surmised that she had perhaps broken passage along the north-west coast of Spain to avoid the tail of a hurricane. When Violet – out of her private concern for William – had pressed her father on the matter, he had confirmed that Captain Noble was a master mariner with many years' experience who wouldn't endanger his ship and everyone on it by putting speed before safety.

Mr Jones and his team of decorators came to the house to paint and hang wallpaper in Ma's bedroom and the dining room. The cat was confined to the kitchen for the week, and Cook wasn't happy because he left his pawmarks in the dough that she'd left to rest before rolling it out for an apple and cinnamon pie. Although Mama grumbled about the workmen being in the way, the work was soon completed.

Once they had left, Mama invited Violet into her boudoir.

'What do you think?' she asked as Violet scanned the freshly painted skirting, the walls covered with the finest paper, the new curtains – or rather the old ones dyed and rehung – and the floral summer coverlet spread across the bed. The carpet had been moved from the dining room, cut to size and the threads knotted to make a fringed edging, something Pa had insisted on, because – so he said – he hadn't forgotten how his parents and grandparents had struggled to make ends meet. Waste not, want not, had been their motto.

'Well?' Mama said.

'It's very green. In a good way,' Violet replied quickly, not wanting to offend her. If Miss Whiteway was right about green being a poison, then there was enough to kill the whole of Dover in this single room.

The cat – a Turkish angora with a fluffy white coat and a ginger splash across his face – looked up from the bedspread, yawned and stretched out one paw. He stared at Violet with his odd eyes – one amber, one blue – without blinking.

'I'm glad you like it,' Mama went on. 'Your father is sending word to my sister and your cousin Jane, the Chittendens and Mr Brooke, inviting them to dine with us tomorrow.'

Violet turned away and looked out of the window. There were two ladies in finery and feathers walking behind an older man in a suit and stovepipe hat, and the vicar of St Mary's taking a brisk stroll by the sea. Several horses and carriages trotted smartly along the road, overtaking a slow, plodding cob pulling a cart laden with pots and pans, and scrap iron.

'I'm waiting for your opinion.' Mama's voice cut into her musings.

'Oh, I've said … yes, I like it very much,' she said hastily, looking back towards her mother who had one eyebrow raised in question. 'The green.'

'I was asking you to help me decide between the duck and the beef.' Mama smiled. 'Sometimes I despair of you.'

'The beef then,' she said. 'It's my favourite.'

'The hostess shouldn't choose the dish that she prefers – she must put her guests' preferences first. Oh dear, you still have much to learn about the art of running a household. Now I must speak to Cook about the menu. Go and tell Miss Whiteway that her presence will be required at dinner tomorrow.'

'Yes, Mama.'

Miss Whiteway and her sisters were delighted at the news, and the following day, they finished lessons at four as the aroma of roast beef and suet pudding began to fill the air. Three hours later, the sound of the doorbell and voices announced their guests' arrival.

'Oh, I'm not ready,' Ottilie wailed.

'You couldn't look any more perfect,' Violet said with a twinge of envy at the sight of her fashionable scarlet gown with its sloping shoulders. 'Make haste.'

Ottilie made one last adjustment to her dark blonde ringlets before following Violet and Eleanor downstairs. The butler had shown the Chittendens and Mr Brooke into the drawing room. Their aunt and cousin Jane arrived seconds later.

Aunt Felicity, a widow who had cast off her weeds many years before, was three years Mama's senior, and similar in appearance except that her crow's feet were deeper, and the lines at the side of her mouth more marked. She was wearing a blush satin dress which didn't suit her grey hair and pale complexion, Violet thought, while Jane – who was twenty-one – looked the same as ever, dressed in brown damask with no other adornment, neither a border of lace, nor a flounce, and with her auburn hair up in a bun.

'Arvin, you have met everyone apart from my wife's sister, Mrs Hewitt and her daughter Miss Hewitt, and our youngest daughter, Miss Eleanor Rayfield,' Pa said.

'It is a pleasure to make your acquaintance, ladies,' Mr Brooke said before turning to Mama who had entered the room. Mr Brooke wasn't wearing black and white evening dress like the other men of the party. Instead, he sported a white shirt, striped silk waistcoat and cravat, and pale pantaloons – he had left his blue tailcoat and tasselled walking stick with Wilson. 'Good evening, Mrs Rayfield.'

'I'm so glad you could come. You must meet our daughters' governess – she speaks a little French. Miss Whiteway, have you found the sheet music I asked for?'

'Yes, Mrs Rayfield,' she said, sorting through a sheaf of papers on top of the piano.

'In that case, leave it there ready and join us.'

Miss Whiteway frowned, and Violet wondered if she was annoyed at being displayed like an ornament. She hadn't considered it before, but Mama's insistence that she meet their guests seemed quite demeaning. Hadn't Miss Whiteway any friends of her own? She wasn't sure. She did leave the house on her days off, but Violet had no idea where she went, except that she had family in Dorset whom she visited twice a year.

'Let us move to the dining room, my dear.' Pa walked across to his wife. 'You may do the honours and open the door with a flourish, so our guests may feast their eyes on the new decoration.'

'Oh, how exciting.' Mrs Chittenden moved up to Mama's side with Aunt Felicity.

Mama rested her hand on the doorknob, turned it and pushed the door open to reveal the updated room.

'It's a truly marvellous sight to behold,' Mr Brooke said after a prolonged exhalation of breath. 'You have an excellent eye.'

'It looks very expensive,' Aunt Felicity grumbled. 'There are people with more money than sense.'

'When one has money, one can afford to show off one's good taste. It is Scheele's green, all the rage in London apparently.' Mama smiled, used to her sister's criticism.

'It's the same as ours—' Uncle Edward began.

'It is quite different,' Mrs Chittenden interrupted. 'Why is it that gentlemen can't understand the subtleties of interior decoration?'

'It is beyond me,' Mama said. 'Please, take your seats. The places are marked with cards – Violet drew the flowers and Eleanor wrote your names.'

Violet blushed, not wishing to be renowned for her hasty designs inspired by the roses in the garden.

'They are gifted young ladies,' Mr Brooke said, finding his place between Mama and Ottilie who was seated opposite John. Violet whispered to Jane beside her.

'Your recent letters have been very entertaining. How is your dear little dog and her puppies?'

'Puppies?' Jane chuckled. 'That isn't possible – my Ruffles is a boy dog.'

'Then why did you invent such a tale?'

'I haven't sent a single letter since I wrote to thank your mother for my birthday gift.'

'How very odd. Ottilie read your letter out to me and Eleanor the other day ...'

'You must have been mistaken,' Jane said.

'Yes, you're right. How silly of me ...' Violet looked across to where her sister was engaged in conversation with John and Mr Brooke. She had lied. She couldn't believe it. Her honest, straightforward elder sister had told an untruth, but why?

When everyone had taken their seats, Pa said grace before Wilson poured drinks, and the maid brought the first course into the dining room. May looked weary, Violet thought – she'd been on her feet all day, cleaning and blacking the fireplaces.

Violet finished her soup before they went on to the next course of roast beef, suet pudding and gravy with three side dishes of vegetables. She talked to Jane and eavesdropped on other conversations at the same time.

'This is formidable,' Mr Brooke exclaimed. 'You have really pushed the boat out, Mrs Rayfield.'

'Why, thank you,' Mama said. 'I will relay your compliments to our housekeeper – Mrs Garling, and to Cook. The servants have taken all day to prepare.'

Pa picked up his glass and swirled the last dregs of his wine around the bottom. 'The tide seems to have gone out – more claret, Wilson.'

The meal continued with desserts, jams and jellies, cake and preserved fruits and coffee before everyone retired to the drawing room for the entertainment.

'My daughters will sing and play the piano,' Pa said jovially. 'It will be good to see some return on the money I've spent on music masters and the like.'

Violet was thrilled at the chance of singing with Ottilie, as Eleanor accompanied them on the pianoforte before duetting with Miss Whiteway.

'Oh bravo! Bravo!' Mr Brooke clapped and cheered.

'This isn't a music hall,' Aunt Felicity muttered disapprovingly.

'One should give credit where it's due,' Uncle Edward said. 'The young ladies play and sing beautifully.'

'We will sing "Leonore, thy voice is music to mine ear" next,' Violet said as the final chords of 'The Hazel Dell' died away.

'I think the singers should rest their voices for a while,' Aunt Felicity said. 'A piece of music allows for a break in conversation, but more than one or two songs in a row is tedious.' Violet frowned, and her aunt continued, 'In my opinion, the level of regard that a musician has for one's audience is in direct proportion to the excellence of their playing.'

'You do have a point.' Mama touched her temple. 'Ladies, we should have an interlude – I have rather a headache.'

'Oh dear, is there anything we can do?' Mr Brooke said.

'No, I will be fine in a while,' Mama said, and Violet went to sit down beside her, worrying that she looked rather pale, but she soon revived when Miss Whiteway spoke out of turn. Mr Brooke had asked her if she enjoyed being a governess, and she had mentioned that she would have preferred to have had the opportunity to become a doctor or engineer.

Both Mama's and Aunt Felicity's eyebrows shot up, and Mrs Chittenden's mouth dropped open.

'You mean you wish you'd been born a man?' Aunt Felicity exclaimed.

'No, not at all. I mean that I would like women to have the same freedoms and chances as men.'

'Oh, how ridiculous. We all have our places in society, men and women in separate spheres, each supporting the other,' Mama said. 'My mother brought me up with traditional values – they have done me no harm, and I wish to raise my daughters in the same way. They will make good marriages – what's wrong with being provided for, in return for making the home a place of glory and repose for one's husband? Look at my hands … they aren't chapped and worn like Cook's, and I'm grateful to Mr Rayfield for that.'

'Why should women have only the prospect of becoming servants to their husbands to look forward to?' Miss Whiteway dared to say.

'It isn't your place to raise this with me as the mistress of this house. Why would I wish to be considered Mr Rayfield's equal when I am content to stay quietly as his inferior, in return for his protection and good sense?'

'There's no reason why men and women shouldn't be treated equally. Why shouldn't women be vicars and prime ministers?'

Violet heard Ma's strangulated snort of annoyance.

'A woman's place is in the home – why would she want to spend hours writing sermons and giving speeches even if that were allowed? How insufferably dull!'

'I believe they would be just as interesting and inspiring as any written by a man.' Violet thought she heard Miss Whiteway continue in a low voice, 'More so, in fact.'

'You have the most peculiar ideas. The very fabric of civilised society would fall apart.' For a moment, Violet expected her mother to send Miss Whiteway to her room, but she backed down.

'I believe Miss Whiteway is playing devil's advocate, all the better to entertain us,' Mr Brooke said, laughing loudly – too loudly to be considered polite, Violet judged, noticing the expression of disapproval on her aunt's face.

'That's right.' Pa guffawed while Uncle Edward looked on, frowning.

'Let's have another song,' Mr Brooke suggested.

'An excellent idea,' Uncle Edward said, and Violet played the piano while Ottilie sang a duet with Eleanor. Letting her fingers run across the keys, the tune so familiar that she didn't have to think about it, she gazed up at the sooty streaks above the gasoliers in the drawing room, wondering if Mama would extend her renovations of the house any further, and then about Miss Whiteway's bravery – or was it foolishness? – in speaking her own mind in front of her employers' guests. As for Mr Brooke, it was kind of him to make light of it – like a decorator, he was skilled in papering over the cracks, his quips and comments smoothing out disagreements and contention.

She played the last chord and let it hang in the air, but before the audience could offer their applause, the sound of a disturbance downstairs stopped them.

'Oh, who is that at this late hour?' Ma sighed.

'It's probably some higgler,' Pa said. 'Don't worry. Wilson will deal with it.'

'Sit down, Violet,' Ma said, but it was too late – she had abandoned the piano, mid-chord, the notes dying away as Wilson's voice rose to a shout. Footsteps came hammering up the stairs towards the drawing room. The door burst open and a young man strode in, his clothes dripping wet from the rain. Violet recognised him immediately.

'Young man! Wilson!' Pa's glass hovered in the air. His hand trembled and a few drops of brandy spilled on to the carpet. 'What is the meaning of this? Oh, it is you, Mr Noble. You have no right to come barging into my house. Wilson, why did you let him in?'

'My apologies, Mr Rayfield,' Wilson said curtly. 'Mr Noble here took me by surprise and forced his way past me.'

'William, this – whatever it is – can wait,' Pa said. 'Call at my office in the morning and one of my clerks will make you an appointment.'

'You can't keep fobbing me off,' William said. 'You've been dodging me for days, which isn't right or fair. Mr Chittenden, you too have unkindly refused to meet me.'

'Oh dear, what an uncouth creature to have walked off the streets, all bedraggled,' Violet heard her aunt say to her mother. 'What on earth can he have to say to Mr Rayfield?'

He was only bedraggled because he'd been standing out in the rain, Violet thought. Their eyes locked briefly –

for just long enough for her to convey her sympathy without words. His face was etched with pain and anger, and her heart went out to him.

'I wouldn't normally disturb you at this hour, but your clerks have turned me away every time I've come to find you at your office. All I want from you is an assurance that you are doing all you can to find the *Dover Belle*. My mother is desperate for news.'

'Return to your mother and give her my personal assurance that all is well,' Pa said sternly.

'How can I take your word for it?'

'Because I am a gentleman of high standing.'

'You have made enquiries as to the ship's position?'

'Of course.'

'And?'

'Nothing.' Pa shrugged.

'I've heard rumours that she wasn't seaworthy,' William said.

'She was overhauled not long ago,' Mr Chittenden exclaimed.

'My brother told me that parts of her engine were worn out.'

'What does he know as a junior engineer?' Pa said scathingly. Violet had no doubt that he knew what he was talking about – he and Uncle Edward had carried out months of research into her fitness for purpose before buying her. 'Within a few days, the *Dover Belle* will be back, along with her crew and precious cargo, and life will go on as usual. You worry unnecessarily.' Pa's expression softened. 'Wilson, take him down to the kitchen and ask Cook to give him some meat and claret.'

'I will not accept your charity – I have my pride,' William said. 'I came here for answers – you can't buy me peace of mind with leftovers.'

'You'll feel a little better when you have some food inside you.'

'I have to get back to my mother. For now, I'm all the comfort she has. I won't be letting this matter rest. I'll call at your office every day, if I have to. Good evening, Mr Rayfield and Mr Chittenden. Goodnight, ladies.'

He looked at Violet who bowed her head, a little embarrassed as their uninvited caller left the house. The two men seemed equally convinced that they were in the right: Pa that the *Dover Belle* was seaworthy and merely delayed coming back to port; William that the ship hadn't been properly maintained by her owners and was likely to have broken down, or worse. She hated the idea that William might think badly of her because he disagreed with her father. 'I think it's time that Jane and I retired to bed. We've had a long day,' Aunt Felicity said.

'I apologise for the unwarranted intrusion,' Pa said. 'It's been an eventful evening.'

'And one to remember,' Mr Brooke added. 'I'm very grateful for your hospitality, Mrs Rayfield, but I too must take my leave.'

When the guests had gone, Violet went upstairs with her sisters.

'What do you think Miss Whiteway was doing, the way she spoke to Mama?' Ottilie said as she changed into her nightgown.

Violet was already in bed, waiting to snuff out the candle on the bedside cabinet.

'I admire her for speaking her mind.'

'But why did she do it in front of our guests?'

'Because she finds evenings like these tiresome. She prefers to stay in her room, reading and preparing lessons. What about William bursting in on the party like that?'

'I thought he was unmannerly. I expect you admire him as well,' Ottilie said.

'No …' Violet said, her cheeks burning.

'I think you do – for his determination to find out what's happened to the *Dover Belle* on behalf of his mother, but that isn't the only reason …'

'Ottilie, please. I'm tired.'

'You are trying to divert me because you know there's some truth in what I'm saying, that you think he's rather handsome.'

'The way you think of John, you mean?' Violet said. 'I have no particular feelings for William. I agree that he has a pleasant countenance and he's a competent dancer, but I have no intention of falling in love with him, or anyone else.'

Ottilie chuckled. 'You protest too much.'

'Ottilie!' Violet suppressed the urge to throw her pillow at her sister, remembering how Mama had cancelled all their outings for a whole month after their last fight when the room had ended up as a sea of goose feathers.

Violet snuffed out the candle, laid her head back on her pillow and gazed towards the ceiling. She couldn't stop thinking about William. Some might consider him to be just a lowly apprentice, but he wasn't afraid to speak up for himself in the presence of the likes of Pa and Uncle Edward. She wished she could help him in some way, but all she could do was pray for the *Dover Belle* to come home.

Chapter Four

The Dover Belle

It was a shame that Aunt Felicity and Jane had been obliged to return to Canterbury early the following morning because they'd often enjoyed their cousin's company when they were younger. Regretting Jane's absence, Violet gazed along the breakfast table: Pa was reading his paper, Ottilie was staring out of the long windows towards the sea with a wistful expression on her face, Mama was sipping at her tea, and Eleanor was picking at some scrambled egg.

'Sidney, we need to discuss the problem of Miss Whiteway,' Mama began. 'I feel that she deliberately showed me up as a bad mother last night. She should go, I think. Her views are troubling and don't fit in with the general consensus in the drawing room.'

'Conversation would be most dull without conflict and disagreement, but you're right, last night was too much. Her opinions don't reflect ours, and she's poisoning our daughters' minds.'

'She's the best governess we've ever had,' Violet interrupted. 'She encourages us to think for ourselves and form an opinion about freedoms for women.'

'Freedoms?' Pa looked up. 'What freedoms?'

'Opportunities to attend university, to work in the professions, to maintain ownership of one's property upon marriage …' Violet trailed off, aware that her father was staring at her.

'You don't believe any of this claptrap, do you? Society has always been like this. Why upset the applecart when we are different? A woman can't possibly match the intellectual capacity of a man.'

'Especially when she's so worn down with raising children and managing a household that she has no time to improve her mind,' Mama interrupted.

Surprised, Violet straightened her spine. She had never heard their mother express any political or controversial opinion. She had always bowed to Pa before.

'Is it right that when a man takes a wife, he also takes her fortune to do whatever he likes with it?' Mama continued. 'Mr Rayfield, is it fair that when I wish to make some improvements to the house, I have to beg you to agree to pay for them, when I inherited the equivalent of several thousand pounds in gold that sits languishing in a bank vault in London?'

Pa chuckled. 'It is precisely to preserve a wife's assets that a husband takes them on. If I'd let you have free rein with the finances, you would have spent every penny on paint and wallpapers, feathers and fripperies.'

'You should give me more credit,' Mama said quietly. 'I am not a fool. None of us are,' she added, looking at her daughters.

'I am outnumbered,' Pa said, growing sombre. 'I'm sorry. I have overstepped the mark in my teasing. It's a serious matter of which you speak. I really don't think it's right to give girls too rigorous an education – it makes them unmarriageable. Not only that, there was talk in the club not very long ago about a physician's theory that study causes the ovaries of the female to shrivel, causing her to become barren.'

'Do you believe that?' Mama said.

'I have no reason to doubt a medical man's opinion.'

'You said it was a theory, not a proven fact,' Violet said, shocked by her father's frankness, but Pa wasn't listening.

'Eleanor is fifteen years old and we have done our duty as far as her education goes. Dispensing with Miss Whiteway will go some way to saving on the general running costs of our household, which have become rather profligate recently.'

'You heard what everybody said last night: that it made the dining room look fit for the Queen herself.'

'I'm glad it pleased you,' Pa said fondly. 'Perhaps we should consider letting Wilson go at the same time – he is a mouse, not a man, for letting Mr Noble into the drawing room last night.'

'He said that William took him by surprise,' Mama said.

'I know. No, I wouldn't replace Wilson for that – he's been a loyal servant. I never had William down as the impetuous sort. His father is a man of quiet authority and competence.' Pa sighed and turned the page of his newspaper, the remains of his devilled kidneys cold and congealing on his plate. 'I've heard that the superintendent of the Packet Yard thinks so highly of him that he's attached him to the drawings office, but let's not talk about this any more.'

'I wish you wouldn't read at the table,' Mama said.

'One has to keep abreast of the news.'

'Why on earth would one want to mix murder, theft and adultery with meal times?' Mama countered. 'It leaves a rather unpleasant taste in the mouth, does it not? Have you no feeling for the poor people who have been wronged?'

'I read and think, there for the grace of God.' Pa smiled. 'Like the devilled kidneys, I take these reports with a pinch of salt. They are written by journalists who are paid for their stories: the more sensational the better.'

'Then what is the point of reading them, if they aren't true?'

'Because they always contain an element of truth. Going back to our original topic of conversation, I believe you are not above a little subversion of the roles of the sexes yourself, Patience. You would argue with me like Violet does!'

Violet wondered if he was going to be cross, but he smiled again, and went on, 'I'm happy for the distraction. I have a lot on my mind with meetings and such, and to that end—' he checked his pocket watch— 'I must hurry to the office.'

While he was folding the newspaper, Wilson showed Uncle Edward into the dining room.

'Oh, what is he doing here at this time of the morning?' Mama sighed.

'You have news?' Pa said, turning pale as Uncle Edward, still wearing his hat, coat and gloves, made his way to the table.

'There's no gentle way of saying this – the *Dover Belle* has been taken down into Davy Jones's locker for certain. Everything is lost – the crew, passengers, cargo and the ship herself, sunk in deep water with just a few bits of wreckage to show where she went down. There's no hope of rescue or salvage.'

Mama uttered a small cry then pressed her fingers to her lips. 'Those poor souls and their families ...'

'They have all drowned,' Violet heard Eleanor whisper from beside her.

'This is dreadful news,' Ottilie murmured.

'Edward, you should have given me this information in private,' Pa said angrily. 'You've upset my wife and daughters.'

'I make no apology – they are going to find out soon enough.'

'There was no need for it!'

'The news is all over town – there's talk of it on the streets, in the bootmakers and the mills – and it will be in tomorrow's papers.'

'You're right,' Pa said eventually. 'We'll retire to my study to discuss what is to be done.'

Holding back her tears as the men left the room, Violet thought of William and his mother. How were they feeling, knowing that their nearest and dearest would not be returning home?

'Mama, would you like us to keep you company this morning?' she asked, but their mother declined.

'I have plenty to do to keep me occupied, thank you. Mrs Green is calling at eleven. Oh, those poor people – I shall have nightmares. Go, Ottilie. And you, Violet and Eleanor. I will see you later in the day. And please don't say anything to Miss Whiteway – I have yet to make my decision.'

Violet leapt to her feet and hurried out of the dining room with her sisters following behind her.

'Why are you in such a rush?' Eleanor called after her.

'You'll see,' she called back.

The maid was walking towards them along the corridor with a tray laden with a coffee pot, sugar, cups and saucers.

'May, let me take that,' Violet said, quickly intercepting her.

'It's for the master.' May frowned as she handed it over.

'Thank you.' Violet turned and hastened along to the study where she hesitated outside the half-open door.

'I have immediate concerns for the captain's wife – now his father and brother have gone, William is wholly responsible for supporting his mother on an apprentice's wage,'

Uncle Edward was saying. 'We should arrange to make an ex gratia payment to the Nobles in advance of settling the matter of compensation, so they don't suffer further hardship.'

'I was about to suggest the very same,' Pa said.

'At least the *Dover Belle* was insured – the financial losses can be retrieved to a certain extent.'

'I'm not entirely sure that she was ...' Pa muttered.

'Not insured? On what account?'

'I believe there was an omission on my part. The cover was arranged, but not paid for. The quote was excessive and I had anticipated negotiating a better price, but other issues took precedence.'

'Are you sure about this?' Uncle Edward sounded aghast.

'I checked the ledgers and paperwork last week.' Now Violet could see why Pa had been convinced in the face of all the evidence that the *Dover Belle* was safe – the alternative had been too much to bear. 'There is a contract, but there are no signatories. The premium was never paid.'

'Then we are in deep trouble. What a disaster! This is all your fault. I place the blame entirely at your door because you've been distracted by other ventures. It's Mr Brooke, isn't it? You've been working with him to feather your nest – and his.'

'Mr Brooke offered you a share in this enterprise,' Pa said.

'Which I declined because I don't trust him. I thought we were partners in the *Dover Belle*, looking after our mutual interests with care and attention. Now I find that you've been neglecting our business and consorting with the enemy.'

'He's no enemy. He came to us with a proposition – a very reasonable one, I should point out – and a share in his wine importing business which fits in with our existing portfolio.'

'The projected figures are all too good to be true. Never trust a man who refuses to drink with you. Your Mr Brooke has too high an opinion of himself,' Uncle Edward went on. 'From what I've gathered of his character here, and the enquiries I've made, I wouldn't recommend going into business with him.'

'What have you found out?' Pa said.

'Nothing. Absolutely nothing, except that he travels two or three times a year between France and Dover on the mail packet, and does a little buying and selling of various fine wines. He isn't the bigwig that he makes himself out to be.'

'Is that all? You'd warn me off because you've found nothing against him? He says himself that he's a straight talker. I find him candid and sincere.'

'I don't take to him and I can't put my finger on why that is. Maybe it's his manners, or his vulgar dress. I've always been of the opinion that a gentleman should dress carefully to avoid attracting attention, yet he doesn't seem to care.'

'He lives in France where they have a different style of fashion. Edward, he's a good man with youth on his side. He has access to great wines, premier cru from the best chateaux in the South of France, and I have no doubt that with our investment and contacts this business will succeed. In fact, it will do more than that – it will make our fortune.'

'Or make you lose even the shirt off your back,' Uncle Edward said tersely.

'You have decided then – you are definitely out.'

'I will have nothing to do with greasing his palms. He has dangled a carrot in front of you, a rotten one at that, and like an ass you have gone trotting after it. But that's enough of Mr Brooke. We have more important fish to fry.'

Violet's heart was almost leaping out of her chest at the revelations as Uncle Edward continued, 'The importers of the cargo that went down with the *Dover Belle* are sure to instruct their lawyers to put in a claim for compensation for the full amount of the loss. There will be claims from the families of the crew and passengers and, as I own half of the *Dover Belle*, I expect you to make sure I'm not out of pocket. Don't scowl at me like that – if you'd fulfilled your obligation of dealing with the insurance, we wouldn't be in this position.

'I've lost all confidence in your judgement, Sidney, and I'm sorry beyond measure that our friendship has had to end like this. I will ask my lawyer to prepare a document stating my intention to dissolve our partnership forthwith.'

Violet heard movement, and realising she was about to be discovered, she elbowed the door wide open and entered the study.

'Your coffee,' she said brightly, noting that Uncle Edward was on his feet and Pa was sitting at his desk, tugging nervously on his moustache.

'No thank you, Violet,' Uncle Edward said. 'I'm leaving.'

'Shall I see you at the office?' Pa asked meekly.

'We have no reason to meet again,' Uncle Edward said. 'I'll see myself out. Good day.'

Violet could hardly believe her ears – did this mean that their friendship had permanently broken down, or was it a temporary state of affairs?

'I'm sorry about the *Dover Belle*,' she began when their visitor had gone.

'Leave the coffee here,' her father said sharply. 'Tell your mother that I'll be back too late for dinner – I have business to attend to.'

'Yes, Pa.' She put the tray down on the red leather which protected the top of the desk.

'And send Wilson to me.'

'Of course.' She fetched the butler before running up to the schoolroom to find her sisters. Ottilie and Eleanor looked up from their books and Miss Whiteway stalked towards her.

'What time do you call this?'

'I'm sorry for being late. I took coffee to my father and Uncle Edward.'

'Why? You are not a maid.' Violet didn't answer, and Miss Whiteway went on, 'Never mind. I'll let it go on this occasion. Now, sit down. We are studying *The Knight's Tale* by Chaucer.'

'I have news,' Violet whispered to Ottilie as she took her place at the table. 'Uncle Edward has fallen out with Pa over the fate of the *Dover Belle*. It's the end of their association. I don't think we'll be seeing the Chittendens here at Camden Crescent again.'

Ottilie gasped. 'That isn't possible.'

'Please share, Miss Tattletale,' Miss Whiteway interrupted, and Violet repeated herself aloud this time.

'How dreadful,' their governess said.

'Are you sure that you heard right?' Ottilie asked. 'Uncle Edward and our father have been partners and friends since before I can remember.'

'I know what I heard.'

'Whatever the truth of it, I fear that there's trouble ahead,' Miss Whiteway said, as the door swung open and Mama entered the schoolroom.

'I've taken the liberty of searching your room,' she said, addressing their governess.

'That's most irregular – it's private.'

'I didn't think it would be a problem, assuming you had nothing to hide, but look!' Mama spread some papers across the table. 'What are these? Explain yourself.'

'That's my personal correspondence and a pamphlet on the subject of the enfranchisement of women.' Miss Whiteway collected the papers up one by one and tucked them under her arm. 'Why do you speak to me like this? I've committed no crime.'

'You will pack your bags and leave our home tomorrow morning. I'll make your wages up to date, but I won't write you a reference – my conscience will not allow it when your character has been found wanting. You aren't to be trusted with a young lady's education and moral development.'

'Mama, you can't do this,' Violet said, outraged.

'As mistress of this house, I can do anything I wish,' Mama retorted.

'What will we do without Miss Whiteway to guide us?' Violet went on.

'You should know better than to question your elders and betters. Go to your room!'

Violet hesitated.

'Obey your mother,' Miss Whiteway said softly, and Violet hitched up her skirts and fled to hide the tears that were welling up in her eyes. Everything was going wrong and there didn't seem to be anything she could say or do to stop it. Filled with despair, she retreated to her room and sat on the edge of her bed with her head in her hands.

'Violet?' The mattress sank. She looked up to find Ottilie beside her, her expression one of abject misery.

'We're both very upset about Miss Whiteway and the fate of the *Dover Belle*,' Violet said. 'It's the worst day of our lives.'

'I'm crying because of John.'

'What's he got to do with any of this?'

'I'm never going to see him again.'

'Of course you will. We all will, when we're out and about in Dover, and in the company of mutual friends. I don't understand why you're making such a fuss—'

'We are engaged,' Ottilie interrupted.

'I beg your pardon—'

'The letters – they were from John.'

'Well, I knew that.'

'We've been making plans for our future and now they are in complete disarray.'

'Does Pa know?' As Violet asked the question, she already knew the answer. 'I don't know why you kept this secret – I mean, I can't see why Mama and Pa wouldn't have approved wholeheartedly …'

'We were waiting for the right time, and it's passed. We've left it too late. This is a catastrophe! I will die if I can't marry him.'

'We can speak to Pa about this.'

'And tell him we are secretly engaged when he has dismissed Mr Chittenden from our acquaintance? I can't possibly do that. It will send him over the edge, and I don't know what he'll do.'

'I don't think Pa has anything against John personally. Perhaps John could speak with him.' Could Pa's permission be given retrospectively, Violet wondered, and what would Uncle Edward's views be on the matter?

'I don't think he'll be very receptive, not when he's broken every link between the Chittendens and the Rayfields. I'm being disloyal, but I believe our father has used Uncle Edward very badly.'

'He'll pay everyone back,' Violet said. 'He's an honourable man.'

'He'll do it because of his fear of losing face,' Ottilie said, her voice faltering as she twisted the corner of her handkerchief into a knot. Violet couldn't imagine the pain she was going through.

'My poor sister,' she whispered.

'Will you help us?'

'I'll do my best, although I'm not sure what I can do.'

'Promise me then that you'll keep your silence for now.' Violet nodded, recalling the joy on their faces whenever Ottilie and John were reunited. They were meant for each other and her heart broke to think of them being forced apart by circumstance. 'And tell Mama I will not come down for dinner later – I am indisposed.'

As it was, Violet arranged for supper to be brought up to them, while their mother dined downstairs with Eleanor. May collected the tray later.

'I'm sorry for your family's troubles. Poor Miss Whiteway – she's distraught,' May said. 'She said to give you 'er warmest wishes, in case she isn't allowed to see you tomorrow.'

'Thank you,' Violet said. 'Please let her know she's in our thoughts.'

The maid left, and Eleanor dropped by as dusk was falling.

'Aren't you going to stay for a while?' Violet asked, thinking that her company might restore their spirits.

'Mama has been complaining all evening: the chicken was tough, the vegetables cold. I'm worn out.' She closed the door behind her, leaving Violet and Ottilie to talk quietly until Mama came up to wish them goodnight.

'What do you think you're doing with candles lit at this late hour?' she said. 'If you must have light at bedtime, you must use the tallow candles like the servants, not the beeswax. Your father isn't made of money.'

'What was that about Pa?' Ottilie whispered when their mother had gone. 'Are things really that bad that we have to endure the stink of tallow on top of everything else?'

'If it's bad for our family, think of Miss Whiteway who has lost her place, and even more of the Nobles and how they must be suffering,' Violet said softly as her sister started to cry. 'I'm sorry, you are suffering too.'

In the space of a single day and night, it felt as if the Rayfields' comfortable life had hit the rocks and was foundering like a stricken ship.

Chapter Five

Every Cloud Has a Silver Lining

Violet gazed out of the schoolroom window – there was no military band playing on the lawn today, just a raggedy old gentleman hobbling along with a black dog at his side. According to May, the regiment had moved on, leaving the women of Dover broken-hearted. She heard the hoot of a steam engine and shouting from a group of navvies on the street.

'What are we going to do without Miss Whiteway to entertain us?' she said, glancing at the clock. They had been upstairs for half an hour and she was already bored. Without their governess and her nagging tongue, she had little motivation to do anything. What was the purpose of painting when there was nobody to pick holes in it? How could they learn any more history without someone to teach them?

'It's a relief that she's going – I can entertain myself,' Eleanor said.

'That's a selfish way of thinking,' Ottilie said sharply. 'You know her situation – she's dependent on others for her living.'

'She will find another place,' Violet said.

'Only if Mama has given in and provided her with a decent reference as to the quality of her character.'

Ottilie's eyes were red. Violet guessed that she had cried all night.

'I'll find out,' Violet offered. 'I should hate to see her wronged because she spoke up for her beliefs.'

'Even though they are completely misplaced. I wish you luck in changing Mama's mind.'

'I don't think I'd bother her with it today,' Eleanor said as Violet walked towards the door, her skirts rustling across the floorboards.

'This can't wait,' Violet said firmly, and she ran downstairs and stormed into her mother's room. 'I need to talk to you. Oh!' She looked down at the rug. *The cat has been sick – I have ruined my slippers*, was on the tip of her tongue, but she fell silent when she saw that Mama was still abed.

'Hush. I have a terrible headache,' she groaned, as she rearranged a flannel compress across her forehead.

'Shall I call for Mrs Garling? Or send word to our aunt?'

'There's no need for alarm – I'm not at death's door, but I'd very much appreciate it, if you'd send May up with a little weak tea and dry toast. And if you would kindly ask Miss Whiteway to take you and your sisters to the apothecary to buy something for the pain ...'

'I can't do that because you have told Miss Whiteway to leave.'

'Have I? Oh yes, I remember now. In that case, you and your sisters will have to go.'

'Please, for the sake of our education, let me ask her to stay.'

'Since when have you been concerned about your education?' Mama began to chuckle, then gasped. 'Don't argue – I haven't the strength.'

'But poor Miss Whiteway ...'

'The decision is made. She will leave the house by noon.'

Violet didn't see how she could continue with her attempt to persuade Mama to change her mind. She was in no fit state.

'What about a doctor?'

'No doctors! I'll be back to my usual self tomorrow.'

'Do you think it might be down to the wallpaper? It seems too much of a coincidence that both you and Dickens are unwell.'

'Dickens is fine – it's just a hairball. As for me, I blame the damp in here. Mr Jones had his men wipe away the mould before they started hanging the paper, but it will have come back behind it. I've been telling your father that it's time we moved.'

Violet pulled the drapes and dragged the window open to air the room.

'No, that's no good – the light hurts my eyes,' Mama complained, so she closed the drapes again. 'Run along and leave me in peace.'

Violet did as she was told, but before she returned to the schoolroom, she made her way into her father's study where she took the key from beneath the brass inkwell and unlocked the top drawer in his desk. She withdrew a piece of his headed paper and sat down quickly to write.

To whomsoever it may concern.

Miss Whiteway has been in our employment for six years. It is only with the deepest regret that I have had to let her go, not through any fault of her own, but because I no longer require her services as a governess. She has shown great dedication to the task of educating my daughters, paying attention to etiquette, conversation, drawing and watercolour, and music.

Violet tried to scratch out a blot of ink.

Yours faithfully,

Mrs P. Rayfield, Dover.

Would it do? she wondered. She hoped that Miss Whiteway's future employer would take the testimonial at its word and not come calling on their mother to ask awkward questions. She folded the paper, put it into an envelope and took it upstairs, where she slid it underneath Miss Whiteway's door. As she hesitated, she thought she heard her crying. Resisting her instinct to go in and comfort her, she rejoined her sisters in the schoolroom.

Did she feel guilty? She was surprised to find that she didn't. She'd done the right thing by Miss Whiteway and her conscience was clear.

'You didn't succeed in persuading Mama to change her mind?' Ottilie said.

Violet shook her head. 'She has asked us to go and buy medicines for her – the three of us, without a chaperone.'

'That's a turn-up for the books,' Eleanor said from the window seat.

'Give me ten minutes – I have a letter to finish and send to Jane,' Ottilie said.

'Wilson will post it for you,' Eleanor said.

'I'll do it myself – we'll be passing the post office anyway.'

It wasn't long before they were waiting at the back of a line of elderly gentlemen – some chewing on tobacco, some leaning on their sticks – queuing for their sailors' pensions, as the post office cat wound around their bowed legs, begging for attention. Violet diverted Eleanor to look at the letter-writing accessories that were on sale: envelopes decorated with flowers and ships; paper knives made from carved wood; colourful enamelled stamp boxes. She glanced towards her older sister, wondering if she dared buy one, but decided it was more than her life was worth, if she spent the money that Mama had given them on a trinket.

The queue gradually disappeared until Ottilie reached the front and began talking to the postmaster. Behind him was a notice to the public: 'Adhesive stamps must be placed in the right-hand corner at the top of the envelope.'

After Ottilie had sent her letter, they set out for Mr Archer's shop. The outside was painted a deep green with lettering picked out in gold, and the bay window was filled with glass bottles containing a veritable rainbow of potions. As they approached, who should emerge but Mr Noble, his eyes downcast and a brown paper bag in his hand.

He glanced up, and at first, Violet wondered if he was going to push straight past them. She wouldn't have blamed him for slighting them after what had happened with the *Dover Belle*, but he stopped.

'The Misses Rayfield. Greetings,' he said stiffly.

'Mr Noble – I mean, William,' Violet said. 'Please accept our condolences and convey our sympathies to your mother.'

'Thank you. Mrs Noble sent me out for sleeping drops, but' – he shrugged – 'there is no medicine to cure grief, only time, I believe, and even then ... Well, I don't think my mother will ever recover from it.' His voice cracked. 'I've never seen her laid so low.'

Violet didn't know what else to say. She turned to her sisters, but they were like the shrunken head in the curiosity cabinet at home, uncharacteristically silent as if their mouths had been sewn shut.

'I wish there was something we could do,' Violet said.

He forced a small smile. 'It is enough to know that my mother and I have your sympathy. Now, I must go – she will be wondering where I am. Goodbye, ladies.'

'Goodbye,' Violet echoed before rounding on her sisters when he had gone. 'Why didn't you speak?'

'Because you said everything that needed to be said,' Ottilie replied slyly. 'We assumed you would be keen to console him.'

'We should go inside,' Eleanor said.

Violet pushed the door open. The bell jangled, bringing a grey-haired gentleman to the counter, on which stood a cast-iron set of scales, a pestle and mortar, and a book.

'Good morning, ladies. How may I help you?' He cocked his head, reminding her of a beady-eyed pigeon.

'It's our mother,' Violet said. 'She is indisposed with a headache.'

'Ah, then tell me what is the nature of the headache … is it to one side? Does it wax and wane? Is it mild or crippling?'

'I'm afraid she didn't say. It's very painful, and her complexion is quite pale.'

'Then I have some patent medicine that will suit her very well.'

'You are familiar with all kinds of illnesses, sir,' Violet said. 'Pray, can you tell me if our mother's troubles could be down to arsenic?'

'Oh no, there's no likelihood of that – we sell Dr MacKenzie's Harmless Arsenic Skin Wafers and toilet soap to whiten the hands, neck and face. It's very popular – in Dover and London. Please be reassured that your mother will have come to no harm from the presence of arsenic.' He turned and pulled a small brown bottle out of one of the drawers behind the counter and placed it in a paper bag. 'Your mother will take this according to the instructions on the bottle, three times a day until her symptoms abate.'

Thanking him, Violet took the bag. Ottilie paid him from her purse, and they made their way back home.

'Quickly,' Violet said, spotting Mrs Pryor, their neighbour, emerging from her house, but it was too late. She came trotting over to them, still quite nimble for a woman in her sixties, the ribbons on her bonnet flying loose and a shopping bag on her arm.

'Anyone would think she'd been lying in wait,' Eleanor said.

'Ah, the Misses Rayfield. Fancy seeing you out and about without your governess. It's most unusual.'

Violet didn't know what to say, leaving Mrs Pryor ready to pounce.

'I thought as much – your housekeeper has been talking to one of our maids. Mrs Rayfield has terminated her employment, but for what reason? Do tell. We are all friends around here.'

'There's no reason except that Mama considers Eleanor too old to need a governess.' Violet knew it was a lie and Mrs Pryor knew it was a lie, but she wished to protect her family. The neighbours didn't need to know their business.

'I've heard a rumour that your father has broken with Mr Chittenden over the sinking of the *Dover Belle*,' Mrs Pryor said, undeterred.

'Our father doesn't discuss business with us,' Violet said sweetly as she tried not to stare at Mrs Pryor's double misfortune: white whiskers on her chin and a wart on her nose. 'You will have to ask him directly. Now we wish you good day, Mrs Pryor.'

'Oh yes. Thank you. A good day to you too,' she said.

The sisters turned away, rang the bell and Wilson opened the door.

'The Misses Rayfield return.' He smiled. 'I knew you would, but the other servants have been fretting about you getting lost.'

They left their bonnets and shawls, and went upstairs to give Mama her medicine. She seemed almost back to normal, Violet concluded, and they spent the day with her, talking, embroidering and playing charades and twenty questions.

However, Mama's health went downhill again over the following days and nights, and one morning – four days after they'd heard about the fate of the *Dover Belle* – she took the medicine and remained in bed, refusing to get up, even when Mr Brooke called to see Pa.

On hearing voices in the hall, Violet – who had been on her way downstairs – stopped and hid in the shadows behind the balustrade on the landing above. She could just see Mr Brooke dressed in his blue coat, dark green trousers and pointed shoes.

'Good day, Sidney,' he said effusively, his voice booming like a ship's horn.

'Ah, welcome, Arvin.' Pa stepped forwards and shook his hand. Violet assumed that the two men would retreat to her father's study, but they remained where they were.

'Did you attend the inquest at the Maison Dieu?' Mr Brooke said.

'Of course – as joint owner of the *Dover Belle*, I was obliged to turn up. It was a straightforward hearing – the coroner stated from the evidence of the wreckage found where the ship was last seen, that all on board had perished from drowning. Little was said about the general condition of the ship, or the reputation of the master, although Mr Chittenden brought evidence of her recent overhaul and the crew's certificates.'

'And everything, naturally, was in order?'

'The coroner was satisfied that the ship was seaworthy, and the master and crew were competent. Mr Chittenden and I were cleared of any blame.'

'As I expected, but I hear through the grapevine that you and Mr Chittenden have had a falling out. I have no wish to interfere in your affairs – I mean, why would I when I have my own business that's making profits of many thousands of pounds a year? However, I wondered if it would help if I acted as mediator between the two of you.'

'No, it's too late. I refuse to have anything to do with him.' Pa's tone brightened. 'Every cloud has a silver lining, though – this means I can give my full attention to our new venture.'

'That's true. However, I've also heard that you're liable to pay compensation for the loss of the *Dover Belle* from your own pocket.' Mr Brooke raised one eyebrow. 'Will that be a problem?'

'It's an inconvenience to me, not an issue for us jointly,' Pa reassured him. 'Is there anything else?'

'There is, and it's a rather delicate matter – William Noble is doing his utmost to blacken your name. We really don't need any scandal, so out of kindness to the young man and to create goodwill, I think it's important for him to be able to complete his apprenticeship while looking after his mother.'

'You're a philanthropist as well as an astute businessman, Mr Brooke,' Pa said. 'You're right – I'll settle the amount in full, out of respect for the families who have lost their loved ones.'

'Society admires private acts of benevolence more than those carried out in the public gaze. You should invite Mr Noble here to give him what he is due, then we can arrange for the details to slip out afterwards.'

'You speak wisely,' Pa said.

'And what about Mr Chittenden? Are you liable for his half of the ship?'

'I accept my responsibility in this and I will pay him back every penny.'

'You are a generous man. Forgive me if I give offence, but it would give me great pleasure to assist you if you are strapped for—'

'No, Arvin.' Pa raised his hand. 'It isn't necessary. We English find it vulgar to talk of money, but suffice to say, I have no difficulty in helping these people – it is a drop in the ocean, after all.' He smiled, but from where Violet was standing, she didn't get the impression that his smile reached his eyes. 'Although my dear wife has spent a fortune on furniture at Flashman's, she has failed to bankrupt me so far. Her father bought gold, a wise investment that remains secured in a London bank – I could buy all the vineyards in France, no trouble. No trouble at all.'

'Then you have reassured me, Sidney,' Mr Brooke said. 'I'm sorry for calling on you at this early hour.'

'Why don't you come with me to the office this morning? I can find you a desk and a clerk, whatever you require.'

'That's very kind of you, thank you.'

'I'll have the contract for our partnership drawn up as soon as possible.'

'Brooke and Rayfield – I like the sound of it. Together we will be formidable!' Mr Brooke pumped her father's hand until he grimaced with the pain. It was all arranged, Violet realised. Pa had quickly replaced Mr Chittenden with Mr Brooke. Was that how business worked? Did he have no sense of obligation or loyalty?

'We'll celebrate – how about dining with the family this evening?' Pa suggested.

'How is Mrs Rayfield, though? Has she fully recovered from her headache the other night?'

'She still isn't herself.'

'Give her my kind regards then. Out of respect for the lady of the house, I regret I must decline your offer of dinner. Please convey my apologies to the young ladies. I know they'll be terribly disappointed – Miss Rayfield, especially.'

In spite of everything, Violet suppressed a giggle. Mr Brooke was deluded if he imagined Ottilie had any interest in him. Whatever had given him that impression?

'I hope that on another occasion, you will allow me to be seated beside Miss Rayfield so I may encourage her progress in French conversation.'

'Certainly …'

Violet heard the men's voices fade as they left the house. She had seen Mr Brooke in a new light. He wasn't merely an acquaintance with no sense of fashion or rhythm, but a thoughtful and well-intentioned gentleman offering her father financial help and showing concern for her mother. Pa was a good man too, she thought, the best father anyone could have, even though his fallibility had taken her by surprise.

Chapter Six

Mock Turtle Soup

A few days later, Violet was in the kitchen with May and Cook, Mama having decided that without a governess to entertain them, her daughters should take turns learning how to prepare a few dishes, so they could talk knowledgeably of the ingredients and costs, in anticipation of them leaving home to run their own households. Would she be baking cherry cakes or gooseberry pies, like Ottilie and Eleanor had?

'Today, we're makin' mock turtle soup,' Cook said, and her heart sank. 'The mistress says you're to get your 'ands dirty, and me and May thought you'd like to have a go at cutting up the 'ead.' She nodded towards the calf's head that was steaming on the marble slab beside the sink. 'Di'n't we, May?'

'Did we?' she exclaimed.

'Hey, you agreed we'd lead 'er on for a bit.'

Cook sounded annoyed, but May winked at Violet and said, 'It doesn't seem right asking one of the Misses Rayfield to slice her own meat.'

'In that case, she can chop the onions – two of them large ones over there in the rack. There's an apron on the 'ook – you can 'ave that one. What are you waitin' for, miss?'

Violet cried while she sliced the onions, but she wasn't unhappy. While she was here in the kitchen, she could put the Rayfields' troubles aside.

'It's easier than breakin' into a green turtle, which is what goes into the genuine article.' Cook handed her a cloth. ''Ere, wipe your eyes.'

Violet went on to prepare some lemon peel while May sliced the meat from the calf's head and Cook prepared a mutton broth, adding sherry, chopped brain and oysters, mace and thyme. Violet hardboiled some eggs and May added the meat to the mixture.

'Oi, that should be on a light simmer,' Cook complained. 'That's bubblin' on a full boil – it'll ruin the flavour. Mind you, if our guest don't like it, he can lump it. I've told the mistress, I'm not cookin' anythin' fancy to make 'im feel at 'ome.'

'You mean, the strange Mr Brooke?' May said.

'I suspect that 'e's considered to be a bit of an oddity both 'ere and abroad, but we mustn't speak ill of 'im in front of the young ladies.' Cook took a whole chicken out of the pantry and put it on the marble slab. 'May, I need you to start on the taters, else this feast isn't goin' to be ready in time, and the mistress and Mrs Garling will 'ave it in for me. Thank you, miss. You're done 'ere.'

'Perhaps I could help with the vegetables,' Violet ventured.

'That won't be necessary. You go and dress in your finery,' Cook said. 'I can't do with people under my feet. I'll 'ave to 'ave a word with the mistress – I'm not trained to learn young ladies, not like Miss Whiteway was.'

Violet decided that it was futile to argue, and she left the kitchen, arriving in the hall as the doorbell rang. Had she learned anything? Only that she would never ask her servants to make mock turtle soup – the sight of the calf's brain had turned her stomach. Remembering that it was Wilson's day off, she opened the front door to find an older gentleman on the step, holding his stovepipe hat in one hand and a leather bag in the other.

'Good day. I'm Doctor Hawkes, here to see Mrs Rayfield.' He looked her up and down. 'Please take me to your mistress.'

'Oh, I'm one of her daughters,' Violet said, glancing down at her old brown day dress. She had forgotten to take off the apron.

'I'm sorry for the misunderstanding,' the doctor said. 'May I ask you to act as chaperone?'

'Yes, of course. Come this way.' She showed him to the parlour where Mama was sitting with Eleanor. 'It's the doctor for you.'

Mama looked up. 'Doctor Hawke, I'm very grateful that you called. I'm sure it's nothing, but my husband and daughters have insisted that I call upon your services.'

'What are your symptoms?' he asked.

'Oh, I have a headache now and again, and—'

'Sometimes she is drowsy and confused,' Eleanor cut in.

'I'm perfectly able to answer for myself,' Mama said. 'I'm sure my daughters will ask if I could be suffering from the effects of arsenic …'

'There are reports of poisoning, but in my considered opinion, they are more likely to be cases of hysteria fuelled by publicity. Allow me to examine you and I will see if I can identify the cause of your poor health.'

Mama allowed the doctor to look into her eyes and study her hands, but, out of modesty, she refused him permission to listen to her heart with his stethoscope, or inspect her ankles for swelling.

'You are a little pale, Mrs Rayfield. I can't comment on the reason for your malaise, but I recommend weekly seawater baths until the end of the summer, plenty of rest and nutritious broth. If you're no better in a month, send for me again, and I'll review your situation. If pushed for a diagnosis, I would suggest that you are merely suffering from women's problems which are perfectly normal and nothing to worry about.'

'I've been taking laudanum for the pain.'

'Extract of willow bark would be preferable, Mrs Rayfield. Opium has the effect of dulling the senses. I hope I have put your minds at ease, ladies.' The doctor packed his bag and wished them good day, saying he would send his bill. Violet saw him out, relieved that he didn't have any real concerns for Mama's health. If he'd said that she'd been laid low by the redecoration, then Violet would have insisted on removing the green wallpaper herself.

By the evening, Mama felt well enough to dress for dinner, and the four Rayfield ladies assembled in the drawing room to await the arrival of Pa and Mr Brooke. It was Pa who arrived first, dressed in his evening wear.

'Good evening, my dears,' he said. 'Ottilie, I'd like you to accompany me to my study. I have business with Mr Noble and Mr Brooke.'

'Before dinner?' Mama said.

'I made the appointment at Mr Noble's convenience.'

'You have no need for my presence,' Ottilie said.

'I'll join you.' Violet was curious to find out what the meeting was about and keen to see William again. Why should Ottilie be invited just because she was the eldest?

'I'm not sure that I approve of you dragging our daughters into this,' Mama said. 'Surely, this is gentlemen's business.'

'Come with me, Violet.' Her father dismissed his wife's concern with a wave of his hand.

She followed Pa into his study and took a seat to one side of the desk, before he welcomed Mr Noble and Mr Brooke into the room.

'Good evening, Miss Violet,' Mr Brooke said with a bow. 'How marvellously marvellous to meet you again.'

She glanced towards Mr Noble whose steely expression softened slightly. He was in mourning, a crape band around the hat in his hand.

'You have met my daughter, Miss Violet Rayfield,' Pa said.

Mr Noble nodded. 'Good evening,' he said, but his fist was clenching at his side. He was angry, and understandably so, and now she realised why her father had wanted a calming feminine presence, and witnesses.

'Do take a seat, William,' Pa said.

'No thank you, and it's Mr Noble to you, sir.'

Violet was surprised at his courage in standing up to her father.

'Mr Noble, I've already expressed my sincere regret,' Pa said. 'Nothing I can do or say will ever compensate you and your mother for your loss, but I have put aside the funds to support you in caring for her while you complete your apprenticeship. After that, I will assist you in securing permanent employment – if you will allow me.'

William nodded.

'Then I will arrange a banker's draft.'

'My mother doesn't hold with banking, sir.'

'I doubt the wisdom of that approach when there are large sums of money involved, but never mind, that is her decision.' Pa went on, 'There are conditions.'

'What do you mean? This is your debt to my family.' William paused. A pulse began to tap at Violet's temple, as his expression grew dark with barely suppressed fury.

'Oh, I see … you wish to bind me to silence so I don't blacken the name of Rayfield?'

'I have a document here for you to sign.' Pa took some papers out of one of the drawers in his desk.

'No, sir, I won't sign anything. I won't be blackmailed. If this money isn't given freely from your conscience, then I will not take it.'

'But you must! I insist,' Pa exclaimed. 'Mr Brooke, you must persuade him …'

A flush of embarrassment and annoyance spread up Violet's neck and clothed her cheeks. What was her father thinking of? If he had just given William what he was entitled to, she was sure he would have accepted it without a fuss and gone away quietly.

'Mr Noble, think carefully about this,' Mr Brooke said. 'This is a generous offer. With Mr Rayfield's patronage, the world will be your oyster …'

'I tell you I shall be beholden to no one, least of all Mr Rayfield, who it transpires is only trying to pay me off for his own ends. What does he care about my grieving ma? What does he care about a young man who is trying to make his way in the world? He cares only for himself and his reputation. I have my pride.' He paused for long enough to incline his head towards Violet, then turned on his heels and walked out of the room, slamming the door behind him, making the walls shake.

'Shall I go after him?' Violet asked. Without waiting for her father's reply, she followed William out to the hall.

'Wait,' she said as he placed his hand on the brass doorknob.

He turned. 'Oh, Violet, it's you.'

She rushed up to him, reached for his arm, then changed her mind. 'I'm sorry about my father,' she began.

'There's no need to apologise on his behalf,' he said softly.

'Won't you change your mind about the money? You have every right to accept it.'

'I can't, not when it has conditions attached. You do understand?'

She nodded.

'Violet! Violet, where are you?' she heard her father calling after her.

'You'd better go.' William opened the front door. 'Don't get into any trouble on my account.' He slipped out and closed the door behind him. Violet returned to the study where Pa and Mr Brooke were still talking.

'He is a fool to turn down money for nothing,' Pa said, glancing towards her.

But it hadn't been for nothing, Violet wanted to argue. It had been offered in exchange for his silence. Would she have been as principled if she'd found herself in his situation?

'I hope this doesn't affect our plans, Arvin,' Pa said eventually.

'We'll make sure that everyone knows you tried to do the right thing by the lad, but being hot-headed and a rather foolish young man, he turned your offer down. Knowing the truth of the matter, they will take your side, Sidney.'

His reassurance seemed to please her father, but Violet wasn't satisfied. She walked beside Pa on their way to take their places in the dining room.

'Far be it from me to question my own father,' she began, but Pa interrupted.

'I know what you're going to ask me: why did I insist on him signing the agreement?'

'Well, yes,' she said.

'Because a businessman lives or dies by his reputation, and I can't afford to lose out because of one young man's vitriol, even though he speaks out of grief. Oh, Violet, I can't expect you not to worry about me and my good name, when of my three daughters, you have the kindest heart.'

She bit her tongue – it was William she was concerned for, not her father.

At dinner, Pa placed Mr Brooke beside Ottilie as he'd agreed. Violet and Eleanor sat opposite him, while Pa took his seat at the head of the table with Mama at the far end. Mr Brooke was indeed an honoured guest, Violet thought, noting that Wilson had put out the best silver and most elaborate epergne with cut roses as the centrepiece.

She hardly touched the soup as she listened to the men talk business.

'You must let me know what space you have available for the cargo coming from France,' Mr Brooke said.

'I can broker as much as is necessary,' Pa said. 'It's no problem.'

'I've heard talk on my travels that there are plans to engineer a tunnel which passes under the Channel. Imagine how much easier it would be to transport goods both ways without having to keep loading and unloading them.'

'People have been suggesting it since the turn of the century, but it sounds rather fanciful to me,' Pa said. 'Everything would have to be right – the geology, ventilation and hydrography.'

'Somebody will make it happen in the years to come. It isn't beyond the wit of man, although it might be beyond his pocket for now.' Mr Brooke smiled. 'Anyway, let's put that aside. I've been thinking about how to promote sales, and one of the things I'd suggest is that we organise wine-tastings on the quay.'

'That's an excellent idea, but how do you stop people taking advantage and drinking too much?' Pa said.

'By paying staff to pour the samples. I've done that many times before and it's always been a great success.' Mr Brooke turned to Ottilie, wiping a dribble of soup from his beard. 'Miss Rayfield, what is your opinion?'

'I shall take guidance from my father,' she said, which seemed to please Mr Brooke.

'There is a sly tactic that the winemakers use on occasion, which is to offer the top vintage for tasting then supply an inferior one when the orders are placed.'

'Mr Brooke, you wouldn't do such a thing,' Mama said.

'*Absolument pas.* I have never made a bad wine. It's all about the quality of the grape. Miss Rayfield, you may be surprised to learn that white wine is created from red grapes by pressing them to separate the juice from the skins before fermentation.'

Ottilie expressed a suitable level of astonishment, Violet observed as she rolled her eyes in her direction. Her sister was humouring their guest for their father's sake, and she continued to do so, until they finished dessert and the gentlemen retired to Pa's study to talk further.

The following morning, Violet was on the balcony outside the drawing room, embroidering a spray of flowers on to a silk panel to use as part of a cushion that she was making for her mother's birthday. The long muslin drapes moved gently on the breath of a light summer breeze and a gull circled overhead. She paused when she became aware of voices from inside. Mama and Pa were in the middle of a conversation.

'I have spoken to Mr Brooke ... dear Arvin ... and he has asked me if I will allow him to ask for Ottilie's hand in marriage, to bind our two families together in good fortune.'

'When did he do this?'

'After dinner last night.'

'You didn't think to tell me before?' Mama sounded most indignant.

'I looked in on you and found you sleeping. Patience, I had thought this news would please you.'

Violet sat bolt upright at Pa's talk of marriage, wondering if she should reveal her presence.

'Oh no, that will not do,' Mama said. 'It isn't what we intended for our daughter. Not a tradesman.'

'How many times? He's a merchant, a renowned businessman.'

'Renowned by whom?' Mama said coldly. 'Tell me one person of our acquaintance who has that opinion from before we met him? You boosted him up.'

'You've always given me the impression that you approved of him.'

'As an acquaintance, yes.'

'How many times have you said that your dearest wish is to see our daughters settled? Well, here is your chance to have Ottilie make what I consider an excellent match. He isn't a baronet or a doctor, or a lawyer with an Oxford education, but he is a good man, the salt of the earth.'

'I shan't contemplate it – how can I tell everyone that our eldest daughter is marrying a tradesman? You can dress it up in any way you like, but that's what he is!'

'You married beneath you – as you never stop reminding me.'

'That isn't fair – you're exaggerating. I've rarely mentioned it in all our years together. Our families were both from Dover – they knew of each other. We know very little of Mr Brooke's background, merely what he's told us himself.'

'It doesn't matter about his background. His actions speak louder than words. In spite of his eccentricities, he's charming, considerate and bears no malice towards anyone. We are business partners – I trust him implicitly. Patience, that must count for something.'

'We haven't been introduced to any of his friends or family. We should meet his sister at the very least.'

'You know that isn't possible.'

'I can't imagine that she remains indoors every waking hour because of her appearance. Why don't I present Arvin with the gift of a veil for her?'

'I think that would be … indelicate. I'm certain that he's left no stone unturned in his search for a cure. He's said himself that he's taken her for consultations with the best physicians in Paris.'

'Then he should bring her to England to consult with our doctors for they are the best in the world. You could offer to pay.'

'Arvin isn't short of a few bob – he'd be mortally offended if I suggested such a thing,' Pa said. 'He's a wealthy gentleman, and not only that, he has a fine countenance.'

'A fine countenance does not make a good husband' – Ma's voice softened – 'although it does help.'

She heard Pa's low chuckle. 'Thank you, my dear.'

'I thought that you favoured John Chittenden for our eldest. I believe that he and Ottilie were sweet on each other at one time. In fact, his mother and I often looked forward to the day when we'd see them walking down the aisle at St Mary's. Ah well, our dream of uniting our families is over. It distresses me deeply to think that they'll never call on us again. Sidney, won't you reconsider? Edward used to be like a brother to you.'

'He has shown his true colours – he's a jealous bigot who has tried and failed to persuade me against going into business with Arvin. There's no way back.'

'Are you absolutely certain?' Mama's voice wavered.

'We'll have nothing more to do with the Chittendens – that's my final decision. Now, we have three daughters, each one an expensive joy who requires a husband, a home and a lifetime of support. We don't have the luxury of turning Mr Brooke's offer down.'

'Would you be as keen to have Ottilie settle for him if you weren't in such a precarious position with the bank? Oh, don't tell me it's fine when I know that it isn't. With the loss of the *Dover Belle*, you're still paying the outstanding loan on the money you borrowed to buy her. You've already paid compensation to the families of the passengers and crew, and for the cargo that went down with her. The value of those shares that you bought on Edward's advice has come crashing down – I heard it from Mrs Chittenden, the last time she called on us, Sidney. I take an interest because the money and assets you have left came from my family. It is a matter of heartbreak to me when I see it disappearing, like water rushing down a drain.'

'It isn't that bad. You're making it out to be a complete disaster when it isn't! We will not talk of this again. I shouldn't have to remind you that our home is supposed to be my sanctuary, a place of peace and sweet delights. It is a failure on your part that you do not trust me to manage my affairs after more than twenty years of marriage.'

Violet had heard enough, but she had to wait a full half-hour before she could leave the balcony without being noticed. She went straight to find Ottilie but only Eleanor was in the schoolroom.

'What's wrong? You are all of a flutter.' Eleanor put down her paintbrush.

'Where's Ottilie?'

'With Cook, according to Mama's new regime.'

Violet knocked over a jar of water which spilled across Eleanor's painting. 'I'm sorry. I've spoiled it.'

'You clumsy clodpole! Oh, I didn't like it anyway – the clouds looked like cows and the cows looked like clouds. What's wrong? What's happened?' Violet felt Eleanor's arm around her shoulders. 'Tell me.'

She looked into her sister's calm blue eyes and took a deep breath.

'I've just heard Pa saying that Mr Brooke wishes to ask for Ottilie's hand in marriage. Can you believe that?'

'No ...' Eleanor said, shaking her head. 'No, that cannot be. It isn't possible.' She moved away. 'She has settled on John Chittenden.'

'How do you know?'

'You two can't keep secrets from me. I've seen you talking together and I know those letters aren't from Jane. I'm not stupid! Oh dear, Pa doesn't expect her to agree?'

'He's made up his mind – he's all for it.'

'Violet, what are we going to do?'

'Stay here and act normally. I'm going to warn Ottilie.'

But it was too late. The sound of shouting reverberated from downstairs.

'I will not marry Mr Brooke!'

Violet ran to find her sister, who was in the study with both of their parents.

'What is going on?' Violet rushed in. 'Pa, can't you see my sister is distressed?'

'You will obey your father,' he bellowed. 'It is your duty.'

'Close the window and moderate your tone, Sidney. People will be able to hear you from Calais!' Mama turned to Ottilie who was standing, shaking and crying, in front of the window over the garden at the rear, where May had paused from hanging out the laundry to listen to the din. Violet pushed past her sister and slammed the window shut.

'Oh, my poor darling,' Mama continued. 'Sidney, what have you done? What have you said to her?'

'I've told her that for everyone's sake she must accept Arvin's proposal when he offers it. We've discussed this, Patience, and you didn't disagree.'

'You didn't let me finish having my say,' Mama argued. 'Let's take some time to—'

'There is no time!' Pa exclaimed. 'Arvin and I want this matter settled before he returns to France to oversee the harvest. Ottilie, pull yourself together – you are hysterical.'

'Who wouldn't be?' she wailed as Mama pressed a handkerchief into her hand and stroked her hair. 'I would rather die than take him as my husband.'

'Your father doesn't mean to be cruel. He isn't in his right mind.'

'There is nothing wrong with my mind,' Pa growled. 'It is clearer than ever. Mr Brooke must marry one of our daughters. If Ottilie won't have him, then Violet or Eleanor—'

'Oh no. Eleanor is not yet of marriageable age and Violet's temperament ...'

Violet took a step towards her father, her heart thudding dully in her chest.

'I would consider his offer if that was your wish,' she said quietly, thinking only of Ottilie and John.

'You would?' Pa gazed at her, his expression flickering from uncertainty to hope and back again.

'I mean it,' she went on.

'Then that is something to think about.' Pa's mood seemed to lift. 'I will have to find out if Arvin's preference is settled, or if there is some leeway for alteration. Thank you, Violet. At least you can see your way to doing your duty by your family. I will go and speak to him urgently. Good day, ladies.'

When he'd gone, she leaned against the desk, her palms damp and her cheeks flushed. What had she gone and done? She felt sick, wretched.

'What a to-do,' Mama said, looking up. 'Although I have reservations, I'm very proud of you, Violet. You have honoured your father's wishes.'

'Why, Mama? What does he see in that man?'

'Arvin has impressed your father with his ambitious plans.'

'He is a leech,' Ottilie said bitterly. 'He has attached himself to our father, ready to suck at his fortune and reputation.'

'You judge him too harshly,' Mama said. 'I find him pleasant enough.'

'Violet, why did you do it?' Ottilie asked.

'I don't want to talk about it,' she said, walking out of the study and hurrying upstairs to the room she shared with her sister. She threw herself on the bed and buried her face in the pillow.

'Violet?' She heard Ottilie's footsteps padding across the rug and felt her hand on her shoulder. 'My dear sister, look at me. Please.'

At Ottilie's third bidding, Violet forced herself to sit up and face her. Ottilie handed her a handkerchief from her pocket. Violet unfolded it and wiped her eyes, but a tiny square of soggy cloth couldn't dry all her tears.

'That's better.' Ottilie knelt at the side of the bed, took Violet's hands and squeezed them, just like their nanny had used to when she had fallen over and scraped her knees as a little girl. 'You mustn't agree to this. You have to pull yourself together, go downstairs and tell Pa that you've made the wrong decision. You can't possibly marry Mr Brooke, because you have no affection for him.'

'How can I do that?' Violet said fiercely. 'How can I go back on it? If I don't marry Mr Brooke, you'll have to.'

'But why do you sacrifice your happiness?'

'For you, Ottilie. For you and John.'

'Oh, Violet.' Ottilie eyes brightened as she released Violet's hands. 'It's the most wonderful gesture, and only what I'd expect from you, but I can't let you—'

'No more!' Violet's heart thudded dully in her chest. 'It is settled.'

'Then I can't find the words to express the depths of my gratitude,' Ottilie said in a small voice. 'There are other obstacles in our way – the consequences of the loss of the *Dover Belle*, for example. Can you see Pa ever softening his stance against the Chittendens and giving me and John his blessing?'

'It isn't impossible.'

'I wish I could believe you,' Ottilie sighed.

Violet found some solace in the notion that her sister would at least have the chance of marrying for love, although she wished she could say that she'd done it out of her own free will so that Ottilie didn't have to suffer from heartbreak. However, when it came down to it, she was a young woman trapped by her situation, her wishes subjugated to the needs of her family and the expectations of society. All she could do now was pray that Mr Brooke, having been rejected by Ottilie, would decide to walk away from marrying any of the Rayfield daughters.

Chapter Seven

The White Cliffs of Dover

Violet realised that her prayers had been in vain when her father gave her an envelope addressed to her when he returned home the following evening.

'Open it then,' he said.

With trembling hands, she placed it on the side table in the hall, took the letter-knife from the drawer and slid it beneath the seal. She pulled out the slip of perfumed paper and let it unfold on her palm.

'Mr Brooke requests the pleasure of Miss Violet Rayfield's company for the afternoon of the last Saturday in July. Oh no, he wishes to walk out with me.'

'What did you expect?' Pa said, his eyes twinkling with amusement. 'Didn't it occur to you that he'd want to spend time in your company? Marriage is a serious proposition – he needs to be sure that you're suited. Don't worry – you'll be chaperoned. I've prevailed upon your aunt and cousin to accompany you and your sisters on this outing, as your mother isn't up to walking. They will be dining with us afterwards.'

The reality of the situation hit her between the eyes. She had a terrible headache and feared that she was going the same way as Mama. For an hour, she was convinced she was going to die, and she wasn't scared because it seemed like the answer to her prayers. She had made a mistake, rushing headlong into courtship with a man she barely knew.

Saturday came all too soon. She took a long time to dress in her Sunday best, trying to delay the dreadful moment when she would have to walk with her suitor. She put on her dress over her corset, camisole and hoop skirt, and Eleanor fastened the back before choosing the sea pearls for her to wear around her neck.

'I must have a bonnet with a large brim. I want to cover my face as far as possible.'

'But Mr Brooke will want to look at you,' Eleanor said.

'I don't want to be seen. I'll be mortified if anyone we know recognises me.'

'If you marry him, you'll have to get used to it. He isn't handsome, but he isn't ugly either.'

That was true, Violet thought, feeling sick as she went down to meet the Rayfields' guests in the hall.

'Good afternoon, ladies,' Mr Brooke said. 'How wonderful to see you … Violet, it is a lovely day for a stroll around Dover, is it not?'

'We will be accompanying you,' Aunt Felicity cut in.

'All of you? I'm deeply honoured to have the company of so many beautiful ladies.' Aunt Felicity frowned as Mr Brooke offered Violet his arm. 'I wish to see the sights, and' – he lowered his voice – 'become better acquainted with you, my dear.'

'That would be most acceptable.' Blushing, Violet stepped back, remembering Miss Whiteway's lessons on the etiquette of courtship. Mr Brooke seemed to have no idea that there should be no physical contact between them before they were engaged. 'Have you any preference for which route we take?'

'I've visited the castle and the Western Heights,' he said. 'I wonder if we might walk up to the lighthouse, if everyone is in agreement?'

There were murmurings of assent before they set out from the house.

'Perhaps we can lose our companions, if we go at a good pace,' Mr Brooke whispered, his breath gusting with garlic and good humour.

Violet smiled at the idea of engaging in a little mischief.

'Your father has said that you are not averse to my suit. *Bon, très bon,*' he said, without waiting for her answer. 'It's a hindrance in Dover society not to be in possession of a beautiful wife, but I am getting ahead of myself. You are turning heads.'

'You flatter me, sir,' she said, but it was Mr Brooke who was attracting the attention for his eccentric way of walking and the oddness of his dress, as they strolled past the baths and turned left along Marine Parade. They must make a strange entourage, she felt.

They headed along East Cliff Terrace and passed the jetty before reaching the cliff path: she and Mr Brooke striding out, their hands behind their backs, with her sisters, Jane and Aunt Felicity trailing along behind. At the top of the white cliffs, they paused to admire the view of the town below them with the harbour and Admiralty Pier beyond.

'I wish you'd slow down a little,' Aunt Felicity gasped as she caught up with them, but they set out again, leaving her, Jane, Ottilie and Eleanor to catch their breath.

Violet and Mr Brooke passed Langdon Hole and made their way to the South Foreland lighthouse where they stopped again to gaze at the lantern on the top.

Mr Brooke mopped his brow. 'If it wasn't for this, I wouldn't be at all happy about crossing the Channel – its light guides the boats past the Goodwin Sands and into the harbour.'

'I'd forgotten that you are a regular traveller,' Violet said, as the seagulls swooped and cried above them. In the distance, she could see Cap Gris-Nez, and a steam-packet's foaming wake.

'You have had no prior attachment?' he asked suddenly.

'No, of course not,' she said, shocked. 'What makes you ask?'

'I saw how you danced with Mr Noble at the ball, and how your manner seemed to demonstrate some affection for him when he met with your father at the house to discuss his offer.'

'I was sorry for him – I am sorry for him,' she said emphatically. 'He has suffered greatly. If my manner suggested anything other than sympathy, it wasn't intended.'

'Then your innocence is beyond doubt, your behaviour past reproach.' Mr Brooke smiled. 'Thank you, my dear. You have given me much encouragement today. Let's amble back through the lanes, giving our companions the chance to keep up. Your father is expecting us for dinner.'

She wondered if she should have asked him about his history, not that it would make any difference to the path she had to tread. Whatever she had felt for William, it was too late. She was set above him, and her father had agreed to match her with a man whose frock coat smelled damp and fruity like an old cellar.

Aunt Felicity and Jane stayed on at the house in Camden Crescent, fearful for Mama's health. Mr Brooke called late one afternoon the following week and Violet's apprehension knew no bounds. She'd never been left on her own in the presence of a gentleman, let alone with the knowledge that his sole intent was to ask for her hand. She didn't know what to say or how to behave when her father ushered him into the parlour and left him there with her.

'Please don't be nervous,' Mr Brooke said. 'I believe your father has mentioned my intentions.'

She cleared her throat. 'Yes, yes, he has.'

'I expect he's raised the subject of my financial security – as you know, I have a chateau in France, vineyards, cellars and an apartment in Paris, much more than a young lady such as yourself could imagine. You won't need to concern yourself with making money, only spending it. I hope this will help you make your decision.'

I believe that we're equal in consideration of wealth, and I scold you for assuming that my heart can be swayed by a disparity of fortune, was what she wanted to say to make herself seem worldly and sophisticated, but instead, she blurted out, 'I wouldn't marry anyone merely for his money.'

'Ah, then you believe there must be some affection between husband and wife.'

'I think so – for a marriage to be a success.'

'I've heard it said that one of the great joys of marriage is getting to know one's spouse, learning about their preferences and dislikes, and discovering what makes them happy. My dear Violet, I realise that we hardly know each other, but I hope that as time passes, we will reach that state of comfortable intimacy that comes with close acquaintance,' Mr Brooke said. 'I pray that you have no doubt about the constancy of my admiration for you.'

'We have known each other but a few weeks,' she said stiffly, *and you wanted to marry my sister*, she thought, her heart pounding as the reality of what she was about to do sank in. She still had time to change her mind, but the consequences were hard to contemplate.

'I knew you were the one as soon as I set eyes on you,' he went on.

'Did you?'

'Perhaps not immediately,' he admitted. 'What does it matter? It is the here and now that counts, and, Violet, be assured there is nothing I wish for more than for you to accept my hand in marriage.' He sank to his knees in the parlour and reached up for her hands, squeezing them tight. 'Will you marry me, my dear?'

'Yes,' she whispered, frozen in fear. She felt no joy nor even relief that everything was settled, that she was engaged to a gentleman who could provide her with everything she could dream of, and that the Rayfields were financially secure. Her father and Mr Brooke would go forward as family and business partners, and one day, Ottilie and John would marry.

'You have made me very happy.' Smiling, he pulled himself up. 'May I kiss you?'

She nodded, and he leaned in to her with his hands behind his back and planted a wet kiss on her cheek.

'Ah, I've made you blush.' He chuckled. 'Shall we go and announce our news? That you are to be the next Mrs Brooke.'

She frowned. 'The next?'

'After my mother, of course,' he said. 'I have a piece of Chantilly lace she would have wished you to wear at our wedding.'

'Thank you.' It was a romantic gesture which made her feel more warmly towards him, although she felt no passion.

'Love will blossom between us – trust me.' He took her by the hand. 'My sole aim will be always to please you, my dear.'

'And I will do my best to make you happy,' she said.

Mama and Pa were so delighted, and Mr Brooke so attentive and kind that Violet began to feel better. Aunt Felicity and Jane congratulated them, and the servants were invited into the parlour to drink a champagne toast to the happy couple, and there was talk of setting a date for the wedding, and how many guests should be invited. Mama proposed that May should go with Violet and Mr Brooke to their new home, and Mr Brooke mentioned that they would rent a house in Dover, one larger and more suitable than the place he was currently renting.

'It's a fresh start,' Pa kept saying.

'It's an event to take our minds off our troubles,' Mama agreed.

'Congratulations, Violet ... and thank you,' Ottilie said, giving her a hug before Eleanor took her aside to give her opinion about her future brother-in-law.

'What does it mean that he can transfer his affections from one to the other so quickly? Don't you yearn for a love match?'

'I can learn to love him.'

'Really? Oh well, I suppose he has a polite way of speaking, but he also has odd manners, bushy side whiskers and a generous beard in which one may find all kinds of unsavoury things.'

'Oh, Eleanor,' Violet laughed.

'You will have to kiss him on your wedding night. There will be spiders and fleas, maybe even a whole live guinea fowl.'

Violet felt a little repulsed at the thought.

'He often scratches his beard when he's talking to Pa,' Eleanor went on. 'He's doing it now. Look.'

Violet peered towards her fiancé. He had a lively look about him, and was charming to Mama and her sisters, but she knew very little about him. Did he wish to have lots of children? Where would they live? He'd mentioned renting a house in Dover, but would they spend time in France as well?

She overheard Pa as he shook Mr Brooke's hand.

'I know you'll look after our daughter – in fact, I don't look at it as losing her, but as gaining a son. Allow me to help you find a house – you will require somewhere to suit your standing.'

'I have no particular requirements,' he said. 'I mean, love in a cottage would be delightful—'

'Only if it were a very spacious cottage,' Aunt Felicity cut in.

'Love in a chateau would be far more enduring,' Pa said with a chuckle.

'Oh Mr Rayfield, don't let him take her away from us,' Mama exclaimed.

'I have great respect for you and your illness, Mrs Rayfield. If I do whisk Violet away to France, it will be only for a few months here and there. I find that I prefer to live in Dover, but not for the weather. The winds are beastly, and I've never known so much rain, but the people are polite and refined.'

'Have you any suggestion as to a date for the wedding?' Pa asked.

'I thought within two or three months – a longer engagement would be trying to me,' Mr Brooke said. 'Unfortunately, I'm booked to return to France on Monday next week, so I will have to let my delightful fiancée make the arrangements.'

'You're leaving so soon?' Aunt Felicity enquired. 'That is such a shame when you are newly engaged.'

'It's unavoidable, I'm afraid. I must be there for the harvest.'

He stayed for dinner before saying farewell, leaving Violet feeling confused. How was it that she was engaged to be married, yet she felt no different? She and her aunt helped Mama to bed because she had worn herself out. She left them talking, but hesitated outside the open door.

'You will soon be better, restored to health?' her sister said.

'The doctor can't give me any reassurance on that matter,' Mama said sadly. 'The headaches are bad when they come, but it's the tingling I can't bear. I feel this pricking in my hands and feet as if someone's stabbing them with pins.'

'I hope Sidney has paid for more than one opinion. I have a contact at a Harley Street clinic – we could make an appointment and spend a few days in London.'

'Thank you, but I really don't feel up to making the journey.'

'Then Mr Rayfield can pay for a house call.'

'I'm not sure that he will – he's been making economies recently.' Ma spoke frankly when she was with her sister, all manners and reserve cast aside.

'Is he in some kind of trouble?'

'He claims that all is well, but I can't help worrying. I don't think he's happy and sometimes I wonder … well, I blame myself. This illness has been wearing me down and wrecking my looks. He doesn't come to me at night any more … he hasn't for a while.'

'I expect he's worried about his dear Violet being married off. I know I would be.'

She was aware that her aunt wasn't impressed by her fiancé.

'I don't trust that man – he has a cast in his eye.'

'Does he? I hadn't noticed. Felicity, I think you are too determined to find fault in him.'

'Why is he in such a hurry to marry her?'

'Because he's set his heart on her, and it isn't hard to see why. She's a rare beauty with her white-blonde hair and blue eyes.'

'That's all very well, but how does she feel about him? He's almost twice her age and he reeks of garlic.'

'You're exaggerating! I confess I wasn't sure about it at first – we hadn't been long acquainted with Mr Brooke before he made the offer,' Mama said. 'Although he's a little eccentric, it turns out that he's quite charming and a gentleman of considerable means. Violet is very happy with the arrangement. What would you have done if he'd offered for Jane? Can you look me in the eye and tell me you would have turned the opportunity down? No, I thought not.'

Violet wished for her aunt's approval, but it wasn't forthcoming. Perhaps it was because she was envious of the Rayfields – after all, poor Jane was well on her way to being left on the shelf.

Later, Aunt Felicity called for her. She found her sitting up at the dressing table in the guest room.

'You asked to see me,' Violet said. 'How is Mama?'

'She's exhausted, but I didn't call you up here to talk about her. I wish to talk about you. I wanted to see how you feel about this situation with Mr Brooke. He is not the husband I would have chosen for any of my nieces, but I'm sure you can make a success of the marriage, with the right approach to it.'

Aunt Felicity seemed to have changed her attitude since her earlier conversation with Mama. Perhaps she realised that this marriage was going to go ahead anyway, and they must all learn to live with it.

'I'm looking forward to becoming a wife and having a household of my own,' Violet said, 'but I can't help feeling that I wrong Mr Brooke, for I don't feel any romantic attachment.'

'It's desirable but not essential in a marriage. You've read too many novels. Marriage is a deal, a transaction of youth and beauty, of feminine perfection for a husband's support. Imagine if love came into it – it would be nigh impossible to organise a marriage, waiting for the whim of Nature, the wave of desire that is supposed to sweep one off one's feet. Your mother was lucky to have a love match, but in my experience it's very rare. Often, couples set out with little affection between them, until at the end they come to fear living without each other.'

Violet wondered if her aunt was talking about her own marriage – she had lost her husband from consumption two years after the birth of their only daughter.

'I am disappointed,' she confessed.

'Life is filled with disappointments – and joys. You will manage your household and bear children. In fact, you will find you don't have to spend that much time together. I don't think I ever saw my husband for much more than an hour a week.'

'In that case, I'd be very lonely. I don't want that kind of marriage.'

'Then you will do your best to make it work. You'll run the house as Mr Brooke wishes, making sure to keep the domestic issues with staff and tradesmen to yourself so as not to bother him. There's nothing a husband dislikes more than coming home after a long day to a tirade of niggles and anxieties. You will have observed, I hope – before your mother became unwell anyway – how she always puts her occupations aside upon your father's return, greeting him with a smile and wearing fresh clothes.'

'Yes, Aunt,' she said, thinking back to Miss Whiteway's views which had been very different.

'And then there is your duty in the bedroom ... When you please your husband, you'll find that he'll be more

cheerful and his character more malleable. Do you understand me?'

Violet was afraid that she did.

It was Arvin's last evening in Dover before he travelled
to France, and he was dining with the Rayfields as had
become his custom. When it was time for him to leave,
Violet's family retreated tactfully to allow them a private
moment to say goodbye. She stood in the hall with him,
wondering what to say.

He put his hand in his pocket and drew out a purple
silk handkerchief. At the same time, she caught sight of a
flash of gold, and heard something scutter across the tiles
and settle beneath the oak hallstand. She ducked down to
find it, running her fingers along the tiny gap between the
umbrella tray and the floor.

'Allow me,' Arvin said. 'Violet, you don't have to do
this. It's rather unbecoming of you to crawl about on your
knees like a maidservant.'

It was too late – she stood up again, holding the locket
between her finger and thumb.

'Give it to me,' Arvin said, but she turned away and
opened the tiny catch, her blood running cold when she
caught sight of the ringlet of dark hair inside it.

'To whom does this belong?' she asked, turning back.

'I could pretend that it belonged to my dearly departed
mother, but I'll be honest with you.'

'Who was she? What was she like?' The sickly sweet
scent of rose petals from the bowl on the hall table filled
her nostrils.

'It doesn't matter.' He grabbed the locket and slipped
it into his pocket.

'You must destroy it.'

'I think you are jealous, dear Violet.'

'I'd be a cold-hearted fiancée if I wasn't.' Her cheeks grew hot at the idea of him courting another woman.

'I had thought that this lady – the one to whom the hair belongs – was going to be my wife, but something happened between us and the wedding didn't go ahead.'

'Why didn't you say anything? Why did you keep it from me?'

'It's a past chapter in an old book. Why should I revisit it when it caused me such sorrow?'

'Oh, Arvin, I'm sorry. It upsets you.'

'It's my fault – I should have got rid of it.'

'It still concerns me that you've had a broken engagement, yet never told me of it.'

'Violet, you know I love your sweet innocence, but sometimes you behave as though you were still a child. However, to prove how much I adore you to the exclusion of all others … You have scissors in your sewing box?'

She fetched them, wondering what he was about to do.

Having taken them from her, he reached out and curled one blonde ringlet around his finger. Then, with a sharp tug, he pulled it straight and cut through her hair, sawing through her thick locks with the scissor blades.

'It will show,' she said anxiously, looking in the mirror. 'How will I explain it to Mama and my sisters?'

'They'll understand – I'll take this with me and keep it close to my heart while I'm away.' He opened his wallet and slipped the curl inside it. 'Now I will bid you *au revoir*, my … love. Even a second's absence is too long for me, but this is business and it has to come first. What is it that Shakespeare said, there is a tide in the affairs of men? Your father and I must take advantage of the flood to make our fortunes, and then you will want for nothing. Oh, you look so sad … your disappointment at the thought of my impending absence pleases me greatly.'

'Really?'

'It means much to me that you've already formed an attachment even though we haven't been engaged for long. It bodes well for the future. I will write to you.' He took her hand and pressed it to his lips. '*À bientôt*. Until we meet again.'

'Goodbye, Arvin,' she said softly. 'I'll write back.'

She touched the corner of her eye, wiping away an imaginary tear. The longer he was away, the longer the wedding could be delayed, and she could continue to live with her sisters and pretend the engagement had never happened.

She watched him walk out of the house and down the steps. He stopped at the bottom, turned and blew her another kiss. With a rueful smile, she closed the door and went to find Ottilie who was in their room, writing a letter.

'What have you done to your hair?' Ottilie said.

'It was Arvin,' she said, flushing. 'He's taken a lock of my hair which sounds romantic, but Ottilie, I have something to ask you – it's of rather a delicate nature.'

'Go on.'

'It's about Arvin. I found him in possession of a locket of hair – he said it belonged to a lady to whom he was previously engaged.'

'It doesn't matter, Violet. He's promised to you now.'

She couldn't explain how she felt: cheated because there had been another woman before her; betrayed because he hadn't seen fit to tell her.

'You're worried that if he's already broken one engagement, that he will break it off with you?' Ottilie tipped her head to one side. 'Or perhaps you're hoping that he will?'

'I don't know,' she confessed. 'He called me his love, but he also talked down to me as if I was a child, and it's always in the back of my mind that he wanted you first.'

'He chose me because I'm the eldest, no other reason. I've been thinking, though – much as I'm grateful for what you've done, you don't have to go through with it. I'll come with you to speak to Pa.'

Violet shook her head. 'When I've said I'll do something, I'll do it,' she said fiercely.

'If you're sure you won't be terribly unhappy,' Ottilie said.

At least Arvin was being attentive to her. He had had at least one affair of the heart before her, which proved that he was capable of love, he had dined with the Rayfields every day since she had accepted his proposal and he had promised to write. She had seen how happy her father was at the prospect of a grand wedding. There was no way she could back down now. She had given Arvin her word.

'He's not so terrible, Ottilie. When we went walking together that day, he put me at ease. He's thoughtful too, and romantic – he's offered me his mother's Chantilly lace to wear at our wedding. Don't worry about me – 1 could do worse than marry him.'

If she wasn't allowed to work for a living or study for a fulfilling career, then she would throw herself into marriage as was expected of her, and she would do it well. She would be the best wife he could possibly have: beautiful, well dressed, a mistress of interesting conversation, yet feminine and submissive. How hard could that be?

Chapter Eight

Marry in White, You've Chosen Right

Aunt Felicity and Jane went back to Canterbury, leaving Violet and her sisters in charge of taking Mama to the bathhouse. When they were about to leave one morning, Violet heard shouting. She went into the kitchen to find that Cook was trying to get rid of a woman wearing filthy clothes and muddy boots, a regular on the streets of Dover, who'd called to sell her besoms.

'I'd like you to leave.' Violet picked up one of the brooms and tried to chase the broom-dasher out. 'You're making a scene.'

'Ah, it's one of the Misses Rayfield,' the woman said, standing her ground. 'Your father 'as sold 'is middle daughter to keep 'is business afloat.'

'Ignore 'er,' Cook snapped. 'She's three sheets to the wind.'

'It's obvious why the gen'leman wants her – 'e's almost twice 'er age.'

'Mrs Wembury, you 'ave a dirty mind,' Cook said, enraged. 'Do as the young lady says! Get out and don't darken this door again.'

The broom-dasher snatched up her wares and stomped from the kitchen, heading out through the back door.

'Good riddance!' Cook snorted. 'Thank you, miss. I'm sorry you 'ad to 'ear that. You'll be back for luncheon?'

'Yes, thank you.' She returned to meet her sisters and Mama in the hall, and they walked down to the bathhouse, one of two such establishments on the seafront. Eleanor carried a bag containing Mama's bathing outfit – a flared dress with long sleeves and Turkish-style bloomers made from flannel – while Mama took Ottilie and Eleanor's arms and struggled along the seafront.

'I'm puffed out,' Mama complained.

'We'll soon be there,' Ottilie said. 'You'll be able to rest.'

They managed to find their mother a place at one of the tables in the busy bathhouse waiting room, where the bathing attendants and waiters were bustling about, trying to keep order among those waiting for their turn in one of the baths or machines. There was an old woman with a terrible cough, and another with bandages around her head.

'I didn't realise there would be so many people here,' Ottilie said.

'Sea bathing is a popular remedy for many ills, but I fail to see how being stuck in here with all these sick people can be good for anyone,' Violet observed, holding a handkerchief to her mouth to keep out the noxious vapours coming from the hot bath in the room next door.

'Violet, can I have a word?' Ottilie went on.

She stepped aside. 'What is it?'

'This way …' They stood in the queue at the desk to book one of the machines outside. 'I'd like you to distract Eleanor while Mama is busy. Tell her I've gone on an errand.'

'What kind of errand?'

'Don't ask me then I won't have to lie.'

'I see. Yes, of course. I'll say we'll wait with Mama. You go, Ottilie.'

'Thank you,' she said softly, her cheeks growing pink.

Violet booked a machine, and they waited Mama's turn, drinking tea.

'Where is Ottilie?' Eleanor demanded.

'She seems to have vanished,' Mama said.

'She's gone to buy mace and sultanas for Cook. The grocer left them off the order by mistake.'

'You are a terrible liar.' Eleanor smiled.

'What are you talking about?' Mama asked.

'Nothing,' Violet said. At least there was no risk that Ottilie would run into Pa. He had an appointment with the solicitor that morning to alter his will. She had no idea about the details – Pa had kept those private – but she trusted him to make sure that her mother and sisters were looked after upon his death.

'Mrs Rayfield. This way, please.' A young woman showed them through to the rear of the bathhouse and let them out on to the beach where a machine, a horse-drawn wheeled wooden cabin with a canvas top, was waiting. Eleanor passed Mama's bag up to the dipper, a middle-aged woman who would push their mother into the sea and assist her in getting out again when she'd had enough. Violet helped Mama into the machine, the dipper closed the door from the inside, and the horses towed it down the beach to the water, heading out some distance before stopping.

'I know very well where Ottilie's gone,' Eleanor observed as the driver unhitched the horses and brought them back to the shore.

'Promise me you'll keep it from Mama,' Violet said.

'I won't breathe a word,' Eleanor said. 'I hope this works. Have you noticed Mama's hair and how it falls out when you brush it?'

Violet nodded. Her nails were breaking too.

While the horses waited, stamping their feet and flicking the flies away with their tails, they returned to the waiting room.

'I wonder what Ottilie is saying to John,' Eleanor said. 'Do you think they will elope? It would be very romantic if they went post-chaise to Gretna Green.'

'Romantic, but foolhardy. One cannot live on love alone. John is dependent on his father. Besides, we would never see them again – Pa would cut Ottilie off for certain.'

'You may be right.' Eleanor looked past her. 'The flag is up – Mama must be ready to come back. I was afraid she might drown with the weight of all that wet flannel. I hope Ottilie turns up soon.'

So did Violet. The longer the horses took to drag the machine back across the beach, the better.

'I'll go and look for Ottilie. You wait for Mama,' Violet said. 'I'll do my best to distract her.'

'Thank you.' Violet hastened outside and looked along the promenade. She walked up and down, searching the crowds for her sister until she caught sight of her straw bonnet and blue dress. As Violet had expected, Ottilie was with John, talking animatedly.

Violet turned back to the bathing house to see Eleanor walking towards her, arm in arm with Mama.

'I tried,' Eleanor mouthed.

'Hurry, Ottilie,' Violet muttered under her breath, but her sister was exchanging a kiss – a kiss on the street with her sweetheart! – and it was too late.

'Where is your sister?' Mama asked.

'She's had to run an errand for Cook – to buy mace,' Violet said.

'Has she? Isn't that John Chittenden over there?'

'Where? I can't see him,' Violet said.

'Neither can I,' Eleanor joined in.

'You two need spectacles. I can see him as clear as day. Who's that with him?' Violet glanced at Eleanor, who frowned. They had run out of options. 'It's our Ottilie. Oh! I was feeling better …' Mama touched her chest. 'All of a sudden, I'm not so good.'

'Please don't upset yourself,' Violet said.

'So she has gone out to buy mace and come back with John instead, when she has been forbidden to associate with him in any way?'

'Hello, Mama,' Ottilie said, walking up to them.

'I saw you,' their mother said coldly. 'How dare you show us up by cavorting in public with your father's enemy!'

'John bears no grudge against the Rayfields,' Ottilie said, her face bright red. 'The argument is between Pa and Uncle Edward.'

'Our families will never reconcile – Mr Chittenden has accused your father of being a thief and a user, even though he's settled almost half of the outstanding debt for his share of the *Dover Belle* so far. John is Edward's son – he is tarred with the same brush.'

'But, Mama—'

'Don't you "but, Mama" me. I'll be speaking to your father when he gets home. No, Ottilie. Don't say a word. You have disappointed me.'

They were banned from leaving the house – all three of them – for a month, Pa having decided that May could take their mother to the bathhouse instead. All they could do was entertain themselves.

'There's a letter for you, Violet.' Eleanor came into the schoolroom one morning and danced around the table, her eyes shining. 'Oh, what intrigue.'

'Anyone would think it was addressed to you.' Violet smiled. 'Is it written in a man's hand?'

'It is doused in the scent of cologne,' Eleanor said.

Violet snatched the envelope and rushed away to the window seat to read its contents.

My dear flower, my little ladybird. I hope you don't mind me addressing you as such.

Arvin expressed his affection in such a dear way, Violet thought.

'Are you there?' she heard Eleanor say. 'I'm sorry for making fun of your letter. It was mean of me.'

Violet pulled the curtain aside and peered out from her hiding place. 'It was indeed.'

'I have your forgiveness?'

'Yes, I think so.'

'May I sit with you?'

She drew the curtain back further, and Eleanor sat down.

'It's from Arvin,' Violet said.

'I guessed so.' Eleanor raised her feet on to the cushion and hugged her knees. 'What does he say?'

'You will keep this to yourself?'

Eleanor nodded. 'At least until I may be allowed to use it in one of my books and under false names.'

'I suppose so.'

'You look sad, dear sister. I'm afraid that Mr Brooke doesn't make you happy.'

'I am content, that's all I can say. I mean, he's an interesting man with a sense of humour, but ...' Her voice faded as William came to mind. She didn't love Arvin – she doubted that she ever could.

'He is very old,' Eleanor finished for her. 'Mr Archer – the apothecary – is twenty years older than his wife.'

'At least.'

'Mrs Archer is waiting for him to drop off his perch, so she can live the life of a merry widow.'

'Your imagination will get you into mischief one day. You know, it isn't so bad – when I become Mrs Brooke, I'll have my own rather wonderful establishment and a husband whose star is rising in Dover society.'

'I'll help you compose your reply, if you like,' Eleanor said.

'I don't know what to say.'

'I'll fetch some paper, a pen and ink.'

They settled down to write …

Dear Arvin,

I find your words most flattering, especially the way you have expressed your sentiments. I am missing you and wish for your safe return very soon. I hope your sister is well. Dover is much the same as when you left. Although Mama is unwell, she is most annoyed because Dickens – you may remember that he is the cat – has scratched the new wallpaper. Pa has refused to pay for the decorator to return to replace it – he says he will wait for the cat's demise which in his opinion can't come soon enough. Mama would be mightily sorry, though, because she loves Dickens as if he were one of her children.

The preparations for the wedding are gathering pace. The invitations have been sent out and I have a dress fitting next week.

Please write more often if you can.

Yours sincerely,

Violet

She crossed out 'Yours sincerely' and put 'From your affectionate fiancée, Violet'.

They exchanged several letters over the following weeks. She received the last one three days before he was due to return for the wedding, expressing his joy at the prospect of their marriage and informing her that he had organised their honeymoon ... to Edinburgh and the Highlands. She brooded on the fact that she had wished to go to France, before realising that she was being churlish. Queen Victoria spent many weeks at Balmoral and if Scotland was good enough for Her Majesty, it was good enough for her.

The day of the wedding dawned and as it was the middle of October, there was a chill in the air. Violet wished that May had been allowed to light a fire in the grate, but Pa had ordered that fires should only be used in the parlour and dining room. He said they were an unnecessary luxury.

'Violet, where are you?' She looked up as Ottilie and Eleanor burst into her room, wearing their matching pale blue dresses. 'You aren't ready? Have you any idea what time it is?'

'You'll be late.' Ottilie drew the curtains. 'Oh, what's wrong?'

'What if I'm making a terrible mistake?'

'You can't think about that now – the time is past,' Eleanor said. 'You can't possibly change your mind on your wedding day. Think of poor Mr Brooke and our parents. You'd be letting everyone down.'

'Mr Brooke's heart is in the right place,' Ottilie said. 'He's sent you those wonderful letters and chosen a lovely house which isn't far away, so we'll be able to see you every day. He has no vices as far as we know.'

'You make him sound like the paragon of virtue,' Violet observed.

'I agree with Ottilie. His manner of dress can be a little flamboyant, but appearances don't matter. It's what's inside' – Eleanor tapped her chest to make the point – 'that counts. Am I beginning to sway you?'

'It's normal for a bride to be nervous on her wedding day. I would be …' Ottilie's voice faded, and Violet's heart went out to her, knowing that she was thinking of John, which reminded her why she had offered herself up for the marriage in the first place. Would it really make any difference? She still harboured hopes that, once she was married off to Arvin and Pa's fortunes improved, he would relent.

'Come on,' Ottilie went on. 'Let us help you.'

'Marry in white, you've chosen right,' Eleanor chanted, picking up the dress from the bed.

'I'd call it ivory,' Violet said.

'Either way, you'll look beautiful,' Ottilie said as she and Eleanor helped Violet into her wedding gown: a concoction of silk and satin trimmed with the Chantilly lace; ruched sleeves; a full skirt over calico petticoats and a crinoline; and with a long train. They placed a coronet of orange blossom and a veil on her head and tied the ribbons on her shoes.

'You have something old, something new, something borrowed, something blue and a sixpence for your shoe, for good luck,' Eleanor said happily. 'Look in the mirror, Violet.'

She gazed at her reflection – she did look well, very well.

'Will Mama be joining us?' she asked.

Ottilie shook her head. 'She's feeling too weak – I've said we'll say goodbye. She's in her room.'

Disappointed, but not surprised, Violet called in on their mother who was sitting up in bed, her hair neatly brushed and set in ringlet papers. She looked up, a smile playing on her pale lips.

'You have remembered what day it is,' Violet said, walking over to kiss her on the cheek.

'How could I forget? My first daughter to be married! I shall be happy and sad at the same time, thinking of the ceremony while I lie here useless in bed. I wish you the happiest day of your life, my dear Violet.' Mama pressed her hand to her mouth to suppress a sudden sob. 'Call on us as often as you can.'

'I promise I will. Mama, you must get well soon so you can visit our new house.'

'I'll try. I don't think the sea bathing is doing me any good.' She sank back against her pillow. 'Run along now.'

'Hurry,' Ottilie said. 'The guests will be waiting, and Mr Brooke will be wondering if you've changed your mind.'

Violet felt a little better at the thought of seeing him again. 'I've missed him while he's been away. That must mean something, mustn't it?'

When she and her sisters went down the two flights of stairs to the hall, they found the servants lined up, smiling and cheering. May ducked towards her in a clumsy curtsey and handed her the bridal bouquet – white carnations symbolising love, bound together with dark green ivy – before the family left the house. St Mary's wasn't far away, only a short walk from Camden Crescent via King Street, but Pa made a show of sending their wedding carriage, drawn by four white horses with silver plumes, along the promenade and back.

When they arrived at the church, Violet gazed out of the window at the crowd which had assembled to catch a glimpse of the bride, and the wedding guests, the great and the good of Dover.

'You have lost your tongue,' Pa observed. 'You are surprised at the turnout?'

She nodded as he went on, 'It goes to prove that the Rayfields are still held in high esteem.'

She nodded again.

When she disembarked, her sisters fussed over her train before she walked into the church on her father's arm. The organist struck up the first chords of a wedding march and rows of faces turned to stare at her. Who were all these people, she wondered, and more importantly, where was her groom?

She caught sight of him, waiting with the vicar at the end of the aisle, half hidden by the array of ferns and flowers that her mother had chosen for decorating the church. He turned and gave her a small smile, seeming as nervous as she was.

The Reverend Green welcomed everyone before they sang hymns and listened to the readings and address. Eventually, the ceremony began with the declarations.

'The vows you are about to make are to be made in the presence of God, who is judge of all, therefore if either of you knows of any reason why you should not lawfully marry, you must declare it now.'

Violet looked at Arvin, standing at her side in a claret frock coat and lavender doeskin trousers – there was no reason why they shouldn't be joined together, and he was hardly the worst husband that Fate could have chosen for her.

They made their vows and Arvin placed a ring on her finger, a plain gold band engraved with the date and their initials. It glinted from her left hand, a symbol of unending love and faithfulness, confirmation that she had done her duty. From now on, she would love and cherish him, and honour him with her body, excluding all others.

The vicar joined their right hands together and said, 'Those whom God hath joined together, let no one put asunder.'

After the blessing, more prayers and another hymn, they walked side by side but several feet apart to the vestry, where she sat down beside her husband and signed the register in her maiden name of Rayfield for the very last time.

'Will you not walk closer to me?' she whispered, as they returned down the aisle, looking neither left nor right for good luck.

'I'm afraid of treading on your dress. You recall what happened at the ball?'

'Oh, Arvin.' She glanced towards him and smiled. He smiled back, and from that moment on, she knew that they would be all right. They would find a way to live happily together, just like the couple remembered in the brass nearby. She wondered if they would be married for even half of the forty-nine years William Jones and his wife Katherine had spent together. How many children would they have? Not ten like they'd had, she hoped. Three or four would be plenty.

Arvin offered her his arm and they stepped outside into the bright October sunshine. While Pa paid for the vicar's services, Arvin having no best man, the congregation threw rice at them. It caught in Violet's hair and her dress, making her laugh. Arvin laughed too, until neither of them knew what they were laughing about.

Even Aunt Felicity seemed to have warmed towards him – her fox fur with its amber eyes seemed to smile when she poked at him with her stick, and said, 'You look after my niece, or I'll have your guts for garters.'

'I will do my best, Mrs Hewitt,' he said cheerfully.

Pa had hired rooms at the Dover Castle Hotel where they received their guests and partook of the wedding breakfast before they cut the cake. Having changed into her travelling dress, Violet prepared to leave with Arvin, but on their way out, she noticed Ottilie looking downcast.

'It will be your turn next,' she murmured to her.

'We'll see. I wish you all the luck in the world. I hope you and Mr Brooke will be very happy.'

'You know, I think we will be.' Violet looked at her husband with pride. He had conducted himself well and seemed genuinely pleased. As for her, she was married to a prosperous gentleman of whom her father wholeheartedly approved. She was eighteen with much to look forward to, her own household among the East Cliff mansions, and the freedom to go out and about unaccompanied. On the whole, she was looking forward to married life, even though in an ideal world she might have chosen differently.

She was excited and nervous in equal measure. They set off on the train at Dover Priory with their luggage to travel as far as London, where they would spend their first night as husband and wife.

They dined together in style before retiring to their suite at the hotel and thence to separate beds, Arvin having changed into a linen nightshirt with lace at the neck and ruffles at the sleeves. He put a black velvet nightcap on his head and sat propped up against three pillows and within seconds he was asleep, snoring like a ... did gentlemen really snore like that?

Violet curled up beneath the eiderdown in her silk night-gown that Mama had insisted she should have for the first night of her honeymoon, relieved yet anxious. Did he not want her in the way a husband should?

The next morning, they had breakfast of poached eggs, ham and sausages and fresh bread with coffee delivered early to their room. The waiter bowed to Arvin before placing the trays on the table, along with a newspaper.

'Is there anything else, sir?' he said, hovering.

'No, thank you.' Arvin hesitated, then sighed. 'Ah, a tip is required.' He stood up and searched through his luggage for a few coins which he handed over to the waiter.

'Thank you, sir. Much obliged, sir.' The waiter bowed again as Arvin waved him away with a scowl of impatience, making Violet feel rather ashamed. Her husband was lacking in manners and she wondered if she could change him.

They sat down to eat and Violet poured the coffee into the tiny cups and saucers before serving up the breakfast on Arvin's plate. With an aching heart, she pictured her sisters at home, eating breakfast together.

'Are you quite well, Violet? You've hardly touched your eggs,' Arvin said, looking over the top of the paper through a pair of half-moon spectacles, which had been another surprise to her.

'I feel a little homesick, that's all.'

'That's only to be expected.' He put the paper down. 'You'll feel better when we get there – I've booked rooms at the best hotel with views of the loch and mountains. There'll be plenty of walks across the moors to keep us amused.'

'Do you think we'll tire of each other's company then?'

'It's the very nature of marriage. Eventually, my presence will grate upon you, and I will find your incessant chatter and questions wearisome.'

'Really?' She saw her expression reflected in the mirror on the wall.

'I'm being sarcastic. You barely speak. Have you nothing to say for yourself?'

Violet bit her lip, upset by his criticism.

'I didn't mean to be so forthright. I am only going on the experience of friends and acquaintances, fine fellows filled with an enthusiasm for life until their wives appeared and sucked all the joy out of them.'

'That will not happen to us. I will not let it.'

He smiled ruefully. 'I know you'll do your best to please me. You're a most obliging and dutiful soul.'

She wasn't sure if that was a compliment.

When they eventually reached their hotel in Scotland, Arvin dispensed with his tweed walking suit and dressed for dinner. They dined again before retiring to bed, and this time, he joined her between the sheets in his nightclothes, and the deed was as dreadful as she'd imagined.

'Arvin,' she whispered afterwards, but he answered her with a loud snore.

At breakfast, he read the newspapers while Violet gazed out of the windows at the sheep grazing among the heather, and the thick grey clouds sweeping down over the mountains.

'What shall we do today?' she asked.

'I thought we'd go out walking, but look at the weather. We'll be washed away. *Zut alors!*'

'We should have gone to France,' she said reproachfully.

'Are you questioning my decision?' He arched one eyebrow, so he must be teasing. 'I've told you we will visit the chateau very soon. In the meantime, we must make the most of these first days as man and wife. As it's raining, we should return to bed.'

'Now? I thought …' She was confused. How had she imagined they would occupy the days and hours?

'I'm sorry, my little ladybird. I forget what a sheltered life you have led.' He took her hand, his fingers sticky

117

with marmalade as he kissed her. 'Did I not please you last night?'

'Oh, Arvin.' She didn't know how to respond. Did one admit the truth and hurt his feelings, or did one pretend for the sake of marital harmony?

'It's all right, my dear. It's natural for a woman not to derive pleasure from the act itself.' He rested his hand on her arm and held it there. 'You will learn to endure it after a while, although it would be preferable for both of us if you could demonstrate some semblance of enjoying it. It's hard to feel passionate about a young lady who lies back with her eyes clenched shut and her body as stiff as a poker.'

As she bit back tears, he reached across and touched her cheek. 'I'm sorry. My poor Violet, I fear that I have rudely shocked you from your innocence.'

'It is my duty as your wife,' she stammered.

'We will go back to bed,' he said, and she turned away to watch the mist rolling across the moor. 'It will be better the second time, I promise.'

The honeymoon passed slowly. Arvin was often out – he was negotiating for a blend of old Scotch that would add to his and her father's enterprise – and Violet grew restless. She asked for stationery and began writing to her sisters but changed her mind. What would it look like, a newly-wed sending letters during her honeymoon? She didn't want to make Ottilie feel guilty about her sacrifice when it had been her decision to marry Arvin. Having put down her pen for the hundredth time, she took luncheon in the dining room, then returned to their rooms to bathe and change into evening wear, before watching the shadows lengthen as the hours slowly unwound.

She let her mind wander back to William, his broad shoulders, dark curls and blue eyes, and most of all his smile. Her conscience pricked as she wondered what might have been, because it wasn't fair on her husband to compare him with another. She blamed her unsettling thoughts on the tedium of Arvin's absences. She couldn't wait to get back to Dover.

Chapter Nine

While the Cat's Away, the Mice Will Play

They went back to the house Arvin had rented for them at East Cliff, not far from Camden Crescent. It was a large residence, furnished with the minimum necessary, and Violet felt lost in the empty, echoing rooms as he showed her around. There was a canvas floorcloth and an odd smell of gas and linseed oil in the dining room. The previous occupant had also left a collection of stuffed birds: owls, gulls and guillemots. She looked out of the long windows towards the sea. Would it ever feel like home?

At least she had May with her, and Arvin had taken on staff – Mrs Davis, a housekeeper with responsibility for cooking duties, whom an agency had recommended, and a man he'd brought with him from France.

After dinner, May helped Violet put her belongings away in her room which adjoined Arvin's.

'I'm very glad to see you, miss. I mean, Mrs Brooke. Married life seems to be suiting you,' May said, more as a question than a statement of fact.

'Ah, there you are. It's time we retired to bed. It's been a long day.' Violet turned to find Arvin beside her. 'Goodnight,' he added, addressing the maid who quickly retreated.

For the next three days, she kept busy, supervising the unpacking of the belongings Arvin had had shipped from France, as well as a few of her own from home. Her aunt had given her a present of *Mrs Beeton's Book of Household Management*.

'It will be useful,' she'd said.

'For the servants?' Violet had responded, and her aunt had smiled and said, 'For you. You'll be able to look everything up and impress them with your knowledge. It's important not to show any sign of weakness, or they'll immediately take advantage.'

She placed the book on a shelf in the library, unsure if she should arrange them alphabetically or by subject. She would ask Arvin when he came back from work, she decided, picking up another book from one of the boxes. She flicked through the pages of Mr Alistair Trent's manual of letter writing. Some of the words seemed oddly familiar, as if she had read them before. She *had* read them before!

She tackled Arvin about it at dinner that evening.

'I found a book that contains the very words you wrote in your letters to me,' she said.

'That can't be right,' he said, frowning.

'I have caught you out in a lie.'

'Dear Violet, one expression of love is very much like another. Those words of affection must have been repeated oftentimes. There is no original thought when it comes to affairs of the heart.'

'I believed you had written those words especially for me, from the depths of your heart, not from Mr Trent's pen.'

She had kept Arvin's letters in a drawer in her room, bound together with pink satin ribbon, just as by writing those sweet words in his absence, he had bound himself into her affections. Now she discovered that it had been rather a sham. She tried to be generous – he had communicated with the best of intentions – but she couldn't help thinking that he'd been lazy in the way he had copied from the book.

'Believe me when I say that it's pure coincidence,' Arvin said.

'I wish that I could.'

'Well, all right. I'll be straight with you – when I sat down to write to you, I couldn't find the words to express the depth of my affection. I turned to the book for guidance. There you go – I used it with the best of intentions. Now, I have had a long day and I'd appreciate some peace and quiet, not the Spanish Inquisition.'

'I'm sorry,' she said. 'Have you any plans for tomorrow?'

'I'm going to Rochester and Chatham to meet with members of the grocery trade.'

'Oh?' She felt a hollow ache in her chest. The honeymoon was well and truly over. 'What shall I do?'

'I don't know. You must entertain yourself, my darling.'

'Perhaps I shall go and visit Mama and my sisters.'

'I'd prefer you not to see them more than once or twice a week. It would look bad if it appeared that you preferred their company to your husband's. You have duties to attend to here: to continue supervising the unpacking; to spend the allowance I've given you on ornaments and pictures to make our house a home.'

Her heart sank a little. She'd liked the idea of having a household of her own, but the idea of running it seemed rather dull.

'In the afternoon, you can do some painting or embroidery, whatever you wish. Don't confront me over my absences, but trust me when I say that your father and I are on the cusp of acquiring great riches.'

In the morning, she was up early to eat breakfast with him.

'I'll be home by six, my love,' he said. 'Oh, and I'd like you to be ready and waiting for me, wearing one of your evening gowns, not an ordinary day dress. We're dining at the Lloyds' – if your father and I are going to make waves in the wine trade, we have to explore all options.'

'Is it a business dinner?'

'In a way – it's an opportunity to make contacts with the right people.'

'Aren't the Lloyds shopkeepers?'

'Oh, that's rather toplofty of you, Violet. We are all the same: flesh and blood.'

'I didn't mean to sound—'

'You will accompany me as my wife – your beauty, if not your conversation, will impress and oil the wheels of any future negotiation. Don't look so anxious – you will do very well, I think. You are such a sweet little thing. *Je t'adore, ma chérie*,' and then he continued in French. He had said that he loved her, but it was as if he had forgotten that she didn't understand much of his native language.

'Arvin, you'll have to teach me more French conversation if I'm to keep up.'

'We'll have plenty of time for that in the future.' He rested his hands on the curve of her waist and planted a kiss on her lips. 'I'll see you later. Enjoy taking charge of your new establishment, Mrs Brooke,' he said with a twinkle in his eye.

She followed him into the hall where Jacques helped him into his black frock coat and brushed some imaginary dust from his shoulders as, like a dandy, he pulled down his wristbands and straightened his necktie.

'How do I look?' he asked her.

'Very … manly,' she said, and she could tell this had pleased him. She waved goodbye and watched him walk down the road in the direction of the office to meet her father. Jacques closed the front door, and she was alone with the servants and wondering what she should do.

'Mrs Rayfield usually went through the menus with Cook on a Monday,' May said helpfully from behind her. 'You could have a word with the housekeeper.'

'Oh, thank you.' Taking a deep breath, Violet went into the kitchen where the housekeeper was whisking eggs in a large blue-and-whiteware bowl. 'Mrs Davis, I'd like to talk about this week's dinners.'

She looked up and stared at her, her eyes narrow and darker than the raisins that were heaped up on the brass scales alongside her.

'I took the initiative and chose 'em myself, according to what the butcher 'ad in 'is shop.'

'Mr Brooke has certain preferences,' Violet began, daunted by the fact that Mrs Davis was at least thirty years her senior, and much more experienced in household matters.

'I'm sure he has, missus,' Mrs Davis cut in. 'But you 'ave to see it from my point of view. Mr Brooke's given me a certain budget that I 'ave to stick to.'

'I see.' Violet felt a little hurt that he hadn't seen fit to mention it to her. 'My husband and I are dining out tonight, so we will not require any dinner.'

'Ah, it would have been useful to have had more notice because I've already started on it. Never mind – the servants and I will eat what we can, and I'll make something of the leftovers tomorrow.'

'I won't have Mr Brooke dining on leftovers,' Violet said rather sharply. 'We will have some fresh fish with a French sauce, a court bouillon.'

'If you want French cuisine, you need to find a chef, a monsieur like the family down the road 'ave – they're frog eaters.' Mrs Davis grimaced. 'I cook plain and simple dishes that are good for the digestion. Tomorrow, you shall dine on pigeon pie and leftovers, and quince. In my opinion, fish should be served as one course of many, not as a main.'

Violet steeled herself against the housekeeper's insolence.

'If I want your opinion, I'll ask for it. I might be young, but I'm mistress of this house, and you will treat me with respect. There are plenty of housekeepers looking for work in Dover.'

'All right, missus, I catch your drift,' Mrs Davis said, backing down.

'I'll thank you to show me where to find the ingredients for peppermint drops.'

'Oh no, I'll make 'em for you. Go on.'

Violet left the room and went upstairs to her boudoir to change into a grey and blue striped dress with beading down the bodice, day wear that was suitable for receiving guests, in case anyone should call. And they did, the ladies of Dover keen to make themselves acquainted with the new Mrs Brooke.

They left calling cards and spent twenty minutes each with her in the parlour, admiring the grandeur and size of the house, marvelling that she had married at eighteen and before her elder sister, and inviting her to various social events: a tea party on behalf of a charity for poor orphans; dinner in Deal; a soiree to celebrate a coming of age.

When the vicar's wife had left, Jacques showed Ottilie into the parlour. Violet breathed a sigh of relief at not having to pretend that she was the sophisticated lady of the house in front of her sister.

'Thank goodness it's you,' she said, greeting her.

'It's lovely to have you back. We've missed you.'

'Do sit down. How is Mama? How's John? Tell me everything!'

They sat and talked for two hours before Ottilie decided she should return home.

Violet promised to call at the house at Camden Crescent within the next few days, an engagement that turned into regular visits on the excuse that Mama's malaise was deepening.

Over the next few months, she settled into a routine of making and receiving calls in the mornings and embroidering with May in the afternoons. She taught her the basic stitches, while she practised gold work and silk shading for a sumptuous wall hanging of Dover harbour with the castle above, but the time seemed to pass very slowly. As the grand longcase clock in the parlour ticked away the minutes and chimed the hours, her thoughts would drift back to William.

Miss Whiteway had been right about women needing an occupation; running a house was not the pinnacle of a married woman's ambition as her parents seemed to think.

She wasn't even yet with child, although not for want of trying on Arvin's behalf. She missed his company when he was out and had grown quite fond of him. The peppermint drops that Mrs Davis made from sifted sugar, egg whites and oil of peppermint, beaten together and dried on top of the range, had done the trick to freshen his breath on the occasions when he took garlic with his meals.

She looked forward, too, to the days when her husband invited people to dine at their house. She took pride in organising the dinner parties where Arvin and her father entertained anyone and everyone who might be persuaded to stock their wines. The proprietors of many of Dover's hotels and hostelries were keen to invest, and Arvin and her father were pleased with the way the business was taking off, and she was delighted to play her part in it as the gracious hostess.

Her sisters looked up to her as a married woman, coming to her for advice on the latest fashion, and Arvin gave her a generous allowance for running the house. As for William, she still thought of him fondly, and always would, but she felt that she'd been right to sacrifice her chance of marrying for love. Through marriage, she had secured the Rayfields' future. Overall she was content.

On a warm afternoon in early July, almost nine months after her marriage, Violet was in the parlour, showing May how to improve her stitches.

'Here, let me show you. The French knot is simple when you get the hang of it. The tension of your thread is too tight which means you can't slide the needle through the loops. Hold the working thread taut as you pull the needle through – that way your knots always look the same. If the knot goes wrong, cut it away.'

'I have a lot more to learn. 'Ow many times should I wrap the knot?'

'Once or twice is best,' Violet said. 'You can change the look of the stitches by loosening the tension. That's right – they make tiny flowers.'

'I don't know 'ow you do it so neat.'

'It takes lots of practice. You're doing well – you have a gift for it.' She heard the clock and counted the chimes: one, two, three, four, five …

'Oh no, Mr Brooke will be home in less than an hour,' she said, securing the end of her thread before removing the needle and putting it away in the sewing box.

May rested her embroidery on the arm of her chair, while the bees crawled around on the hydrangeas outside the open window.

'Can I help you dress for dinner?'

'Yes, thank you.'

On her way upstairs, Violet noticed Arvin's post on the silver tray in the hall – there were two letters: one which looked business-like, addressed in a masculine hand; the other sent from France. She picked it up and held it to the light, then guiltily put it down again, before going up to her room where May did her hair up for her, parting it in the middle and creating low chignons at the nape of her neck. May fastened the buttons down the back of her bodice while Violet adjusted her lace collar.

'You look beautiful, missus,' May said. 'I've always envied you for your hair – it's such a wonderful colour, like white gold.'

Violet gave her a wry smile. It was a shame that it wasn't enough to keep her husband at home. He was late again that evening, heading straight upstairs to change, and although she tried to hide her irritation, she didn't quite manage it.

'Arvin, do you really need to work all the hours God sends?' she asked when he joined her in the parlour to escort her to the dining room. 'I was under the impression that we were already comfortably off.'

He frowned.

'I'm doing this for us. I'm compelled to work hard to prove myself. All I want is for the gentlemen of Dover to accept me as one of them.'

'At least you are here now,' she said, noticing how weary he looked and feeling guilty for riling him. 'Let's dine – Mrs Davis has cooked sole meunière.'

His expression brightened.

They took their places at the long table in the dining room which was adorned with one of the cloths that Violet and May had worked on together, and she added, 'May I remind you that we have an invitation to dine at the Churchwards' this Saturday.'

'Ah, I'm sorry. I should have said. We will have to decline.'

'At this late notice?'

'I'm afraid so.'

'Why?'

'I've received a letter from Claudette.'

'There is something wrong?'

'I must go home. The roof of the chateau is falling in.'

'Can't she take on a builder to do the repairs?'

'She's afraid they'll take advantage.'

'Surely this can be negotiated through correspondence! The builders can write to you.'

'The last time I left my sister in charge of emergency works, the men concerned left it half finished, and I ended up paying over the odds to have it made good. The fabric of the chateau is in a delicate state. I'll book my ticket for the mail packet to Calais first thing tomorrow.'

'Oh, but I will come with you.'

'I think it would be a great sorrow to your mother, if you should leave Dover while she's in such a poor state of health.'

'I'm married to you – it's my duty to be companion to my husband, not my mother.'

'Could you live with the regret if she should pass away while you were abroad? No, I thought not.'

'I don't understand – you ask me not to spend time with my sisters, yet you're prepared to drop everything when your sister asks for you.'

'What do you expect when she's on her own?'

'She should come and live with us – she wouldn't be obliged to show her face.'

'It's a kind offer, Violet, but no. The weather wouldn't suit her – she likes the warmth. Now, I have responsibilities to you, my sister and my family home.'

'And to the business,' she added for him.

'That's right. Although it's a nuisance, this trip will kill two birds with one stone because I'll be able to check how last summer's wine is maturing, and visit some of the local vintners. Your father expects me to apply pressure on them to keep their prices down.'

'Shall I come with you next time then?' she asked hopefully as May brought the first course, a salad with salad dressing. It wasn't her favourite by any means, but Arvin had persuaded her that eating lettuce and herbs was beneficial to correct the tendency of meat to become putrid when inside the stomach.

'I expect so,' he said.

'How long will you be away for?'

'At least five or six weeks, if not longer. Let's face it, it makes sense for me to stay on for the harvest.'

'I see. Well, what can I say? I can't change your mind. Arvin, I'll miss you.'

'And I'll miss you too, my little ladybird.'

Arvin left for France the following day, wearing a hat cover over his white hat so that it wouldn't be discoloured by the smoke from the funnel of the mail packet, and Violet was alone again. Never mind, she thought. She would miss him, but she would make the best of it. While the cat was away, the mice would play.

She sent a note inviting Ottilie to call on her to make the arrangements, and on the servants' half day, she let her into the house.

'You look ... well, you will take his breath away,' Violet said, closing the door behind her sister, who had taken great care with her appearance. 'Is that rouge on your face?'

'No. It's the heat ...' Ottilie said, touching her cheek. 'Are you sure about this? What about your neighbours? Won't they talk? I don't want you to get into any trouble.'

'It's none of their business – you've called to assist me in choosing a piece of bespoke furniture from an artisan's catalogue, or—'

'You sound like Eleanor, making things up,' Ottilie laughed.

'Anyway, I'll be here – upstairs with my embroidery,' Violet added quickly. 'I'm not going to play gooseberry, but my presence in the house will dispel any gossip.'

'What about Arvin and Pa?'

'Arvin won't be back for weeks and Pa doesn't call here very often. He's been left to run the business while Arvin looks after his sister and buys wine in France.'

'Then I am reassured,' Ottilie said, smiling. She removed her gloves and checked her bracelet watch. 'He will be here soon. I can't thank you enough for this, Violet. I haven't dared meet with him since Mama caught us out.'

'That was months ago.'

'We write to each other once a week and we've run into each other in town a few times, but it isn't the same as talking face to face. Sometimes ... sometimes I worry that he will lose patience and someone else will catch his eye and capture his heart.'

'I think that very unlikely. He loves you. He always has.' Violet felt a pang of envy as Ottilie gazed at her, her eyes questioning.

'What about you?' she said. 'Are you happy?'

'I am.' She smiled as she heard a knock.

'It's him,' Ottilie squealed as Violet opened the door. 'Dear John.'

John Chittenden, dressed in a coat, waistcoat and checked trousers, stepped inside, keeping his hat on until Violet closed the door behind him, when he took it off. He tried to smooth down his hair and dropped his hat.

'Oh, I'm sorry,' he said, diving down to pick it up at the same time as Ottilie bent to retrieve it. They both stopped, each with a hand on the hat, looking at each other.

'My love, I am so glad to see you,' Ottilie whispered. 'You wouldn't believe how much I've missed you.'

'Oh, I can,' he said in a low voice.

'I'll leave you,' Violet said, choking up.

She didn't think they'd noticed her disappear upstairs to her empty room where she sat down and picked up her hoop and thread. Her heart wasn't in it today. She could hear low murmuring and laughter: John's voice and her sister's. She turned her mind to Arvin – what was he doing today? Barking orders in French to the roofers? Walking through the vineyards, arm in arm with his sister – she tried to imagine what she was like, but only conjured up a picture of an anonymous young woman in a veil. Did she miss her husband? It was quiet without him – she missed his company at the breakfast table, and at dinner, but apart from that, life was no different.

How would she have felt if she'd loved Arvin with a passion in the same way that Ottilie regarded John? Briefly, she wondered what would have happened if Arvin and her father had never met. Would she have married William? If she had, her life would have been very different. A tide of heat spread across her skin as she imagined William leaning down to kiss her.

Angry at herself for thinking such a thing, she flung down the hoop and thread. She was married to Arvin and it was far too late for regrets. She had to make the most of what she had, and she knew she was one of the lucky ones. When he was at home in the evenings, engagements permitting, they would sit together on the chaise. Arvin would put his arm around her and she would rest her head on his chest and listen to him tell stories about his childhood and the characters he'd met in the winemakers' caves in France. She had grown affectionate towards her husband, much as Aunt Felicity had predicted.

Glancing down towards the street, she watched a child, barefoot and dressed in rags, being chased away by a constable for selling matches, and she recalled the filthy urchin who'd accompanied the chimney sweep to unblock one of the fireplaces not long after they'd moved in.

She sighed – she'd asked Arvin if he could contribute to some of the ladies' charitable efforts for the poor of Dover, but he'd refused, saying that people had to help themselves. She'd felt sore about it, but what could she do? She had no money of her own. Everything they had belonged to her husband.

Eventually, when it was time for John to take his leave, Violet showed him out and Ottilie stayed on for tea.

'I notice that John's beard has grown at last,' Violet said, smiling as they sat in the parlour with cucumber sandwiches and ginger cake. 'Do you remember how Uncle Edward used to make fun of him?'

'The scanty herbage? Oh yes. I don't care for John's father's opinion. We're making plans. I don't know quite how it will work out but I'm hopeful. John and I have accepted that our parents will never give their blessing – they're too far apart, even though Pa has apparently made overtures to Uncle Edward to try to restore their friendship.'

'Has he really? Has he paid what he owed?'

'In part. He offered Uncle Edward shares in his partnership with Arvin, but he turned it down. He won't have anything to do with either of them, and he wants money in his hand, not shares.'

'Arvin hasn't mentioned it to me.'

'Perhaps he doesn't know.'

'Pa wouldn't keep secrets from him – they are bosom friends. They keep saying that business is brisk and on the rise, which suggests that Pa will soon be able to pay Uncle Edward back in full, and then your troubles will be over, Ottilie.'

'We're preparing for the worst. John is working all hours for his father, putting as much money as possible aside so that one day we can move away. It grieves me to do this behind Pa's back, but we have no choice.'

'What about Mama?' Violet felt guilty at not having asked after her before.

'She hardly knows night from day. I won't be made to feel bad about it.'

'You'll write to me and Eleanor?'

'Of course I will. This isn't going to happen immediately – John and I have a long way to go.' Ottilie looked up at the clock as it whirred then chimed four o'clock. 'I should go home.'

'I'll walk with you, but I won't stop,' Violet said. 'A breath of fresh air will do me good.'

She and Ottilie walked to Camden Crescent with their parasols up to divert the seagulls which were flying low along the seafront, diving at the stallholders who were selling off the last of their wares for the day.

'Cockles and mussels – buy an 'a'porth.'

'Chestnuts all 'ot, penny a lot.'

'Dover sole! No ornery flounders.'

'Are you sure you won't stop for a while?' Ottilie asked when they reached the house.

'Another time.' She would have loved to have stayed, but she needed to go back to supervise Mrs Davis who was supposed to be preparing for visitors the following day – the vicar's wife and some of her ladies. 'Tell Mama and Eleanor that I'll call in soon.'

'Thank you for everything you've done for me, Violet,' Ottilie said, before wishing her farewell and disappearing into the house.

Violet walked slowly back along Marine Drive, taking in the panorama of the sea and sky, illuminated in the soft golden light of late afternoon. A steam packer was on its way towards France, its funnels pouring smoke, and closer to the shore, a fisherman was casting his net from a small skiff. She hesitated, feeling a strange pang of yearning when she spotted a group of children playing a game of dare with the waves.

'Miss Rayfield? Violet, it is you.'

She turned to find William smiling and doffing his hat.

'Good afternoon,' he went on.

'Hello, Mr Noble. It's Mrs Brooke now,' she corrected him gently, at which his expression grew serious. Was it possible that he felt the same sense of regret? 'It's lovely to see you.' She didn't know what else to say as she tried to slow her racing heart.

'The feeling is mutual,' he said. 'You married your father's business associate.'

'That's right.' She found that she didn't want to talk about it. 'Are you still working at the Packet Yard?'

'I'm junior engineer on the *Samphire*, one of the mail packets.'

'Congratulations,' she said. 'Your mother must be very proud.'

'Oh, she is.'

It was on the tip of her tongue to ask if his sweetheart was equally proud of him. She was sure he had to be walking out with someone. He must have had many admirers to choose from.

'I read that you were one of the winning crew at the regatta again this year.'

'My heart hasn't been in the rowing recently, but I couldn't let the side down. My cousin was right – getting back on the water helped me find a sense of perspective after everything that's happened, but you know all about that.' He gave her a baleful smile. 'Let me assure you that whatever I feel about your father, I will never hold a grudge against you, Violet. You are entirely blameless.' His face turning pink, he changed the subject. 'I wish you every happiness.'

'As I do you,' she said, echoing his sentiments. 'Good day, William.'

'Good day.' He turned abruptly and walked away. She watched him striding towards the town until he disappeared, her brief joy at seeing him again crushed by a deep sadness.

Afraid that Pa would find out, Violet had mixed feelings about having encouraged the course of true love, but John and Ottilie met the following week and the next, and Violet soon became complacent. Her plan had worked very well, she concluded as she threaded a piece of pure white silk through her needle, but the sound of a stick rapping at a door alerted her.

Who could it be? She wasn't expecting any callers and the servants weren't due back until late that evening. She got up quickly, smoothed down her skirts and headed downstairs. Having checked the parlour door was firmly shut, she opened the front door to find her father on the doorstep.

'Pa? What are you doing here? I mean, what a lovely surprise.'

He touched his hat and her palms grew damp. What was she supposed to do? Invite him in?

'It seems you have forgotten, Violet,' he said, smiling. 'Have I woken you from a nap? You seem flustered.'

'No, I was—'

'Never mind,' he interrupted. 'I should have reminded you – there's a consignment of wine at the warehouse. Arvin wanted me to supervise the tasting he'd had planned before he left for France. You must come along to represent your husband – it will make a good impression on the buyers.'

'Who will be there?' she asked, feeling daunted.

'It's a private event, by invitation only, for the mayor, hoteliers, grocers, publicans and some shopkeepers from further afield.' He paused. 'Did I hear voices? Oh, my dear, you have company. You should have said.'

'No, Pa,' she said quickly, praying that John and Ottilie wouldn't reveal their presence. 'It's only the servants,' she lied. 'Let me go and change into something more suitable.' She began to push the door closed. 'I'll meet you at the quay.'

'I'll wait for you.' Pa held out his hand to stop the door. 'I'd rather hoped to make an entrance with you on my arm.'

'I'm sorry, but I can't come dressed like this.'

'The mayor is announcing the event officially open at three o'clock. It is now' – he checked his pocket watch, a gold timepiece which was attached to his coat by an Albert chain – 'five minutes past two. There's plenty of time.' He pushed past her. 'I'll wait in the parlour.'

'No, don't,' she said hurriedly. 'The servants are spring-cleaning – the carpet has been taken up and the curtains and antimacassars sent for laundering.'

Pa frowned. 'It's rather unusual to be spring-cleaning in the autumn.'

'I want everything to be perfect for when Arvin gets back.'

'I knew you'd make him a good wife – you've taken after your mother,' Pa said gruffly.

'This way,' she said, showing him into the dining room. 'Take a seat – the newspapers are on the sideboard.'

He thanked her, and she left the room, promising to be back shortly. On her way past the parlour, she knocked softly at the door.

'Ottilie!' she whispered as she opened it. Her sister peered out with John standing right behind her, looking red-faced as he fastened the top button on his shirt. 'It's Pa – I knew Arvin had arranged a wine-tasting, but he didn't give me the date and I certainly didn't realise that I was expected to attend. I'm sorry, but I must make haste. Another time.'

'We'll take our leave,' John said, tying his cravat. 'We'll use the side door. Thank you, Violet.'

'I'll help you with your dress and let myself out later,' Ottilie offered.

Within twenty minutes, Violet was ready, dressed in iridescent blue taffeta and lace, the skirts so full she could barely move, and her corset so tight she could hardly breathe. She used the glove stretcher to put on her new silk gloves while Ottilie placed her matching bonnet on her head and laid her shawl across her shoulders.

'Will I do?' she said.

'You look wonderful.' Ottilie kissed her cheek. 'Oh, now I have disturbed your bonnet.'

'No, leave it. I must hurry. I'll see you when I visit Mama.'

Violet left Ottilie in her room and went downstairs to meet her father in the dining room where he looked up from his paper.

'Your servants are like a herd of elephants,' he observed, standing up. 'You are ready?'

She nodded, and they left the house, walking briskly along Marine Parade to reach Commercial Quay, and the forest of masts and funnels of the boats in the Pent and Bason.

'Mind your backs!' warned one of the porters as a batch of crates came swinging across on a crane from one of the ships. They moved away as the crane lowered the crates, and a team of men removed them from the sling, pushing them away on a horse-drawn trolley into one of the warehouses, while the customs officer stood watching. Violet turned to her left and spotted a small crowd of smartly dressed gentlemen standing outside another warehouse, a sign outside it reading 'Brooke and Rayfield: Importers of the Finest Quality Wines'. There was a line of bunting fluttering above the double doors which were wide open.

'What do you think, Mrs Brooke?' Pa said, taking her arm and steering her inside.

The first section of the warehouse was decked out with tables – wine tables, ornately inlaid with rosewood, ebony and walnut, with silver spittoons on top. There were waiters lined up, dressed in black and white uniforms holding trays of glasses.

'I'm very impressed,' she replied. 'It is a far more elaborate occasion than I imagined it would be.'

'Thank you, my dear. It's taken me a lot of time and effort.' Pa introduced her to the guests before the mayor, dressed for the occasion in his robes and chain, made his address, standing on an upturned half-barrel to give him extra height and authority.

Violet's heart filled with pride at what her father and husband had achieved as the mayor announced that the tasting could begin. The waiters would bring glasses and pour the wines which would be clearly labelled. The guests would have a printed list, so they could write notes and place their orders at the end of the event.

'This is going swimmingly,' Pa said as the buyers began to taste. 'It will be the talk of the town.'

Violet saw the landlord from the Cause is Altered inn tip his head back, swill wine around his throat and noisily spit it out.

'Ugh! Did you say that was a claret?' He came across to where Violet was waiting with her father. 'Mr Rayfield, this 'as gorn off.'

'Oh no. This is a new consignment. Mr Brooke – an expert vintner – sent it directly from one of the great cellars in Bordeaux.'

'It's vinegar, only fit for sousing mackerel.'

'Please, sir. Keep your voice down. Allow others to make their own judgement. What do you think of the white?' Pa called one of the waiters over. 'Pour the one from the Médoc. You'll find it most agreeable, I'm sure.' He muttered aside to Violet, 'I wish Arvin was here – he has the gift of the gab.'

'You taste it, sir,' the landlord said. 'Give me your opinion.'

Pa was forced into sipping at a glass of the red. His cheeks reddened, and his eyes seemed to bulge as he forced it down, then he slapped his lips together and smiled as if he'd partaken of the sweetest nectar. 'It is wonderful,' he exclaimed. 'I'd be more than happy to see that served at my table.'

'You should be on the stage, Mr Rayfield. I'm sorry, but this is a waste of my time. Good day.'

'What's happened, Pa?' Violet asked as the landlord scurried away.

'Nothing, my dear. This isn't about the wines – it's merely sour grapes because these people don't want our business to succeed. I know what will happen next – they'll fill in their order forms then demand a price cut. That's what they're up to.'

Violet wasn't sure that this was the case. If the gentlemen were enjoying the wines, they would be drinking them, not spitting them out. Within an hour, the spittoons were filled to overflowing and the order forms left blank on the tables. Pa looked dejected as the last of the guests left.

'We've been had. The casks have been swapped somewhere along the line. Arvin won't be happy about this – it's done nothing for our reputation. Importers of fine wines indeed! We should turn our minds to selling vinegar, because that's what it is. Vinegar!' Pa took her arm. 'Let's go home.'

Violet wanted to call on Mama and so they returned to Camden Crescent. Wilson let them into the house and took her shawl and bonnet. Pa retired to his study to lick his wounds while Violet went up to her mother's room where Eleanor was scribbling in a notebook. Mama was lying on her bed with her eyes closed, propped up with bolsters and pillows with Dickens curled up on her feet, purring.

'Hello, Violet,' Eleanor said. 'Didn't Ottilie call on you earlier?'

'She did, but I thought I'd come and see Mama. It's quiet at home without Arvin and there's only so much sewing one can do to fill in the time. Where is Ottilie?'

'She's helping out in the kitchen. May I be excused for a while as you're here? Much as I find satisfaction in caring for our mother, it's ... well, it can be trying.'

'Yes, of course. You go. I'll sit with her for a couple of hours.'

'Thank you.'

When Eleanor had left the room, Violet opened the window and pulled a chair up beside the bed. She reached out and held Mama's hand.

'It's been quite a day,' she said. 'How are you?'

Mama opened her eyes, then frowned.

'Eleanor ...' she muttered.

'Oh, you have been asleep. It's me ... Violet. Your daughter, the middle one,' she went on when Mama stared at her without a flicker of recognition. 'Don't be silly. You know who I am, Mama.'

'Eleanor,' she said slowly.

'No. Violet.'

'Eleanor,' she repeated, and a brief smile crossed her face.

At the same time, Violet's heart broke.

Chapter Ten

The Samphire and Fanny Buck

When Arvin came back from France, he was delighted to see her, and very passionate, making her wonder afterwards if she could possibly be with child. She sincerely hoped so as it might give him reason to stay in Dover.

When they dined at the Rayfields', Pa spoke of the disappointing wine-tasting event, but Arvin wasn't discouraged. He thought the casks could have been tampered with, and suggested that they take on a man to guard the next consignment. They needn't worry, he said, because during his stay, he'd managed to find the wine that would make their fortune. They would need to raise the money quickly to purchase it before anyone else did, though, as Arvin had persuaded the winemaker to give him first refusal.

Her father had seen no difficulty in this. He would call on all his resources, arrange for a bill of exchange from the bank and sell his shares in the railway if need be.

Violet ventured to suggest that they should be more circumspect, but neither of them would listen to her.

'This is it,' Pa said. 'This is the big one. I can feel it in my bones.'

'Then as soon as we have the funds, I'll return to France to complete the deal.'

'I shall accompany my husband this time,' Violet said. 'Mama no longer recognises me. There's no reason for me to stay at home.'

For once, Arvin didn't try to persuade her out of it, and Violet threw herself into the flurry of arrangements that she had to make – notifying her friends that Mrs Brooke would not be at home, making sure the servants were organised, and packing everything she would need for a trip abroad. She couldn't wait.

At last! They were on their way to France to see Paris and meet Claudette at the chateau. It was just a shame that Arvin had chosen the middle of a damp and dreary December to make the trip, Violet thought. It shouldn't be too bad a journey, though – Arvin had assured her that it took less than three hours to cross the twenty miles to France.

The paired funnels of the steam packet rose above them into the night sky as they followed the porter who was struggling with a trolley laden with their luggage: various boxes and a trunk from home, along with a small chest bound with chains and padlocks. Arvin had collected it in person from the guard's van of the mail train while Violet waited for him at the Warden Hotel. He had insisted on keeping it in sight, making her wonder what its contents were.

Pulling her fur hat down over her ears, she slipped her arm through her husband's and they made their way by gaslight along Admiralty Pier and across the walkway on to the *Samphire*. When the inspector checked their tickets, Arvin glanced towards her with a look of mild surprise as if he had been lost in a trance and forgotten she was there.

'You seem distracted this evening,' she observed, as the water slapped against the quay.

He patted her hand. 'My mind is much occupied with business that you need not be concerned with. Don't fret, my dear! Once we are safely through Calais, we'll take the train to Lille where we change for Paris. I'll feel much more at ease when we arrive at our destination.'

She couldn't help wondering if he was anxious about the crossing – he would never admit to it, of course. Smiling to herself, she walked with him along the deck, listening to the sound of manly voices: the captain's orders to the sailors and their calls back; the laughter and swearing from some passengers who had clearly emerged from one of the nearby inns; the shouting from where the mail master was stowing the bags which had been unloaded from the train alongside, its engine hissing and belching steam and smuts.

The porter stopped outside one of the doors towards the bow of the ship, unlocked it and showed them inside. He tipped his trolley, depositing their belongings in a neat stack on the floor.

'Can I help you stow this away, sir?' he asked.

'No, that will be all,' Arvin said.

There was an awkward moment when Violet found herself compelled to give her husband a hard stare to remind him to tip the poor man. Arvin dug around in the pockets of his greatcoat and found a shilling.

'Thank you, sir. I wish you a pleasant crossing.' The porter's expression was one of indifference as he left with his tip, and Violet supposed that her husband's generosity had not been enough to make up for his initial faux pas.

Removing her gloves, she looked around the cabin where the sconces flickered, making reflections in the brass fittings and woodwork. The upholstered seats were clean and well padded, giving an impression of luxury, but the air reeked of tar and bilge water.

Feeling sick, she sat down.

The boat juddered as the engine cranked into life. Soon, the pistons began to pound, powering the steam packet away from the quay and into the Channel. The unrelenting noise made her ears hurt and the quaking of the ship brought a fresh wave of nausea welling up in her gullet.

'Please, fetch me my smelling salts. Arvin!' She raised her voice to attract his attention from where he was testing various keys on a ring from his pocket in the padlocks attached to the chains on the trunk. 'I'm not well. I think a breath of hartshorn will revive me.'

'Where is it?' he said grudgingly, over the sound of the engines.

'In my reticule over there,' she said, not trusting her legs to hold her up. 'I would fetch it myself, but … Oh dear, I feel such a fool.'

'I hope this isn't a sign of things to come.' Arvin fetched her beaded purse from which she extracted the silver vinaigrette. He opened it for her and held it under her nose, the sting of the sal ammonia in her nostrils making her feel worse than ever. 'We've barely left Dover and you are pining for home. I think that we should ask the master to turn about.'

'Oh no, I am not going to miss out on our grand tour,' she said, upset that he would contemplate leaving her behind. There was no way she was going home now. She was determined to meet Claudette, stay in the chateau and walk through the vineyards he had talked about so much. 'I'm not homesick like I was before – that would be ridiculous.'

'You'll be unhappy without your mother and sisters' company. Sometimes I wonder if we can really be married when you spend more time with them than you do with me.'

She found it hard to explain how deeply that comment hurt her feelings. Her husband was her priority, but he was away more than she had expected, and she had found herself depending on her family to combat the loneliness. There were only so many letters one could write, and Arvin didn't often respond because he was busy. She didn't feel that it was polite to pick people up and put them down whenever it suited her, which was why she maintained her visits to the Rayfields even when he was at home, but she wished that he didn't take them as a kind of rejection when she was fond of them all: him and her family.

'It's late,' she said, not wishing to argue. 'Usually we are abed by now, my love.' In the excitement and anticipation of their journey, she had tired herself out. 'I wish we could have taken the earlier crossing.'

'You are being petulant,' he said. 'You know I had to wait for the mail train from London.'

'Perhaps you could have had the chest sent on after us,' she suggested.

'Your father has entrusted me with its contents.'

'Pray, tell me what they are.'

'Just papers. No more questions. I've had a long day. The steward will soon be here with refreshments and I wish to sit quietly for a while.'

He was keeping secrets from her, she realised, and lowered her gaze. For now, it seemed wise to let the subject of the chest drop.

She looked towards the door again – Arvin had locked it behind the porter – and then at the porthole through which she could see only blackness. The engines continued to rumble. Everything around her was vibrating, churning her insides. She stood up quickly, gathering her skirts.

'I need some fresh air,' she muttered. 'Will you come with me?'

'Passengers aren't allowed on deck at this hour. It's too dark out there.'

'I wish to go outside. I cannot breathe in here,' she said, her heart racing with panic as the low ceiling seemed to press down on them.

'Violet, do as I tell you!'

'Oh, Arvin, I can't stand another minute in this godforsaken cabin.'

'Go then.' His eyes flashed from the shadows where he knelt by the trunk. 'On your head be it, if you fall overboard! Nobody will see you're gone.'

'If you're trying to frighten me, it isn't working.' Her need to escape was more pressing than obeying her husband.

'You would make a fool of me?' he said coldly. 'I forbid you to step outside.'

Her hand was on the key. With trembling fingers, she turned it. What was wrong with him?

'I'm grateful for your concern for my safety, but I won't go far, only up the steps to the deck to take a few breaths of air.'

'If you walk out through that door, I swear I will not follow you. I've been charged with looking after this, and I will not let it out of my sight.'

She let herself out and made her way up to the main deck where the cold night air caught her by the throat. She took a deep breath as her eyes began to make out shapes emerging from the darkness: the mast for when the *Samphire* went under sail; a rope coiled around a capstan; the railing defining the perimeter of the deck. She walked across and grabbed on to the top rail with both hands, glad that she'd left her gloves on. Gradually, she began to feel better as the steam packet thrashed through the mild swell with her running lights – brass lanterns – shining brightly: red on the port bow and green on the starboard. One of the sailors topped up the oil in a third lantern, adjusted the wick and lit it. He closed the hinged door and tightened the wingnuts to secure it, then carried it up to the masthead where it gave out a reassuring arc of white light.

She glanced back towards Dover where the moonlight caught the breaking crests of the waves before disappearing behind a skein of fog which obscured the South Foreland Lighthouse where she and Arvin had walked together, light-hearted as they'd tried to escape their companions. She had grown fond of him, but his devotion to her now appeared to be fading, like the colour in a plucked rose. What had she done wrong? Could it be that he was unhappy that she wasn't yet with child?

She turned to face France. All would be well once they reached the chateau and Arvin had had time to put business aside for a while and return to his normal self. The lighthouse on Cap Gris-Nez twinkled then disappeared, and the *Samphire* carried on through the bank of sea haze.

'Look harder!' came the sound of shouting. 'There are herrin' boats about. Who's the forrard lookout?'

'Here—' The rest of the response was drowned out by the engines, but Violet was no longer listening. Sick at heart over her marriage and disturbed by the renewed rocking of the boat, she retched miserably and clung to the railings, wishing she was back on dry land.

'Hey, miss!'

She tried to ignore the voice at her shoulder, but the man was most insistent.

'Miss, go back to your cabin immediately. You shouldn't be out here!'

She turned to face the speaker, a young man in a dark coat and hat.

'Mr Noble!' she exclaimed.

'Mrs Brooke. I'm sorry for speaking roughly to you, but there are rules,' he said. 'Oh dear, it seems that one hasn't found their sea legs yet. Never mind, we'll be in Calais before you know it.'

'I truly hope so.'

'I'll escort you to your cabin.'

'Thank you, but I don't wish to trouble you while you're at work. I can find my own way back.'

'May I be so bold as to take your arm to help you down the steps at least?' he asked as the mist swallowed the *Samphire* and the lights from her lanterns for a second time.

Before she could give her assent, another shout rang out.

'There's a sail off the port bow!'

'Lord have mercy on us,' her companion muttered, and she followed his gaze towards the bow where a steamer under sail was looming out of the darkness, heading straight for the *Samphire*. It came so close she thought she could reach out and touch it, but she didn't feel any fear until she heard a second voice.

'Hard to port!' the captain bellowed from the bridge. 'Hard to port!'

She glanced behind her and caught sight of the reflections of his night glasses from the bridge. As she turned back, she saw the name of the ship in front of her and heard her sailors shouting a warning, as the *Samphire* swung to one side, throwing her off balance and into William's arms.

'Hold tight, missus,' he shouted, and she clung to him with her hands locked around his neck as the *Fanny Buck* bore down on the *Samphire*, striking her with a deafening crash on the port bow.

'Steamer ahoy! Back engines!' The crew shouted and screamed at each other.

'It's too late.' William clasped her to him, so close that she could feel his heartbeat pounding in time with the pulse in her ears.

Two of the *Fanny Buck*'s sailors came falling barefoot from above them when the ship's bow rode up and scraped across the *Samphire*'s, coming to rest on her deck. Someone blew a whistle and people began shouting for help.

'There is water coming in. She's holed!'

'Not us. They mean the *Fanny Buck*,' William reassured her as the steamer rose with the swell of the sea and slipped from the *Samphire*'s deck. There was a grating and groaning sound as it fell back on to the water while the *Fanny Buck*'s crew began to take down her sails.

Violet stared at where the *Samphire*'s fore-cabin and compartment should have been. They were under water, crumpled by the contact with the other vessel, the occupants surely having perished, crushed or drowned. The cabins to the aft of it were above the surface of the waves, but she couldn't tell in the confusion and chaos who had escaped and who was trapped.

'I have to find my husband.'

'Where is he?'

'In our cabin. Down there …' She tore herself away from William and pointed towards the steps, but they were broken, made unusable by the impact.

'Arvin!' she called. 'Are you there?'

'Stay with me, Mrs Brooke,' William said, reaching for her arm to restrain her.

'I have to do something. I can't just stand here,' she cried, as the *Samphire*'s pistons ceased pumping and the engine fell silent.

'The chances are that he's already made his way out. It isn't safe. You'll break your neck trying to go down those steps.'

'Please, let me decide for myself. You go and attend to your duties. There are so many people …' Other passengers pushed past her, shouting for their friends and dear ones, milling back and forth looking for the lifeboats, their eyes white with fear.

'There's no danger!' William shouted. 'We are not taking on water! The *Samphire* is not about to sink.'

'We're drifting without power,' the captain shouted back. 'Man the lifeboats and cutters. Some of the crew will row to Dover for assistance while the rest remain here.'

'There are four boats – plenty of room for all,' William said as one of the crew yelled, 'Ship ahoy!'

'It's the *Belgique*,' somebody else shouted with relief. 'She'll give us assistance.'

'No, she isn't stopping. She's steaming past us,' William said.

'She can't see us. Fire the rockets!' the captain ordered. 'Lower the boats without delay.'

'We can't get to the rockets. They're underwater,' one of the sailors said. 'Where is the *Fanny Buck*? Why hasn't she come back for us?'

'She's holed,' William explained. 'All hands will be repairing the breach in her hull with canvas cut from her sails, but as soon as she's watertight, they'll make their way back. I'm sure of it.'

'William, I'm grateful for your attention, but you have to go back to your work.' In desperation, Violet caught the sleeve of a passenger's coat and added, 'This is the ship's junior engineer – he'll help you.' She pushed her way out of the crowd of people who surrounded him, begging for help with their luggage and shouting to be let on to the boats, but William had been right – she couldn't get near the cabin, only see from a distance that the door had been broken off its hinges and cast aside. Arvin had escaped – she just had to find him.

'I'm looking for my husband, Mr Brooke,' she kept saying as she made her way aft, but it seemed that no one cared. The rules of polite society were ignored as everyone – man and woman, old and young – cried and fought for a space in one of the boats. Violet counted three people – none of them Arvin – sitting in the first cutter before the crew had a chance to lower it on to the water.

'Captain Bennett, these people won't move even though I've asked 'em to,' one of the sailors shouted.

The captain stepped in. 'Ladies and gentlemen, please get out and leave your possessions on the deck, so we can take more passengers.'

'We aren't getting out,' one of them said. 'And we will not leave our luggage behind. We've paid for our tickets just like everyone else has – I don't see why we should have to forfeit our valuables.'

Violet wanted to urge the master to be more forceful but he conceded quickly.

'Lower the cutter,' he barked at the crew, and they let it down into the sea with the passengers inside it. 'There's no time to waste. I want five of you to row to Dover to find help ...'

Offering silent prayers for everyone on board, Violet continued to search the deck for her husband, and then she saw him with his back to her.

'Arvin,' she called. Relieved, she hurried on, bumping into an elderly gentleman who was supporting his wife.

'Have a care, my dear,' he said.

'I'm sorry.' She rushed forwards to let her dear Arvin know she was safe. 'My darling,' she exclaimed, but as he turned to face her, a quizzical expression in his eyes, her heart plummeted. 'I thought you were my husband,' she stammered, realising from the stench of whisky on the stranger's breath that he was soused to the eyeballs.

'Madam, I wish that I was, and we would go down together.' He raised a silver hip flask to his lips, took a swig and tried to hand it to her. 'This will make you feel better.'

'No, thank you.' She recoiled.

'I would that I had a whole bottle – I believe oblivion is a better prospect than to be drownded conscious.'

'The crew are rowing to Dover to fetch help,' she said, trying to remain optimistic.

'Ah, I swear the boat is taking on water and I've heard there are over seventy passengers on board tonight and there isn't enough room for all on the lifeboats.'

'Sir, please keep your opinions to yourself,' she said sharply. 'The *Samphire* isn't sinking, just drifting. We must stay calm and not arouse further panic. Now, I have to find my husband.' She looked along the railings and there he was, staring at the captain. She hastened towards him and flung her arms around his neck.

'Violet!' He extracted himself from her embrace and glared down at her, grim-faced. 'Have some restraint. There are people watching.'

'I was afraid you'd been killed.' She bit her lip, drawing blood.

'We must make our way into one of the boats,' he said. 'Why didn't you board the first one? I saw you nearby.'

'Because I was waiting for you, my dear. I wouldn't abandon you, just as you wouldn't leave the ship without me.' She looked down towards his feet, spotting a bag and the locked chest. 'You have our luggage?'

'I have the papers and personal items at least. Hurry, or there will be no space for us. Bring the bag! I'll carry the chest.' He leaned down and dragged it along the deck towards the remaining boats, beads of sweat glistening on his forehead, while she followed with the bag.

The second cutter was full, and a passenger was sawing at one of the lines with a knife.

'Put that away, sir,' Captain Bennett shouted. 'Sit down and the crew will lower the cutter.' The sailors released the lines to let the boat on to the water with a soft splash, and the crew who were already on board picked up their oars to row. 'Go after the *Fanny Buck*. Tell them to heave to and help us as soon as they can. The ladies who are left on board should get into the next boat.'

Violet glanced towards Arvin, who was barging his way to the lifeboat, shouting, 'Let me through. My wife will not go without me.' When he reached it, he stowed the trunk in the bow.

'Arvin, wait for me,' Violet called, but he didn't look at her while other men pushed and shoved and clambered into the boat. No one offered her a place and her husband didn't appear to have heard her. She caught sight of the glint of metal through the darkness as he removed the chains from the chest, then started to stow its contents – small packages of papers, she guessed – into the pockets of his greatcoat.

'What about the ladies?' asked the sailor who was at the bow, struggling to reach the lowering gear. 'Gentlemen, you must allow the ladies on to the boat.'

'We will not be moved,' the men said, looking away.

'If you won't get out, you must sit in the thwarts at least, the same number each side or you will capsize the boat,' Captain Bennett joined in as the sailor reached the lowering gear at the bow, and another took hold of the rope towards the stern. 'The ladies will take the next one. Hurry! We are wasting time.'

'Please remain seated,' the second sailor shouted. 'Sit down!'

'What do you think we're doing?' came a yell back. 'Get on with it. We are frozen to the bone.'

'Arvin!' Violet shouted again. 'You are leaving me behind.' The water below was black, a monster lying in wait for its prey, its chest rising and falling. 'Somebody help me!' She stared towards her husband, making out his shadowy silhouette in the gloom. He would be worried sick when he found out that she hadn't made it on to the boat with him.

'Lower the boat!' The sailor at the bow put the line one turn round the cleat and slowly slackened it off, so the lifeboat dropped a few inches. 'Is all well?' he shouted as a fracas broke out aft.

'I can't sit here with you elbowing me in the face,' one of the passengers shouted. He stood up and clambered along the lifeboat, pushing the sailor aside, giving him no option but to let go of the line. The rope slipped through the cleat, the boat tilted then dropped at an angle. For an agonising moment it held, but suddenly the rope flew up and the boat tipped aft, sending the passengers and their bags tumbling backwards and sideways through the air, splashing and crashing into the icy water.

'No!' Violet screamed and pressed herself against the railings, searching for any sign of her husband as the water foamed and swirled around the thrashing men. 'Arvin!'

Some of the crew were in the water, helping those who weren't able to swim to the upturned lifeboat. The sailors who remained on the *Samphire* threw down ropes so they could clamber back on board, where they stood shivering and waiting for the steward to hand out blankets.

'There's somebody left in the sea!' someone shouted.

Was it her husband? Violet ran along the deck to find one of the sailors and William throwing lifebuoys towards a figure disguised by the swell and the darkness of the night. Even the moon seemed to have taken against them, hiding once more behind a veil of fog.

William took off his jacket and tied a running bowline around his waist. The sailor did the same before they dived together and swam across to the man, securing a rope around him and creating a harness to tow him back towards the boat.

Was it Arvin? She couldn't be certain as the man struggled to make his way back, gasping and spluttering through the swell. She hung on to the rail, willing him to reach the side of the hull. He made it and the crew began to haul him up by the rope, but as he rose out of the sea, his body jerked, slipped from the harness and plunged back into the water.

Violet cried out.

William dived under, and after what seemed like an age, he resurfaced, struggling to hold the man's head above water as he reattached a rope to his arm, so the crew could make a second attempt at hauling him in, but it was too late. His limp body collapsed in a shadowy heap on the deck nearby. His lifeless eyes stared at the night sky.

'He was too heavy.' William hawked and spat as he scrambled back on board. 'His boots filled with water.'

'Turn your eyes away, miss,' the steward said kindly. 'A drowned man is not a sight for a lady's eyes.'

But she was compelled to keep looking. Was it her husband?

'That's Monsieur Duclercq, I do believe,' someone said. 'He's a merchant, a regular traveller.'

'There's another!' the steward shouted. 'Man overboard! Ten yards aft.'

At first, Violet could only see the whites of the man's eyes and the reflections of the sailors' lanterns in the water.

It wasn't until a beam of light caught the man's face that she recognised him.

'Arvin! Don't give up,' she shouted as he rose to take a breath before sinking underwater. 'Keep swimming. Somebody will come with a rope.'

The *Samphire* drifted back towards him.

With their hair slicked back and grim determination etched on their faces, William and the sailor dived in for a second time and swam slowly towards Arvin as he floundered and thrashed in the water.

'You must take off your coat, sir.' She heard William's voice caught up and carried on the wind.

'I will not!' Arvin disappeared for a full minute before resurfacing.

'Hold on to the rope then and I'll tow you in!'

Did he not understand a simple instruction? she asked herself, as Arvin threw his arms around William's neck, dragging him down again with him. They were fighting the sea and the icy chill, fighting for their lives and now they were fighting each other.

'Unhand me ...' She heard William's strangulated cry and saw Captain Bennett leap into the sea to go to the engineer's aid, but Arvin was having none of it, and all Violet could do was pray that all four men would make it back to safety.

Chapter Eleven

Between the Devil and the Deep Blue Sea

The crew were treading water, staring as one at a patch of sea, waiting for Arvin to reappear at the surface. After the longest minute of Violet's life, they turned with one accord and swam back to the *Samphire* without him.

'You must go back,' she wanted to shout, but she knew from the fear on their pale faces and their chattering teeth that there was no hope. If they stayed in the water any longer, they would all die.

The crew pulled William up to the deck. He looked straight at her, shivering under his sodden shirt.

'I'm sorry, missus. I did my best, but he wouldn't listen. He wouldn't take off his coat and in his panic to stay afloat, he put his hands around my neck, half strangling me so I couldn't catch my breath. If I hadn't fought him off, he would have drowned both of us. He wasn't thinking straight – the cold must have got to him …'

What other reason could there be? She felt as if her ribcage had been stoved in like the *Samphire*'s bow. Hot tears ran down her cheeks as she stared wildly across the water, lost and not knowing what to do, while the captain and the other sailor were helped on to the deck, gasping and blue with cold.

She was only vaguely aware of the second lifeboat being launched and of an argument and raised voices over whether there was room for the mail sacks.

'How many passengers are left on board?' the captain said as it drifted away from the *Samphire*, the sea having calmed since the fateful collision.

'Just the ladies.' William approached, with a blanket around his shoulders. 'This is a poor show, a very poor show indeed.'

'All the gentlemen have taken to the cutters and life-boats, leaving us without means of escape,' the steward said.

'It's shocking. I'm ashamed of my sex,' William said.

'You shouldn't be. You and the captain and the crew who remain here to look after us are true gentlemen. The others ...' Violet's voice trailed off. She couldn't find the words to describe the men who had abandoned them, more concerned with the fate of their luggage and how they would reach Calais than saving lives.

'Can I do anything for you?' he asked her.

'Nothing,' she said faintly. Thanks to an unfortunate series of events, she had lost Arvin. If it hadn't been for the chest coming from London, they wouldn't have been on the late mail packet; if the mist hadn't fallen, the other ship would have seen the *Samphire*; if Arvin had waited for her they could have boarded the other lifeboat.

'I'm sorry ... was that your husband?' She turned to find a young woman with tears in her eyes, touching her shoulder with her gloved hand. 'My name's Beth. I can't find my governess, Miss Ayres – she was accompanying me to Lyons. I was wondering if anyone had seen her.'

'I'll help you look,' Violet said. 'Hold my hand – we will give each other courage.'

'I'm ever so grateful, missus. What a night, eh? I tell you, I will never travel by boat again. We must beg the Prime Minister to make a tunnel under the sea to France.'

'I think that's rather ambitious.' Violet recalled Arvin talking of the very same thing, and then she remembered that he was missing. Was he dead? she wondered, her heart filling with grief.

'I don't know if we will get home – we are drifting,' Beth observed.

Violet squeezed her hand. 'We must be brave,' she said, even though she felt anything but. 'The crew are doing their best to get us back to Dover.'

'Where is our Junior Engineer?' somebody called.

Violet glanced to where William was finding chairs and brandy for the ladies on deck. He had been a hero, determined and indefatigable.

'Who wants to know?' he called back.

'You're needed. The steering gear's failed, we can't find the First Engineer, and the captain wants to know if you can do anything about it.'

He disappeared into the darkness, and the ship continued to drift.

'We will end up on the other side of the world,' Beth said with a shiver, as they stood side by side, staring towards the water. How on earth they would get back to dry land? Violet started to panic. For the first time in her life, she felt as though she was staring death in the face.

The minutes turned into hours, until one of the crew started shouting, 'It's the *Belgique* – she's come back for us!'

There was clapping and cheering as the mail packet drew alongside and the passengers began to transfer with their luggage to the ship, but Violet didn't want to leave the *Samphire*, not without Arvin.

'You should go with the other ladies,' William said. 'There is nothing you can do here.'

'Please come with us, Violet,' Beth begged. 'It isn't safe to stay on the boat.'

'I promise I'll send word as soon as there's any news on the fate of Mr Brooke and Miss Ayres,' William said.

'I'll go back to Dover then, but I will not think him gone until I see his body with my own eyes,' Violet said fiercely, clinging to hope, the one thing she had left. 'What will you do, William?'

'The captain of the *Belgique* has given us a stock of lights to warn other ships that we're disabled. He'll come back and tow us into Dover after you've been safely delivered to shore, unless we can repair the steering beforehand.'

'I wish you luck,' she said.

'Don't worry about us. You look after yourself and the young lady here.'

Before she could thank him again, she and Beth were whisked on to the *Belgique* and shown to one of the empty cabins. They sat down side by side with cups of hot tea and a blanket that one of the crew gave them across their knees. When anyone spoke, they did so quietly.

Why had Arvin not waited for her? Violet reflected bitterly. If he'd been patient, he would be sitting here with them. And then she felt guilty for forgetting that her companion was suffering too. 'Let's hope that Miss Ayres is trapped in her cabin and can be released unharmed,' she said, wishing that she could believe in happy endings like some of those in Eleanor's books.

'Why didn't the captain delay the mail because of the fog? What was he thinking of, leaving harbour in such weather?' Beth asked.

'I don't know.' Violet half expected Arvin to appear at her side as the gleaming lights of Admiralty Pier came into view through the porthole.

The *Belgique* docked in the early hours before dawn began to break, and the ladies were escorted off the ship. A small crowd of well-wishers and the Marine Superintendent greeted them.

'I can arrange passes for any passengers who wish to return to London,' he said. 'For those who prefer to continue their journey to France, they may wait at the hotel and take the next boat to Calais.'

Violet decided to wait at the hotel for news of Arvin.

'And I will wait there too,' Beth said. 'I must send word to my father in London because my governess is missing, and I have no chaperone.'

'I'll stay with you until someone comes for you.'

'Oh, thank you. That's very kind, but you have enough to deal with …'

'I can't possibly abandon you now. Let's speak to the superintendent's assistant and find out how we can get a message to your father.'

'May I offer to stay with you?' came a voice from behind them. Violet turned to find the elderly couple she had accidentally bumped into on the boat. 'We are going to London – there's no way you'll ever persuade me back on to the mail packet,' the wife said. 'What do you think? We can take the next train together. It's no trouble at all.'

Beth looked at Violet, who nodded. 'If that suits you better.'

'It means I'll get home sooner,' Beth said.

'Then travel safely.' Violet wished her farewell and watched her go to collect a pass.

'There you are.' She heard her father's voice and made her way to where he stood, his eyes dark with concern. 'The news is already all over town. Are you hurt?'

'I'm ... I'm still in one piece,' she said weakly as he embraced her, 'but I've lost Mr Brooke.'

'I expect he'll be in the hotel waiting for you.'

'He is gone,' she said, breaking down.

'All are accounted for – I have it on good authority.' Pa's voice faltered. 'Tell me what you know.'

'I saw the body of a Frenchman brought back on to the *Samphire*, and a young lady's governess is missing. And Arvin – he fell from one of the lifeboats and although the crew tried to rescue him, he panicked and disappeared under the water without trace.'

'Our Arvin? Our dear boy?' Violet nodded and Pa's complexion blanched under the gaslight.

'Where is the chest?' Pa said suddenly. 'Your luggage?'

'I don't know. Arvin took what he could carry on to the lifeboat with him. Everything went into the water. You can't imagine what it was like out there.'

Pa began to pace up and down the quay, agitatedly picking at his nails.

'This is a tragedy, a complete disaster,' he muttered. 'Violet, as you've said, all hell had broken loose, and in the chaos and confusion, you imagined you saw Arvin in the water. Isn't it possible that your eyes deceived you?'

'No, Pa.'

'Well, we will not rest until we find him. As you say, there is no absolute proof of his demise. All is not lost.' He took her firmly by the hand and started walking towards town.

'Where are we going?' she said, pulling against him.

'Back to the house at Camden Crescent. I can't let you go anywhere else – you need your family around you now.'

Not having the strength to argue, she gave in and returned with her father to the family home where Ottilie, Eleanor, Wilson and the maid were waiting up for them.

'My dear sister,' Eleanor cried, throwing her arms around her. 'We didn't think we'd see you again.'

'Oh, it is dreadful ...' Violet started to sob. 'My poor husband has drowned.'

'No!' Ottilie exclaimed. 'Tell me it isn't true.'

'We don't know anything yet,' Pa interrupted. 'Nothing is certain.'

'He has gone. I saw him ...' Violet's throat closed, and she couldn't catch her breath. Her head began to swim, and everything went black.

She woke to find herself in her old room with Eleanor asleep under a blanket in a chair at her side. When she sat up, her sister stirred.

'Violet, you are awake. Can I fetch you a drink?'

'No, thank you. What time is it?'

'It's the middle of the afternoon. You were exhausted ...'

The memories of the night before came flooding back into her sleep-addled mind.

'Arvin,' she cried.

'Hush.' Eleanor stood up, walked to the bed and hugged her trembling shoulders. 'There's no news, but Pa is still hopeful. Shall I ask him to call the doctor?'

'No,' she responded. Her heart was in agony, but there was nothing that a doctor could do about it. 'Please, fetch me some paper so I can write to Arvin's sister.'

'I'll help you with that. Pa has requested that you dress and come downstairs to be measured up for your mourning clothes. The seamstress is calling at four.'

'I can't bear to see anyone.'

'Then I will have the seamstress sent up to you.'

'If Pa is still hopeful, why does he want me to go into mourning?'

'It has to be done out of respect for Mr Brooke, for what if he should return and find you in your ordinary day dresses? I think he would be disappointed that you thought so little of him that you didn't bother with wearing black in his memory.'

'I will come down then, if I must,' Violet sighed.

'Pa asked me to give you this. It belongs to Mama, but she doesn't need it.' Eleanor dug around in her pocket, pulled out a piece of jewellery and handed it to her. Violet bit her lip at the sight of the jet beads in her palm: black beads for a widow.

Later, she and Eleanor wrote to Claudette, and the seamstress came to take measurements with a tape and write them down, but her grief couldn't be recorded in inches. It was infinite. She supped a little chicken broth, but there might as well have been bones in it because it seemed to stick in her craw.

She didn't go downstairs until the following day after the dresses had been delivered, and she was obliged to be present when people called to offer their condolences.

Aunt Felicity was one of them, eager to hear a first-hand account of the accident. Violet sat in the parlour with Ottilie and Eleanor, and Mama who stared mutely towards the window, unable to contribute anything to the conversation. Wilson brought tea and brandy, then left the room.

'Is there anything I can do, my dears?' their aunt asked. 'I am at your disposal.'

'It's very kind of you to offer, but we have everything in hand,' Ottilie said.

'Have you any idea when we might expect the date of the funeral?' she went on.

'Don't you know? His body hasn't been found.' Ottilie poured the tea and passed round the cups.

'Oh, I see. He is still out there.' Their aunt stared towards the sea. 'How dreadful. Will there be a memorial service instead?'

'We haven't decided – it's too soon,' Ottilie said. 'But the vicar is going to remember Mr Brooke this Sunday. There will be no funeral or wake until he has been returned to us.'

Violet toyed with the jet beads at her throat, her mind drifting. Oh, Arvin. She remembered how she had rebuked him over copying out the love letters from the book, how she had complained of his prolonged absences in France, and the harsh words they had exchanged when boarding the steam packet. How she regretted them now.

'The inquest is being held today, and one of your father's acquaintances, the Mayor of Dover himself, has mooted an inquiry by the Board of Trade,' their aunt said. 'They will find out who is to blame for the accident and they will be punished.'

Through the mists of her sorrow and uncertainty, the heat of a slow burning anger began to sear through Violet's veins. If she ever found out who was responsible for the accident, she would seek them out and make their lives a misery, just as they had ruined her future.

'Excuse me,' she said, standing up and putting her tea back on the tray.

'Where are you going?' Eleanor said.

'To my room.'

'Leave her be,' she heard her aunt say. 'All this talk is upsetting her. I dare say she needs time alone to grieve.'

She would end up like Queen Victoria who had lost her beloved Prince Albert a few years ago – they'd had twenty-one years of married life while she'd had only one. She

167

would wear black and remain in seclusion for ever. She hadn't exactly been prepared for widowhood. She didn't know what to do, how to behave, or what she wanted. Without Arvin, she felt she had lost everything, her status and hopes for the future.

The next morning, she was sitting at the dressing table in her nightgown and slippers, resting her head on her hands as daylight tried to make its way around the chinks in the curtains.

'Violet, it's me.' The door opened a crack and Eleanor's face appeared. 'It's gone ten. I hope you don't mind me disturbing you. I've brought tea, toast and the newspapers.'

'Can't you see I'm in no mood for reading or company?'

'I thought it might help if I showed you this …' Eleanor brought the tray across to her. 'Oh, I'm so sorry for what happened to Mr Brooke.' She burst into tears and Violet's resolve to remain in isolation and in widow's weeds for the rest of her life wavered.

'Come here.' She took the tray and put it down on the bed, then got up to embrace her sister.

'I wish … it's too late. Poor Arvin.' Eleanor cried against Violet's shoulder. 'To have gone like that, swallowed up by the ocean. And it wasn't even a romantic way to die, not a proper shipwreck on a stormy night—' She broke off suddenly. 'I'm making things worse for you. I should go.'

'No, I'm glad you came to find me.' Violet tucked a damp lock of Eleanor's hair back behind her ear and released her. 'What was it you wanted to show me?'

'There's an article about the inquest held yesterday at Dover Town Hall,' Eleanor said, recovering her wits. She picked up the newspaper, smoothed it out and tapped her finger against the front page. 'It names the coroner, the crew and those who lost their lives … and the name of the poor governess.'

'Don't read them out,' Violet said quickly. 'I can't bear it.'

'The crew of the *Samphire* were there to give evidence in front of a jury who decided that no one was to blame for the accident. The only fault to surface was that the *Fanny Buck* didn't show sufficient light – one of the lanterns had run out of oil and the glasses were dirty.'

'The only fault? How can that be? What in God's name is that all about? Why didn't she show sufficient light? Who is responsible? Someone must accept the blame. Where is Pa? He will know what to do.'

'Let me finish. Pa has gone out to Whitstable on some errand. He will be back later. The jury praised the intrepidity of Captain Bennett in particular, and the rest of the crew for saving so many lives that might otherwise have been lost.'

The words didn't touch her. Yes, they had done their best, but Arvin was dead. Had he really expired for the lack of a lantern?

'It sounds as though everything is settled, but I don't think that is the end of it,' Eleanor said. 'Pa doesn't think so either. He is like a dog worrying at a bone.'

'He is sad about—' His name caught in Violet's throat and brought fresh tears to her eyes. 'He thought of him as a son.'

'I know, and although it took me some time to get used to him, I thought of him as a brother.' Violet gave her a handkerchief from the drawer beside her, and Eleanor blew her nose. 'I'll send May up with some hot water, so you can wash.'

'May? She is here?' Violet was surprised because she and Arvin had left her looking after their house at East Cliff while they were away.

'Pa sent for her. He let our housekeeper go last week.'

'Mrs Garling? Why?'

'He said we didn't need her, but I think he made the decision due to lack of funds. Shall we go to church to pray for Mr Brooke? Perhaps you'd feel better if you took some air.'

'I can't bear to see the pitying looks on people's faces.'

'They have the best of intentions – everyone is hoping for the matter to be concluded quickly for your sake. Perhaps you'd like to sit with Mama for a while instead? It would be a favour to me.'

'Of course,' Violet said. 'Thank you, Eleanor.'

She took Mama out on to the balcony, making sure she was comfortable on the chair that Wilson put out for her. Her mother didn't utter a word, and Violet was grateful to be left quietly with her thoughts. Whenever she heard the bell ring, she was on tenterhooks, still half expecting somebody to announce that her husband had been found alive and her tears had been for nothing, but the longer time went on, the more likely it seemed that he had gone for ever.

Chapter Twelve

Dead Reckoning

Violet spent the Saturday and Sunday quietly at home with the Rayfields, declining to attend the service when the Reverend Green was due to honour Arvin's memory. She slept fitfully that night. Each time she woke, she remembered that Arvin had gone, and she was overcome with a fresh wave of nausea and grief. Eventually Monday dawned, heralded by a knock on the door.

'Yes?' She sat up and rubbed her eyes as May came into the room.

'I'm sorry for disturbing you at this early hour.' May brought a ewer of hot water and placed it on the wash-stand. 'Your father requests your company in his study within the half-hour, dressed warmly ready to go out.'

Violet sighed. 'What for? I have no desire to leave the house – I'm coming down with a chill.'

'I'm just the messenger, missus.' May looked flustered. 'What shall I tell 'im?'

'Let him know I'll be down soon.'

'Would you like me to bring you breakfast?'

'No, thank you.' She couldn't eat a thing, she thought, hearing Ottilie stir as the maid closed the door.

'I wonder what Pa wants to see you about,' Ottilie said, from under the covers.

'I'll let you know later.' Violet assumed that it was about the arrangements for her future. Someone had to pay the bills until Arvin's will had been dealt with by the executors. Slowly, she got up then washed and brushed her hair. She put on a second layer of stockings under her mourning dress and petticoats, before she went downstairs to find Pa waiting not in the study, but in the hall, dressed in his coat, scarf and hat, and carrying his silver-topped ebony cane and a small leather bag.

'Ah, there you are. Thank you for humouring me at this early hour.'

'What's going on?' Violet put on her crape bonnet and veil, and black kid gloves. 'Are we going to see the solicitor?'

'Not yet. This is more urgent – I'm sorry in advance for upsetting you anew, but I need your help to identify precisely where you saw Arvin disappear. I have a boat ready and waiting at the pier.'

Fresh tears pricked at her eyelids as she glanced at her reflection in the mirror – she looked drawn, and older than her years, her brow furrowed and the corners of her mouth turned down. What was the point of Pa's quest? A body would be long gone, carried away by the currents in the Channel, and she could hardly remember where they were when it had been pitch-black.

The events of that night flashed before her eyes: the sensation of nausea and the stench of the tar and bilge; the cold seeping through her flesh and deep into her bones; the fear and panic as the boat crashed into the *Samphire*; the shouts and screams; the sight of the drowned man and the utter despair as Arvin's head disappeared beneath the black water one last time. She couldn't do it. She couldn't go back.

'Pa, don't ask me to go on a boat. I couldn't possibly,' she said, trembling.

'I need you to do this – for my sake as well as yours, dear Violet. I can't rest until we find your husband, God rest his soul.' His voice broke. 'I'm finding the sorrow hard to bear, but it must be much worse for you. I'm haunted by the fact that I encouraged this marriage.'

She reached out for her father's hand. 'I beg you not to torment yourself over it. It was God's will. I find that difficult to accept, but I have to, or I will never find peace.'

'Then you will join me today and put this all to rest.' Her father's eyes were wide in entreaty. 'I will be on that boat with you.'

'I wouldn't refuse your request without good reason – you know that. I would rather die than—'

'You have always been a dutiful daughter,' Pa interrupted. 'You are naturally disposed to do the right thing. Please, don't go against your instinct on this occasion when there is so much at stake – your peace of mind, if nothing else.'

She hesitated for a moment, picking a stray hair from the lapel of his coat. If they found him, it would put a stop to the dreams where he came back to her, alive and kicking as though nothing had happened. She would know for certain that he had perished, and in a strange and unwelcome way, it would put her mind at rest. She would be able to mourn him properly.

'I will do my duty to my husband, and come with you to look for him,' she decided. 'Let us make haste – the sooner it's over with the better.'

'Thank you. Take my arm.'

They hurried on foot along the streets to Admiralty Pier, passing beside the railway line where the mail train from London was in early, exhaling black smoke while its passengers disembarked. The porters were bustling around

173

unloading goods from the guard's van while a tall gentleman in uniform stood watching, with a whistle dangling from a cord around his neck.

'I know the chances of finding him are small, but I'm very grateful to you for not giving up hope,' she said, trying to keep up as her father strode past where one of the steam packets was moored, awaiting her passengers.

'We must pray for a favourable outcome. Ah, there is our hire for the day.' Her father pointed to a herring boat that was tied up further along the pier.

'Oh?' The sight of it changed her mind about the wisdom of her decision. She felt sick at the notion of bobbing up and down on the water in a small boat stinking of fish, because she could smell it already, even though the deck, glistening in the pale winter sun, had been scrubbed down. 'I can't,' she said, quivering with fear. 'Don't make me do this.'

'Don't let me down,' Pa said, sounding irritated.

'It is such a tiny boat compared with the *Samphire* … Why can't you show me some compassion? I am afraid this is another accident waiting to happen. My husband is missing after the incident with the *Fanny Buck*. The *Dover Belle* was lost with all hands. I will not risk my life on some wild goose chase across the Channel, because that's what it is.' She gestured towards the sea. 'How will we ever find him in all this water?'

Pa's eyes flashed with frustration. 'You will come with me. I need you to show me where Arvin fell into the sea.'

She stared at him in disbelief. 'How can I? It was dark and chaotic.'

'I'm sure that when we're out there, something will jog your memory.'

Violet couldn't understand why her father was being so insistent. Arvin's passing – because she was sure he had drowned – had affected him deeply, turning him into a raving lunatic.

'Is everything all right, Mrs Brooke?'

She turned at the sound of a familiar voice. William – dear William, who had risked his life trying to save Arvin – had appeared at her side, dressed for the weather in a sou'wester, long oilcloth coat and boots.

'Yes, yes, all is well, thank you,' she said, even though it wasn't.

'Good morning, Mr Noble,' Pa said smoothly. 'You are ready to join us on our expedition?'

'Yes, Mr Rayfield,' William said stiffly.

Violet found that she couldn't read his expression. She wondered what he was thinking. How much had he heard of her father's conversation? How had her father managed to persuade him to join them on this expedition after what had passed between them with the loss of the *Dover Belle*?

'I came down here this morning ready to tell you that I wasn't joining you on this fool's errand after all, seeing how you bullied me into it, but' – he gazed at Violet with tenderness – 'I've changed my mind.'

'You don't have to come,' she said. 'You are under absolutely no obligation.'

'Violet, you heard what Mr Noble said,' Pa interrupted. 'He has decided to join us.'

'That's right,' William said, 'and nothing will stop me now.'

'Thank you,' she whispered, knowing that she would have William to protect her. If there was any problem with the boat, he would know what to do.

'Mrs Brooke was just saying how nervous she is of the water,' Pa said more cheerfully. 'Perhaps she will be reassured now she knows that you are to accompany us on this mission. Let us waste no more time.'

Reluctantly, with heavy limbs and a leaden heart, Violet made her way to the herring boat where a small group of men were waiting for them.

'Good morning, Mr Rayfield,' one of them said.

'I'm very grateful for the loan of your boat, Captain Merriweather,' her father said. 'Allow me to introduce you to my daughter, Mrs Brooke, who will be accompanying us.'

'It's a pleasure to make your acquaintance, but it isn't wise for a woman to come aboard. You would have your daughter spend a day in the cold with no comforts?'

'I have commissioned this boat and her crew, therefore I shall invite anyone I like,' her father said. 'Don't waste any more of my time – I'm paying for a full day.'

'Very well, sir. Welcome aboard. Mrs Brooke, allow me.' The captain helped Violet on to the boat. Her father and William followed.

'I've been given the coordinates of the place where the *Fanny Buck* hit the *Samphire*, but the latter would have drifted some distance after the impact,' her father said. 'I've made some calculations based on the speed and direction of the wind and currents to pinpoint the exact location where Mr Brooke was last seen, but I can't be sure.'

'You think you're an expert in dead reckoning then, sir?' the captain said. 'Leave it to me – that's what you're paying me for. We'll make our way to the *Samphire*'s last recorded position before the collision, then we'll take soundings and ask our witnesses where they last saw the unfortunate gentleman.' The captain began to organise the crew who cast off and started to row the boat away from the pier.

As the boat caught the swell, it rocked, and Violet's heart began to race, remembering how the *Samphire* had been caught up by the waves as she'd drifted on the sea, on that fateful night.

The boat entered the Channel, where the sailors in their caps, navy woollen ganseys and wide-bottomed trousers hoisted the sails to take advantage of a brisk wind.

'Mrs Brooke' – William walked up beside her as she stood on the deck, frozen with fear – 'I wish we were meeting in better circumstances.'

She nodded in agreement.

'Come and sit down.' He caught her by the arm. 'You aren't well?'

'The motion of the sea makes me feel sick, and I'm scared,' she admitted, as he gently led her to a bench where they sat down side by side.

'It isn't surprising that you're worried about being back on the water, but I can assure you that all will be well on this occasion – Merriweather is an experienced master. I used to find that it helped to keep your eyes on a fixed point like the white cliffs.'

'Did you used to suffer from seasickness, then?' she asked, surprised.

He nodded, a half-smile on his lips.

'I haven't had the chance to thank you for what you did … You risked your life.'

'I'm sorry it didn't work out. I did what I could, but—' He shrugged. 'The sea is a cruel mistress at times. She looks benign, even kindly, then turns quickly to spite.'

'I know.'

'I admire your bravery too. You were very kind to the other young lady in her hour of need. You know that her governess didn't—'

She nodded.

'I've heard that the captain of the *Fanny Buck* was to blame for the accident,' she said.

'It's all speculation for the present – everyone is looking for somebody to blame. Never mind. It will all come out in the wash.'

She turned away, letting her gaze settle on the French coast in the distance. She and Arvin should have been leaving Paris by now on their way to the chateau to meet his sister, she remembered, unsure if the salt she could taste on her lips was from the sea spray or fresh tears.They'd been tacking back and forth, making slow headway for about half an hour when the captain gave the order to heave-to to bring the boat to a steady position. Having consulted with his sextant and chronometer, he concluded that they were at the place where the *Fanny Buck* had hit the *Samphire*.

'Then we must start making our search here,' her father said, his voice taut. He called for William. 'Tell me where you last saw Mr Brooke.'

'I can't say exactly, sir,' he responded, standing up with his gloved hands in his pockets. 'It was dark and foggy, and there was much confusion at the time. I would guess that we'd drifted a little further north-east by the time we had the trouble with the lifeboat.' He pointed towards a buoy floating on the surface of the water, as two men emerged from the fore-cabin, wearing heavy-booted brown canvas suits which covered everything except their heads and hands.

'How sure are you?' Pa moved across and caught William by his coat lapels. 'Come on, my man. Think!'

'I've already explained why it's impossible to be certain of the exact position.' William stood tall and straight, staring down at Mr Rayfield. 'Unhand me.'

Pa continued to cling on.

'I said, unhand me.'

Pa took one hand off William's coat and clenched his fist.

'I see that I'm going to have to knock some sense into you!' he growled.

'Pa, leave him alone! Let him go!' Violet shouted, hot with shame at her father's behaviour, and worried that he was about to lose his temper completely and knock William to the deck. She rushed up to them and grasped her father's arm, at which he seemed to recover his wits, releasing the young engineer.

'As you aren't going to help me, I'm going to make sure you suffer,' Pa went on, spitting fury. 'I'll have you taken off the *Samphire*'s crew. I'll make your life a misery.'

'Father, stop this!' Violet snapped. 'You are making a scene. Whatever has happened to you? Mr Noble has stated that he doesn't know where to look for Arvin. Threatening him won't make any difference.' She despaired of his lack of manners. In fact, at that moment, she despised him. She turned to William.

'I'm fine,' he said with a half-smile. 'I'm grateful for your intervention but I can fight my own battles, you know.'

'Violet, where is your loyalty to your father?' Pa interrupted.

She glared at him – he didn't deserve it.

'We'll discuss it later,' he went on impatiently. 'There's no time now. What do you think? Is this where the lifeboat fell into the sea?'

'I concur with Mr Noble – this would be as good a place as any to start the search,' she said coldly, siding with William.

'Then prepare the divers,' her father said as she scanned the surface of the water, which was a murky grey-green beneath the winter sun, much calmer and less malign than it had been on the terrible night of the accident.

'Divers?' Violet couldn't help herself. She hadn't imagined that her father would invest in an underwater search for Arvin. What about these men? Why would anyone make a career of putting their own life in danger? And why would they risk diving in the winter? They would freeze to death.

She looked up to find a man of about her father's age, dressed in a cap and overalls, placing a heavy copper helmet over one of the diver's heads. He tightened the bolts that held the corselet to his diving suit while the diver fiddled with his dark leather cuffs. He connected a hose to the helmet, and shouted and gesticulated to the diver inside.

'Forgive me for raising such an indelicate subject, Mr Noble, but wouldn't a body have floated away by now?' Violet whispered.

'I think so, if it were not weighted down.' William cleared his throat. 'I wonder if you might address me as plain William, as you did once before? Please forgive me if I've been too forward in assuming we are friends of sorts. It's the situation that we find ourselves in. I feel – wrongly, perhaps – that we are kindred spirits, having survived that night. I'm sorry, Mrs Brooke, you are suffering ...'

'I will call you William, if you will address me as Violet,' she said softly.

'You aren't offended?'

She shook her head. He was right – they shared a bond, and although she would always be Mrs Brooke, she felt safe and at ease with him.

'How deep is the water here?' she asked.

'I don't know – Mr Johnson will have looked at the charts,' he said as one of the divers disappeared into the water with a soft splash, the umbilical unwinding behind him. The second diver followed immediately after.

Violet shivered with cold.

'May I suggest that we take shelter in the cabin?' William said.

'No, I couldn't ...' her voice faded.

'It's freezing out here in the wind.' He fetched an oily canvas sheet from the fore-cabin. 'You can have my coat.'

'Oh no,' she said. 'That wouldn't be right.'

'I insist.' He took off his coat and placed it around her shoulders. 'I'll sit under the canvas – it's windproof.'

Grateful, she pulled his coat around her chin, inhaling its scent of musk and engine oil as she waited for the divers to return to the surface.

'I'm sorry about my father. He had no right to threaten you like that.'

'There's no need for you to apologise on his behalf. I had always thought of you as sweet-tempered and mild-mannered, but you are quite a fighter.'

'Oh dear,' she said. Was he trying to say that he considered her unfeminine?

'What I mean is that I admire the way that you stood up for me. It takes guts to confront one's father.'

'Did you ever ...?'

'On a few occasions. I feel terribly guilty because we had an argument over – oh, it was something trivial – before he left on his last navigation with the *Dover Belle*. I only hope that he knew how much I loved him in spite of his flaws.' He swallowed hard.

'How is your mother?' she asked, feeling a little guilty for having focused on her troubles when he obviously had challenges of his own.

He smiled. 'She's as well as can be expected, thank you.'

'How does she feel about you going to sea? I mean, perhaps you don't want to talk about it. I'm sorry.' She blushed at her insensitivity as the wind whistled around the mast.

'Don't be. Ma and I talk of my father and brother often. I'm sure she doesn't let a moment go by without thinking of them. We remember them fondly.'

'Aren't you scared of the water?'

'No, my family have been seafarers for generations – it's in our blood. In fact, my grandfather used to say that if you cut into his veins, the sea would drip out of them. My mother would be much happier if I found a shore-based position, though.'

'I would be too, if I were her. She must be afraid of losing you as well.'

He nodded. 'You speak frankly – I like that.'

'I miss my husband,' she said, trying to control her trembling lip. 'We were supposed to grow old together ...'

The boat rocked and creaked beneath them, and eventually William broke the silence. 'Here they are.'

'Well?' said her father as the divers dripped water across the deck, and the man in charge, whom they called Mr Johnson, helped them to remove their helmets.

'There's no sign of what you're looking for, Mr Rayfield,' one said, shivering, his hands blue with cold.

'You've been all the way to the bottom of the sea?'

'We have, but the visibility is very poor today as we told you it would be. It's like diving through pea soup down there.'

'But you have been to the bottom?' her father repeated. 'You weren't down there for long.'

'It was long enough,' Mr Johnson said. 'The water is extremely cold, the visibility is terrible, and we're looking for a needle in a haystack. I told you that this mission was unlikely to succeed, yet you wouldn't listen.'

'You will dive again and again until you find what we're looking for.'

'I won't send the divers down a second time. It's taking an unnecessary risk.'

'Mr Johnson,' one of the divers interrupted, 'I'm willing to give it another go. Mr Rayfield's paying us a year's wages for this.'

'I know that, but your life is worth more.'

'I have a wife, children and bills to pay. I want to dive again – I know what I'm doing.'

Mr Johnson gazed at the two divers. 'All right then. Dive closer to the buoy, but don't expect to be able to see any better this time.'

Violet waited as they dived twice more and returned to the boat without success.

'This is impossible,' she said quietly aside to William. Her father didn't appear to have thought his plan through. Was he expecting the divers to search the whole of the Straits of Dover?

'I'm afraid so. I admire your father's determination in trying to find your husband, but, as I've said, I think he is on a fool's errand. Forgive me for talking in such a way.'

'You are only stating the facts,' she said, looking towards her father who was arguing with Mr Johnson again.

'Let me go down.' Mr Rayfield raised his voice. 'I'll borrow one of your suits with the helmet and airline and go and see for myself.'

'It isn't safe for someone with no experience to dive on a day like today. It's easy to become disorientated.'

'It's my choice. In fact, I insist on it.'

'I can't let you take this risk,' Mr Johnson said. 'If anything happens to you, I'll be ruined.'

'Your reputation is already at stake – your divers must be blind!'

Violet didn't know what to do. At the moment, she didn't like her father much, but she didn't want to lose him as well as her husband, for her family's sake. They needed him. She stood up and walked across the deck.

'Listen to what Mr Johnson says,' she said. 'It's too dangerous.'

'I will go!' her father bellowed. His face was a deep crimson, and beads of spittle adorned his whiskers as he went on, 'Mr Johnson, I know what you're up to – I'm not stupid. Your men are lying, pretending they've seen nothing, when tomorrow or the next day, you'll come back and pocket the gold for yourself.'

'What gold?' Violet exclaimed. 'I know nothing of this. Why did you keep it from me?'

'Because we didn't want to trouble you with it. To be honest—'

'Honest? What do you know about honesty? You've been lying to me! To us all!'

'Allow me to explain – Arvin was carrying it on my behalf, with the intention of depositing half in a bank in Paris and using the rest to invest in wine.'

'That was what was in the chest – not papers, but gold.' That's why Arvin had guarded it so fiercely. It was Mama's gold, the dowry she had brought into her marriage, and which her father – by the law of the land – had appropriated. She wasn't sure how she felt about that. 'Mama doesn't know about this, does she? You haven't told her either.'

'What's the point of worrying her with it? She wouldn't understand and besides, she's suffering enough.' Her father turned back to Mr Johnson. 'You are trying to deceive me, sir!'

'We have been bringing treasure trove to the surface for almost thirty years and returning it to the rightful owner,' Mr Johnson said. 'How dare you suggest that we would act dishonestly!'

Mr Rayfield was shaking with anger as he removed his hat and coat and flung them on to the deck.

'Give me a suit and helmet,' he ordered. 'You gave me assurances of your professional competence, and you've let me down.'

'We're the best people for this enterprise. When we dive to retrieve treasure from shipwrecks we generally know exactly where the lost ship lies, but here we are relying on guesswork.'

Pa turned to Violet and William. 'You are both my witnesses – I have chosen this course of action by my own free will. Hand me a suit. I cannot rest until we have retrieved the gold – my life depends on it.'

'If that is your will, Mr Rayfield, I won't stop you, but I'm telling you now that I wash my hands of all responsibility for your safety.' Mr Johnson turned to one of the divers with a resigned shrug. 'Davy, you'll dive with him.'

A short while later, her father was dressed in one of the suits which was clearly made for a smaller frame, the canvas stretched so he could barely move, and the cuffs halfway up his forearms. Mr Johnson secured the corselet, helmet and airline.

'Remember to take your time. Guard your umbilical with care – you are dependent on it. If by any mischance you should lose sight of your guide, follow the rope back upwards to the boat. It is all too easy to become disorientated and panic. I've known men to suffocate and die from losing contact with the surface and heading further into the depths.' He gazed at Pa through narrowed eyes. 'Are you sure about this?'

Pa gestured his assent.

'Let's not delay then – the weather is coming in.' Mr Johnson glanced back towards Dover where dark clouds were shrouding the tops of the cliffs.

'I can't watch.' Violet turned away and held on to the side, a wave of grief washing through her at the thought of Arvin lying cold and alone at the bottom of the sea, and her father about to join him.

She became aware of William standing beside her.

'I had no idea about the gold,' she said, not wanting him to think ill of her.

'I believe that wives are not always privy to their husbands' affairs, although it isn't how things happened in my family. I don't think that my father ever withheld anything from my mother, although he didn't always treat her kindly,' he said. 'How is your ma? Is she any better?'

'She is much changed, I'm afraid. She doesn't recognise us – her daughters – any more, but we still have hope that she will recover.'

'I'm sorry. How are your sisters?'

'They are well, thank you.'

'Is Ottilie walking out with John Chittenden? I saw them on the promenade not very long ago. At least – perhaps I'm being presumptuous ...'

'Can I trust you with a secret?'

'I know how to hold my tongue. You can rely on me, Violet.'

She looked up into his eyes. His gaze was steady.

'My father mustn't know. They are engaged.'

'It is a love match then?'

'Well, yes.' Violet recalled her dutiful marriage to Arvin. 'Mr Brooke and I ... I miss him. I didn't love him, but I came to look upon him with affection ... and now ...' She swallowed hard. 'I don't know. I don't know anything any more.'

'It's very distressing, and being out here isn't helping you,' William said. 'What is your father thinking, bringing you back to the scene of the accident?'

There was a sudden series of splashes from behind them as Mr Rayfield and his diving companion emerged from the swell a few feet from the bow of the boat. The diver shoved her father up on to the deck where he collapsed in a heap, his chest pumping up and down like a set of bellows. Mr Johnson hauled him up to a sitting position then removed his helmet, revealing his face, purple from the lack of air.

'Nothing!' he gasped. 'It is hopeless! It is all over for me.' He bent double, clutching his knees, and broke into great raking sobs before dragging himself up again. 'We must go home,' he said abruptly. 'We have finished here. I am finished. Ruined.'

There had been a time when her heart would have gone out to him and she would have run up to him and put her arms around his neck to console him, but Violet couldn't do it. She felt nothing, no pain or distress at seeing a grown man cry for the very first time, only embarrassment at this expression of emotion in public. She had done her duty once too often and all it had brought her was grief. She wouldn't do it again.

William and the other men were watching her, waiting for her to help her father, but she would not. The deck shifted beneath her feet, seeming to emphasise the point: their relationship had changed for ever.

Captain Merriweather turned the boat about and they headed back to Dover. Her father didn't say a word until they reached the quay and William helped her disembark.

'Where do you think you're going, Violet?' he said.

She turned and glared at him. 'Home, and it's Mrs Brooke to you.'

'You can't ask me to change a habit of a lifetime.' He offered his arm and she pushed it away. 'I'll walk you back to your house. We have much to discuss on the way.'

'I don't want to have anything to do with you, the way you've treated me and Mr Noble today.'

'You are a traitor to me and the rest of the Rayfields,' Pa said. 'The way you allied yourself with that uncouth, ill-bred upstart as opposed to your own flesh and blood is a disgrace.'

'You gave me no choice. If you'd behaved like a gentleman …' She stepped back, her heart pounding. She could sense his anger in the tautening of the muscle in his cheek and the black fury in his eyes, and she hated him for it.

'If you turn away now, I will disown you. I'll cast you off and leave you to manage your affairs by yourself,' he went on bitterly.

'I am perfectly able to cope,' she said, but he added one final blow.

'And I'll make sure you never see your mother and sisters again.'

'How could you? You don't mean it.'

'I mean it,' he confirmed.

A bilious mixture of grief, anger and resentment rose in her throat. How dare he control her like this! She wanted to give him a good shove and push him into the water. She would watch him drown.

'I'll come with you then, Father,' she said coldly. The scales had fallen from her eyes, and she doubted she would ever be able to bring herself to call him Pa again. She was almost in tears, but she wouldn't cry. Not this time. 'I will never look at you in the same way.'

'I'm glad that you've seen reason,' her father said as they moved away from William who was watching them closely and the crew who were within earshot. 'This is another occasion on which you must do your duty.'

'What duty? I have done my duty in marrying the man of your choice to help the Rayfields out of their financial difficulty. I've done my part – I'm not obliged to do any more.'

'But family is family – it never goes away. You were born a Rayfield – you will always have ties and obligations to me, your mother and sisters. We need you now, more than ever.'

She knew what he was going to say, what he was going to ask of her.

'At least you will not want for anything,' he began as they walked back into town.

'Apart from the company of my husband,' she said curtly.

'I beg your pardon. Naturally you will suffer, but after a while, you'll start to feel better. Arvin has left you well provided for. Being party to his financial situation, I can confirm that you will be very comfortably off. It is better to be a rich widow than a poor one.'

'I assume that I will receive a jointure to live on, that's true, but no amount of money can make up for my loss.' Her voice wavered. She was a widow. There was no way – she accepted it now – that Arvin could have survived. He had drowned that night.

'I know, but he has entailed almost the whole of his estate to you, his wife.'

'I didn't know … It is most unusual, isn't it?'

'Most husbands leave an allowance and an arrangement wherein their widows may remain in their home while holding the majority of their estates in trust for the eldest sons when they come of age, but Arvin was most insistent that his assets should pass to you, Mrs Brooke.'

'How do you know about Arvin's will?' Violet asked, put out that he hadn't shared it with her.

'I asked him when we were arranging the details of your marriage and financial settlement. I had to make sure that your future was secured, and to that end, I gave Arvin an extra twenty per cent share of our business.'

Violet felt her brow tighten.

'Now you own a share in Brooke and Rayfield, but don't worry about it – I shall manage it on your behalf. There's also the property in France; an apartment in Paris; the castle and vineyards.'

'What about his sister?'

'As I've said before, you have a kind heart – I know you'll make sure that Claudette's provided for too. You can draw up a contract allowing her to have the apartment for the rest of her natural life.'

'I see. Perhaps she would prefer to stay on in the chateau – in fact, I might go and live there to keep her company.'

'I think it must be sold to release the capital,' Pa said quickly.

'It will be my decision.' Violet began to feel an unusual sense of power, being in control by virtue of inheriting a fortune.

'Listen, I'm in deep water ...'

'An unfortunate turn of phrase, considering the circumstances.'

'It was your husband who lost the gold—'

'It wasn't his fault.' She had never felt so angry with anyone before. 'If I were a man, I'd call you out.'

Her father lowered his eyes. 'I apologise, but I'm in dire straits. I'm on the verge of bankruptcy, and if that happens, we'll lose the house at Camden Crescent. Please, I'm begging you to do everything within your reach – as you've done before – to help your father who has fallen on hard times through no fault of his own ...'

'If Mama was well, she would beg to differ,' Violet observed. 'You've been foolish and downright unpleasant, taking advantage of me and Arvin for your own ends. If it hadn't been for you encouraging him in this scheme, he would still be alive.'

'He played his part in it.'

'This situation is a result of your greed.'

'I wanted to secure my family's future,' her father argued. 'It's part of a man's nature to look after his nearest and dearest. I've only gone along with the normal way of things, but Fate has played against me. You wouldn't let your mother and sisters suffer in poverty?'

Torn between wanting to punish her father and look after the rest of the family, she agonised over her response. She had done her duty before and look how it had left her. The grey stone walls of Dover Castle glowered down at them against the wintry sky.

'I need to think about it,' she said eventually. 'I'll give you my answer within a few days.' She would let him stew in his own juice – as far as she was concerned, he deserved it.

Chapter Thirteen

A Most Disagreeable Caller

Dejected and frozen to the bone, Violet returned to the house she'd shared with Arvin, before remembering that she had no key. She went back to the Rayfields' where she packed the few belongings she had there, and asked May – with her sisters' permission – to accompany her.

Ottilie came to the bedroom to help her fold her clothes: her mourning outfits, nightgowns and slippers.

'Pa's in a right state – I can't get any sense out of him,' she said.

'It's been a terrible day. You aren't going to believe this, but our father chartered a herring boat with divers today.'

'He did what?'

'He refused to take no for an answer when I said I didn't want to go and he threatened Mr Noble who came with us with all kinds of trouble when he stood up to him. He's a bully who's threatened to disown me, his own daughter. I've tried to understand his point of view, but I can't. I was under the impression that he was hiring the divers to look for ...' Violet's voice broke, and she struggled to regain her composure '... Arvin, but all he wanted was to find the gold. That's what pains me the most.'

'What gold are you talking about?'

'The bullion, Ma's dowry. From what I can gather, he gave it to Arvin to take to France where he was supposed to deposit some in a bank and use the rest to buy wine. At least' – she bit her lip, drawing blood – 'that's what I would like to think. Ottilie, I have lost faith in our father's goodness, and what's more, I can't help doubting my husband's motives in all this.'

'Oh Violet, I know you're upset, but you can't go accusing Arvin of anything, not when he isn't here to defend himself.'

'He behaved very coldly towards me when we boarded the boat – Arvin, that is. It was almost as if he didn't want to know me. All his attention was on the trunk which I found out today contained the gold.'

'That doesn't surprise me – he knew he couldn't afford to lose Pa's fortune,' Ottilie said. 'They were partners – he had a vested interest. Violet, you must remember better times: the day Arvin proposed; your wedding day; the love letters he sent you.'

'The ones he copied from a book, you mean?' They had been an indication of his feelings for her, his young bride-to-be, and he'd said he'd done it because he couldn't find the words to express his affection. Was that the truth? She hadn't loved him, but she'd grown fond of him, and now she felt sick as she began to wonder how well she'd really known him.

'Nobody is perfect. He was trying to do the right thing,' Ottilie scolded, making her feel guilty for judging her husband.

'I realise that.' It had been her father's behaviour which had unnerved her and made her start questioning Arvin's attitude to her while they'd been travelling on the *Samphire*. Of course he would have been careful with the gold. She just wished he'd explained the situation to her – she would have understood.

'Pa says that you will be well provided for. At least you'll be able to afford to keep the house on, and ... I know it's too soon to be thinking about it, but you will find plenty to keep you occupied, and one day in the distant future, you'll marry again and bear children.'

'Marry again? How can you talk of that when Arvin isn't yet buried?'

'Forgive me for speaking frankly, but you are young, far too young to spend the rest of your life on your own. One day, I promise you, we will go out walking together with our husbands and children.'

'I'm sorry,' Violet said. 'I'd forgotten to ask you – how is John?'

'He is well. All I wish for is Pa's blessing, but it's never the right time to ask him. Firstly, he and Uncle Edward part company over the *Dover Belle*, then Mama falls ill, and he starts to worry about our financial security, and then we seem to begin to get back on to an even keel with your marriage and his partnership with Arvin, and now this … Never mind. I will never give up hope. Why don't you leave your packing and stay here?'

'My life is unravelling. I don't know what to do or where to go, but in the meantime, I find it untenable to continue to live under the same roof as our father.'

'Are you sure?'

'Don't worry about me. I'll take May with me as agreed.'

There were no other staff left – both Jacques and Mrs Davis had taken their holidays when Violet and Arvin were supposed to be in France. Violet supposed she would have to contact the housekeeper through the agency to inform her of what had happened. As for Jacques, she had no idea how to get in touch with him.

'I didn't think we'd be coming back here today,' May said as they walked up the steps to the house at East Cliff. 'You should have sent me ahead to air the rooms and light the fires to chase the damp away.'

'I didn't plan it in advance,' Violet said wryly as she stepped inside, shivering.

May put her bags down in the hall and Violet followed suit.

'Let me take your coat,' May said. 'Can I get you some brandy? It'll take a while to boil a kettle for tea.'

'No, thank you.' A lump caught in her throat at the sight of the empty hooks on the hallstand where Arvin's coats should have been.

'I'm very sorry for your loss. The master, although I 'adn't known 'im long, often had a kind word for me.'

Keeping her coat on, Violet made her way to the parlour.

'I'm sorry to have to ask this, and I know it's probably too soon for you to have made any plans. I mean, I don't think Mr Rayfield's too keen to keep me employed over at Camden Crescent, and you might wish to give up the lease on this 'ouse ...' May said.

'I want to stay here for a while. I'd give you plenty of notice if I decided to move somewhere smaller and more modest.' *Or go to France*, she thought, *to start a new life and forget about this one.*

'Then I'm very grateful.' May walked over to the fireplace, her long black skirt dragging across the carpet.

Violet slumped in a chair with her legs tucked underneath her. She stroked the locket at her throat – engraved with a skull and containing a miniature of Arvin's portrait – while she watched May light the fire, using the tinderbox to create a spark to ignite the kindling.

Gradually, the coals began to smoke and glow orange on their undersides, but it wasn't until the clock chimed, tolling the passing of another hour, that the room began to warm up.

Violet had been transformed from wife to wealthy widow, and now she had to make something of her life

195

while waiting for her time to be taken up to Heaven. She teased out a loose black thread from her sleeve, picturing days, months and years of sorrow, tedium and idleness. Could she use some of her inheritance to help both the Rayfields – for her mother's and sisters' sake, not her father's – and the families of sailors lost at sea? It seemed like a reasonable idea, but grief had taken hold of her – body and soul – and she couldn't see how on earth she would find the energy to instigate it.

The following afternoon, Violet was sitting in the dining room alone at one end of the long table with the gas lamps burning to brighten the winter gloom. Picking at a light luncheon of ham and scrambled eggs that May had prepared, she gazed towards the aquatint photograph of her and Arvin which she'd turned to face the wall because she couldn't bear to look at it. As for the pretty arrangements of pressed flowers from her wedding bouquet, the delivery of which she had looked forward to with great anticipation, she had put one in Arvin's place at the dining table, and the other in her bedroom.

She stifled a sob. She was confused: still mourning her husband and feeling affection for him, as she believed a good wife should, but – she felt guilty for it – angry about what had been revealed during her father's expedition to try to find him.

'Oh, Arvin, I'd do anything to be able to talk to you now,' she whispered, picturing him sitting opposite her, scraping his plate and getting on her nerves. 'There's so much I need to know. Why did you lie to me about the gold? Why did you treat me so unkindly when we were on the mail packet? Why did you seem to care more for the contents of the chest than your wife?' She had listened to any number of sermons on how riches were to be found in human relationships and family ties, not gold and silver. She supposed that the tendency for men to think the opposite was the reason for the vicar's frequent reminders.

The harsh ring of the doorbell and the sound of the maid's footsteps on the tiles in the corridor disturbed her solitude.

'No, Mrs ... Ma'am ... I'm sorry, ma'am.' She heard May's frantic calls.

Quickly, Violet stood up from the table and ran from the dining room to find a woman pushing her way past the maid in the hall. Was there news?

'At least wait 'ere until I've spoken to my mistress. This is 'er private residence.'

'I must speak with Mr Brooke *tout de suite*,' the woman said, dismissing Violet's hopes that Arvin's body had been found.

'My mistress is in mourning and entitled to 'er privacy. If you wish to call on 'er, please leave your card and make an appointment.'

'I'll deal with this,' Violet said, recognising that the woman wasn't going to take no for an answer. 'May, bring some tea.'

'Are you sure?' The maid raised her eyebrows in surprise at this breach of social propriety.

'Quite sure, thank you. This way, miss ...' Violet showed the woman to the parlour, noting how her navy coat with brass buttons was cinched in at the waist, making her seem waspish. Her eyes were blue, her cheekbones highlighted with rouge, and her hair coal-black and falling in ringlets from beneath her hat. Who was this petite stranger with a French accent? Could she possibly be Arvin's sister? She was quite a beauty, a little faded and older than Claudette by at least ten years, and certainly not disfigured.

'How shall I address you?' she asked, showing the woman to one of the chairs beside the fire. A shiver ran down her spine even though the room wasn't cold, as the stranger removed her grey kid gloves, using her teeth to pull them off before taking them in one hand.

'I've come to see my husband, *mon mari*. Je suis Madame Arvin Brooke,' the woman said.

'How strange. I am Mrs Arvin Brooke,' Violet said, rather aggrieved at the way the stranger had entered the house under the false pretence of an association with Mr Brooke. 'I don't understand.' She'd made a mistake in letting her in – she was a fraud and a charlatan. 'I'd like you to leave.'

'I will be staying here tonight – Arvin and I will dine together. This is his house?'

'It is our house.' Violet's brow tightened and her head began to ache. Something wasn't right. Was it the custom in France to invite oneself into any old stranger's home? Was this woman referring to a different man of the same name?

'I'm sorry to be the bearer of bad news, but I married this man …' The woman showed her a carte de visite from her reticule. The subject was undoubtedly Arvin – he stood with one foot in front of the other, resting one arm on the back of a chair. He looked rather smug.

'That's Mr Brooke. That's my husband,' Violet said curtly. She glanced down at her widow's weeds – she didn't need this intrusion.

'You can't be – Monsieur Brooke and I are married.' Her unwelcome visitor dropped her gloves on the low table next to Violet's embroidery where her needle glinted from the fabric, like a dagger through her heart.

'No, we are married. I am the widow of the very same gentleman.'

'Widow? Oh!' The woman paled. Fearing she was about to collapse, Violet took her arm and sat her down.

'Tea isn't adequate for a situation such as this. I'll call for some brandy instead.' Watching the tears catching in the woman's long dark lashes, Violet picked up the brass bell from the table and rang for May.

'The rumours are true. He has perished?'

Violet nodded. This wasn't happening. The woman was deluded. She should be committed to the asylum.

'Then it is no wonder that he didn't arrive in Paris as we arranged.' The woman's expression hardened, and Violet felt as if she had stepped straight on to the pages of a sensationalist novel as she went on, 'Where is the gold? He was bringing gold bullion over to France. Where is it?'

Violet decided to keep some of the truth to herself.

'The gold belongs to my father. I don't see that this has anything to do with you. Arvin didn't get the chance to arrange the purchase of goods so the gold remains the property of Mr Rayfield.'

'Oh, you are so naïve, you poor little Englishwoman,' the woman sneered. 'My husband was never going into business with your father – he didn't need to.' The coals sank into the grate with a menacing clink. 'Once he'd won Mr Rayfield's trust and persuaded him to let him carry the gold, he planned to abandon you in Paris ...'

'I don't believe you,' Violet said acidly. 'He treated my father with great respect, and we were going to do some sightseeing in Paris before going to stay at his home in France. It was all arranged.' The implications of what the woman had said began to sink in. Had they all been taken in by Arvin's quick tongue and smooth talking? Had their marriage been a sham, part of a plan to defraud the Rayfields of what was left of their money? She couldn't believe what she was hearing. 'What is your name?' she asked.

'Madame Arv—'

'No, not that.'

'Claudette,' the woman said quietly, looking her in the eye.

Violet almost laughed, the story was even more preposterous: Claudette, the disfigured sister, hidden from view, was in fact Arvin's wife.

'You rang for me,' May said from the parlour door.

'Forget the tea. Fetch some brandy and two glasses, please,' Violet said, and the maid frowned and scurried away.

'I wasn't happy when I found out that my husband had become involved with another woman, but I didn't imagine that he'd married her! He told me you were ugly and flat-footed like a duckling. I should have guessed that he was lying.' She uttered an epithet in French. 'I could wring his neck! He has betrayed me and been the ruin of you.'

'I wish you wouldn't speak so harshly of him,' Violet countered.

'Because he is dead? Oh dear, when you have had time to reflect, you will feel the same. Where do you think your beloved was last summer, for example? He was overseeing the harvest and the pressing during the day, and spending the nights in my bed, of course.'

How indelicate, Violet thought, but it made sense. Those prolonged trips to France: to check on the grapes; for business; to see his sister. But when he'd come back he'd been passionate and affectionate ... How could he have been so duplicitous?

'Brandy, missus,' May said, interrupting the conversation.

'*Merci*,' the other Mrs Brooke said, as May poured two glasses from the decanter. As she watched her take a sip, Violet hoped she would choke on it.

'Please leave us,' she said firmly when May stoked the fire and put a log on top of the coals, then hovered, ready to pour out a second glass of brandy for their unwanted guest. The maid made herself scarce.

'I expect you married in the Chantilly lace,' Claudette said.

'A gift passed down from Arvin's mother.' As soon as she said it, Violet realised it had been another lie.

'He gave it to me first.'

'Arvin and I are legally married,' Violet said, remembering how the fragrance of lilies had lingered on the lace, the perfume which Arvin said his mother had used to keep it fresh. Even though the idea of him lying with another woman cut her to the quick, she would maintain her dignity. She had done nothing wrong. 'We said our vows – sacred vows – in church and signed the register in front of witnesses. I am his true wife. There is no over-turning it.'

'I'm sorry to disappoint you. He married me first and there's proof of our union in France. I intend to remain here in Dover – don't worry, I'll take a room at the Warden Hotel – until I have proven my claim and collected his possessions. I intend to return to France as soon as possible. I have no desire to embarrass you, although perhaps my departure might be hastened upon a small payment from your dear father.'

'That is extortion.' Violet began to shake uncontrollably.

'It is common sense on my part.' Her tears for her lost husband appeared to have completely dried up as she stood from her chair. 'I will take my leave now. I'm very grateful for your hospitality, Miss Rayfield. I'll see myself out.'

Violet stayed sitting in her chair, staring at the fire until the sound of the woman's footsteps faded, and the front door clicked shut. A log cracked, throwing a cinder on to the rug, and gradually the smell of burning replaced the scent of the woman's perfume and the rug began to smoke. She watched a tiny flame grow and begin to take hold of the fibres, just as the woman's revelations had set alight a fire of confusing thoughts in her head.

Which of them was right? Which of them would be recognised as the true Mrs Brooke and what fate would befall the other?

'Oh dear, oh dear. Forgive me, but what are you thinkin'?' May came rushing in, holding up her skirt and stamping on the flames to put them out. 'I dread to think what would 'ave happened if I 'adn't come in when I did. The whole place would 'ave gone up.'

'I'm sorry,' Violet whispered.

'You are unwell? Shall I send for the doctor? Or your sister? You really shouldn't be left alone at a time like this.'

'I am quite well, thank you.' It had been an odd sensation, watching the potential disaster gradually unfolding, knowing she should have stopped it before it had gone this far, but being unable to move, her limbs weighed down with shock and renewed grief. For she had no doubt that what the stranger had said was true. That she believed she was Arvin's true wife.

What kind of man had Arvin been that he would willingly enter into marriage with her, knowing that if the truth came out, she would be ruined? She couldn't believe that. The carte de visite had been a fake. She wouldn't slight her husband's reputation by entertaining doubt when he was dead and couldn't speak for himself. She would have to speak for him.

'I just want to say that I'm very sorry,' May said. 'Will you be wanting dinner this evening?'

She deliberated for a moment. She needed time to let the detail of the visit sink in, yet she wasn't sure how long she would have to investigate the woman's claims and overturn them. It wasn't an issue one could wait upon to see what happened next because, even though she judged the woman's claims a mistake, much damage could be done to her family's reputation if she should continue repeating them to all and sundry in Dover.

She consoled herself with the idea that the situation was so far-fetched that it couldn't possibly be real. She needed to speak to someone, but to whom could she turn?

It was something that should be kept within the family. No one else must know, apart from May. She could guess what Miss Whiteway would have said on the matter – that it wasn't right for a woman to be shamed because of a man's dishonesty, but it was the way of the world.

'Mrs Brooke. Mrs Brooke!' May's voice cut into her consciousness. 'Forgive me for saying this, but you are away with the fairies. I asked you if you require dinner.'

'I'm sorry. You're right – I'm not quite myself. As for dinner – not tonight, thank you. I'm going to call on my father.' She would take the information to his door and let him advise her. He would know what to do and he owed her. Not only had he threatened to cut her off from her family, he had allowed his affection for Arvin to overwhelm his better judgement. If he had been more careful with his dealings with the *Dover Belle*, and his investments in the railway, then he wouldn't have ended up in such dire straits that he would marry off one of his daughters to a man he didn't know to restore the family's fortunes.

It had turned out to be a disastrous error – for all of them – and it was up to him to sort it out.

'I trust I can depend on your discretion, May,' she said. 'If anyone asks, I'll say that nobody called.'

'That will be all then. Take the rest of the evening off. I'll take a key and let myself back in.'

Flushed from the brandy and the heat from the fire, Violet pushed herself up from her chair, and fetched her coat, muff, hat and button-up boots before heading out. She pulled up her coat collar against the icy chill and walked along Marine Drive under the gleaming gaslights to the Rayfields. When she reached the house, she ran up the steps and rang the bell.

Wilson opened the door and showed her through to the parlour where her father was sitting in his favourite leather chair. When he saw her, he stood up and rushed over to greet her, grasping both her hands.

'You have come! You have come to the right decision! I assure you of my deep and everlasting gratitude for agreeing to do your duty to your family.'

'No.' She shook her head to emphasise the point. 'I'm here for another reason entirely.'

'Oh? What a pity.' He gazed into her eyes. 'I had such hopes ...'

'How is Ma?' she asked.

'She's sleeping. According to Eleanor, she has had one of her good days.'

'That's something to be thankful for, then,' she said. 'Father—'

'I wish you would call me Pa again,' he said mournfully, but she dismissed his plea. It was too late for that. What had been said and done could never be taken back.

'I came because I need your advice on a matter which affects us all. I received a visitor this afternoon, a most disagreeable and unpleasant woman.'

Her father released her hands.

'Come and sit down. Tell me all about it,' he said gruffly, and they sat down side by side on the chaise. He looked grey and drawn, a man who had been much altered by circumstance. His figure was slimmer, shrunken as if, like an old piece of furniture, he'd had all the stuffing knocked out of him.

He sat in silence, his hands pressed together as though in prayer, while she told him the story of what had happened that afternoon.

'Why did you sit and listen to her lies? Oh, this is preposterous.' The knotted veins at his temple stood out from his skin. 'She will be after his money. That's what it's all about,' he said a little more cheerfully. 'There is no other explanation.'

'Except the one that she put forward,' Violet said softly. 'She was very convincing.'

'But she's a fraudster all the same. Arvin wouldn't have done something like this – I always found him to be a decent and honest man. Did this woman say where she was staying? I assume she is still here in Dover.'

'She told me she would take a room at the Warden Hotel.'

'My dear—'

'I am not your dear,' she said sharply.

'I'm determined to redeem myself. Violet, don't worry about this woman. I'll call on her first thing in the morning and persuade her out of this delusion.'

'I'd like to come with you – this is my business.'

'No, this is my fault. Let me go and put a lid firmly on top of her ridiculous claims. Why don't you stay here tonight? Your sisters will be pleased to see you – they're upstairs with your mother.'

She wanted to see them, but she couldn't face having to explain why she had called, nor did she have the strength to pretend that all was well.

'Give them my regards,' she said. 'I'll walk myself home.'

Chapter Fourteen

The Truth Will Out

It was raining stair rods when her father called on her the next day. Violet guessed from his expression that he had bad news.

'She is certain she is the true Mrs Brooke,' he said, mopping the rain from his face as he stepped inside the parlour. 'I've offered to pay her off, but she won't budge. She says there's nothing I can do to persuade her to let the matter rest – she wishes to prove her case for the sake of her reputation. I'm afraid that if she carries on like this, it's going to be most unpleasant. The matter may well end up in court.'

'Why's that? Arvin is gone, missing presumed dead. You can't prosecute a dead man.'

'I'm afraid that it will be you who goes on trial.' Pa picked at his nail, leaving it blunt. 'I'm going to hire Mr Wiggins to look into this properly and challenge her position.'

'Can you afford it, Father?' she said frankly.

'I'll borrow the funds.'

'Is that wise?'

'We have nothing much left to lose and everything to gain, because when we prove that you are his true wife – and I have no reason to doubt that the court will rule in our favour – then you will inherit Arvin's estate.'

'And I'll be able to pay off your loan with interest,' she said, not wanting to be obliged to him in any way. 'What if the court finds against us?'

'That won't happen. Arvin would never have set out to deceive us. I knew what kind of man he was as soon as I clapped eyes on him. Was he not the perfect husband?'

She couldn't answer. It was too painful.

'You blamed him for the loss of the gold,' she said defiantly, 'and this woman claims that he was going to take it and abandon me on the way to Paris.'

'Whom would you believe? Your husband or a stranger? She's out to make some money, that's all. It's a case of extortion, pure and simple.'

'I don't see what we can do when it's my word against hers.'

'If Mr Wiggins decides that it's the correct procedure, then we will attend court. It's your duty to defend yourself – for your own interest and that of the family.'

'I've told you before – I'll have no more talk of duty. I owe you nothing.'

'But you owe it to yourself. I can't afford to support you – you are reliant on your husband's inheritance. What would you do, if you lost that?'

She shivered, realising that she was caught between the devil and the deep blue sea.

'How about witnesses?' he went on. 'I think we should be prepared.'

Her brow tightened.

'I mean, there are people who can testify that they have seen you and Arvin together, behaving in a kind and affectionate manner to one another?'

'Well, yes.' She blushed at the memory of how they had held hands at the breakfast table while on honeymoon at the hotel in Scotland, how he had showered her with kisses in front of the guard on the train on the way back home. He hadn't behaved in such a husbandly manner on the *Samphire*. In fact, he had neglected her. 'Those things don't hold any weight anyway. We have our signatures witnessed in the register at the church. Our guests saw us marry – there is no question—'

'Except for the claims of this Frenchwoman …' Her father swore – he actually cursed out loud in front of her. 'I suggest that we don't speak of this to anyone yet – let's keep it under wraps.'

'I shall continue to consider myself the true Mrs Brooke,' Violet said fiercely. 'I will not be cowed because I know it's the truth.'

'I admire your strength – I'm afraid that you're going to need it. I'll send word when I know more.' Her father bade her farewell, and Violet retired to the parlour where she spent the rest of the day, lost in her embroidery and her thoughts.

She knew why her father was worried – if the Rayfields did turn out to have been tainted by a bigamous marriage, it would be a scandal. She would be shamed, and her sisters would suffer. It would reflect badly on her father, too.

The next morning, she and her father hurried to the solicitor's where they took their seats with Mr Wiggins at a vast mahogany table in a high-ceilinged room.

'I'm afraid that what you feared has come to pass, Mr Rayfield,' the solicitor said without preamble. 'The secret is out.' He waved to his clerk who had been loitering at the door. The young man brought an armful of newspapers over to the table and laid them out. 'The Frenchwoman has sold her story to the pedlars of sensation and rumour.'

'Turn away, Violet – I'd hoped to keep this from you,' her father said, but she refused to be spared the vicious headlines.

Bigamy! A Cruel Deception! Miss Violet Rayfield. The Two Mrs Brookes.

Her name was all over the papers from *The Times* to the *Dover Chronicle* and *Cinque Ports General Advertiser*. She pictured people at home swallowing the lies over breakfast and chewing over them in the inns and eateries. She felt like a criminal, yet she'd done nothing wrong.

'These are wicked, scurrilous stories,' she exclaimed. 'How can they do this?'

'We can sue for libel – defamation of your character and reputation – as long as we can demonstrate that Madame Brooke, as she calls herself, is lying,' Mr Wiggins said. 'However, I will tread carefully and ascertain all the facts, Mrs Brooke. As I said to Mr Rayfield yesterday, this unfortunate situation may be settled without recourse to the courts, but there are difficulties. Firstly, that the gentleman who is alleged to have committed bigamy was certified dead by the coroner – that may have to be reviewed. Secondly, Madame Brooke has already lodged a caveat at the Probate Office to contest Mr Brooke's will before probate can be granted.'

'I knew it. She is a chancer, a crook out for his money,' Violet's father said crossly. 'She's already made a tidy sum from the newspapers, raking our good name through the mud, and now she wants Arvin's estate.'

Violet didn't know what to think. It seemed extreme to risk one's own reputation without having good grounds.

'I need to ask you some questions. Mr Stone.' Mr Wiggins gestured to his clerk to sit beside him. He picked up a pen, dipped it in the inkwell and began to screeve a note of the conversation. 'Mrs Brooke, no matter how painful this is, now is the time for you to be completely frank with me. I must have all the facts so that I can create a watertight case against Madame Brooke.

'Let us start at the beginning. How did you meet Mr Arvin Brooke?'

The solicitor's question took her right back to the night of the ball, how she'd danced with the clumsy man who was to become her husband. More questions followed: what kind of man was he?

'He was a good man, the best,' her father interrupted.

'Please be silent, Mr Rayfield,' Mr Wiggins said. 'All in good time – I will interrogate you later.'

Violet knew why her father wanted to protect Arvin's reputation – he still couldn't believe that he would have wronged him. It seemed ironic that Arvin had been so busy plotting Pa's downfall that he'd walked straight into his own.

She went on to answer in the affirmative when Mr Wiggins asked her about the wedding ceremony and the signing of the register, and whether or not they had consummated the marriage. There was no sparing her blushes – it had to be done and in the presence of three men. By the end of the meeting, she felt like a wet sheet put through the mangle.

'I'll dictate a letter to be delivered by hand to Madame Brooke to see how she wishes to proceed with this matter,' Mr Wiggins said. 'If at all possible, we will settle this quietly, but if she insists on pursuing her claim through the courts, I will prepare papers to present to the bench.'

'Will Mrs Brooke here be subjected to cross-examination?' her father asked.

'I think we should bear that possibility in mind. Before you leave the office, I'd be grateful if you can arrange payment of my initial fee and an interim amount towards the incidental expenses.'

'Of course. I'll walk my daughter home then call on the bank.' Her father forced a small smile.

Violet walked back to Camden Crescent with him. She declined his suggestion that she should move back in with the Rayfields, or at least spend the night there.

'You could sit with your mother for a while, in any event,' her father said.

'Are my sisters at home?'

'I've sent them to your aunt's for a few days – until after Christmas, maybe longer.'

'You haven't told them?'

'Not yet.'

'But Aunt Felicity knows?'

'She is furious – she blames me. I suppose I'm clutching at straws when I say that I'm hoping the storm will blow over. In the meantime, I've engaged two nurses to care for Patience …'

Reassured, she spent the rest of the morning with Mama, washing her hands and applying cold cream to moisten her skin. She seemed to enjoy the attention and Violet imagined that she heard her whisper, 'thank you', when she wished her goodbye.

A couple of weeks of negotiation between the lawyers acting on behalf of the two Mrs Brookes went by before it was deemed that the matter should go before a judge.

'Lawyers – they are lying, thieving bastards,' her father kept saying. 'Now we will have to find money for the court fees, but never mind, Violet. We will win this case and you will be confirmed as the rightful Mrs Brooke. Poor Arvin – he would never have put us in such a bind.'

Like the lawyers, Violet reserved judgement, continuing to live quietly with May at the house at East Cliff while Ottilie and Eleanor returned from their stay at Aunt Felicity's, having insisted on coming home to Mama.

One dull February afternoon, Violet's father sent Wilson to fetch her.

'I've invited Mr Noble to the house – I wish to persuade him to give a statement to Mr Wiggins on your behalf,' her father said when she arrived.

'What can he say? What does he know about my marriage?' she said hotly.

'There's no need to be shy about it. You'll suffer worse indignities in court. He was on the *Samphire* that night. He saw you and Arvin together. Let's go to my study.'

She took a seat while her father stood waiting with his hands behind his back. A few minutes later, Wilson showed William into the room.

'The vicar is here to see you, sir,' the butler said. 'Shall I ask him to wait?'

'I'll see him straight away. Please excuse me, Mr Noble. This will take only a few minutes.' Pa and Wilson left the study, and Violet found herself alone with William.

'How are you, Mrs Brooke?' He seemed apprehensive, not knowing why he was being received, and she suspected that he would be remembering what had passed between him and Mr Rayfield the last time they had met.

'I am as well as can be expected.'

'It's always a pleasure to see you,' he said softly, and she had to turn away to hide the tears which sprang to her eyes. Others had been cruel, mocking her behind her back, yet William was the same as ever. 'I'm sorry for your recent troubles. It's unfair that a blameless woman has been judged in the way that you have. I don't understand it. I want you to know that whatever the outcome,

I shall never think any less of you. And remember, whatever your father wants from me, I do it only for you, nobody else.'

She turned back to face him when her father returned.

'Thank you for accepting my request,' he said.

'Make this brief – I have to return to work shortly.'

'You are back at the Packet Yard?'

'I've been promoted to the boiler-making department.' William changed the subject quickly. 'You've heard the latest news from the hearing?'

'I sent a representative on my behalf. You understand why I couldn't attend.'

'Your wife is ill and … well, I can see that you are a man under pressure. Anyway, I can't help thinking that the Court of the Admiralty influenced the hearing unduly. Those gentlemen behaved just as badly as the Board of Trade who put the blame for the accident on the captain, saying he was travelling too fast for the conditions.'

'It's a fair judgement – he was in charge.'

'They didn't consider how the Government Packet contract was set up, but then you are part of that, Mr Rayfield.'

Violet noticed how her father's spine straightened as William continued, unafraid.

'As a shareholder in the railway company, you have corporate responsibility for the accident.'

'How dare you make that accusation without proof?'

Violet wondered if her father was about to throw William out of the house.

'Mr Rayfield, I thought you wished to know the outcome of the hearing …'

'Yes, it's important. Go on,' he said impatiently.

'Captain Bennett is a hero – it's the Postmaster General who's the villain of the piece. If the voyage exceeds the length of time he has set – two hours and five minutes precisely – then money is deducted from the crew's wages. They have criticised everyone except the Postmaster General: the crew for not keeping the passengers under control; the railway company who own the *Samphire* for not maintaining the cutters and lifeboats. But then you know that – you attend the meetings held by the railway company.'

'The accident has been mentioned, but not discussed in any depth because we're still waiting for the outcome of the Court of the Admiralty hearing,' Pa said dryly.

'Then you shall hear it now … the hearing was due to decide whether or not the *Fanny Buck* was properly illuminated as there was some question about the navigation lights being bright enough.'

Her father nodded. 'If her crew had looked after the lanterns, kept the glasses clean, then the lookout would have seen her, fog or no fog.'

'Ah, that's irrelevant – according to maritime law, steam must always give way to sail whatever the situation.'

'The *Fanny Buck* was under sail – she had no time to alter her course,' Violet said, remembering. 'So her crew were not at fault. The blame for the accident lies with the *Samphire*.'

'That's right – that's the Admiralty's verdict,' William said. 'The London, Chatham and Dover Railway Company have been charged fourteen hundred pounds – that's to be paid to the owners of the *Fanny Buck* for her repairs. Not that that will be anything but a drop in the ocean for the railway company and its shareholders. It must be rolling in money and assets.'

'The Board will sign that off at our next meeting.'

'Though there are rumours that the company's in financial difficulty,' William said, challenging her father.

'They are rumours, that's all. The shipping operations are heading to make a profit, after the high set-up costs, and the trains – well, everyone travels by train nowadays.'

'What was it you wanted to ask me, Mr Rayfield?' William changed the subject.

'Ah, yes. Down to business … You will have heard of my daughter's predicament.'

William nodded.

'We are going to court to prove the legality of her marriage – I'm asking you to give a statement regarding what you saw on the boat that night. What I mean is, how Mr and Mrs Brooke were together, the depth of their mutual regard …'

'I cannot swear on oath that I saw them together, but I can confirm that Mrs Brooke behaved just as a wife should, her immediate thought being for her husband when the *Fanny Buck* struck the *Samphire*.' He paused before continuing. 'I can't say the same for Mr Brooke. He showed little or no concern for Violet – I mean Mrs Brooke. Forgive me, but he played the part of a callous, ungallant and boorish husband.'

'Then that's most reassuring as it isn't unusual for a husband to act in that way,' Mr Rayfield said. 'You're willing to meet with my solicitor and stand up in court if necessary?'

'If you think it will help Mrs Brooke's case. Let me know when you require me to give my statement. I wish you good day, Mr Rayfield. Good day, Mrs Brooke.'

'Violet, one more thing,' her father said when William had gone. 'This is a delicate subject, but I have to ask you if there's any chance you are with child?'

'I don't think so,' she said softly. She had wished that she was. Holding Arvin's child in her arms would have softened the blow of his loss. Since the accident, the spells of nausea had worn off, and although her monthly course had not yet returned, May had told her that a shock could put it off for some time. She'd had enough shocks to have put it off for ever. 'I'm not,' she confirmed.

'That's a shame,' her father said. 'The court is always particularly concerned with the fate of any children. Never mind. I have high hopes of a rapid and painless resolution. Everyone I've spoken to is behind us. Our case is watertight, just as Mr Wiggins hoped.'

Was it, though? Violet had her doubts.

The dreaded day of the court hearing arrived. The early March winds were whistling from the east along the Straits of Dover, gusting and rattling the windows of the house in Camden Crescent where Violet had stayed overnight so that she'd be ready to leave with her father first thing in the morning. Ottilie helped Violet dress while Eleanor and the nurses looked after Mama.

'You can borrow my velvet dress,' Ottilie said. 'The navy one.'

'With the matching hat and cloak?' Violet said, looking at her reflection. 'Thank you, but I intend to wear full mourning dress with Mama's beads.'

Ottilie fetched her black silk crinoline from the wardrobe. Violet hated it – the colour sapped her pale complexion, making her look even more washed out than she felt.

'I'll be able to go into half mourning later in the year,' she said as Ottilie helped her into the dress, spreading the wide skirt over layers of petticoats. She scraped her hair back from her face and put it up in a bun covered with a piece of black lace. Her lips were dry, so she opened the pot of balm on the dressing table, but there was an iridescent fly in it which reminded her of the Frenchwoman, so she didn't use it.

'It will be over soon,' Ottilie reassured her. 'Tonight, we'll celebrate the judge's verdict.'

'It won't be a celebration.'

'I chose the wrong word. I'm sorry. What I meant was that we'll be able to carry on our lives without this terrible slur hanging over our heads. The papers will have to print an apology and our good name will be restored.'

'I hope so, but there's no woman on earth who would expose herself to such scrutiny if she didn't think she had a good case.'

'She's trying it on for the money … and the notoriety. Apparently, she's loving the attention of the press – she's even been well received by some of Dover society. Well, it's all going to come tumbling down around her. Pa has left no stone unturned in your defence. There.' Ottilie fastened the last hook on the back of Violet's dress. 'You are ready.'

She might be ready to face the court, but she realised as she and her father disembarked from the cab outside the Maison Dieu, the new Town Hall, that she wasn't prepared for the onslaught of renewed interest. The lawyers had decided that, although the accused had been certified dead, the case should go before the bench at the Borough quarter session to decide who was entitled to inherit his property.

'Steel yourself,' her father said, taking her hand and leading her through the crowd.

'That's 'er – that's Violet Rayfield.'

'It's Mrs Brooke, you mean.'

'We don't know that. She says she di'n't have any idea 'e was married before now, but I don't believe 'er. How can any man 'ide a second wife? 'E'd always be flitting from one to the other.'

'I can't think why any man would inflict a second wife on 'imself. One is more than enow,' one said wryly amid runnels of laughter.

'For variety,' said another. 'The two women – the Mrs Brookes – are chalk and cheese in appearance. Mr Brooke's a hero, taking on two wives for pleasure and profit.'

'She and her father encouraged it, so I 'eard. I reckon nothing would stop 'im getting his 'ands on Mr Brooke's money.'

'A man drownded while carrying more gold in 'is pockets than's in the Bank of England.'

'The coroner says 'e's dead, but what if he i'n't? What if 'e chose to disappear, avoiding the women 'e's wronged? What if 'e's set himself up in a new life with another woman?'

'If 'e has, then 'e's a felon of the first degree.'

'Violet, this way.' She looked up at her father's urgent tone, and he led her inside. 'Don't listen to them. They know nothing.'

They took their places in the ancient chapel which had been converted into the town's court. Violet sat with her head held high – Mr Wiggins might have preferred her to pose with her head bowed, but she felt that it would give the impression she was hiding her face out of shame. As she rested her hands in her lap, she felt something flutter in her belly. It was like a butterfly, confirmation of what she had begun to suspect, that she was with child, which meant there was even more at stake.

The Recorder, Mr Bodkin QC, presided and began proceedings with some legal discussion with the lawyers about the Bigamy Act, and how if any married person went on to marry again, their former spouse being alive, then that offence was an indictable felony, the punishment ranging from hanging to seven years in gaol, or branding on the thumb. As Mr Brooke couldn't be tried, having been declared dead, the Recorder would restrict his judgement to the simple matter of which of the two Mrs Brookes was Arvin's *de jure* wife, and therefore entitled to his estate, according to his will.

Madame Brooke's lawyer was interrogated first, but her evidence was straightforward. She had met and married Monsieur Arvin Brooke ten years previously and had the legal documents to confirm the marriage had taken place in France. There was no record of a divorce having been sought or granted.

'It was painful for me to discover that my husband had become involved with a younger woman,' Madame Brooke said. 'I found out about his deception, but I never imagined he would be so *stupide* as to enter into a bigamous marriage.'

'That is not yet proven,' the judge warned her. 'The court will now hear the evidence presented by Mrs Brooke.'

The parish clerk produced a certificate of marriage – he had examined it against the register and stated that it was a true copy. A witness gave evidence that they were present at the marriage of the man they knew as Mr Arvin Brooke, bachelor, and Miss Violet Rayfield, spinster, while her father explained that he had given his blessing, having made enquiries beforehand as far as he could as to the man's background and character. William wasn't in court – it was a relief that Mr Wiggins had decided that they could do without his statement.

Violet had deemed that she was prepared, but when she was called up to be cross-examined, she faltered. The words and sentences she had committed to memory evaporated as she faced Claudette's lawyer, a well-spoken, well-dressed gentleman from London. Mr Carrick surveyed the court, then turned his head and looked straight at her.

'When did your alleged marriage take place?'

She stated the date, and the lawyer made a play of counting the months on his fingers.

'Did you have full physical relations with Mr Arvin Brooke?' His style of questioning was blunt and brutal, and the way he stared at her reminded her of how a hawk locked its eyes on to its prey.

'Yes,' she said very quietly, wondering why she should be ashamed of that admission when they had been husband and wife, and she too had legal documents and witnesses proving their marriage.

'Speak up, madam. I can't hear you.'

'Yes,' she repeated, having no intention of revealing her pregnancy to the court.

'Your response goes to show that there was desire on your part. I put it to you that Mr Brooke did tell you of his prior marriage, but you wanted him for yourself. Knowing that his wife was out of the way, living in France, you coerced him into an illegal marriage to maintain a veneer of respectability. Miss Rayfield, you were driven by lust.'

'How dare you!' Violet couldn't stop herself, and the court erupted into gasps and sniggers of shock and amusement.

The Recorder's gavel came down with a crack. 'Order. I will have order in this court! This lady is not on trial. If you continue with this line of questioning I'll hold you in contempt, Mr Carrick.'

'No more questions, your honour,' Mr Carrick said smugly, aware that he had already made his point, that Violet may have been complicit in Mr Brooke's crime.

'I will sum up. One must accept that Mr Brooke entered into a bigamous marriage with Miss Violet Rayfield. We cannot ask him why he did not seek a divorce, but it seems to me that he didn't desire one. He was content to remain married to Madame Brooke, because he didn't want to damage her reputation and status, or lose his marital benefits.'

Violet began to offer up prayers. She was losing the battle. She could tell.

'I rule that Madame Brooke is his wife *de jure*, and Miss Violet Rayfield's marriage to the aforesaid felon is null and void. Null and void,' the Recorder repeated as Violet grasped the railing in front of her. 'Unfortunately, this isn't an unusual crime. It has devastating effects on the women concerned. There is no retribution, no recompense, nor even the satisfaction of bringing Mr Brooke to trial so he can explain himself. I'm sorry, Miss Rayfield. You aren't the first to be dishonoured in this way, and you won't be the last.'

Violet glanced towards the Frenchwoman who smiled back: she actually smiled. She had no delicacy of feeling, no compassion, Violet thought, turning away with tears in her eyes. When she looked back, she'd gone.

Violet let her father lead her out of the courtroom and was forced to listen to the jeers and catcalls from the jostling crowd outside as he helped her into a cab for the journey home. The driver sent the horse forward and the yells of 'Whore!' and 'Slut!' followed them down Priory Road towards York Street.

'How did I not see through that man's trickery? He was a rat. No, a weasel.'

Violet put her hands over her ears, trying to ignore her father's ranting as the cab rattled and bounced along Dover's cobbled streets.

'Violet.' She felt her father's hand on her wrist. 'Violet, listen to me.'

'No, I will never take notice of you again. You said all would be well, that you'd protect me.'

'I did my best,' he said dully, 'but it is done and now we must plan for the future.'

'What future?' She dropped her hands and glared at him. 'I have no future. I'm ruined. You heard them!'

They headed along the seafront.

'I have another appointment with Mr Wiggins – I'm reviewing the contents of my will to make sure that you, your mother and sisters are properly provided for should anything happen to me.'

'I'd assumed that you'd made sure of that before,' Violet said as they passed Camden Crescent.

'I had,' her father said, sounding hurt, 'but after recent events, I've realised that one can't be too careful.'

'Where are we going?'

'To your house ...' Mr Rayfield corrected himself. 'To the house Arvin rented for you ... I think we should collect your valuables and any other small items that we can manage. Tomorrow, I'll send removal men to collect your clothes and the furniture. We will take what we're owed.'

'I don't want anything except my sewing box and personal effects.' She didn't want anything which would remind her of the duplicitous Mr Brooke.

'This is our only chance to obtain any recompense and we're going to make the most of it.' Mr Rayfield called up to the driver through the trap-door in the roof. 'Stop here, sir.'

The cab pulled up outside the house at East Cliff, and the driver leaned down from his raised seat behind the passenger compartment to ask for his fare.

'Release the doors, so my daughter can get out – she needs air,' her father said.

'I will have my fare first, thank you,' the driver said.

'Please, have some consideration for the young lady.'

Violet wasn't sure if it was the driver or the horse who snorted with derision.

'My fare?'

Her father paid through the trap-door and the driver released the doors. Violet struggled out with her heavy skirts, and looked across to find that her father was already on the pavement. He was waving his fist at the Frenchwoman who was on the doorstep of Violet's former marital home, talking animatedly to a man with an oil can in his hand. May was standing beside the railings outside the house, surrounded by several bags and a suitcase.

Her father had been thwarted – they were too late.

As the cab turned on a sixpence and set off back along the seafront, she went to try to drag her father away, but he pushed her aside, almost knocking her off balance.

'My daughter wishes to collect her possessions.'

'I can speak for myself, thank you,' Violet said crossly.

'Your maid has packed your valuables,' Claudette said.

'I have the sewing box and your embroidery,' May interrupted.

'I've had the owner of the house change the locks, so don't even think about coming back. Everything inside was my husband's property and therefore belongs to me.'

Somehow it didn't matter – Claudette had not only appropriated the items she and Arvin had chosen for their home, she had stolen Violet's life, her honour and self-respect. Unknowingly too, the true Mrs Brooke had condemned an innocent child to a lifetime of shame. Violet's blood started to boil. The situation had been Arvin's fault, but this woman was revelling in it.

'You are an evil witch!' she shouted. 'You have no heart!'

Chapter Fifteen

Bags o'Surprises

Of course, there was no way that anyone could keep the court's verdict from her sisters. When Violet returned to Camden Crescent with her father, he went straight out again while she hid herself in the kitchen, reluctant to face them, but it had to come.

'There you are,' Eleanor said, pushing the door open.

'We're very sorry.' Ottilie walked past her and pulled one of the wheelback chairs up to the table so that she could sit down. 'I can tell from the look on your face that it didn't go well.'

Violet didn't know what to say to them as they gazed at her, their eyes dark with concern. She picked up the rolling pin and began shaping a pat of pastry into rounds for a pie.

'I'll put the kettle on,' Eleanor said, and she started making tea. She put out the Chinese cups and saucers which reminded Violet of Arvin and how the cups used to rattle when he sneezed. 'Is Pa at home?'

'He has an appointment with Mr Wiggins. He's very downhearted.'

'Arvin deceived us all,' Ottilie said.

'I don't know why I didn't see it.' Violet took a handful of flour out of the bag and scattered it across the tabletop, so the rounds wouldn't stick.

'You're making a mess,' Eleanor observed.

'I don't care. My marriage is null and void.' She pressed too hard on the rolling pin, tearing holes in the pastry. She screwed it up into a ball and started again. 'Arvin seemed genuine, but there were clues, little things that he said and did that didn't ring true.' A tear dripped into the flour. 'When I asked if I could travel with him, he said he couldn't drag me away from Mama when she was so ill. I've been a fool.'

'Wouldn't you have been horrified if he'd insisted on you travelling abroad in those circumstances?' Ottilie asked.

'Well, yes, I suppose so.'

'Then you mustn't blame yourself.'

'What I can't reconcile is …' She glanced towards Eleanor who was measuring loose tea from the caddy into the pot. There was no point in holding back – the reports of the hearing would be in all the newspapers tomorrow. 'I can't get past the fact that Arvin was having relations with me and Claudette.' The thought of his infidelity, of him lying with another woman, made her feel nauseous.

'My John wouldn't do such a thing, but he did tell me once that there are some men who like to eat their cake and have it too.'

'We are all ruined,' Eleanor said dramatically over the kettle's shrill whistle. 'What decent man will have us now, any of us?'

'You're right,' Violet said bitterly. She hadn't just lost Arvin, she had lost her good name, status and her establishment, and let her sisters down. Her ruination was their ruination too. 'My marrying Arvin was supposed to have freed you, Ottilie, but it's only made things worse. I wish I'd drowned in the sea that night, then our troubles would have been over.'

'You don't mean that,' Ottilie said quickly. 'The Frenchwoman would still have turned up to put in her claim against you, and Pa would still be out of pocket.'

'I'm spoiled goods.' Violet recalled the failed wine-tasting and consignment of vinegar. 'I'll never marry again, even if I want to, which I don't. And I'll never be forgiven for ruining the Rayfields' good name. My poor sisters ...' Gazing through a veil of tears from one to the other, she couldn't bring herself to tell them about the infant which had quickened inside her. There would be no more balls and dances, no more privilege born of their association with their father. Their lives as they knew them were over.

'We will be three spinsters growing old together,' Eleanor sighed.

'Only two,' Ottilie said as Violet picked up the bag of flour to put it away in the pantry. 'I'm still determined that John and I will get married, even if it has to be over the broomstick. What's that? May?'

May looked into the kitchen. 'I'm sorry to disturb you, but there's a gentleman at the door who says 'e's a reporter from the *Dover Chronicle*. 'e wishes to speak to Violet to 'ear 'er side of the story. I wanted to send 'im away with a flea in 'is ear, but 'e's most insistent.'

'Let me deal with him,' Violet said, fresh ire rising in her breast.

'Are you sure?' May asked.

'Oh yes.' She made her way to the hall where a middle-aged man with brown teeth and yellow fingers, dressed in a long coat, stood with one foot in the doorway. He beamed when he saw her, walking with her head held high and her hands behind her back.

'Thank you for agreeing to give me this interview, Miss Rayfield,' he said. 'You have proved elusive.'

'How can you pretend to be surprised, considering the terrible lies you have printed about me?' she said coldly.

'Then this is your chance to have your say. May I come in?'

'No, sir. I came out here, so I could have the satisfaction of sending you on your way. Go!'

His brow furrowed. 'Give me just five minutes of your time. Please.'

'Go away.' She gave the door a shove, but it wouldn't shut because his foot was in the way. 'Oh, all right then. If that's how you want it.' She opened the mouth of the bag of flour behind her back and threw the contents at him, right over his head.

'Miss Rayfield. My coat! What have you done?' He tried to dust himself down as the cloud of flour settled in his hair, his hat and his clothes.

'Don't darken our doorstep again,' she snapped.

'All right. I'm leaving.' He hurried down the steps, turning at the bottom. 'You should be locked up.'

She stared at him. He looked pathetic, comical. She began to laugh, and he hurried away.

In spite of having turned the journalist away, Violet's name was back in the papers, thanks to the court hearing. There were stories of how Madame Brooke had returned to France, confirmation that the coroner would not reopen the inquest into Mr Brooke's disappearance, and that Miss Rayfield had wanted him anyway, that she'd taken him as a lover and made the sham marriage for the sake of her reputation.

Violet stayed on at the house in Camden Crescent, with her sisters and her father, who was happy to dispense with Mama's nurses and employ May instead. He had already given notice to Mrs Garling – the housekeeper – some time ago and Cook who'd left in tears. With her experience of running a household, Violet stepped into her mother's shoes, but she resented being dependent on her father, the man she blamed for most of the Rayfields' difficulties. She felt guilty for thinking it, but she was thankful that her mother was oblivious to her fall from grace.

Two weeks went by and the March winds were replaced by April showers.

Violet was with her sisters in the parlour while Mr Rayfield was out.

'You have spoiled me for making up stories.' Eleanor looked up from a blank page. 'I can't think of a plot to better what's gone on in real life.'

'Don't say that – it's mean,' Ottilie scolded her.

'All right. I take it back, but it's true. You can't make it up.'

'We were all caught up in Arvin's web of lies. I remember the efforts he made to impress us, the assurances he gave about his prospects,' Ottilie went on. 'He was very convincing.'

Violet felt a fresh pang of confusion and grief – and anger too – as she recalled how they had stood on the cliffs in front of the lighthouse and he had declared his affection for her. '*Je t'adore*,' he had once told her.

She heard footsteps and May entered the room, breathless and wiping her hands on her apron. 'I'm sorry for disturbing you, but the butcher is 'ere, demanding 'is money. I asked 'im to come back another day, but 'e won't 'ave it.'

'Thank you. I'll come down,' Violet sighed. 'I thought Father had paid all the tradesmen.'

Mr Young, the butcher, stood blocking the light from the door.

'This won't do, miss. This really won't do,' he said, his side whiskers bristling. 'I gave you my invoice two weeks ago – I put it into your hand and you promised me you'd give it to Mr Rayfield.'

'And I kept my word – you have my assurance that I gave it to him.'

'He hasn't paid it, and he hasn't paid the one before that either.'

'I wasn't aware of that,' she said quietly.

'That old chestnut – I've heard them all before, every excuse under the sun. Well, I tell you, miss, the finest cuts of beef, the fattest legs of lamb and the most exceptional sausages in Kent come at a price. Tell Mr Rayfield that I'll be back tomorrow morning for my payment in full. If it isn't here, I'll be taking steps. You tell him, I'll be taking steps,' he repeated with menace, his words sending a shiver of fear down her spine as she pictured him standing over her father with his butcher's knife.

'I'll make sure you receive your money, even though your sausages are very ordinary bags o'surprises,' Violet said. 'Good day, Mr Young.'

She closed the basement door, shutting him out.

'I'm sorry for putting you through that, miss,' May said from behind her. 'He wouldn't take no for an answer.'

'It won't happen again – I'll speak to Father.' It wasn't the only invoice he had left unpaid – she'd spotted the final bill for the nurses on the desk in his study and a letter from Mr Johnson requesting immediate payment for the diving trip.

'Forgive me for saying, but I was under the impression that Mr Rayfield weren't doin' so well. I 'eard talk of it when I went to the bakers – I didn't say nothin', but I couldn't 'elp listening in. They say he lost all your mother's gold, and before that there was the trouble with the *Dover Belle*—'

'My father has many business interests – he was never one to keep all his eggs in one basket.' Violet chose not to mention that she knew he'd taken out a loan with the bank to pay Mr Wiggins and the other expenses he'd accrued in fighting her case. He'd done it on the basis that they would win, and he would pay it back plus interest with the inheritance she would have received from Arvin. She couldn't see how he'd ever pay it back, especially now that Claudette held the greater share in Brooke and Rayfield. 'I'll speak to him later.' She placed her hands on the slight curve of her stomach.

'You're putting on weight,' May observed. 'Do you think ...?'

'I'm not. I'm sure I'm not.'

'It wouldn't be the end of the world, miss.'

'Oh, it would.' She hated lying to May, but she knew full well that she had to keep it to herself until she absolutely had to admit it to anyone else – if her father thought she was carrying Arvin's bastard, she would be out on her ear. As it was, the few ladies who used to call on Mama, bringing calf's foot jelly, herbs and special remedies as gifts for the invalid, had made excuses to stop their regular visits. They sent their regrets instead.

The gentlemen didn't associate with her father either – there was no more dining at Camden Crescent.

That afternoon, he requested her company for a walk down to the quay, saying that he wished to check on the casks which had remained unsold after the disastrous wine-tasting.

'I would have preferred not to go out,' she said, looking at the weather. The road was gleaming after a short, sharp shower, and the sea spangling in the sun.

'I have an umbrella,' he said, putting it up as the rain began to fall again. 'And it won't take long. Come on, there aren't many fathers who would welcome their daughter back into the fold after what has happened.'

'Am I supposed to be grateful?' She glared at him, hating being beholden to him and expected to work as house-keeper, cook and nurse with her sisters.

He didn't answer as they set out along the promenade.

When they reached the quay, they made their way through the chaos of sailors, fishermen and porters to the warehouse, tripping over ropes and crates of all kinds. Her father stopped abruptly and stared at the doors. Somebody had bolted and padlocked an iron bar right across the front and affixed a sign with 'Warehouse to Let. Apply to Mr Turner, Dover Harbour Board.'

Violet watched her father's face turn puce and his hands clench with anger.

'How can they do this? They have stolen my wine – it belongs to me now that Arvin is gone.'

'There's been a mistake. Let's find this man and explain. I'm sure it can all be sorted out very quickly.' She paused. 'You aren't behind on the rent?'

'I may have missed a payment,' her father said.

'And the wine – well, everyone said it was vinegar.'

'It has some value for pickling eggs and walnuts. I don't want to give it up when I need every penny I can get.' Violet watched on helplessly, wishing he wouldn't cause a scene as he ran around frantically asking for Mr Turner, who turned out to be away on other business.

'Father,' she said eventually, when he was standing in the middle of the quayside, with his head in his hands. 'We should come back another day. Please, come home.'

He turned to look at her, and quietly acquiesced.

As they walked along, she was aware that people were looking at them. She could hear a group of low-born women chattering without caring who heard them.

'There's Mr Rayfield and 'is daughter, the infamous Mrs Brooke.'

'I'm surprised she dares show 'er face.' One spat, her spittle landing just in front of Violet's feet. ''Usband thief!'

'You can see why 'e did it – look at 'er.'

''E was bewitched.'

Mortified, Violet hurried her father along.

'Why didn't you speak up for me?' she asked him when they reached the seafront and there were fewer people around. It crossed her mind that William would have done, had he been there.

'What can anyone say to change their opinions when they believe in gossip and rumour, not fact?' he said glumly. 'There's no point in me wasting my breath.'

She bowed her head. He had let her down again, her own father.

'I need money to pay Mr Young tomorrow morning,' she said.

'You must ask him to extend credit for another month, sweet-talk him into it, if necessary.'

'He won't agree to that. He made it very clear,' she said, but he wasn't listening, his attention drawn to a couple who were walking towards them.

'Edward, Mrs Chittenden, good afternoon. I was planning to call on you,' he said, raising his hat.

Violet gripped his arm and looked away. 'Please, don't.'

'Out of compassion for your old friend who was like a brother to you, give me a moment of your time. I need money, a loan,' Pa blurted out. 'Just a few hundred.'

'How much? You are joking?' Uncle Edward said as his wife tried to jostle him away.

'Edward, we mustn't be seen associating with these people – a dishonest tradesman and a woman of dubious repute.'

'I'll pay you back, with interest,' Pa went on.

Ignoring his wife, Uncle Edward smirked as he leaned on his stick.

'Come on, Sidney, I wasn't born yesterday. You're on the verge of bankruptcy. Your ship has sailed, and everyone knows it. Why on earth would I lend you a single penny?'

'Because I'm desperate,' Pa begged, almost on bended knee. 'I've lost money hand over fist.'

'Which is entirely your responsibility. You put your trust in a scoundrel and dropped your old friends. I'm warning you now that I've commissioned a bankruptcy order to claim back the rest of the money you owe me for the *Dover Belle*. You've made a right royal mess of things and I shan't give you a spade to dig yourself out of the hole you're in because you'll only use it to dig yourself deeper.' Uncle Edward poked him in the chest with his stick. Pa didn't move. 'You are a disgrace of a father, a husband and a friend. Good day, sir.' He turned to his wife. 'Come along, my dear.'

The Chittendens crossed the street and by the time a coach and horses had driven past, they had disappeared from view.

'Father, are things as bad as Uncle Edward says they are? Did he mean what he said about making you bankrupt?' Violet trembled – the confrontation had been most unpleasant. 'Tell me the truth,' she went on, before realising that it was unlikely that her father, whose shoulders had sagged like one of May's cakes, would come clean.

'They aren't good, but something will turn up – all I need is a little windfall.'

'What can we do in the meantime? There are bills to pay.'

'I have some shares in the London, Chatham and Dover Railway. I'll find a broker who will sell them – that will bring in enough to keep the wolf from the door.'

Violet didn't trust him any more. She understood Miss Whiteway better now. She'd been right to teach them to question their decisions, to be inquisitive about the world and develop the means of supporting themselves. She remembered her in the schoolroom, how she had suggested that one day she might use her embroidery skills to make a living. She might need them after today, because she couldn't see how they could continue to rely on their father.

Chapter Sixteen

Tea with Milk and Plenty of Sugar

Several days had passed since her father's confrontation with the Chittendens, and Violet had barely spoken to him since, even though he'd started spending more time at home than at the office. In the mornings, he hid himself away in his study, and in the afternoons, he sat quietly holding Mama's hand.

'There you are, Violet. You can't keep avoiding me, you know.'

She turned at the sound of her father's voice, saying, 'You scared the life out of me. Excuse me.' She made to continue into the kitchen on an errand to fetch cake for her sisters.

'Wait. This is important.'

She froze as her father placed his heavy hand on her shoulder.

'Let me go.' The hairs on her neck stood up on end. 'I can't bear to look at you. Let me go,' she repeated.

He stepped away, his hands at his sides.

'I want to say how sorry I am,' he said in a low voice.

'It's too late for that. You've failed me, your daughter.'

'I know, and I'll never forgive myself. I'm not asking you to forgive me for the way I've behaved, just for you to listen. Give me a minute of your time. Please …'

There was something in the tone of his voice that made her hesitate. Was there any harm in hearing what he had to say? She nodded her assent.

'Thank you,' he sighed. 'I've been a fool and a terrible judge of character. I encouraged you to marry Mr Brooke, a thief and a conman – I was flattered by his attention – he chose me above others as the man he wished to do business with, he treated me as a son might treat his father, with great respect and affection, and deep consideration for the fortunes of the Rayfields.

'I'd always been careful in matters of business, but with the loss of the *Dover Belle* and the downturn in our fortunes, I threw caution to the wind. Mr Chittenden and I looked into his background and tried to check his stories – he was a great raconteur – but we didn't find out much about him. To my regret, I ignored Edward's reservations against engaging with him.'

Violet noticed that her father smelled of claret.

'He put you through immeasurable torment and there will be more to come. I'm so ashamed that I can barely look you in the eyes, and as for your mother and sisters ... well, I'm grateful that my dear wife doesn't understand what has gone on. I've been sitting with her and dwelling on what has passed between us – we married for love and against her father's wishes, but it turned out for the best. I've never stopped loving her ...' He swallowed hard. 'I remember how she used to take such care in her dress, matching the colour of her jewels with her skirts every time she accompanied me to a ball or a dinner. Oh yes, we had our differences, but how I miss her sharp wit and humour! How I wish I'd insisted against the green wallpaper, but she would have it!'

'Ma's illness has nothing to do with it,' Violet said. 'Doctor Hawkes said so.'

'He was wrong. It's become generally accepted in medical circles that Miss Whiteway's views on arsenic were right.'

'Then we wronged her when she was only trying to help.'

'I know that now and I'm truly sorry.'

'You realise what this means, Father. We can have the paper replaced and Ma will be cured.'

'It's true that the house can be redecorated, but it's too late for Patience. I have it on good authority that her health will never be restored even by removing the source of the poison. Her nerves are irretrievably damaged. She will never be herself again.'

'How can we know that without trying?'

'Because it is certain. There is no point ... She is on her way out.'

'Then there is no hope for her,' she said, her optimism dashed.

'Everything has gone awry.' Her father held out his hands, but she didn't take them.

'I'll never forget how you threatened to disown me. You were concerned only with the loss of the gold, not me, or Arvin. Why do you expect me to feel any compassion for you now?'

'Because you are still my daughter, and I love you with all my heart.'

She gazed at him, sensing his anguish. Could she forgive this broken man?

'Oh, Pa,' she said softly, remembering back to a time before Mr Brooke had come into their lives. 'I love you too and I forgive you for everything that's happened. We both did what we thought was right out of regard for our family.'

'Thank you, my dear Violet. Your forgiveness is more than I deserve. I'm deeply grateful, even though I can't forgive myself for what I've put you all through,' he said, his voice breaking as he turned away and headed for the door.

'Where are you going?' she said, following him.

'Out,' he replied.

'You are going to St Mary's?'

'That's a good idea. I will go and pray.'

'And you will be back by this evening, so we can all dine together?' Violet went on, but he didn't stop to answer. She watched him put on his coat and shoes, then pick up his cane and leave the house with Wilson fussing and closing the door behind him. She had capitulated, but on her terms, and she felt much better, having found it in her heart to forgive him for the way he had treated her and William. Perhaps he would return home in a better state of mind than he'd been in for a while, and she would be able to broach the subject of her unborn child.

'Where's Pa?' Eleanor asked a while later as dusk began to fall, and the gaslights began to glow on the streets.

'He's gone to church,' Violet said. 'He'll be back for dinner.'

But he didn't turn up and May was grumbling that the roast chicken would be dried out by the time it reached the table.

'Should we go ahead?' Eleanor asked. 'I'll take some broth up to Mama later.'

'Perhaps we should delay another half-hour. I'm not hungry,' Violet said.

'I am,' Eleanor said, so Violet gave in and the three sisters sat at the table, chewing on stringy chicken and burned potatoes.

'I'll have yours if you don't want it, Violet,' Eleanor said. 'We have to make the most of what we have, if we're going to be poor and live on scraps and go about in rags, begging on the streets.'

'Who on earth put that idea into your head?' Violet asked.

'Mrs Pryor said something the other day. It's common knowledge that Pa's in trouble.'

'He won't let us starve,' Ottilie said fiercely. 'You shouldn't listen to the likes of our nosy neighbour.'

'Don't talk to me like that,' Eleanor said snappily. 'I have more intelligence in my little finger than you have in your head.'

'Sisters, please don't quarrel. Father will be upset if he comes home to find you've fallen out,' Violet interjected, wondering how bad things would get. Would they still have a roof over their heads at the end of the year?

'Where is he? He always lets us know if he's going out for dinner.' Eleanor looked up from her plate. 'Oh, he's back. Listen.'

'He must have forgotten his key.' Violet frowned as the ringing of the doorbell was replaced by a hammering sound. A few minutes later, Wilson appeared, showing William Noble and a police constable into the dining room.

'These two gentlemen wish to speak to you, ladies,' he said. 'I asked them if it could wait, but—'

'Is your mother at home?' William stepped forwards.

'She isn't to be disturbed,' Violet said quietly, her strength deserting her at the sight of their sombre expressions. Something was terribly amiss.

'Then I'm forced to break the news to you and your sisters.'

'It's Pa, isn't it? Our father?'

'There is no gentle way to say this ...'

'Oh no,' she gasped.

'It isn't possible. You've made a mistake!' Eleanor exclaimed as Ottilie stood up and moved round to comfort her.

'Are you sure that it's him?' Ottilie asked.

'I saw Mr Rayfield walking through town earlier, heading for the cliffs. I greeted him, and he nodded back. Not imagining that he was about to do anything untoward, I carried on with my business. I'm very sorry ...'

Frozen with shock, Violet stood stock-still. Why hadn't she seen this coming? Why hadn't she suggested that she accompany him earlier that afternoon? All his talk of love and forgiveness – he had been saying goodbye.

'I've identified him – I felt it was for the best,' William said. 'The constable here says the body can be released as soon as a doctor certifies the cause of ... your father's passing.'

'He must have fallen by accident,' Ottilie muttered.

'The unfortunate gentleman was seen in an agitated state,' the constable said. 'I have witnesses who say they saw him walking back and forth along the cliff path before he stopped, turned and took a running jump.'

This was getting worse, Violet thought, looking at the tears running down Eleanor's cheeks.

'He wouldn't have done it,' Ottilie said. 'He loved us – he'd never abandon us in this cruel way. It's impossible. This is a malicious rumour, constable. You must take it back.'

'Miss Rayfield, please,' William said. 'I've seen your father's body with my own eyes – he must have died instantly without suffering, so that part I can vouch for myself. Who were these alleged witnesses, constable? You have their names?'

The constable took his notebook from his pocket, opened it and read out the names of a lady and two gentlemen, and the lady's statement, describing her distress at having seen a person running full pelt towards the edge of the cliff with neither the means nor the intention of stopping.

'My apologies for causing you further upset, ladies, but it's important that you hear the full circumstances of the manner of your father's death,' he went on.

'Thank you,' Violet said, her mind racing ahead.

'There is much to do,' William said softly as though reading her thoughts. 'If you have no objection, I'll take it upon myself to arrange for the vicar of St Mary's to call on you tomorrow. The constable here is familiar with these cases and has advised me of the possible complications which may arise.'

'Will there be an inquest?' Violet worried that the Rayfields would be exposed to further notoriety if the coroner decided to interview the witnesses and the family in front of a jury.

'The coroner may be satisfied with my report – I'll see what can be done. Is there anything else?' the constable said.

'No. No, I don't think so,' Violet said. 'We're very grateful for your assistance.'

'Then I'll take my leave.'

'We'll see ourselves out. If there's anything I can do, you must contact me at this address.' William handed her a card from his inside top pocket, his fingers brushing hers. 'Please, don't hesitate. It's no trouble to me.'

'I appreciate your offer,' she said, thanking him, yet certain that she wouldn't take it up. She and her family had imposed on him enough – he had no obligation to them after what had happened with the *Dover Belle* and her father's subsequent behaviour. The difficulties and challenges that lay ahead were down to him and it was up to the rest of the Rayfields to overcome them.

She showed William to the front door and watched him descend the steps, turn and doff his hat, and her heart clenched with grief. Without her father, with Mama ill, and Ottilie in a state of denial, and Eleanor being so young and having led a sheltered life, she felt responsible for the rest of her family – and much older than her years after everything she'd gone through, thanks to Arvin.

'Miss, is there anything I can do?' Wilson joined her in the hall.

She took a deep breath and composed herself.

'I'd be grateful if you'd send word to our aunt and cousin, so we can receive them tomorrow morning. I'm sure Aunt Felicity will want to comfort Mama in her hour of need.'

'Consider it done.' Wilson was nearly in tears. 'I'm sorry for your loss – the master was a troubled man, but I can't believe that he went and jumped.'

'Neither can I.' Was it her fault? Should she have been kinder to him, even after the way he'd threatened William when he was chasing after the gold? With a heavy heart, Violet returned to the dining room where Ottilie and Eleanor were holding hands, with tears running down their faces. Tonight, she would mourn their loss with Mama and her sisters. Tomorrow, she would turn her mind to practical matters.

Aunt Felicity turned up on their doorstep the next morning. Wilson relieved her of her luggage.

'Oh, my dear Violet. How are you and your sisters, and my dear Patience? I can't believe that Mr Rayfield has gone!'

'You don't know the half of it,' Violet said, unsure if she was pleased to see her. She hoped that her presence would soothe Mama, but it rattled Violet's nerves. Not wanting an inquisition or advice, she had laced her stays a little tighter than usual and arranged a shawl across her shoulders, letting it drape across her front to hide any tell-tale curves from Aunt Felicity's enquiring eyes. 'Come in – you can't have had time for breakfast.'

'Tea with milk and plenty of sugar would be most welcome.'

'Where is Jane?' Violet asked.

'I judged it best that she remain at home at this difficult time.'

Was that because she didn't want her daughter mired in the Rayfields' troubles? Was it because she was afraid that Jane's reputation would be ruined by association?

Violet showed her to the parlour where Mama was sitting propped up in a gown and bedcoat. Eleanor was beside her, holding a bowl of porridge and a silver spoon.

'She won't eat a thing,' she said mournfully.

'Oh dear,' Aunt Felicity said. 'I didn't realise – my poor sister, she has lost so much weight. Allow me …' She took the bowl and raised the spoon to Mama's lips, but the porridge merely trickled down her chin.

'She's been bad recently,' Eleanor remarked.

'Do you think she knows about …?'

'We've told her, but we don't think she understands.'

'What about calling the doctor? She can't go on like this.'

'They've already confirmed that there's nothing they can do,' Violet said.

'Even though Patience is wasting away? Where are the nurses?'

'Our father dismissed them. He thought we should care for her ourselves.'

'What made him think you could do it? You have no experience or training.'

'We've done our best,' Violet said sharply.

Her aunt looked suitably contrite. 'I'm sorry – it's just such a shock to see her like this. The last time I called on her, she was speaking a little. Now she is mute and unlikely to recover …'

'She is fading,' Ottilie confirmed.

'Oh, this is too much,' Aunt Felicity pulled a lace handkerchief from the sleeve of her dark grey travelling dress and dabbed at the corner of her eye. 'My dear nieces, what happened to your father? Pray, tell me that he passed away peacefully.'

'His mind was tormented,' Violet murmured, hardly able to bring herself to utter the terrible truth. 'His body was found at the bottom of the cliff – there are witnesses who say that he jumped ...'

Aunt Felicity sat silent for once, her mouth dropped half-open. 'Then maybe it is best for Patience that she doesn't understand,' she said eventually. 'What was your father thinking of, going against the Ten Commandments and the will of God? He's a coward!'

'He had a lot to bear,' Violet said. 'He'd spent all his money – the only assets he had left were the house, personal effects and a few shares. His creditors were circling like vultures, ready to tear their share of flesh from his bones, he'd fallen out of favour with his friends and acquaintances, and Mama was ... well, she is dying. He did love us – we didn't always see eye to eye, but he did what he felt was best for us.'

'Whatever his motives, I fear that he's left you in the lurch,' Aunt Felicity said. 'There'll be an issue with any inheritance or jointure he has settled on you and your mother, because in this situation, anything he does have left will revert to the Crown – suicide is illegal and immoral, and as your father was not insane ...'

'Can't we find a doctor who's prepared to state that that was the case? There are grounds for it,' Violet said, remembering his frantic behaviour and the bizarre expedition diving for gold.

'The problem with that idea is that insanity is known to run through families – who will want to marry any of you when there's a possibility that you and your children will develop the same madness?'

'He was sound of mind at the start,' Ottilie interrupted. 'It was only circumstance that changed him. We can't ask a medical man to lie for us.'

'Who will want to marry us anyway?' Eleanor said. 'Violet's put paid to any chance we had of that.' Her comment knifed through Violet's heart, and even as she said it, Eleanor seemed to realise that she had spoken out of turn. 'I'm sorry. I didn't mean it,' she stammered.

'I think you did, or you wouldn't have said it. I can't believe that even my sister blames me for what happened with ...' Violet couldn't bring herself to say his name.

'No, really,' Eleanor said. 'I'm upset – it just slipped out. It was Mr Brooke's fault – he is entirely to blame, and I wish that he hadn't died, so we could confront him over it.'

Violet welcomed the interruption when Wilson showed the Reverend Green into the parlour. The vicar removed his hat and brushed back his greasy dark hair, then addressed Mama, apparently unconcerned that she wasn't properly dressed.

'I'm deeply sorry for your loss, Mrs Rayfield,' he said.

'She is much worse,' Aunt Felicity pointed out.

'In that case, allow me to offer my prayers and condolences to the Misses Rayfield. I assume that you are making plans for a quiet funeral.'

'We haven't thought about that yet,' Violet said.

'It is something which should be carried out quickly and without ceremony.'

'Our father was a respected businessman with many friends and associates in Dover,' Ottilie said. 'He should be buried according to his status.'

'You understand that there is some difficulty. Having died by his own hand, he cannot be buried in consecrated ground ...'

'Is there any way round this?' Violet ventured, feeling lower than ever. 'My father was a God-fearing man who attended church all his life. How can he be cast out now?'

'I think I may be able to help for a small honorarium and a promise that my involvement in this goes no further.'

'What are you suggesting?'

'That I could arrange for him to be buried at Cowgate – and say a few words over his grave with only close family present. Would that suffice?'

Violet glanced towards Ottilie who nodded. If that was the best he could do, then they would have to accept, but how would they find the money for his burial?

'I'll contact the solicitor about Father's will and see if I can make an appointment with the bank to find out how much money there is in his accounts,' she said after the vicar had left. 'We'll have to pay for the funeral and then there are the other bills – the servants' wages, the cost of gas for the lamps, the rates ...'

'We'll all have to go into mourning too,' Ottilie said. 'That's going to be expensive.'

'You still have your clothes from before, Violet?' Eleanor asked.

'Of course not. I threw them out when I found out that I wasn't Arvin's wife – it would have brought bad luck if I had kept them.'

'You can order dresses made from bombazine – they don't have to be made from parramatta silk,' Aunt Felicity said. 'Why don't I lend you the money to pay the reverend?'

'That's very kind of you,' Ottilie said. 'We're very grateful, but we'll find the money ourselves.'

'You must let me do this for my sister. It's better for everyone that your father is laid to rest quickly and quietly. We can put a notice in the paper after the funeral. Nobody needs to attend, least of all the family.'

'I shall go,' Violet said.

'Women aren't expected to be present.'

'I can't let him go alone, no matter what he's done,' she insisted, and her aunt backed down.

The following day, Violet stood side by side with Ottilie and Eleanor at their father's graveside in the cemetery beneath the Western Heights. The vicar prayed for Mr Rayfield's soul and the sexton covered the wicker coffin with earth. They left the grave unmarked except for a spray of roses which they'd bought on Mama's behalf.

Chapter Seventeen

By Order of the Lord Chancellor

'The Misses Rayfield are here to see you, sir,' the clerk said, showing Violet and Ottilie into the solicitor's office one morning not long after Mr Rayfield's burial. Violet touched the jet beads at her throat as she followed her older sister past the glazed bookshelves filled with legal volumes. They were both dressed in black, in deep mourning for their father.

'Thank you. Do sit down.' Mr Wiggins gestured towards two chairs and the clerk dived forward to clear them of paperwork and an empty pewter tankard. 'It's a matter of sorrow to me that we meet again under such … miserable circumstances. You are in possession of Mr Rayfield's death certificate?'

Having sat down beside her sister, Violet removed it from her bag and handed it across the desk. Mr Wiggins put his monocle up to one eye and began to read.

'This is all in order.' He looked up and the monocle fell out. 'Death by misadventure. I'm sorry for your loss.'

Ottilie pressed a handkerchief to her mouth.

'Then there's no likelihood of a claim on our father's estate by the Crown,' Violet said, her mind flooding with relief. They'd had so much bad luck – they didn't deserve any more.

'The doctor has been kind to Mr Rayfield, but other forces have not been so generous to the rest of your family.'

'What do you mean?' Violet asked.

'You should prepare yourselves to lower your expectations of what you and your mother might receive in the way of a jointure or inheritance.'

'We have no great expectations, just that we'll be able to live comfortably, as our father would have wished,' Violet said.

'Allow me to read out the salient terms of his will.' Mr Wiggins opened a file of papers and took the first from the top. '"This is the last will and testament", et cetera, et cetera. There is much wordy preamble that we can ignore ... ah, here we are. "I leave an annuity in perpetuity for my wife, Mrs Patience Rayfield, and the use of the house at Camden Crescent until either her death or such a time as she should remarry. I leave an annuity for each of my daughters, the Misses Ottilie, Violet and Eleanor Rayfield to be paid until marriage. The remainder of my estate is to be held in trust for the first male heir until he reaches the age of twenty-one."

'However, I'm afraid this is all hypothetical. Having made enquiries into the extent of your father's assets, I've found out that he's in debt to the bank, his former associate, Mr Chittenden, and many other creditors, including my firm. After those debts are paid, there will be precious little money left.'

'There will be an income from Brooke and Rayfield,' Violet observed.

'You haven't heard, then – Madame Brooke has wound up the business – her decision, not Mr Rayfield's. There was nothing he could do to prevent it, being the minority shareholder, and she was keen to hurry the process because she wished to return to France. She had already stayed in Dover longer than expected.'

'He told me about some shares that he bought from the railway company,' Violet said.

'You mean the London, Chatham and Dover Railway?'

'That's right. He reckoned they were worth something.'

'Unfortunately, the company is bankrupt. According to the committee looking into their finances, their shipping service is in debt and the shares they sold to their investors have turned out to be false. Thanks to an intervention by Parliament, the company will survive, but people like your father who put their trust in them have lost their money.'

'We have nothing?' Ottilie's face was white with shock.

'The only consolation is that Mama still has use of the house,' Violet said. 'I'd fear for her life if we had to move her.'

'You can stay there for now, but I can't guarantee for how long,' Mr Wiggins said. 'I would advise you to do everything in your power to find alternative accommodation. There must be family you can call upon to assist you and your mother. Mr Rayfield had many friends and acquaintances who would take pity on you out of respect for his memory.'

Unfortunately, her father and Arvin were the kind of men who'd done everything for themselves. They'd never acted out of charity or compassion for anyone who had fallen on hard times. Look how Pa had treated William when he lost his father and brother on the *Dover Belle*. He hadn't seen the error of his ways until after the trial when it was too late. Why should anyone help their nearest and dearest in their hour of need? Violet felt sick.

On the way home, she and Ottilie turned out of Pencester Street into Cannon Street, and passed the Royal

Oak and the corn market, before entering the square where the Wednesday market was in full swing. Some of the stalls were in the open, some beneath the arcade above which stood the museum.

'It's all very well, continuing to live in Camden Crescent, but how will we manage?' Violet said as the magnitude of Mr Wiggins's revelations began to sink in.

'You can sell our mother's jewellery and trinkets – that will bring in a tidy sum. She has no need for it any more. We'll have to let Wilson and May go, I think.'

'Not May. She's been loyal, a true and faithful servant, and a friend to me when Arvin was away.'

'We can't let sentiment interfere with common sense. She will have to go.'

'Her wages won't make much difference in the scheme of things, but you're right. We could rent out a room or two – to respectable ladies only.' The word 'respectable' caught in Violet's throat. What respectable lady would choose to live in the same house as the Rayfields where the father had killed himself, the mother was sick, and the daughter was ruined? 'I will have to go out to work, if anyone will have me ... There will always be people talking behind my back.'

'Hopefully, it won't come to that,' Ottilie said.

Violet slipped her arm through her sister's while they made their way through the throng, dodging the horses and carts, and barrows. Further along, under the arcade, a stall selling pats of golden butter caught her eye.

'Ottilie, stop. Look at those.' Her stomach growled as she imagined molten butter dripping across a toasted muffin. 'Can't we buy one?'

Ottilie smiled wryly. 'How can you be hungry at a time like this? Anyway, you heard what Mr Wiggins said – we have no money. We're going to have to make economies in running the household, or rather you and Eleanor are.'

'What do you mean? Where are you going?' Violet took a step back and gazed at her sister whose eyes were shining with tears, not of sorrow, but joy. 'Is it John?'

'We're getting married at long last and there's nothing I'd like more than for you to come to our wedding – if you can bear it, that is. I'll understand if you—'

'When? When is it?' Violet demanded.

'Tomorrow morning at ten o'clock, quietly at St Mary's.'

'That soon?'

'It's been planned for a while – we applied for a common licence two weeks ago to avoid having to have the banns read in church. I'm not going to postpone it. We've waited long enough – John's stood by me through thick and thin. I know it seems heartless to think of it so soon after losing Pa, but I've learned that life is short, and you have to make the most of it.'

'Will you invite our aunt?'

Ottilie shook her head. 'Just you and Eleanor. We don't want any fuss. Afterwards, we'll catch a train to London.'

'You are leaving us?'

'It's for the best. John is parting ways with Uncle Edward – he wishes to start in business on his own account. With me gone, there'll be one less mouth to feed.'

'I'm pleased for you, over the moon, in fact. I wish you were staying nearby, though.'

'We'll come and visit as often as we can, and when we're settled, you'll be able to visit us.'

Having torn themselves away from the stalls, they crossed the square to King's Bench Street and walked across New Bridge over the river and home to Camden Crescent, where they paused to look up at the terrace, its grandeur heightened by the golden rays cast by the midday sun. Thanks to their father's errors of judgement, their house was at risk of being seized by the bank.

Violet's pulse fluttered with panic. What were they going to do?

'What if the house has to be sold?' she said.

'You can always come and live with me and John once we're settled. We've decided to rent a small house while he sets up his own shipping agency.'

'Thank you for the offer.'

'I mean it, Violet. Anyway, I think everything will turn out all right in the end. One day, you'll marry again.'

'I was never married in the first place.' She turned to her sister, her vision blurring with sudden tears. 'Mr Brooke has ruined me for anybody else,' she went on bitterly.

'Even William Noble?'

'That's an odd thing to say.'

'I'm your sister – I know you better than anyone else. I've always thought you had a fancy for him.'

'If I did, it doesn't matter now. When we danced together at the ball, and I saw him at the regatta, I considered him very handsome. Since then, I've grown fond of him, but I think William blames Pa for the deaths of his father and brother, so why on earth would he want to marry me, a Rayfield?'

'And you went on to sacrifice your happiness for me and John, by marrying Mr Brooke,' Ottilie added.

'I was doing my duty, and to be fair, I did think that Arvin and I would find a way to rub along and be content. Life would have been very different if I could have married someone like William. He's a wonderful man – kind, chivalrous and brave.'

'So you do like him?'

'Yes, very much, but it's too late, and besides, I will never know if my feelings are reciprocated. There's been too much water gone under the bridge. We've been through this before – what respectable man would have me now?' Violet took a deep breath. 'Ottilie, I should have told you before – I'm with child.'

'Oh Violet, I thought you were looking rather matronly, and I wondered how you could bear to wear that shawl indoors when our aunt called on us. How long have you known?'

'Since the court hearing. I had my suspicions before then, but it wasn't until the infant quickened that I knew for certain.'

'Why didn't you say anything before?' Ottilie's expression was a mixture of shock, hurt and concern. 'You should have confided in me. How many times do I have to say: I'm your sister!'

'I'm sorry. I couldn't bring myself to tell anyone. I felt as though I'd already brought more than enough shame to our door. I'm at least six months gone. I've been lucky so far, but I can't hide it for much longer, so even though people are beginning to forget about the scandal, my swollen belly will remind them of it. I'd hoped to live quietly as Miss Rayfield, spinster of this parish, not Miss Rayfield, unmarried mother.'

'It isn't your fault,' Ottilie said, catching her fingers and giving her hand a brief, but reassuring squeeze.

'I intended to say something, but I was afraid that Pa would put me out on the street if he found out, and then I didn't want Aunt Felicity telling me what to do. Knowing her, she'd have me sent away for my confinement, then insist on me giving up the child, something I could never do.' She was close to tears again. 'Will you forgive me for not letting on?'

'My dear sister, there's nothing to forgive. It's me who should be asking your forgiveness for abandoning you in your hour of need.'

'You mustn't change your plans on my account,' Violet insisted, relieved that she had shared her secret at last. 'I will cope very well with Eleanor helping to look after Mama and the baby when it comes.'

'Have you told Eleanor yet?'

'Not yet. All in good time. Let's look forward to tomorrow – we must prepare for your wedding.'

It felt as though her family was falling apart and not for the first time, she wondered what on earth her father had been thinking. His greed had been his downfall, along with his propensity to succumb to flattery.

The wedding was simple and straightforward, with none of the pomp and ceremony which had attended Violet and Arvin's union. Ottilie wore mourning dress and carried a small spray of lilac flowers, and May and Wilson waved them off as they left the house on foot. At the church, the only witnesses present were Violet, Eleanor and the sexton.

When the vicar spoke, he said that he always did his best for his flock, with God as his guide. He was aware that some churchmen might find his decisions unconventional – even objectionable – but his conscience was clear. Violet guessed that he was referring to the outrage surrounding their father's death and her marriage. His words weren't soothing – they merely rubbed salt into her wounds.

But Ottilie was happy and that was all that mattered today, she reasoned.

After the service, they went to a local hostelry for a modest wedding breakfast, before John embraced his new sisters and apologised to Violet for what had happened with Mr Brooke, saying that if he'd known what he was like, he would willingly have punched him on the nose. Violet and Eleanor cried when they watched Mr and Mrs

Chittenden leave for the station to catch the late morning train to London.

'We should go home,' Violet said.

'At least Mama won't be upset,' Eleanor said. 'That is the one thing we can be thankful for.'

'You've been very brave.' Violet linked arms with her. 'I'm proud of you.'

'We've all had to find the courage to get through this, most of all you. Don't worry, my dear sister. At least we have each other.'

'You're right. We'll make the most of what we have left.'

When they reached the house, there were horses and carts outside, and Wilson was on the doorstep arguing with two men, both swarthy and wearing sombre clothing. Violet hurried towards them with Eleanor trailing along behind.

'Let us in, sir! By order of the Lord Chancellor!' the taller of them shouted.

'We have no business with him, or anyone like him,' Violet called from behind them.

They turned to face her. 'Good day, madam. Are you the mistress of this house?'

'I'm one of Mrs Rayfield's daughters. Who are you?' She felt faint, but she would not fall. The men stared at her, and she wondered if they knew who she was. She felt her face flush hot as they took in her figure and the tell-tale curve of her belly.

'Mr Toke and Mr Tipstaff, bailiff and under-bailiff,' said the taller one.

Her heart sank. 'You can't come in. Wilson, you are right not to let them in.'

'We have a warrant to remove goods to the value of' – he named a figure – 'and evict anyone living at this property forthwith.'

'That isn't possible. The house is subject to probate and due legal process,' Violet said. 'In the meantime, my mother is permitted to live here. Go and see Mr Wiggins – he'll confirm what I say. You can't evict us without notice at least.'

'I'm afraid you've been misinformed. Mr Chittenden started bankruptcy proceedings against your father recently. The notice has just been published in the newspapers. Probate won't be granted until Mr Rayfield's debts have been settled.'

She looked up at Wilson. 'Did you know about this?'

'I was aware of it,' he replied. 'I gave my word to the master that I wouldn't mention it in front of the ladies of the household. He wanted to protect you, miss.'

'I shouldn't speak badly of the dead, but he wanted to protect himself,' Violet said crossly.

'He was in dire straits by the end,' Wilson said. 'That's why he jumped – he couldn't bear the shame of being incarcerated in a debtor's prison.'

'I wish he'd thought of us and Mama.'

'He was devastated when he knew she wasn't going to recover, and then there was all that trouble with Mr Brooke. It broke him,' Wilson said.

Violet turned back to the bailiffs. 'You heard all that – you understand how we're suffering. I beg you to show us compassion. My mother is dying and we have nowhere to go.'

'We've heard it all before, every excuse under the sun, and it makes no difference. May we come in now? It would be better, more discreet.'

'Won't you give us another day, just tonight so we can find somewhere to live? You can't cast my mother out on the street. You wouldn't treat a dog like that.'

'You must have relatives you can put her with,' the bailiff said, his manner softening slightly.

'She has a sister in Canterbury, but it all takes time …'

'We're only carrying out our duties, Miss Rayfield.'

Wilson let them into the house, closing the door behind them as Mr Toke went on, 'We never enjoy doing this to a respectable family, but Mr Rayfield was declared bankrupt and it's his creditors now who suffer.'

'Isn't there any way?' she tried again.

'The house is mortgaged almost in full. It belongs to the bank. Anything left after it's sold will be used to pay the creditors. Now, down to business. How many people live here, including servants?'

'There's Wilson here, and one maid, my mother, my sister and me.' Violet slipped her arm around Eleanor's waist to comfort her. The bailiffs were about to evict them and now her shame knew no bounds.

'May has gone away, miss. I believe that somebody told her that the master had been declared bankrupt.' Wilson gazed down at his shoes, and Violet couldn't help wondering if that was the whole story.

'Where is your mother?' Mr Toke asked.

'In the parlour – she has her day bed in there.' Violet headed towards the foot of the stairs.

'Where do you think you're going?'

'To pack – you can't possibly put us out of the door with nothing.'

'Go and wait with your mother. Both of you, and the manservant! You must allow us to get on without interference.'

'I wish to go upstairs – you can't stop me.'

Mr Toke stepped up close to her until she could see the brown stains on his teeth and smell his stale tobacco breath. 'I can, and I will.' He took her arm. 'Show me to the parlour.'

'I won't go with you, sir,' she snapped, feeling his fingers bruising her flesh.

'Mr Tipstaff, go upstairs and search the rooms – go through the chests and jewellery boxes.'

'The valuables belong to my mother,' Violet argued. 'Unhand me!'

'We're authorised to seize all assets of value from this address,' the man said. 'In the eyes of the law, a wife's property belongs to her husband. You haven't the luxury of picking and choosing what to keep.'

'You are vultures!' she exclaimed.

'Call us what you will. We're used to it.'

He was serious, she realised as his grip tightened, and if she continued to fight him, he would certainly win.

Giving in, Violet accompanied Eleanor and Wilson to the parlour where they waited with Mama, listening to the sound of the bailiffs stripping the house of their belongings: the furniture; their mother's trinkets and curios; her father's books; the dinner service, cutlery and fire dogs. The carts came and went, laden with the Rayfields' possessions, and soon there was very little left. They even took Mama's day bed, having lifted her bodily into her bath chair, a carriage mounted on three wheels with blue velvet cushions.

Mr Toke came in to speak to them.

'Where does the missus keep her jewellery?'

'In the box in her boudoir,' Violet said. 'You must have found it.'

'We found a box, but there isn't much in it. Did Mr Rayfield have a safe?'

'Not as far as I'm aware.'

The bailiff walked across to Mama and picked up her left hand. 'Where is her wedding ring?'

'How dare you, sir?' Eleanor said. 'You're scaring her.'

'I don't think she knows I'm here.' He dropped her hand which flopped back into her lap. 'The ring? She must have had a ring, and brooches at least. Has she put them in some other hiding place?'

'Not to my knowledge.'

'Nor mine,' Eleanor added. 'She never was one for wearing jewellery, was she, Violet?'

'No, she didn't condone vanity in any form,' Violet elaborated.

'I wish I could believe you.'

'You have no choice than to take me at my word. You must have more than enough to satisfy the creditors – you've taken nearly everything except the clothes from our backs.'

'We've turned everything out, Mr Toke,' Mr Tipstaff said.

'In that case – out of the goodness of my heart – the young ladies can have the half-hour that remains before the locksmith arrives, to pack anything they want from what's left. You'll be gone by then or we'll forcibly evict you, according to the terms of the warrant.'

'You've made it very clear,' Violet said stiffly.

She and Eleanor ran upstairs and threw some clothes into bags.

'My embroidery and the sewing box? They've gone. They've taken them. Oh, this is the end ...' Violet burst into tears.

'They are just things,' Eleanor said gently. 'They can be replaced.'

'But they are precious to me – the box belonged to Mama and her mother before her. Without it, well ...'

'We will buy another one. Hurry, we haven't got very long.'

Returning to the parlour, they dressed Mama in her day clothes, a coat and a big blanket over her knees. Violet put on Mama's gloves, noting how her soft white fingernails were peeling away from her fingertips.

'I'm mightily sorry about this,' Wilson said as he helped them carry Mama and her bath chair from the house and pile up their luggage on the pavement outside. 'What are your plans?'

'All I can think of is to take Mrs Rayfield to our aunt's and throw ourselves on her mercy.' It was that, or a night on the streets. 'I have a few coins in my pocket. What will you do, Wilson?' Violet asked, putting the bath chair's canvas hood up. 'Have they seized your valuables too?'

'Knowing for a while how the land was lying, I took the precaution of sending my possessions to my sister in Deal for safekeeping. Don't worry about me, ladies. Let me help you to the station – where do you wish to go?'

Violet gave him her aunt's address.

'Where's Dickens?' Eleanor said suddenly. 'Have you seen the cat?'

'He must have taken fright,' Wilson said.

'We have to find him – he's always been Mama's favourite.'

'We can't take him with us,' Violet said.

'He'll die if we leave him behind – he's too stupid to catch mice. Wilson, there's a basket in one of the attic rooms. Fetch it while I look in his favourite spots.'

Violet didn't know whether to be relieved or annoyed, when her sister reappeared with the cat trapped in a wicker basket, the lid tied down with string. Eleanor put the basket on Mama's lap and held her hand as they waited on the pavement, attracting a small crowd of onlookers, curious to find out why an invalid would be out on the street in the rain.

'She's taking the air,' Violet kept saying. 'Doctor's orders.' She couldn't wait to get away, but Wilson was taking his time to leave the house.

'Good afternoon.' Mrs Pryor, their neighbour, came stalking up to them. 'Oh, you are in a poorly way, Mrs Rayfield. I saw the removal men outside and I said to myself, they're moving without telling me. Well, I shall find out where they're going, so I can keep in touch.'

Violet had no idea why she'd want to do that when Mrs Pryor had been avoiding her and the rest of the family as if they'd been suffering from a fatal contagion.

'We're taking my mother to stay with our aunt for a while.'

'I heard from the maid that Ottilie's married her sweetheart. That was done very quietly considering the celebrations your father had for your marriage ...'

Violet knew very well what she was suggesting.

'Would you celebrate within a week or two of your father's burial? No, I thought not.' She turned away, not caring that she appeared rude. Mrs Pryor wasn't worthy of her attention. She, Eleanor and Mama would leave, their heads held high, carrying two bags and a suitcase containing a few chemises, odd stockings, and a vanity set that the bailiffs had left behind in the empty bedrooms. She looked down at the basket – and a cat.

Aunt Felicity would take care of them for a while, at least, but what would happen after that? Where would they go? How would they live?

'It's time to leave, miss,' she heard Wilson say. 'I'll help you as far as the station.'

Chapter Eighteen

A Peculiar State of Affairs

Did she have enough money for three tickets to Canterbury? Violet counted the coins from her purse and put them on the counter at the ticket office.

'One way?' the ticket seller enquired.

'Thank you.' She nodded, feeling a pang of regret that they wouldn't be returning for a while, if ever. Dover had been her home all her life. Apart from the vague notion she'd had of moving to France, she'd never expected to have to move away. She thought of William and her heart broke in two – she doubted she would ever see him again.

'Miss, your tickets,' the ticket seller said, pushing them towards her.

'I'm sorry. I was miles away.' She picked them up and returned to where Wilson was waiting with Mama and the bath chair, and Eleanor was talking to one of the porters.

'The last train from Dover Priory to Canterbury arrives in five minutes,' Eleanor said, turning to Violet.

'Then I'll leave you ladies to it,' Wilson said. 'I wish you all the best ... If only things had been different ...'

'We're very grateful for everything you've done for us.' Violet swallowed a sob. 'I hope you find another situation very soon.'

'I've received an offer of employment from a mutual acquaintance of ours, Mr Chittenden. His butler's on his last legs and he wants to put him out to grass, so to speak.'

'Good luck then, Wilson.' Violet stepped back as the train, painted in gleaming black livery, came squealing and hissing into the station. When it came to a halt, the station boys ran alongside it, opening the doors to let the passengers off.

'Can I help this lady into one of the carriages? The chair can be stowed in the guard's van for the journey,' the porter said.

'She must stay in her chair,' Violet said. 'She can't sit up by herself.'

The porter pushed the chair along the platform and shoved poor Mama up a ramp into the guard's van with Dickens still in the basket on her lap. A young man loaded a box of live lobsters with their pincers tied shut, three sacks of flour, several boxes of new shoes, and a crate of walking sticks on after her.

'Where should we travel?' Eleanor whispered in her sister's ear.

'With Mama, of course. I'm not letting her out of my sight.'

'Ladies, please take a seat in one of the carriages,' the guard said, joining them. He was wearing a peaked cap with lettering on the front, an enamel badge, and a jacket with brass buttons which barely did up across his large belly. 'I can't let you travel in the van. Rules and regulations.'

'We can't possibly leave her on her own – she's ill,' Violet argued.

'Don't you worry – I'll keep an eye on her.'

'No, sir. She must have one of her daughters with her at all times. It isn't right to treat her the same as a box of lobsters. It's disgraceful. I'll be writing to the manager of the railway company.' Violet stopped abruptly. She could see from the guard's expression that it was no use arguing.

'In you get, or the train'll go without you,' he said, and Eleanor grabbed her arm and pulled her towards the adjacent carriage. They clambered on and the door slammed behind them. As they took their seats, the guard blew his whistle and the train pulled away, the engine settling into a pounding rhythm which reminded Violet of the *Samphire*. She felt a sense of foreboding which she couldn't shift.

'We're on our way,' Eleanor said. 'This has been a terrible day, one of the worst, but now we're on our way, it can only get better.'

'I wonder what's happened to May,' Violet said. 'I expect she did a runner when she saw the bailiffs. It's a shame she didn't leave word about where she was going. She's been very good to me and I consider her a friend, not just a maid. I don't mean to sound superior when I say "just a maid". She's the most capable woman I've ever met – she can turn her hand to anything except for baking cakes. When we were at East Cliff together, she took to embroidery like a duck to water. Her work is flawless.' Violet gave her sister a nudge. 'Eleanor, are you listening to me?'

She answered with a quiet snore.

'Oh, you poor thing. You're worn out.' Letting her sister sleep, Violet looked out of the window, counting down the stations to their destination: Shepherds Well, Adisham, Bekesbourne ... The train rattled and lurched through the Kent countryside, which was turning gold in the evening sun. They passed the hop gardens where the bines were twiddling up the chestnut poles, and the orchards where the blossom was drifting from the trees. Eventually, the towers of the cathedral came into view.

'Eleanor,' she said, gently shaking her shoulder. 'We're nearly there.'

Eleanor yawned and stretched as they got off the train in Canterbury. The guard and one of the porters struggled to unload Mama, because she'd been blocked in by more boxes and crates since they'd left Dover. Dickens yowled as they jolted the bath chair on the platform.

'There you are, ladies,' the guard said. 'I wish you a pleasant onward journey, wherever you are going.'

'Thank you,' Violet said, feeling guilty because she couldn't afford to tip the porter.

'Do you want to push or shall I?' Eleanor asked.

'We'll take it in turns.' Violet gathered up their luggage. 'You first.'

On leaving the station, they passed the city wall with the Dane John Gardens above them. On reaching Castle Street, they wended their way through Beer Cart Lane and Stour Street where the houses seemed to be built on top of each other, blocking out the light.

'This can't be right,' Eleanor said, trying to pick her way around the puddles and excrement with the bath chair.

Violet wanted to put her handkerchief across her nose to block out the stench of rotten eggs, but she had too many bags, and she didn't dare put them down even for a second, not only because of the filth underfoot, but because of the people. There were so many of them, staring at the strange entourage, watching and waiting. She didn't feel safe among the beggars and lunatics, and the barefoot boys dressed in their rags with their ravenous eyes. One limped over to them.

'I'll 'elp yer with yer bags, missus.'

'No, thank you.' She clutched them more tightly as he tried to snatch them away. 'No! Go away!'

'Give us a penny then … an 'a'penny? Some bread? Just a bite.'

'Leave us alone or I'll scream the place down,' she hissed.

'I'll 'ave my ma put a curse on you,' the boy said darkly.

'Keep walking, Eleanor,' Violet urged, shocked by his threat and the squalor. 'I'm sorry you have to listen to this, Mama. We'll soon be at Aunt Felicity's. Don't you worry.'

They continued past Eastbridge Hospital and the Weavers House on St Peter's Street where Violet saw a landmark she recognised from past occasions when the Rayfields had taken a coach to Canterbury. It was a medieval gatehouse, built from ragstone, with an arch through the middle and battlements on top. It reminded her of Arvin and his chateau.

'Eleanor, it's the Westgate Towers,' she said, returning to the present. 'All we have to do is go along St Dunstan's and we'll be in Orchard Street. Let me push Mama now. You take the bags.' They swapped places, and she gave the bath chair a good shove to get it going again.

'I wish more than anything that we could have stayed at home,' Eleanor said sadly, as they stepped aside to allow a cart filled with squawking chickens to pass. 'How did we sink to this? We had everything we needed and more, and now we are homeless.'

'We have Mama and each other.'

'And Dickens.'

'And Dickens,' Violet echoed. 'Here we are. Our aunt's house is just along the road.'

They stopped outside a handsome yellow brick house which had a green door with a stained-glass fanlight above.

'Ring the bell then,' Violet said.

Her sister rang four times before their aunt came to the door with her hair tied back, and her silk wrapper pulled tightly around her slender frame.

'What are you thinking of, turning up unannounced on my doorstep like a pair of bad pennies?' Aunt Felicity's face turned pink with annoyance when she saw them, and deep scarlet when she noticed the bath chair. 'What on earth possessed you to drag an invalid all this way?'

'We didn't drag her. We took the train,' Eleanor said.

'Patience, my poor dear.' She pushed past her nieces, leaned beneath the hood of the bath chair and touched her sister's face. 'Oh, you are cold … so cold.' She uttered a blood-curdling scream, loud enough to bring the neighbours to their windows. 'Oh my lord. She is dead!'

Violet's heart missed a beat. 'She can't be. She was alive when we put her on the train.'

'And when we took her off,' Eleanor contributed.

'Was she? I didn't check.'

'Aunt Felicity, you are hysterical.'

'You are mistaken,' Violet said, refusing to believe her. Eleanor hadn't devoted the past few months to nursing their mother, only for her to go and die on them now.

'Oh no, I've paid my respects to the dearly departed often enough to know …' Their aunt turned to where Jane had appeared behind her with her dog in her arms. 'Fetch a mirror immediately.'

'Yes, Mama,' Jane said, frowning. As she put the dog down, he ran forward and started yapping at the cat, who spat and hissed from the basket.

'We have a mirror here,' Violet said, scrabbling through their luggage to extract it while Eleanor picked the basket up out of the dog's reach, and Jane looked on. Violet gave the mirror to her aunt and pulled the hood of the bath chair down.

'Oh, Mama,' she gasped when she saw that her eyes were wide open, and her mouth contorted as if she was about to give her a good telling-off.

Aunt Felicity held the mirror to Mama's face, and Violet could only watch for the tell-tale frosting of the glass, with her hand across her mouth to hold back a cry of anguish.

'She is gone,' her aunt whispered. 'Oh, my dear sister, what happened to you?' She turned to face Violet and Eleanor, her eyes flashing with distress and fury. 'You have killed her. Explain yourselves.'

'We had nowhere else to go,' Violet stammered. 'The bailiffs put us out of the house today. I didn't know what to do – I thought it best to come to you. You're the only family we have left ...'

'You'd better bring her inside,' Aunt Felicity said, her voice like ice. 'We must decide what is to be done.'

Jane recaptured the dog, and Aunt Felicity took the cat basket and left it in the hall. Violet helped Eleanor push the bath chair through to the parlour.

'We must send for the doctor.' Aunt Felicity wrung her hands. 'He will advise us. Jane, go and ask Annie to fetch him.'

'I can go myself,' Jane offered.

'We can go together,' Eleanor said.

'No, I don't want my daughter mixed up in this. Annie will go. She's in the scullery, washing the dishes.'

Jane hurried off to the back of the house from where Violet heard exclamations of shock, horror and, 'Well, I never did!'

'She'll go straight away.' Jane rejoined them.

'Thank you,' Aunt Felicity said. 'Now, we must decide what to do with the two of you. Where is Ottilie? Why is she not with you?'

'She's married. We went to her wedding only this morning.' Violet couldn't help thinking that her mind was playing tricks on her because it felt like a lifetime ago.

'To whom?'

'John Chittenden,' Eleanor said. 'Ottilie said it was the happiest day of her life … and now we're going to have to send word that our dear mother has fallen asleep.'

'Oh, my goodness. What a peculiar state of affairs! They are staying on in Dover, I presume.'

'They've gone to London. John has broken away from his father.'

'Then I wish them luck – they're going to need it. Ottilie has made her bed and now she must lie in it. As for you two …' Aunt Felicity glared at them. 'Eleanor, you can stay for as long as you wish – I do this for your dead mother's sake. But Violet, you and the cat must go. I can't have you here.'

'Why not? We're family,' Violet said. 'Aren't families supposed to look out for each other?'

'I'll do my duty by my sister. I'll make sure she's treated with respect and buried with dignity – even though she brought this on herself by marrying Sidney, whom I always regarded as a most unsuitable husband. She would have him, though, and look where it got her, taking her last breath in the compartment of a train.'

Violet didn't like to enlighten her about the guard's van. She felt bad enough about that already.

'Eleanor, you will make a gentle companion and maid for your cousin.'

'I won't stay without my sister – and the cat,' Eleanor said. 'Mama adored him.'

'I won't have that filthy, flea-ridden creature in my house – besides, the dog will have him for breakfast. You can let him go down by the river to fend for himself. As for you,

271

Violet, you're asking the impossible. The scandal isn't over, is it? You are with child. I have to ask – is it Mr Brooke's?'

'What are you suggesting? That because I was wronged, I have no morals?' Violet was distraught. 'It's come to a pretty pass when your aunt considers you a harlot.'

'How dare you speak in such a way!' her aunt exclaimed.

'You are with child?' Eleanor said, her eyes wide with disbelief.

'Yes,' Violet said, in tears. 'Mr Brooke left me with one more little surprise, something I can do absolutely nothing about. It is cruel of you to lay the blame on my shoulders.' She walked across to her mother, her skirts dragging across the floor. Leaning down, she kissed her cold cheek, whispering, 'Goodbye, Mama.' She stood up straight, struggling to tear herself away, but she had to leave. She knew when she wasn't welcome. 'I bid you farewell, Eleanor,' she muttered, heading for the parlour door.

'Where are you going?' Jane interrupted.

'Away from here. I'm sorry, I'd expected to find some respite and kindness here, but it wasn't to be.'

'Don't blame me for it. I can't have an unmarried mother and an infant born on the wrong side of the blanket living under my roof, while your cousin is on the verge of making what I hope will be an excellent marriage. I can't have even a hint of scandal ruining Jane's prospects.' Aunt Felicity's voice softened slightly. 'Do you understand?'

'Perfectly.' Violet picked up the bags, and went out to the hall to collect the cat.

'I'm coming with you,' Eleanor said from behind her. 'We'll take Mama away from here.'

'We can't,' Violet said sadly, turning to face her sister. 'She has no need of us any more – she's at peace at last.'

'I can't leave her,' Eleanor sobbed.

'You heard what Aunt Felicity said – you are welcome to stay here.'

'I don't want to.'

'You have to,' Violet said firmly. 'Stay and you'll have all the home comforts you're used to. You'll have company, occupation and a roof over your head. I can't promise you anything.'

'Except a sister's love,' Eleanor said quietly. 'That means more to me than anything in the world at this moment.'

'Oh, Eleanor.' Violet gazed at her through a blur of tears, as her sister continued, 'You're all I have left. You're going nowhere without me.'

Half an hour later, they left their aunt's house in Orchard Street, Violet walking with the basket and bags, ahead of Eleanor who carried the suitcase and a small purse containing a few shillings, a gift from their aunt to salve her conscience.

'We have riches beyond compare,' Eleanor said with a spring in her step, as they reached the centre of Canterbury. 'Is it wrong not to feel all that sad about Mama? I mean, I feel sorrowful now and then because I miss her, but I feel as though I've mourned for her already. I grieved when she first got sick and was taking laudanum for the headaches, and then when she started to lose her beautiful hair and fingernails, and then when she turned into a shell of her former self. The worst time was when she couldn't remember any of our names. I cried all week after that.'

'I know what you mean. It's a relief knowing that she's no longer in pain. She's been taken up to a better place.'

'And we don't have to look after her any longer,' Eleanor said in a small voice. 'I'm going to miss sitting with her on the balcony. Oh Violet, for a moment I imagined we could go home ... Do you think she'd still be with us, if

273

she'd been allowed to stay at the house? Do you think it was the shock that finished her off?'

'It doesn't matter now,' Violet said. 'We've got to find some way of making our living. Where are we going to stay tonight? Tomorrow night?'

'I could write and be published,' Eleanor said quietly.

'How will that work? We'll have starved by the time you've finished the first chapter. Oh, I'm sorry for being snippy with you. I'm tired, hungry ... and anxious beyond measure, because try as I might, I can't think of a way forward. How will we survive?'

'There's somewhere down there.' Eleanor pointed along a narrow side road which led towards one of the cathedral gates. They followed a sign to West's Dining Rooms along Mercery Lane, where the old timber-framed shops leaned in towards each other as if a team of drunken builders had had a hand in their construction. The aroma of braised beef and suet drew them to the eatery, but the patron turned them away because of the cat.

'If Dickens had stopped yowling, we would have been allowed in,' Eleanor grumbled as they went on towards the cathedral. 'Slow down – I'm famished.'

'We'll buy coffee from a barrow, and bread from the bakery.'

'And some cheese from the market, and some fish heads for Dickens, for he will surely starve if we leave him in the basket without food.'

It was too late for the market – it had closed – but they bought a ham hock pie from an inn. They ate it on the street – something their parents and polite society would have frowned upon – but Violet didn't care. Food had never tasted so good. When they had finished and Dickens had had his share, she brushed the crumbs from her face and put the remaining piece into one of their bags.

'What are we going to do now?' Eleanor asked.

'I don't know. It's getting late.'

'Should we set out for London to find Ottilie?'

Violet shook her head. 'We don't have a forwarding address, or money to get us there. Ottilie's supposed to be writing to us to let us know where she's living. I hope she thinks to contact Aunt Felicity or Jane when she doesn't hear back from us.' Even if they did know where she was, the newly-weds wouldn't want them getting in the way, and it wouldn't be fair to impose on John when he was setting up in business. Not only that, she would be bringing her shame with her – she couldn't escape it. 'I want to go back to Dover, where our memories are.' Where William was. The thought came unbidden into her head. She remembered dancing with him at the ball, happier times when Pa had been wealthy, Mama well, and life filled with promise. 'Dover is home.'

'I agree with that. What times are the trains?'

'We should make our way as far as we can on foot.'

'That's madness – we aren't dressed for walking.'

'How much money is in that purse?'

Eleanor counted it out, as Violet lugged the cat basket and luggage along.

'Oh dear,' she said.

'Exactly. We can waste what's left on our train fare, or travel by shanks pony and keep the money aside for when we get back to Dover.'

'How far is it?'

'Fifteen or sixteen miles, thereabouts,' Violet guessed. 'I don't know how long it will take. If we set out now ...' Her strength was beginning to fail her after the events of the day. She could barely put one foot in front of the other.

'We can't walk all that way now – you're worn out. Look at you,' Eleanor said gently. 'We should rest and set out in the morning. If we leave now, we'll be walking in the dark.'

'You're right, but we haven't anywhere to stay.'

'Listen to me. You're in no fit state. Think of the infant that's growing inside you – you have to look after yourself.'

'But where will we sleep? It isn't safe to be here on the street.'

'We'll find somewhere, and I'll stand guard while you rest. Trust me.'

They wandered through the narrow alleyways and squares which led down to the river, where they found what looked like a disused doorway overgrown with grass and ivy.

'I can't go any further.' Violet's feet were aching, and her head was swimming.

'We'll stop here. We can let the cat out for a while. It's all right, I've got some string – I'll make a collar, so he can't go too far.' Eleanor took the basket and bags, and made a makeshift cushion for Violet to sit on. 'There you are. I'll unpack a couple of our dresses for blankets, not that it's all that cold.'

'It will be by dawn,' Violet muttered.

Later, they huddled together in the doorway, hidden in the shadows with Dickens in his basket looking out, his eyes glowing green from the darkness. A rat squeaked and scuttled across their feet and an old grey-muzzled dog ambled along and cocked its leg against the suitcase. Violet hugged her sister tight and kissed her cheek, and after a while – in spite of her fears of being attacked by thieves and men out to have their wicked way with them – she fell asleep.

She was woken with a jolt and a yelp of protest.

'Hey, what do you think you're doing?' She was aware that Eleanor was on her feet, chasing down the street.

Having opened her eyes, Violet saw a tin bucket lying on its side, and two laughing urchins disappearing off around the corner, and Eleanor standing with her hands on her hips. She could smell the stench of river water seeping into her clothes.

'The little tykes,' Eleanor exclaimed as she returned to the doorway. 'It isn't funny. It's a disaster. Look at us.' A black liquid was trickling down her face on to her blouse. 'We stink.'

Violet handed her a handkerchief. 'Here. Use this.'

'Oh, what good will that do?' Eleanor took it anyway and did her best to clean herself up. 'That's the last straw.'

'A little bit of dirty water never hurt anyone,' Violet said, trying in vain to cheer her sister up. 'Let's pack our things and move on.' She was even more determined to get back to Dover to breathe the sea air and hear the rush of the waves dragging at the shingle. 'We'll buy some ginger beer and have a picnic with the food we have left.'

'You can't fool me, Violet,' Eleanor said. 'We are in a dreadful pickle, and I can't see any way out of it.'

Chapter Nineteen

The Dover Road

'I wish I'd worn my walking shoes, not my best boots,' Violet said as they made their way out of Canterbury, passing the cricket ground. 'They're pinching my toes.'

'You wouldn't have chosen to wear them, if we hadn't gone to Ottilie's wedding,' Eleanor pointed out.

Violet was hobbling by the time they reached Bridge, where she decided that she'd had enough of her footwear. They stopped for refreshment they could ill afford at the White Horse, then paused again in the shelter of a hedge at the side of the road so she could take them off.

'They're no use now,' Eleanor said grimly, as Violet unfastened the buttons on her lovely French silk boots. One of the heels had come off, and the material was in tatters. Violet tossed them into the hop garden behind them. 'Don't throw them away, though. What are you going to wear on your feet?'

'Petticoats. I'll tear them into strips and bandage my blisters. What choice do I have? There's nowhere to buy shoes in the countryside, and we couldn't pay for them if there were.' Violet felt the consequences of being poor beginning to sink in. The bandages were not a success. By the time they realised that they'd taken a wrong turn and were heading towards Selstead and Swingfield Minnis rather than Lydden, her feet were bleeding through the cloth.

An elderly woman with white eyes, a stick and a bag of lavender, tried to persuade them to cross her palm with silver, but Violet refused, and Eleanor spent the next few minutes worrying that she would place a curse on them out of revenge.

'What difference does it make? We are cursed already,' Violet said as a carter drove up behind them, calling, 'Ladies, was that woman making a noosance of 'erself? She's always makin' trouble.' He hauled on the reins, slowing his piebald cob to match their pace as he came alongside. 'Can I be of assistance? You seem to be in some kind of trouble.'

'We're trying to get to Dover,' Violet said.

'Ah, you're 'eading in the direction of Folkestone. Where 'ave you come from?'

'Canterbury,' Eleanor said.

'Why don't I give you and your' – he stared into the basket – 'livestock a ride? I don't expect any reward except for your company.'

'Thank you, mister,' Violet said. 'It's very kind of you.'

'Whoa!' The horse stopped, and the carter – a red-faced, middle-aged man in a straw hat, long shirt, twill trousers and boots, jumped out and helped them into the cart, loading the cat, along with the rest of their luggage. Violet glanced at Eleanor, who gave her a quick smile of reassurance. The man seemed harmless enough.

He flicked his whip at the cob's rump and the cart jolted forward and rumbled down the hill.

'It seems odd to find two refined young ladies like yourselves out 'ere,' he bellowed over his shoulder.

Violet gave Eleanor a warning glance to keep her mouth shut.

'We've been visiting our aunt,' Violet said.

'For pleasure or out of dooty?'

'Our mother passed away yesterday,' Eleanor blurted out.

'I'm sorry to 'ear that. I'm always putting my great big foot in it.'

'We've lost everything,' she went on.

'It's a shame. Life's 'ard – the best anyone can 'ope for is to be 'appy and live without sin. I reckon I've achieved the former, but I'm still working on the latter.' He chuckled to himself. 'I take it that your 'ome's in Dover?'

'Yes,' Violet said. 'Where are you heading to?'

'Just the other side of Hawkinge – I'm delivering a couple of wheels and picking up some tools to take back to Denton. Are you two all right in the back? It isn't the most comfortable ride, but beggars can't be choosers,' he said brightly. 'I've got two grown-up sons, and a daughter who's about your age. In fact, you remind me of her. I'm giving 'er away next month and I'm going to be the proudest father in the county.'

Violet felt a pang of regret, remembering how her father had given her away to Arvin.

'It's getting dimpsy – you really shouldn't be wandering about at night.'

'We can make our way to Dover – it can't be much further,' Violet said, aware that Eleanor had fallen asleep, slumped over Dickens's basket.

'It's far enough, and considering the state you're in, if I were your father, I'd tell you to stop somewhere for the night before setting out again,' the carter said sternly.

'I appreciate your concern, but—'

'My brother runs the Valiant Sailor on Dover Hill. I'll drop you there. Really, miss, let me 'elp you. I couldn't have it on my conscience if anything should 'appen to you. It's what any decent father would do on finding another man's daughters in need of assistance.'

'You are a true gentleman,' Violet said.

'We're few and far between, but we do exist.' The carter clucked at the horse, encouraging it to walk out faster.

'I'm truly grateful.'

'Your pa would 'ave done the same thing in my position,' he said, but Violet was afraid that he wouldn't.

The lights of the inn were glinting in the dark. Somebody was shouting and laughing, hanging out of an upstairs window. A cow mooed from nearby, making Violet jump.

'Don't you think it looks like a place for common people?' Eleanor said after he'd dropped them off.

'That's what we are now: common people, keeping themselves to themselves and living quietly.' Violet pulled her bonnet down so that it shaded her eyes. The last thing she wanted was to be recognised: the infamous Miss Rayfield. She wished she had Arvin's ring to put back on her finger so that she could pass herself off as a married woman, but the bailiffs had taken it, along with the rest of the Rayfields' jewellery.

The carter had spoken to his brother, the landlord, who'd said that there was a room available with one bed, and that the cat could stay for an extra sixpence. He showed them upstairs and opened the window for them.

'It looks out across Steddy Hole,' he said. 'Two sisters were murdered there – stabbed to death. You might 'ave heard of it.'

'We haven't, sir.' Violet refused to be cowed.

'The soldier who did it was hanged outside Maidstone Prison a few years ago. If you don't believe me, just ask some of my regulars who went along to watch. I'll 'ave your supper sent up.'

'We didn't order food,' Violet said quickly.

'My brother ordered it on your behalf, and he's paid for it too. I've always said that he's too soft in the 'eart and 'ead for his own good. Goodnight, ladies.'

After a supper of soup and cold meats, they let Dickens free to wander around the room, and retired to bed. As Violet lay beneath a sheet with her arms around her sister, listening to the unfamiliar sounds of the inn, she felt the baby kicking in her belly.

'The baby – he, or she – won't let me sleep,' she said, in wonder.

'Are you scared?' Eleanor asked. 'I would be. It's daunting enough to think you're going to become a mother, but when you haven't … I'm sorry.'

'It's all right. I know it'll be a terrible struggle, bringing up a child out of wedlock and without its father's support, but I'll do my duty.'

'You'll do your best,' Eleanor said, 'and when the infant arrives, you will adore it, and everything you do for it, you'll do out of love.'

'I'm afraid that I won't look at the infant with any fondness.'

'But you will. It will all work out.'

'You can write happy endings for the heroines in your books, but not for real life, not for us,' Violet said sadly. 'I don't know how I'll manage. I don't know anything about bringing up children.' She could recall Eleanor's arrival, the hushed tones of the midwife, the sudden squall of an infant, and the nurse whisking her sister away to be raised in the nursery.

'I'll help you. We'll take it in turns to soothe him, or her.'

'How do you know these things?' Violet said.

'I watch and listen, and I read.'

'What you read isn't the truth.'

'It always contains elements of reality. Writing is like baking a cake – you take handfuls of raisins and nuts, and stir them together so you end up with the finished article looking very different, but essentially being the same. It's like a riddle.'

'It's too much for me at this time of night, and the thought of cake – even one of May's – is making me hungry again.' Violet recalled the warmth of the kitchen at home, and the way the maid used to run around after them. Even May had abandoned them, but she didn't blame her. She had done more than enough for Violet and her sisters, and poor Mama. Who else could they turn to? After everything that had happened, nobody favoured the Rayfields. They were on their own.

In the morning, Violet paid their bill and they did without breakfast. They repacked their bags, leaving a few odds and ends behind to lighten the load. They tried to clean the stains from their clothes with some fresh water, but it did little for the smell.

'I wish we had some lavender,' Eleanor said.

'And soap,' Violet added, putting on her slippers for the walk.

Eleanor caught Dickens and pushed him back, protesting, into the basket.

'We could leave him behind,' Violet said tentatively.

'No, absolutely not. I know he's an extra burden, but when Mama first fell ill, she made me promise I'd look after him.' A tear trickled down Eleanor's cheek.

'Look, now you've started me off.' Violet blew her nose. 'You carry the cat. I'll take the rest.'

They trudged up Dover Hill to Capel-le-Ferne, turning off the turnpike road to walk along the top of the cliffs: Abbot's Cliff then Round Down Cliff, where they paused to watch the samphire gatherers taking their lives into their hands, climbing down the cliff face from ropes attached to iron bars lodged in the rock.

'I don't like it up here,' Eleanor said with a shiver, as they passed one of the gun emplacements left over from Napoleon's time. 'It reminds me of Pa.'

'The good times and the bad,' Violet said.

'And Mama.'

'I know.' She took a deep breath of fresh air as a train belched smoke from the railway line which ran on the chalk bank hundreds of feet below. In the distance, past the coastguard station, she could see Dover. They were going home, but to what? Violet wished she could write to Ottilie to ask her her opinion about what they should do, but she didn't know where she and John lived, and Ottilie couldn't send word to her and Eleanor without a forwarding address.

'Where shall we stay tonight? The Lord Warden or the Dover Hotel?' Eleanor said.

'We can't—'

'I know. I'm teasing, but seriously, Violet, I don't like the idea of sleeping on the street after the other night.' She sniffed at her sleeve. 'We stink to high heaven.'

'We'll see if we can find a room, so that we can leave Dickens behind while we look for work.' Violet felt guilty – she couldn't protect her sister from the real world, for that was what it was. She could see that now. The Rayfields had been living on a cloud, a frail construction of their imagination which had evaporated bit by bit with each misfortune they had suffered. She and Eleanor had tumbled to the ground where they had landed, bruised and battered, yet still alive.

'Do you think the Chittendens would take pity on us? Or Mrs Pryor?' Eleanor said. 'I think I could be a maid for them, as long as I didn't have to empty their pisspots and launder their clothes.'

'Whoever you work for, you'll have to do as you're bid.'

'I could apply to be a governess or work in a shop.'

'You'd need a character reference for that.'

'I could ask Aunt Felicity …'

Violet gave a dry laugh. 'I don't think so – we've burned our bridges with her.'

'What will you do? Nobody will employ you now you're with child.'

'I know – I've been thinking about little else. How are we going to support ourselves, and an infant?' Her worst fear was that they would end up in the Dover Union with the wretched and insane.

They went down towards the Western Docks and made their way into the Pier district, a maze of streets and alleyways where the houses and inns were crammed together, as if they were fighting for space. It wasn't the Dover she recognised, not the grand mansions and crescents, and the sweeping promenade in front of the white cliffs. There were slopsellers, selling clothing and bedding for sailors and workmen; a herbal shop with grimy glass bottles in the window; a pawnbroker. Street sellers accosted them, trying to sell their wares, from candles to salted cod.

They found the address, from an advertisement in a corner shop window, of a 'respectable' landlady who had rooms for rent. Continuing through the narrow streets where the drains were overflowing with stinking black liquid, and men in rags and boots with holes sat on their doorsteps, chewing baccy and smoking pipes, they went to look for it. On their way, a child came running out of one of the houses, shouting and screaming.

'Hey, what's wrong?' Violet caught hold of him as he came running headlong into her, but she let go quickly: he was an urchin with one eye half closed, snot pouring from his nostrils and his hair … crawling with lice.

'It's Ma. She 'it me again.'

'Norman, come here.' A young woman appeared, wearing a filthy apron. 'What do you think you're doing?'

'He says he's been hurt,' Violet said.

'An' so 'e 'as! I've given 'im a good 'idin' for gettin' up to no good, but don't you go tellin' me 'ow I should treat my son.' She had just two blackened stumps for teeth. 'What are the likes of you doing 'ere anyway? You don't belong around 'ere.'

Violet felt Eleanor's hand on her arm.

'Leave it,' she said, and they walked on. 'Let's find somewhere to put our heads down. I'm worn out.'

They called at the address they'd found, but the rooms had already been let. The landlady sent them to another lodging house where her friend, Mrs Chapman, had space available, thanks to one of her tenants having dropped dead from an apopleptic fit the day before. They found Mrs Chapman sitting in a chair outside her home, a four-storey building with several windows boarded over, and the drainpipes hanging off. She looked rather regal, though, Violet thought, waving them across to her as if she was the Queen on her throne.

'Good morning. We've been told that you have a room available – please can you tell me how much it is?' Violet said.

'Don't you want to see it first, ducky? I don't think it's what you're used to.' She smiled kindly. Her clothes were not à la mode – she wore a cape-jacket, a bell-shaped skirt and pins in her hair.

'We don't mind what kind of room it is, as long as it's clean and furnished.'

'Well, I pride myself on keeping a tight ship. Come on in, ladies.'

'What about the cat?' Eleanor said.

'I don't normally accept animals – they don't make good tenants, but this one can earn its keep. It's a good mouser?'

'Oh yes, the best,' Eleanor said, and Violet looked at her. The spoiled Dickens had never caught a mouse in his life. 'He'll keep the rats at bay.'

'That makes him useful – we are often racksened with vermin.'

It wasn't a good advertisement for the landlady's premises, Violet mused as they followed Mrs Chapman into the house, and down a dark corridor all the way to the back, where she opened the door at the end into a yard.

'The privy's down there.' She pointed along a muddy path to an old shed. Violet could smell it from where they were standing, and she began to doubt Mrs Chapman's assertions of cleanliness. She wasn't very clean herself, wearing a grubby lace cap and dirty apron. Her dress appeared to have been repaired many times, patched with different materials and patterns.

'The cat can have the run of the garden. Oh, you mustn't mock my illusions of grandeur, but this is my kingdom, my own little empire. When you've worked your way up from nothin' to this, it's a miracle indeed.' She turned and unlocked the adjacent door. 'This is the room. It's nothin' special, but it fulfils your basic requirements: a bed with a mattress – so it's stuffed with straw, not horsehair, but it's perfectly adequate; blankets in the chest over there; a mirror, rather foxed, I'm afraid; one stickback chair. The previous tenant burned the other in the grate, something that is expressly forbidden, according to the rules of this house. The rest of the regulations are on the back of the door.' She eyed them curiously. 'Where 'ave you come from?'

'It's a long story—' Eleanor began.

'And one which we prefer to keep to ourselves,' Violet said. 'How much is the room?'

'Three shillin's a week, paid in advance. Take it or leave it.'

That was close to all they had.

'You won't find anything cheaper.'

'Then we will take it, thank you.'

The landlady held out her palm and Violet counted out the money.

'Why did you silence me?' Eleanor asked later. 'I was playing on her sense of pity – I hoped she might offer us a little charity.'

'She's a businesswoman. Eleanor, do poor people really eat and sleep, and wash in the same room? And where do they receive visitors?' Violet felt claustrophobic as she sat on the edge of the bed, watching a fly struggling to escape from the sticky grasp of a spider's web. The more it fought, the more tangled it became, until eventually, it gave up and fell still. She couldn't be like that fly, she decided. Poverty was like a spider preying on the weak, and she wouldn't let herself and Eleanor be caught up in its web.

But they had no money, only their wits to fall back on.

During the week when April turned into May, they discovered that they were far from being the only tenants. The house had a cellar, coal store and kitchen on the first floor, a living room and bedroom on the second, and a total of four bedrooms on the remaining two floors. There were families in each of the four bedrooms, and a husband and wife lodging in the cellar. Eleanor had spoken to the wife who'd told her that her husband had fallen on hard times when the oil mills in Limekiln Street had burned down some years before. Even though the mills had been rebuilt, he hadn't got his job back and now he worked as a bone gatherer, scratching through the ashes and dirt for a living.

'What can we do for work?' Eleanor asked when they were sipping at mint tea and eating a slice of bread at breakfast. 'I've considered every possible occupation. I could be an authoress, but I don't think there's any call for books around here. I could be a mush-faker, but I don't know how to repair umbrellas. Oh look, there's Dickens.'

The cat came leaping up through the open window with something hanging from his mouth.

'He's got one – he's caught a mouse!' she exclaimed.

'He must have been hungry,' Violet said as he landed on the floor, crouched and ate it, leaving just the tail on the rug.

'Ugh, you'll have to pick that up.'

'So you couldn't be a street-sweeper, then,' Violet said, amused. 'You'd have to clear up far worse.'

'It isn't funny. We have to find work, or we'll starve to death.'

'I know. It's no laughing matter.' Violet had been sick two days in a row, and confined to their room, while Eleanor had gone out looking for employment. 'I have a plan. As soon as I'm well again, I'm going to offer my services as an embroideress.'

'How, when we have no linen, or thread? And who will buy your work?'

'I haven't worked out the details yet, but there's plenty of demand. We can hawk the finished pieces door to door, or I can apply to become an outworker.'

'We need money to buy supplies for samples.' Eleanor got up and put up her hair.

'We'll have to be prepared to do anything ... well, not quite anything,' Violet added, thinking of the woman next door who entertained any number of men for financial reward.

'I'll go out again. Wish me luck. Perhaps today will be my day.'

Violet watched her sister go. The end of the week was fast approaching, black Monday when Mrs Chapman would come to collect the rent or turn them out on their ear. She lay down on the bed, feeling useless and hungry, listening to the drawn-out, wracking coughs from the children in the room above and a baby's feeble wail. If only she could afford a needle and silk, she could sew her way to a better life.

She blamed her father and Arvin for their situation. Mr Brooke had been a cad, a conman and a common thief – by his actions he had stolen everything from her, everything except her self-respect. He'd seen an opportunity and taken it with both hands. Knowing that her memories would destroy her if she kept returning to them, she tried to dismiss them, praying instead that Eleanor would find work, but at the end of the day, she returned empty-handed.

As they ate the last crust of bread, Violet wondered if their torment would ever end.

She fell to her knees that night and prayed for anything that might help them. Anything would do. She wasn't asking for much, only a thimbleful of hope.

Chapter Twenty

A Thimbleful of Hope

Violet stayed in bed the next morning, too weak from hunger to move, while Eleanor stirred and dragged herself up. The bedclothes were warm and damp with perspiration and the room smelled of dirty laundry, making her yearn for the fresh, sharp scent of the sea.

'Where are you going?'

'Out,' Eleanor said. 'We have no food.'

'What are you going to do?'

She shrugged. 'I'll beg if I have to. You need to eat.'

'I can't bear the thought that we've been brought this low,' Violet said, her voice breaking. 'I've failed you, my poor sister.'

'Don't think like that,' Eleanor scolded. 'I chose to come with you, not stay with Aunt Felicity and Jane.' She put on her dress and left her hair unkempt. 'Will I do?'

'Please don't do this. What will I do when Mrs Chapman comes for the rent?'

'Pack our belongings, bring Dickens and wait for me – we'll meet on Limekiln Street. I'll see you later.' Eleanor leaned down and kissed Violet's cheek.

'Take care,' Violet whispered.

The dreaded knock came at midday. With her heart in the pit of her stomach, Violet went to unbolt the door.

'Mrs Chapman,' she began. 'Oh, it's you.'

'Of course it's me.' Eleanor was grinning from ear to ear.

'You have good news?' Violet hardly dared hope.

'The best. Look who I've found ...' Eleanor showed her companion into the room. 'I ran into her in the street.'

'May! How wonderful to see you, but you find us in straitened circumstances.'

'I've been searchin' for you 'igh and low. Mr Wilson gave me your address in Can'erbury, but when I called, your aunt pretended she didn't know who I were.'

'I'm sorry to have given you the runaround,' Violet said, embarrassed at the state of her dress. 'I'm afraid we have no work for you. We're just about to lose the roof over our heads.'

'I'm not expecting you to give me a place.' May smiled. 'No, I 'ave something to your advantage. When Mr Wilson spotted the cart outside the 'ouse, 'e knew the bailiffs 'ad arrived – 'e'd been expectin' it for some time, to be honest. Anyway, 'e thought it wa'n't fair that you were left with nothin' so he put them off while I grabbed what valuables I could and climbed out of the window at the back ...'

'How did you manage that?'

'I've done it before, years ago when I first worked for the Rayfields. The rules were that you couldn't 'ave followers, but I did 'ave one for a while ... I used to see 'im sometimes.'

'May, you are a dark horse,' Eleanor said.

'I didn't do it more than three or four times. Cook found out and read me the riot act – she said the family 'ad been good to me, and I shouldn't break the rules, or I'd lose my place. 'e weren't up to much anyway.' She beamed.

'You don't know that Mama is dead,' Eleanor said. 'Our aunt wouldn't have told you.'

'I'm sorry about that, but I can only think that it was a blessed release for all of you.' May went back into the corridor and returned, shoving a battered pram in front of her. It was quite a fancy pram, consisting of a wicker basket on top of a frame, an elaborately curved handle and four wheels, the front ones smaller than the rear, like a carriage. 'I can't tell you 'ow relieved I am to 'ave found you – I've bin so worried that I was going to get caught out and accused of thievin'.' She pulled off the shawl that was covering the pram's contents.

'Is that my sewing box?' Violet exclaimed, peering in. She was overjoyed, having expected never to see it again.

May began to divest herself of some of her clothing – her cloak and bonnet, her blouse and her socks, which smelled of mouse and strong cheese. She shook the contents of her socks out on to the table, revealing a string of pearls and a ring. There were pieces of jewellery tucked into the hems and pockets, and inside her bonnet.

'There you are. It's all yours.' She slid it across the table. 'Safely restored to its rightful owners, the Misses Rayfield.'

'May, I think you have saved our lives,' Eleanor said.

'Do you remember when Ottilie wore this pendant to the ball?' Violet murmured, picking it up and turning it over, wishing that she could spend time with her elder sister. She missed her. 'And here's the wedding ring Arvin gave me. It's a shame, but we're going to have to let everything go.'

'You can pawn them,' May said, putting her blouse back on and fastening the buttons. 'You don't 'ave to sell what's rightfully yours.'

It wasn't theirs, Violet recalled. If May and Wilson hadn't had the presence of mind to take the jewellery, it would have been sold to pay their father's debts.

'Miss Rayfield – oh, you 'ave company,' Mrs Chapman said from behind them.

May quickly scooped the jewellery into her bonnet.

'I've come for the rent.'

'I haven't got it,' Violet said, 'but I'll have the money by the end of the day.'

'That's no use to me. I've already got new tenants lined up.'

'Please have some compassion ...'

'If I 'ad compassion, I'd be standing in your shoes. I don't want to be penniless, thank you very much. Pack your bags, take your cat and push off.'

'I'll pay the rent for another week,' May offered.

'I can't let you do that,' Violet said.

'I have a bit put by – all I ask is that I can sleep on the floor for a few nights.'

'Well, I don't care who stays 'ere, as long as I get my money,' Mrs Chapman said impatiently. Feeling faint, Violet swayed as May handed over the three shillings from her pocket.

'My sister isn't well.' Eleanor caught her and helped her to the bed.

'When did she last eat?' May asked.

'Yesterday. I've been out every day to look for work, and today, I tried begging for food, but I've had no luck.'

'Here, Eleanor. Take these coins and fetch us some bread, beef and stout,' May said. 'Don't be long.'

Mrs Chapman left them to go and harass some of her other lodgers, and presently Eleanor returned with the shopping. As they golloped the food – as May described it – Dickens mewed and jumped up on to May's lap, swiping at her hands in a vain attempt to steal a morsel of beef. In the end, Eleanor dropped a small piece on the floor. The cat leapt after it, pounced and carried it away.

'Do you feel better now?' May asked. Violet nodded as she went on, 'You're with child. It's all right – I've known for ages.'

'I'm sorry for not telling you the truth – I wanted to keep it to myself for as long as possible, but the secret's out now. Eleanor knows.'

'Have you thought about what you're going to do?'

'I've thought of little else, and I keep coming back to the same conclusion.'

'Which is?'

'To get back to my embroidery. It's the only way I can see us making an income.'

'It's no use you creating your beautiful designs and hoping somebody will buy them,' Eleanor said, somewhat scornfully.

'I know that. No, we'll only sew pieces to order. I wonder what is in most demand?'

'Gold work for uniforms, I should think,' May said.

'Ladies always want fine white work for christening gowns and household linens,' Eleanor added.

'We can try the dressmakers as well,' Violet said, remembering her ballgown. 'They're bound to have customers looking for bespoke patterns.'

'You're right. Oh, this is very exciting – my 'eart is pounding like a steam engine! To think that I won't 'ave to spend the rest of my life on my knees, blacking grates and scrubbing floors.'

'May, I think you're running before you can walk.'

'Not at all. We'll still have to work from dawn to dusk, but we'll be doing it for ourselves.' Her eyes were shining. 'This will be my first chance at independence, not being reliant on a master or mistress, but of course, you'll be in charge, Violet.'

'Thank you,' she said. 'However, I expect to divide any profit equally between the three of us.'

'And we'll share the loss,' Eleanor piped up. 'I'm sorry to stop you in your tracks, but we will have expenses.'

'We have no choice but to give it a try,' Violet said. 'I'm willing if you are.'

'We have the benefit of Pa's experience,' Eleanor said wryly. 'He gave us quite an education in how not to run one's business affairs.'

They drank a toast in stout.

'To a monsterful future,' May said. 'Where shall we start?

'At the beginning,' Eleanor said, 'like a book.'

'We'll need somebody to box the orders, deliver them and do the accounts. The workshop will need to be organised, supplies of thread and material bought in ...' Violet could hardly believe her own words. Was it possible? She felt a frisson of fear laced with anticipation. She hadn't been brought up to run her own business, but to marry and live like a pet kitten supported by a husband.

Her confidence had taken many blows in the recent past. Had she enough faith in herself to see it through?

'We'll stay here for the rest of this week while we get ourselves organised,' she said.

'I don't think we'll be able to work from here,' Eleanor said doubtfully. 'It's too dirty and too small for a workshop – there's barely room to swing a cat.'

'You can look for rooms that would be more suitable, but not too expensive,' Violet said.

'That woman – Mrs Chapman – is a twink,' May said. 'I've met 'er kind before, shrewish, grasping creatures. We don't want to be givin' 'er our 'ard-earned shillin's.'

'May, you can investigate suppliers of embroidery materials. I'm going to make a start on the samples, but first things first ...'

'You need to find "uncle",' May cut in. 'That's got you confused. You've never 'ad to go to a pawnbroker before in your life, 'ave you?'

'Have you?' Violet asked.

'How do you think I've survived this far? My ma used to send me off to see "uncle" almost every week. My pa – he weren't good at managing 'is money in the normal way. On payday, he'd go and redeem his belongings and spend what was left of his wages, then I'd 'ave to go and pawn his belongings again, so we 'ad enough to live on for the rest of the week. Some people were shy about it, but we were regulars. Anyway, I've been asking around, and there's a shop run by a Mr Cove, just across the alley and around the corner. Just remember to take your ticket when you're done and keep it safe.'

'Thank you for the benefit of your experience,' Violet said dryly.

'Would you like me to come with you? The two of us will be more than a match for anyone who tries to rob us.'

'I think that would be wise.'

Violet and May set out with the jewellery and found Mr Cove's premises up a side street opposite a gin shop. When she saw the brooches and watches glinting through the grimy window, Violet almost changed her mind, but the door was open and a silver-haired man – she wasn't sure if he was a gentleman – called her in to the open counter while May looked on.

'There's no need to be bashful, miss.' He was a walking display of precious metals with his gold teeth, a chain around his neck and several rings on his fingers. 'Come on in ... Don't I know you?'

'We've never met,' she said curtly.

'Ah, it doesn't matter who you are – you can rely on my discretion. Everyone is welcome here from lords and ladies, to paupers and freaks. Everyone's gold is the same to me. In fact, I advance money on any kind of property from apparel to a workman's tools. Everything has a value.

Anything pledged and unredeemed after one year and seven days will be kept or sold, either privately or by public auction.'

'I wish to redeem my belongings eventually,' Violet said.

'They have sentimental value ... in that case, you will pay interest when you collect them. The rates are on the board behind me.'

She extracted the jewellery from her pockets and placed it on the counter. His eyes latched on to the sapphire necklace and her gold ring. He took the ring first and examined it with a magnifying glass held to his eye, tipping his head from side to side like an avaricious magpie.

'The hallmarks are present and correct, but don't get your hopes up. They aren't worth much, these thin bands of gold. As for the chain and pendant – the chain is of a good weight and quality, but the stone is polished glass, a common or garden object.'

'My grandmother said it was a sapphire.'

'Oh no. It doesn't have the required depth of colour and purity for that.' He named the price he was willing to pay.

She felt disappointed, but also suspicious. There was a time when she had believed that a gentleman's word was his bond, but she knew better now. She showed him the pearls and various other pieces.

'I will pawn everything but the ring and the gold necklace,' she said.

'Oh?' He looked up, surprised. 'Are you sure?'

'You don't offer me enough for them.'

'I see. You drive a hard bargain,' he said, but she knew that he was acting, even when he raised the amount he would lend against it, telling her that she was a hard woman. She wouldn't allow herself to be fooled again, not after Mr Brooke. He named a better price for the sapphire which she accepted. 'To whom shall I make out the ticket?' he asked.

'Miss Violet Rayfield,' she said.

'Miss Rayfield,' he repeated, placing emphasis on the 'miss' as he glanced towards her belly. He put down his pen and handed her a copy of his terms and conditions to sign before he counted out the money, which she put away in her purse. 'It's a pleasure to do business with you.'

She slipped Arvin's ring on to her finger.

On the way back to the room, she and May haggled with a stallholder for a pair of second-hand shoes to replace the ones Violet had ruined, then dropped in to the haberdasher's and bought a small frame and stretchers, and some coloured silks. They were ready to make a start on the samples. She opened the sewing box – her needles, chalk and scissors were still inside, resting on the velvet lining. At the bottom, she found a piece of her embroidery, a butterfly she'd made for practice before she'd sewn the train on her gown for the regatta ball, and her silver thimble. She smiled as she held it up to the light.

Violet, May and Eleanor sewed day and night to make the samples, burning tallow candles down to stubs.

They needed to show the samples to likely customers, but Violet wasn't sure where to start. How did you contact the army? The fire brigade? Dressmakers? The suppliers of uniform for railway drivers and guards? May went out to ask around, and came back with the name and address of several contacts.

Violet dressed in the cleanest dress she had and washed her hair, adding a little beer to the rinse to give it more shine before letting it dry. Having brushed it thoroughly, she put it up, checking her appearance in the hazy reflection of the mirror.

'Aren't you worried about this?' Eleanor asked.

'Not at all,' she fibbed. 'Do you think I'm ready to impress?'

'You'll do very well.'

'I hope so – I don't think I've left anything to chance.' She touched the wedding ring on her finger, then picked up the bag of samples and the price list.

'All the best.' Eleanor hugged her. 'I'll go and pay the deposit on the rooms in Oxenden Street. May is going to help me move Dickens and our belongings with the pram. Remember not to come back to Mrs Chapman's later.'

'Oh, I'll remember all right. Why on earth would I want to come back here?' Violet smiled. 'I look forward to moving into our palace.' She only hoped that they would be able to afford it – Eleanor, May and the baby were depending on her to obtain some orders today. It wouldn't be long before the infant was born, and she was under no illusion. The more she worked now, the better, because when it came, it would fret and cry to be fed and changed, and life would never be the same again.

If she'd imagined that the dressmakers of Dover would be interested in her designs, she was wrong. They took one look at her dowdy dress and swollen belly and turned her away, and even though she flashed her wedding ring, they seemed to know that it was a front.

One of them – a Mrs Kinnaird – recognised her name when she introduced herself, gave her her card, and showed her the butterfly sample.

'The infamous Miss Violet Rayfield! I can't believe your brazenness in coming here. I dress your neighbours in Camden Crescent. There is no way I'll have anything to do with you, no matter how remarkable your work may be.'

Filled with renewed shame, Violet walked on and knocked on the door of Mr Oliver's, supplier of embroidery for the shipping trade.

'I wish to see Mr Oliver,' she said to the clerk who answered.

'Whom may I say is calling?'

'Mrs Rayfield, embroideress. I have business with him.'

'I'm sure you'd *like* to have business with him, but we have plenty of skilled outworkers already, thank you.'

'I have a small workshop and two others working for me – we make badges, epaulettes and other piecework of the finest quality,' she was saying, as the door closed in her face. Shaking her head at the clerk's rudeness, she turned and went on to the next place on her list, where a Mr Evercreech allowed her five minutes of his time.

He ushered her through his shop and into his office, where he offered her a seat to take the weight off her feet. He was older than her by at least twenty years, and when he smiled, he showed three gold teeth. She unpacked the relevant samples of their goldwork to show him. He picked them up and scrutinised them with a magnifying glass.

'These are better than I'd expected, almost too good really for my requirements. I've won a contract for railwaymen's uniforms – I need more ladies to sew the letters, the small ones on the cap bands. The way I work is to provide the raw materials for a modest price, then buy the product back from my outworkers. You are new to this?'

'It's a new venture,' she said, not wanting to reveal too much.

'What about your husband? Does he approve?' He gave her a searching look. A well-spoken married woman who was with child wouldn't be out and about trying to earn money.

'I don't need to ask his approval. Tell me what you charge for materials and the price you pay for each finished piece.'

He gave her the figures.

'If I pay that for the thread, there will be little profit in it for me and my ladies. It would behove you to reduce your prices.'

'You speak wisely, but I have children to feed …'

And an expensive taste in suits, she assumed, noticing the cut of his clothing.

She ran through the figures in her head for a second time. The margins were tiny. There was no way they could support themselves even if they sewed the letters on a thousand caps every week. Her heart was heavy. She'd thought that she was getting somewhere, but it seemed that she would have to turn his offer down.

'I'm sorry for you, Mr Evercreech. I'm going to have to take my business elsewhere. I can't afford to waste any more time.' She made to rise from the chair.

'No, Miss …'

'It's Mrs Rayfield,' she said, removing her glove to show her ring.

'Then, Mrs Rayfield, it appears that you employ some very skilled needlewomen indeed, but can they maintain this quality with volume?'

'Of course.'

'I beg to differ – how can you guarantee it?'

'Give us a month to prove ourselves. We won't let you down, I promise.'

'In that case, I'll give you a better deal, but if you fail to deliver, I'll have to let you go.'

Mr Evercreech shook her hand when she left his office.

'If you see my clerk, he'll draw up my contract with you, and set you up with instructions and materials. Make sure you get the finished goods back in a timely manner.'

She thanked him, met with the clerk, then went back out into the bright sunshine. She'd done it. She'd signed their first contract! She would return to pay for the materials and collect them in the morning. They were on their way.

Walking along Snargate Street, she passed the noisy Packet Yard which stood at the foot of the cliffs, and opposite the dock where the ships came in for repairs. She could hear the cacophony of steam engines, men shouting and blacksmiths hammering metal into shape.

Continuing along the road, she came to the bottom of the Grand Shaft, an arched passageway dug into the cliff which led up to the barracks on the Western Heights. There were people about, workers from the yard taking a break, some rough navvies, and a constable leading a drunken sailor away in handcuffs. She noticed the sentry on duty, and the railway line ahead, but she missed the sound of a galloping horse coming up behind her at full pelt, until it was almost upon her.

'Beware! Runaway 'orse!'

'Ladies, out of the way.'

When she turned, she saw the white of the horse's eye, the scarlet flare of its nostrils and the veins of its chestnut skin standing proud. It dropped one shoulder as though it was trying to avoid her, but this sent the cart behind it off to one side. Its wheels were heading straight for her, and she knew she couldn't get away in time.

Just as the wheel touched her arm, something – someone – snatched her away, pulling her off balance so she was falling backwards. She landed on her back, winded and looking up at the sky, a pair of arms around her waist, hands on her belly and the sound of the horse's hooves disappearing into the distance.

Slowly, she sat up.

'Are you all right, missus?'

She turned as her saviour moved away and stood up, brushing the dust from his trousers and waistcoat.

'William?' she breathed. 'Is it really you?'

'Violet? I've been looking out for you. I didn't know where you'd gone.' He took her hand and helped her up. 'Are you all right? Do you need a doctor?'

'I'm fine,' she said quietly. She was aching all over. She would live, but what about the child growing inside her? Having longed to see William again, she was suddenly overwhelmed with mortification. 'I'm sorry,' she muttered, and she picked up her skirts and fled.

'Violet,' he called after her, but she kept moving, half running, half walking, until she reached the warren of alleyways in the Pier district. Catching her breath, she found her way to Oxenden Street where she met Eleanor and May at their new lodgings.

'What happened to you?' Eleanor said, letting her in.

'It's been a day of mixed fortunes,' she said, going straight to sit down on one of the chairs in the ground-floor room.

'You're shaking,' May observed. 'Let me put the kettle on.'

'Let me tell you my news first. I'm a little disturbed because I was almost run over by a bolting horse, but I'm well, apart from a few bruises.'

'What about work? Did you find any?' Eleanor asked.

'I have a contract.'

'Oh, Violet, that's wonderful,' May said.

'I shouldn't get too excited – it's only for sewing the letters on railwaymen's caps.'

'That'll do,' May said. 'When do we start?'

'Tomorrow.' Violet gazed around the room, taking in the cracked window, the soot in the grate and the dust on the floor. 'In the meantime, we'd better get this place into shape.'

When she had recovered her composure, Eleanor showed her around. As well as the room they would use as a workshop, they had a kitchen, an outside privy in the small backyard where Dickens was sunning himself, and a room upstairs.

'What do you think?' Eleanor said.

'It has potential,' Violet said guardedly.

'It isn't quite what we're used to, is it?'

'It isn't, but we'll soon make it home. We'll know we're back on our feet when we can buy furniture at Flashman's.'

They had sheets, but no other linen for the bed – a double bed with a plank base and a thin mattress. May decided she would sleep on the settle in the kitchen.

Eleanor took charge of the dusting and removed the creepy crawlies which emerged from the cracks in the walls and wainscoting. May swept the ashes out of the fireplace, and blackened, brushed and polished the grate. She sprinkled the floor with tea leaves to settle the dust and make it smell better. Violet sorted through the cutlery and crockery that had been left behind by previous tenants. The plates were chipped and the knives blunt, but they would do.

Later, she and May went out to buy hot meat and vegetable stew for supper, bread and eggs for breakfast, and plenty of candles, along with paper and ink for Eleanor to write to their aunt to give her their address and ask if she had received any letters from Ottilie. Having dined, there wasn't much left to do except retire to bed. In the morning, they were woken early by the knocker-upper with his peashooter, aiming dried peas at the upstairs window which they'd left half-open overnight.

Violet looked out.

'What do you think you're doing, sir?' she called down to him.

'This is on my round.' He frowned briefly, then grinned. "As Mr Clarke got a lady friend? Well, I never.'

'Mr Clarke doesn't live here any more.'

"E owes me money.'

'He isn't here!' Violet said quickly.

'Are you sure 'e hasn't put you up to this?'

'Quite sure. Please go away and leave us alone. We won't be requiring your services, thank you.'

'You're a polite one, quite the young lady with your pleases and thank yous.'

'Good day, sir,' she said, closing the window.

Violet couldn't get back to sleep, so she went downstairs into the workshop to plan where they would keep the needles and threads, and the finished orders, and make a list of the other items they needed, such as a ledger for their records, and a book for invoices and receipts. They would need an area where they could welcome callers who might drop by to offer them commissions, and boxes in which to pack away their finished work. She felt a thrill of excitement and anticipation as she pictured the three of them, happily sewing and talking together, as the orders – and the money– came flooding in.

None of them would be depending on the whims of a father or husband to support them. She couldn't wait to get started.

Later that morning, Violet took Eleanor with her to Mr Evercreech's, where she handed over most of what was left of the money from the pawnshop in return for the materials they needed for their first week in business.

Life as an embroideress wasn't easy, though. By the end of each fourteen-hour day, Violet's eyes were stinging, her fingers aching, and her back was so painful that she could hardly move.

They lived on Eleanor's egg curry, onion soup and the cheapest cuts of meat, and May melted down the candle stubs to make new ones.

The long days were brightened by the arrival of a letter from Ottilie.

Dear Violet and Eleanor,

I hope this letter finds you well and happy in Dover. I can't tell you how relieved I was to hear back from Aunt Felicity who sent me your address. Although it had been coming for a long time, the news of our poor mother's passing was still a shock to me. I pray that you will forgive me for not being there with you.

I was wondering if I would ever find you again, having corresponded with Mrs Pryor, our former neighbour, who took great delight in writing about how she last saw you and Mama outside the house at Camden Crescent, and how she had no idea where you went after that. I wrote to Mrs Chittenden, but she sent my letter back, return to sender. It pains me deeply that she refuses to have anything to do with us.

John and I are living in Woolwich in a small but handsome house which suits us very well. I couldn't have a better, more loving husband. He has made some excellent contacts while setting up his agency and everything is looking rosy.

I'm pleased to hear about your plans for a workshop and wish you and May every success. Mama and Pa would have been very proud of you. Embroidery is a very respectable way to make a living.

You are welcome to visit at any time. Let me know when you can come, or when I can come to you. I can't wait to see you.

Your loving sister,
Ottilie
P.S. Jane is engaged to be married, not only a great joy
to her, but a relief to our aunt, I suspect.

Eleanor wanted to go straight to London, and was upset
when Violet advised that they should write back, saying
they would wait a while. They couldn't afford to take a
couple of days off while they were establishing themselves,
and they couldn't expect Ottilie to stay in their rented
accommodation – there just wasn't the room. At least,
that's what Violet told Eleanor. She didn't want Ottilie to
see how they were living. She didn't want to worry her.

All the while, Violet's child was growing so big inside
her that she had to let out one of her dresses at the waist.
But even though it was a struggle, she didn't yearn for
the long, lonely days that she'd spent in the house at East
Cliff, waiting for Arvin's return from his trips to France.

Chapter Twenty-One

Shipshape and Bristol Fashion

The month of June came and went, and Violet began to understand her father a little better. She had assumed that he'd taken risks out of greed, but she could see that it was more likely that he'd done it out of a sense of insecurity. Having run the workshop for a few weeks now, she had experienced the cold sweats and panic, worrying that their orders would dry up and she wouldn't have enough income to support the three of them, and the cat.

They fulfilled their orders every week, but how were they going to improve their lives by sewing letters on caps? It was tedious, repetitive work for a wage on which they could barely survive and, even though she went out one day a week to look for other, more lucrative commissions, she failed to convince anyone else to take them on.

July was ushered in with long, sunny days and oppressively hot nights when Violet would dream of the accident: the darkness, the lights and the fog, and the man she'd grown fond of, who had claimed to love her, falling into the sea, then William trying to save him before he was engulfed by the black swell. She would wake, the bedsheets damp with perspiration, remembering the way that Arvin had betrayed her.

He had taken her to bed and made her his, and then ruined her, but in spite of everything she had gone through since, he hadn't broken her spirit.

One morning, she was woken by pains dragging through her loins and thighs. Her belly ached and she wasn't hungry, but she forced herself to sip at some tea and take some bread soaked in milk. She couldn't afford to rest when there were orders to be fulfilled – Mr Evercreech would be waiting. Downstairs in the workshop, she sat down and picked up her needle and thread.

May sat down beside her. 'How are you feeling today?'

'I'm fine,' she said irritably.

'You're all wittery.' May smiled. 'I expect you're tired of people asking you.'

'You haven't eaten much,' Eleanor said, joining them.

May gave her a knowing look. 'That's because she's about to drop. Look at the size of 'er. And she can barely sit still for the pains. I know what I'm talking about – a friend of mine had three littl'uns: with the first one she almost died from the pain, the second she pushed out and the third popped out like a cork.'

'Oh May, we don't want to hear the details.' Eleanor winced.

'I don't see why you're so sensitive about childbirth when you write of monsters and murder,' May said. 'It's the natural lot of womenfolk to suffer. Look at our poor queen – she's borne nine children.'

Violet stared at the letters she was supposed to be working on. A pain caught her in its tightening grip, and her needle fell to the floor.

'It will be spoiled,' she gasped, leaning down for it, but she couldn't reach with the pain stabbing into her stomach. Forcing herself to straighten and stand up, she moved to the workbench where the completed orders were boxed ready for delivery, and the raw materials of their trade were arranged ready for use. Violet gripped the edge with both hands.

'The babe is coming and there's nothing you can do to stop it – it will be 'ere by this time tomorrow,' May observed, moving up to the bench. 'If it isn't, we'll be in trouble.'

Violet felt May's hands massaging her back, as a rush of wetness drained from her body.

'Let's get you back to bed. Help me, Eleanor. Don't just stand there gawping.'

'I need to finish—' Violet looked towards the embroidery that Eleanor had picked up from the floor and placed on her chair. 'If these orders aren't completed in time, we won't be paid.' She groaned as another wave of pain took over.

'I'll go and fetch a doctor,' she heard Eleanor say.

As May said there was no need for one, Violet found herself being ushered up to the room she shared with her sister. She could barely crawl up the stairs and fall on to the bed. The pain! Other women had warned her about its intensity, but she hadn't believed them. She couldn't have imagined how terrible it was, as if she was being crushed through her middle by a road roller.

As her labour progressed, she began to lose track of time and who she was.

She drifted in and out of consciousness as the pains gradually squeezed the life from her. It grew dark, and then light again.

'We have to send for the doctor.' She heard Eleanor's quavering voice. 'Even then, I'm afraid we have left it too late.'

'If you can't say anything useful, hold your tongue,' May said. 'The babe is almost 'ere now. You must use the pain to bring it into the world. Shake yourself, Violet, or you will both die.'

She closed her eyes and summoned the little strength she had left. As the next pain began to build, she took a breath.

'That's good.' May shouted into her ear, sending a tremor through her weary body. 'Now push the babe out. Push for all you are worth. 'Arder! Ah, there's the 'ead. Rest for a moment. Rest until the next pain comes and use it to push again.'

'I can't,' she whimpered, limp with exhaustion.

'You must,' Eleanor hissed. 'One more. Squeeze my hand and push.'

And as though from a great distance, she heard Eleanor shout in triumph.

'It's born. It is done. A boy. He isn't crying, May. Why is he so quiet and still?'

Violet didn't hear any more, slipping away into delirium: sometimes sleeping, sometimes dreaming. She was burning up: she was frozen. She was heading for the grave ... like Arvin and her father, and poor Mama.

'May the Lord save her soul,' she heard somebody say, and just as she began to fade again, a baby cried. It was the thin, plaintive wail of a helpless creature calling out for its mother's love.

She would not die, she told herself. How could she have come this far only to give up? She had a child who needed her. She could hear him. Opening her eyes, she saw her sister at her bedside, like an angel with a halo of light around her head, holding a bundle of white swaddling in her arms.

She opened her mouth to speak, but no words came out.

'Violet, what are you trying to say? Oh, my dear sister. You have come back to us. It's a miracle.'

'The baby?' Violet murmured.

'He's as well as can be expected, considering the start he's had. Look at him, the poor little mite.' Eleanor leaned down and showed him to her. He was pale and scrawny, not round and plump like other babies she had seen before. All her fears of not wanting him were washed away by an overwhelming rush of maternal love. He looked so vulnerable and innocent that all she wanted to do was hold him in her arms.

'You look as if the vampires have dined well recently,' Eleanor said. 'I'll fetch you some broth – you need to get your strength back so you can feed him. He will do better on his mother's milk than pap and goat's milk. Come on, dear Joe, let's put you back in your crib. I'm afraid your mama might drop you – she's been in a faint for two days.'

'Joe? Did you say he is called Joe?'

'I hope you don't mind – we took the liberty of giving him a name. We can change it if you don't like it …'

'No, it's a lovely name.' Violet was at a loss, not knowing which way to turn, yearning to hold her tiny son, yet afraid of hurting him because he looked so delicate. She pulled herself up and pushed the coverlet aside. 'How am I going to cope?' she murmured. 'How can I look after him when there are orders to be met?'

'I'm going to help you,' Eleanor said. 'I owe you a great debt, and this is my way of repaying it. I'm going to work through the night, so that you can take a day or two to recover – you're no good to anyone if you make yourself ill again.'

Violet gave in gracefully.

'I'll fetch you something to eat and drink, then I'll show you how to bathe and dress the little one.'

Eleanor returned with beef broth and bread, then while Violet was eating, came back again with a ewer of warm water which she poured into the basin on the washstand.

'Let me show you what to do – May has been giving me the benefit of her experience.'

'I'm sure she has,' Violet said wryly. 'She's a great one for giving instructions.'

'You must be kind to her,' Eleanor chided. 'She's been a great friend to us.'

'I know. I don't know what we'd have done without her.'

'What are you waiting for? Bring Joe over here.'

'I can't,' she stammered. 'I don't know how to pick him up.'

'You can do it.' Eleanor chuckled as the baby sniffled from the middle drawer of the oak chest where she'd left him for safety. 'Go on.'

Violet peered down at where he was peeking out from under his blanket, his button nose beaded with perspiration.

'I wonder if he's too hot,' she said tentatively.

'Carry him over to the bed – you can undress him.'

She bent down and lifted him up, uncertain how to hold him. He gazed into her eyes and frowned, and from that minute she knew she would do anything for him.

'Hello, my handsome boy,' she murmured, tears of joy trickling down her cheeks. 'I'm your mama.' Carefully, she carried him to the bed where she put him down on his back. 'I wish Ottilie was here to see him.'

'She would adore him,' Eleanor said. 'I hope all is well with her and John. I miss her.'

'So do I. She's in my thoughts every day.'

'I'll write to her and let her know about Joe. I'll invite her to stay as you won't want to travel with a newborn.'

'I'd rather not invite her here just yet. Wait until we are more settled.'

'We are settled. This is our home.' Eleanor raised one eyebrow. 'Are you ashamed of it? Ottilie will take us as she finds us – you know that.'

Violet sighed. 'You're right.'

'I will ask her to pay us a visit.'

Violet didn't argue as Eleanor changed the subject.

'May says one must bathe an infant every day. And you must sing to drown out his cries and teach him to get used to it. According to her, babies should be toughened up, but I don't believe that, do you?'

Violet glanced across to where Eleanor was checking the temperature of the water with her elbow. She didn't believe it either. Having unwrapped the shawl that Eleanor had put round him, she unfastened the binder around his middle. A shilling fell clattering to the floor.

'May says that applying a coin to where the cord was cut makes for a well-shaped belly button,' Eleanor explained. 'I haven't put him in a nappy yet this morning. Now you must pick him up and bring him over here.'

Violet carried him to the washstand and lowered him into the basin, where he wailed and wriggled, then screamed, his face turning dark purple like a ripe damson.

'He's getting stronger,' Eleanor said in awe. 'May wasn't sure he'd make it this far. Oh, Violet ...' She burst into tears. 'There were times when we didn't think either of you would survive. All we could do was pray.'

Touched beyond measure, Violet didn't know what to say.

Joe's crying settled to a whimper, his belly hollowing in and out beneath his ribcage. She rinsed his scant brown hair, and his tiny hands and feet, then picked him up, wrapping him in a soft cloth which her sister gave her to dry him with. Once she was happy that he was dry all over, she placed him back on the bed.

Eleanor passed her a pot of what looked like lard. She sniffed it. It *was* lard.

'What do I do with that?'

'It's nappy cream – smear that on his bum.'

'Eleanor!' she exclaimed, shocked.

'There's no point in beating about the bush.' Eleanor laughed. 'You can't be all refined and ladylike when you're looking after a baby. Quickly, put on his nappy before he—'

'Too late,' Violet sighed. She wiped him and put on his nappy, folding it to fit as Eleanor showed her, and pinning it at his bony hips with large safety pins before putting on the cover to stop the leaks.

'I remember Mama telling me how we didn't have safety pins when we were little ones and how she worried that our nurse would stab us.' Eleanor handed her a cream flannel dress. 'This is his barracoat to go on next.'

Violet turned it inside out before she worked out how to slip it over Joe's head and pull it down to cover his feet. She tied the cotton strips at his shoulders.

Eleanor handed her a tiny cap. 'I don't think he needs his petticoat and frock – he'll roast in this weather.'

'Where did these clothes come from?'

'May and I have been doing some extra sewing in the evenings after you've gone to bed. You've been so tired, you didn't notice.'

Violet began to thank her as Joe started to cry again.

'He's hungry,' Eleanor said. 'You must feed him. May says that the more he sucks, the more milk you make.'

Violet had expected to be repulsed by the idea, but she found that there was nothing she loved more than holding her baby close and nurturing him. He was a darling.

*

316

Little Joe slept through the days and kept Violet up at night. It meant she could get on with her work, but she was exhausted. They still weren't bringing in enough money, and she had to pawn the very last of Mama's jewellery to pay the rent. To her relief, though, Ottilie declined their invitation to visit because she was indisposed. She gave no reason, only reassured them that she wasn't seriously unwell, just reluctant to travel. She asked them to visit her when they could, but Violet had to explain that they were overwhelmed with work, so she didn't have to confess that they didn't have the money for the train fare.

One morning towards the middle of August, Eleanor had boxed the latest batch of embroidery, and Violet was ready to deliver it to Mr Evercreech.

'Will you look after Joe for me?' she asked, keen to get away from the sweltering confines of the workshop for an hour or two.

'Of course. He loves his auntie.' Eleanor smiled. 'Don't be long, though.'

'You know I'd never leave him for long.'

Violet put on her bonnet and the best of her black mourning dresses before setting out with her arms full of boxes. She threaded her way through the narrow streets to the seafront where she paused to look out across the Channel where the sea was an expanse of sapphire blue and jade beneath the blazing summer sun. She couldn't help sparing a thought for William Noble. She was a fool, she knew, but she imagined she could detect his scent on the sea breeze and hear his voice in the waves as they washed back and forth across the shingle.

'Violet?' She turned on hearing her name. Was she dreaming?

'How lovely to see you, William,' she said, as he strode up to her and doffed his hat.

'Would you allow me to carry your boxes?'

'I'm very grateful for the offer, but I can manage.' She felt awkward, recalling the last time they'd met.

'I know you can – you're obviously more than capable … Here. Let me take half.' He took the top ones from her before she could protest. 'Where are we going?'

'Up to the other end of town. It's a little way from here.'

'I don't mind. I was hoping to see you again. How should I address you now?'

She frowned as they started walking along the promenade.

'What I mean is, are you … have you remarried, or anything?'

'Oh no. Do you really think I'd take a risk on marrying for a second time after what happened?'

'Maybe not,' he admitted, glancing down at her hand, making her feel shy that he'd caught her out not wearing gloves to hide her roughened skin. 'I apologise for bringing it up. I'm an idiot.'

'You can address me as "Violet",' she said, watching how he blushed. 'Plain "Violet".'

He gazed at her as if he regarded her as anything but.

'Look where you're going.' She smiled.

'I haven't seen you in such a long time. I've often thought of you.'

'That's very kind,' she said politely. Was it wrong to tell him that she'd thought of him too?

'I wasn't expecting to see you again. When you disappeared last time, I made some enquiries, but nobody knew where you'd gone. I came to the conclusion that you'd moved away, but I didn't give up hope.'

'I'm afraid that I took off in rather a hurry.'

'It doesn't matter. I understand, I think. The last thing you wanted was your name in the newspapers again, for whatever reason. I'm sorry, I shouldn't have said ...'

'It's all right.'

He smiled, and her heart turned a somersault.

Keep calm, she told herself. She had liked him before, admired him for his heroism and good sense, and now the sight of him filled her with warmth and affection, but nothing could come of it. They were from two different worlds, separate layers of society. William's fortunes were on the rise while hers were in the doldrums. She was proud of what she'd achieved, keeping her head above water by her grit and determination, but she had no expectation beyond that now. She was Miss Violet Rayfield, embroideress and unmarried mother of an illegitimate child.

'You are still in mourning?'

'For my parents, Mama especially,' she said.

'I'm sorry. I hadn't heard.'

'Are you still working at the Packet Yard?' she asked.

'Yes, I'm still there. Although I say it myself, I've worked hard and succeeded on my own merit. I acknowledge that I might have climbed the ladder more quickly if I'd accepted your father's offer, but I have my pride.'

'I admire you for not compromising your principles. I regret how my father behaved towards you.'

'You weren't to blame,' William said.

'I seem to remember you saying that you worked at the boiler-making department. What do you do there exactly?'

'I'm foreman. I order the best wrought-iron plates from Staffordshire and Yorkshire, then I direct the men to cut out the shapes from them, using the drawings given to me by the superintendent of works, and the sketches I make to guide them. The plates are moved by crane to the forge to be flanged and curved, before they're riveted together. After that, they go to the fitting department to be finished. It gives me great satisfaction when I see one of my boilers installed and working on one of the ships. But that's more than enough about me. What's in your boxes?'

'I have an embroidery workshop in Oxenden Street. Our former maid and my sister, Eleanor, work with me. These are the orders we've finished this week.' She wondered what more they could have to say. What did they have in common? 'How is your mother?' she began.

'Ah.' He looked away, but not before she caught the glistening in his eyes. 'She left this life over a month ago. It was a relief in a way because her struggles were distressing to see. I miss her – I tended to her every day.'

'What was she like?' she asked gently.

'She was the best ma in the world and I miss her terribly. I don't miss my father in quite the same way – he spent many months away at sea. I remember how Ma would dress me and my brother in our sailors' outfits when we went down to the dock to meet him. She'd scold us for shouting out loud and running too fast to greet him. Pa would swing me up in his arms and sit me on his shoulders and I would cling on tight, running my fingers through his rough whiskers, while he picked up my brother and carried him on his hip.

'He was incredibly strong and handsome, and my mother would lean up and kiss him full on the mouth without regard for anyone else who happened to be looking on.' He sighed. 'Her joy never lasted long. After a few days, Pa would start beating her – out of kindness, he used to say.'

'That's dreadful,' Violet said.

'He left her with a black eye on more than one occasion. When he went back to sea, she would cry, but as soon as he'd gone, we'd feel this great sense of relief because our mother would be young and gay again.'

'Your father was not a good man, then?'

'He was a loyal husband and father, but he was a stickler for discipline. Maybe that's what made him such an excellent master – he liked everything to be shipshape and Bristol fashion. When he was at home, my brother and I had to stand to attention beside our beds while he checked that the sheets were tucked in and there were no dirty socks left lying around. But he inspired us with his tales of brave sailors and audacious engineers, and after listening to him, I wanted to follow in Brunel's footsteps.'

'You enjoy your work?'

'I couldn't live without it. It gives me a purpose, a reason to go on. I think I can understand your father's desperation towards the end. He'd lost his business and the prestige that comes with it.'

She caught a glimpse of the sadness behind his eyes.

'We have both been through the mill,' she said.

'I have to console myself with the fact that I had my family around me for over twenty years. I have fond memories of them and I cling to the hope that one day I'll have a new family to love and cherish: a wife and children.'

As they approached Mr Evercreech's shop, she felt a pang of regret that William's new family would be nothing to do with her.

'This is where we must part. Thank you for helping me,' she said, stopping outside.

'I'd be honoured if you'd agree to meet with me again soon,' he stammered.

'I don't think it's a good idea.'

'Why? Is it because you still have feelings for Mr Brooke? I'd be grateful if you spoke frankly.'

There was something in his tone – an urgency and firmness – that made her change her mind about the wisdom of unburdening herself. She could trust him to keep her secrets.

'I have regrets, of course, and I'm still angry at him for his deception, and at myself for not seeing what he was like, but this isn't about Mr Brooke. This is about my regard for you.'

'You have little regard for me?'

'I admire you greatly, yet I'm not worthy of you. You saved my life. Hush,' she said, when he opened his mouth to speak. 'Let me finish …' There was a time when she would have added *if I may*, but not now. Never again. She would make herself completely clear. 'It is because of my regard and affection for you that I decline your suggestion of friendship. The people of Dover still see me as a fallen woman, the duped daughter of a greedy bankrupt. I have a child out of wedlock, a bastard. You see, I'm tainted. People will turn their backs on you if you are acquainted with me.'

'My true friends won't. I have my own mind. Life is precious, and I live it my way, with kindness, generosity and joy. All I'm asking for is your friendship, nothing more. What harm can there be in that?'

She scanned his face. There was no guile in his expression.

'Then you have persuaded me. I'd like us to be friends.'

'You've made me very happy.' He smiled as he handed back the boxes. 'May I call on you?'

Violet's mind raced. Where on earth would she receive him? What would he think of their cramped workshop and lodgings? How would he deal with Joe? It was all very well meeting here, just the two of them, but her life was too involved, too complicated for her to contemplate inviting William to Oxenden Street, even as a friend. When she wasn't embroidering and doing the accounts, she was nursing the baby.

'I'm sorry, I don't think that will be possible,' she said.

William looked at her beseechingly. 'The last thing I want is to make things more difficult for you, but I would simply be calling as a friend.'

'Much as I like the idea, it would not be suitable for you,' she replied. 'It's for the best, William. I am truly sorry.'

It tore her heart to shreds as she walked away. William was honest, ambitious and caring, but she couldn't see how a friendship would work. How would she have felt, falling in love with him, knowing that they had no future together? Her sorrow knew no bounds.

Chapter Twenty-Two

When it's Dark in Dover, it's Dark All the World Over

A month passed, and Violet found that she was always worrying about money, even though they were frugal with food, oil for the lamps and coal for cooking. When she'd set up the workshop, she'd envisioned creating her own designs and losing herself in embroidering items of beauty. Instead, she was stuck sewing letters and numbers, and the occasional badge for Mr Evercreech.

One morning, Joe was lying asleep in the drawer they used for a cot. They had taken it from the chest upstairs and placed it across two chairs in the workshop.

'Oh, Joe, you look so handsome.' Violet sighed from where she sat close by, as he opened his eyes and yawned. She rested her sewing in her lap.

'He's the sweetest child,' Eleanor joined in.

'One day, he'll be crawling around the workshop and then what will we do?' Violet said, smiling.

'We'll cross that bridge when we come to it,' Eleanor said. 'I wonder how Ottilie is. Perhaps she is with child and Joe will have a cousin within the next few months.'

'We'll write to her again.'

Joe began to sniffle and cry and, feeling his anguish as her own, Violet put down her embroidery, went over and picked him up. She held him close, pressing her mouth to his cheek, and he began to quieten.

'He's got you wrapped around his little finger.' Eleanor chuckled.

''E wouldn't do that,' May said, looking up from her sewing. ''E's a little cherub.'

'How are you getting on?' Violet asked her. May stopped, snipped a thread and checked her work, holding it up to the light, before laying it carefully in one of the packing boxes.

'My fingers are raw and I'm goin' boss-eyed, but don't you worry, I'll get this order finished by the end of the day if it kills me. I mustn't grumble. We must be grateful for what we 'ave. That's how I've got through, by bein' thankful for the small things. I 'ave everything I need and more 'ere in these rooms.'

'It saddens me that we have no control over our destiny,' Eleanor said. 'We're subject to the whims of men like Mr Evercreech, and the demands of the market. We do the same thing every day.'

'Except on Sundays,' Violet pointed out. She looked forward to their days of rest when they went for long walks along the cliffs, pushing Joe in the pram, which had seen better days.

Eleanor went to answer a knock at the door.

'Who's that?' May said. 'We don't usually receive visitors.'

'Oh, do come in,' Violet heard her sister say, and her heart sank, because the workshop was a mess with boxes and clutter everywhere, and Joe was in her arms so she couldn't do anything about it. She slid a box under the table with her foot and Dickens shot out with a yowl.

''Ere, let me take Joe for you,' May offered.

Reluctantly, Violet handed him over, and turned to see Eleanor showing a woman through to greet her.

'Good morning. My name is Mrs Kinnaird,' she said.

She was about forty years old and bore an air of unmistakable superiority. She seemed familiar, Violet thought, and then she remembered that she was one of the dressmakers who'd turned her away when she'd first started looking for business. She had skin like porcelain, a straight back and small waist, and was the perfect mannequin for the dresses that her seamstresses sewed in the room at the back of her shop.

'Good morning,' Violet responded stiffly, noticing how her bonnet was adorned with lilac beads which matched those on her dress.

'I have something for you,' Mrs Kinnaird said, looking through a purple cloth bag embroidered with silver thread. She pulled out a folded slip of material and handed it to Violet.

'Oh, it's my butterfly. Thank you for returning it.'

'You left it behind and I put it in a drawer where I keep various designs and samples for safekeeping. I'd forgotten about it, but when one of my ladies saw it, she said that she must have a gown made with butterflies exactly like this one flying up from the hem. I've been in touch with my usual embroideresses, but none of them can produce sewing of this quality. It's so very fine ...'

Violet smiled to herself, delighted that someone had appreciated her art.

'Would you accept this commission?' Mrs Kinnaird went on. 'My seamstresses will make the gown while you create an overlay of butterflies.'

Violet hesitated. They had Mr Evercreech's orders which kept them busy, and she wasn't sure about working for Mrs Kinnaird after the way she'd treated her.

'It will be very lucrative. My customer will pay whatever it costs.'

'How lucrative?' Violet asked, tempted not so much by the money, but by the chance to do something different, a job she would enjoy.

Mrs Kinnaird named a price, and Violet remembered a time when Mama wouldn't have thought twice about paying the same for a gown for herself or her daughters. It seemed outrageous now – she, May and Eleanor would be lucky to make that in a month. How could she refuse?

'This will do wonders for your business,' Mrs Kinnaird said. 'Your reputation will spread by word of mouth.'

As it had before, Violet recollected dryly. She glanced towards the door into the kitchen where May was singing to Joe. If she took this on, she would be able to provide more for her son: toys; clothes; maybe rent a whole house. Money didn't buy happiness or love, but a little more put by would help.

'I'll accept your commission, thank you,' she said.

'A wise decision. I'll send one of my girls round with the design and fabric later. You will supply the silks. It's a pleasure to do business with you, Miss Rayfield. I wish you a good day.'

'Just a minute,' Violet said. 'When does it need to be done by?'

'My customer needs the dress ready for a fitting a week on Wednesday.'

'That soon.' Violet glanced towards her sister, whose face said it all. She was aware of a sense of mutiny in the ranks as Eleanor showed Mrs Kinnaird out.

'Who does she think she is, waltzing in here and throwing her weight around?' Eleanor exclaimed. 'Violet, you're exhausted. How do you think you're going to finish this commission by next week?'

'We can't afford to turn it down. Mrs Kinnaird's right – it could lead to a change in our fortunes. A few pieces of work like that, and we can forget about Mr Evercreech's orders. Instead of bread and butter, we'll have fish in court bouillon, and sole meunière.'

'We can do it,' May said, bringing Joe back. He squirmed and stuck his fist into his mouth, wanting his mama.

Violet took him into the kitchen, sat down on the settle and let him suck until he fell asleep and she was able to put him back down in his crib. How long would it be before he outgrew it? she wondered. Yawning, she returned to the workshop, leaving the door into the kitchen open so that she could listen out for him.

The following day, having bought the silks and received the fabric and instructions from one of Mrs Kinnaird's girls, Violet made an immediate start, turning the design into a pattern which she traced on to the fabric.

As she sat down with her needle and thread, making the most of the light from the window, she wondered if they should take on a girl to train up when they could afford it. Soon, though, she was lost in another world, creating the delicate beauty of myriad gossamer butterflies.

'I envy you,' Eleanor said, looking over her shoulder. 'You make them look real, as if they're about to stir their wings and take flight.'

She could picture them, hundreds of colourful butterflies lifting off from the fabric and rising out through the open window, dancing and fluttering along the streets of Dover …

'I wonder who will wear them and for what occasion?'

'A society lady.' It was strange to think that someone who would turn away from her if they met in the street would be wearing her embroidery at some social event like the regatta ball, or the Lord Warden's dinner.

Having worked day and night, in between attending to Joe, and supervising May and Eleanor, Violet began to hallucinate. At dawn on the morning she was due to finish the commission, she had just one wing to go.

'Tea?' Eleanor said.

'No, thank you. I can't risk spilling anything on this.'

'Stop then – for five minutes.'

'I must keep going.'

'What about Joe? He's hungry.'

'He'll have to wait,' Violet said harshly. 'If I don't get this to Mrs Kinnaird's this morning, all this work will have been wasted.'

'You would neglect your child? He's bawling his eyes out.'

'I can hear him. Give him some pap and close the door.' She paused, his cries tugging at her heartstrings. She couldn't do it. She couldn't ignore him any longer. She put the sewing down and went to feed him, cuddling him to her breast. 'I'm sorry, little one,' she sobbed. 'Forgive me, but I'm doing this for you.'

'Oh, Violet.' She felt Eleanor's arm around her shoulders. 'This is too much.'

'I can do it,' she said. 'I will do it. This could be the making of us.'

She delivered the commission to Mrs Kinnaird just in time, and she – perhaps out of relief that there would be no unpleasantness between her and her demanding customer – paid Violet's invoice in full.

On her return to the workshop, there was no respite. Violet helped May and Eleanor catch up with the rest of Mr Evercreech's regular order, embroidering by candle-light until after midnight. She fed Joe, fell into bed and was up again at the crack of dawn.

*

By the end of October, the chestnuts were falling from the trees in Connaught Park. Two weeks had passed since she'd delivered the commission and the money she'd received hadn't gone as far as expected. She'd had to buy medicine for Eleanor who had been unwell, and extra coal for the fire to keep them from freezing in the workshop. Violet began to lose hope that her work for Mrs Kinnaird would bear fruit. The dressmaker didn't call again, nor did she send any of her customers their way.

One morning while checking the boxes, Violet contemplated the possibility that they were doomed to continue with Mr Evercreech and the railwaymen's caps for the foreseeable future. With a heavy heart, she took the latest batch of finished pieces over to Mr Evercreech's shop. She knocked on his office door, then put the boxes on the side table as she'd always done.

'Greetings, Mrs Rayfield. Do sit down for a moment,' he said from where he was sitting behind his desk. 'This won't take long,' he added when she hesitated, wanting to get back to Joe.

With reluctance, she sat down and watched him slide the piece of paper with the next order across his desk, then form a steeple with the fingers of both hands. It reminded her of one of the rhymes that Eleanor loved saying to Joe and, smiling, she picked up the paper and read it. Mr Evercreech's figures were no laughing matter.

'This order is for less than a quarter of the number of pieces we normally make,' she said, frowning.

'I'm sorry. It's pure economics, nothing personal. There's a workshop that's just been set up in Maidstone and their prices are lower.'

'How can they do that without reducing the quality?'

'They haven't.' He showed her a sample from his desk. Violet stared at it, noting the regularity of the stitches. She had to admit that it was as good as anything that came out of her workshop. 'They've offered me a better deal.'

'How much are you buying this for?'

He named a price. 'It shocks you,' he said as her spirits fell.

'It does. How can I compete with that? I have overheads: rent, ladies who work for me. What am I supposed to do?'

'I'm sorry, Mrs Rayfield, but I can't help you there. Let me know if you decide that you can match or better their price, and I'll reconsider.'

She thought for a while, adding and subtracting various figures in her head. She couldn't do it. She couldn't offer to work for less. They would run out of money and starve.

'I'll take this for now,' she said, feeling sick at the prospect of having to explain the situation to Eleanor and May.

'I'll see you next week, usual time,' Mr Evercreech said.

'Yes. Yes, you will.'

The following week was the last time that she delivered boxes to Mr Evercreech because when she went back, he had no orders for her. All the work had gone to Maidstone. Like a ship, holed on the rocks of sharp business practice, their enterprise had sunk.

'We mustn't give up, no matter what life throws at us,' Eleanor said when Violet gave her and May the news. 'This will give me time to clean the workshop – I'll make it spotless.'

'May, if you'd like to look after Joe for an hour or so, I'll go and knock on some doors. There must be someone who needs our services. Perhaps we can embroider children's clothing, or do the monogramming on gentlemen's handkerchiefs? I'll see what I can do.' Violet took a few cards with her and traipsed around Dover, putting them up in shop windows and handing them out to anyone who'd listen to her sales patter, but she had no luck.

The next morning, when she went downstairs with Joe, she found May in the workshop, tying a piece of string around a package wrapped in brown paper.

'What are you doing?' she asked.

'I'm packin' my things and leavin'.' May burst into tears. 'We've 'ad a wonderful time during the past months, but I can't stay any longer. You'll be better off if it's just the three of you. I can see what's going on. We 'ave no work – embroidering a littl'un's name on its bib won't bring in enough to keep us all. And nothin's come of Mrs Kinnaird. I expected we'd 'ave a bit of a chance with 'er and she'd bring us more commissions, but the ladies of Dover are strange like that.'

'There isn't anything odd about them – they don't offer us work because they know who I am,' Violet said sadly. 'But, May, we sink or swim together, don't we? Please, stay – at least until you have somewhere to live. Think of Joe. He loves you. We all do.'

'Well, I don't want to leave,' May said eventually.

'Don't, then. Put your belongings back and come and have some breakfast. We'll make a plan.'

May stayed with them, but their plan didn't work out. Nothing worked out. As the days shortened, Violet's worries continued to grow.

They were living hand to mouth on the income from small orders for embroidering children's clothing and house-hold linens, and it didn't seem that anything was going to change. Dickens brought a whole circus of fleas into the workshop, making them itch. The bread they bought started to taste of dust, not flour, and made Eleanor sick again.

By the middle of November, they were almost penniless. Joe was now four months old and Violet wanted to buy him a second-hand high chair – a wooden one on brass wheels with a hole in the seat for his pot – ready for when he started crawling and they needed to keep him safe in the workshop, but she couldn't afford it.

On the third Monday of the month, she spent the day in the workshop with May and Eleanor, embroidering and singing to Joe, but although she presented a brave face, she spent the whole time praying that the landlord wouldn't turn up. He was a strange little man, a widow according to May, who had had the misfortune of having to listen to his life story. Whenever Violet had seen him, he'd been wearing the same neckerchief, brown shirt and braces. His teeth had been stained from years of smoking baccy, and his back was hunched.

'Hey diddle diddle, the cat and the fiddle, the cow jumped over the moon,' they sang as Joe lay on a blanket on the floor, waving his arms and cooing. 'The little dog laughed to see such fun, and the dish ran away with the spoon.'

Joe grinned.

'Do you remember Mama singing to us?' Eleanor said.

'It wasn't Mama. It would have been one of the nurses who looked after us in the nursery. Oh no, not a hairball.' Violet went to grab Dickens who'd started to choke. She whisked him on to the table and opened his mouth, catching sight of the eye of a needle at the back of his throat. She grabbed the end of it and pulled. Dickens turned and swiped her.

'There's gratitude for you,' Eleanor said. 'Poor Dickens.'

'We must be more careful.' Violet watched the cat settle down and start washing his paws. 'What if that had been Joe who'd found the needle?'

'It doesn't bear thinking about,' May contributed.

Violet picked Joe up and let him nap, tucked inside her cloak for warmth, as dusk began to fall. Eleanor lit a candle.

'Can we light the fire now?' she asked. 'It's getting cold in here.'

'No, if you're feeling the chill, you must go to bed instead,' Violet said. 'The choice is stark – food or fuel.'

'Is it really that bad?'

'I'm afraid so.'

'I hate being poor. It's like being a parrot stuck in a cage – there's no escape.' Eleanor rested her head in her hands. 'Is this how it's going to be for the rest of our lives?'

'Not if I have anything to do with it. We must continue to be brave.' Violet wasn't sure if she believed her own words any more. How could she go on giving encouragement to the others when she saw her son growing less strongly because her milk was too thin, and her sister had had to take in the seams of her dress, and she had cankers in her mouth from lack of nourishment?

'Something will turn up,' May said.

Violet heard footsteps outside. 'Quick, snuff out the candle and hide.'

'I know you're in there,' came the landlord's voice. 'I want my money and I shall get it.'

'It's Black Monday,' May whispered. 'He's a right squeeze-crab of a man: sour-looking, short and shrivelled.'

'I'll bring you the rent tomorrow,' Violet shouted. 'I promise.'

'You'd better, or I'll 'ave you out on your ear. All of you!'

'How on earth are you going to do that?' Eleanor said as the landlord stomped away.

'I'll pawn Arvin's ring. It's the only thing I have left. It has no sentimental value, but I find it helps when I'm out looking for work. People look on me more favourably if they think I'm a married woman, not that it's been of any benefit recently.'

'We'll find you a curtain ring,' May said. 'That will do.'

'It will have to.' For the first time, Violet felt completely without hope. After her visit to see 'uncle' the next day, she would be reduced to begging on the streets.

Chapter Twenty-Three

Make Do and Mend

'That's all you'll give me for it? You offered me more before,' Violet said, staring at Mr Cove who was making a great play of examining the ring through his magnifying glass. She knew he was toying with her. He could read her desperation as she stood there with Joe cuddled against her breast, the cuffs on her black dress frayed to bits and her shawl too thin to fend off the winter cold.

'I'll give you what it's worth,' he said, 'but if you think you can do better elsewhere, you know what you can do.'

'No, Mr Cove. I'll take it, thank you,' she said quickly. It would be enough to cover the rent, a pot of stew and maybe a small bag of coal.

'Very good.' He wrote out the ticket and gave it to her, along with the money. 'Take some advice from me, my dear. Give the child up. I know of someone – of good repute – who's happy to take a boy from a mother who finds herself in dire need. She'll pay a few bob.'

'I beg your pardon,' Violet said, shocked.

'Think about it. Let me know if you're interested.'

'I am not, and never will be. How dare you make such a wicked suggestion! I wouldn't be that cruel.'

He smiled. 'Sometimes you have to be cruel to be kind. I wouldn't dismiss the idea out of hand.'

'Come on, Joe.' She turned on her heels and walked out, pushing past the queue of Mr Cove's shabby and unwashed customers, her eyes blurred with tears. She would never come back to redeem the ring, or any other of the Rayfields' valuables. He could keep them.

She put Joe back in the pram which she'd left outside the pawnbroker's and headed along the street, not caring where she was going.

Somehow, she found herself walking along the quay towards the Packet Yard. As she passed the warehouses, she recalled the disastrous wine-tasting, and her embarrassment and sorrow at seeing her father's humiliation. Perhaps she shouldn't have come back to Dover at all. It held too many sad memories.

Joe didn't share her mood – he was lying propped up against a pillow, gazing at the people on the street, beaming from ear to ear from beneath his felt bonnet.

As she pushed the pram along, it gradually grew harder to move and then it stopped with its wheel caught on a stone, or so she guessed. She gave it a good shove and the front collapsed, and Joe and the blankets began to slide over the edge of the wicker basket. With lightning speed, she caught hold of her son, snatching him up before he fell.

'My darling boy, you could have been hurt,' she whispered, kissing the top of his head as a pair of elderly sailors stopped to stare, adding to her distress.

'I wasn't expecting that,' one said. 'Well, I never.'

'That ironwork's rusted through.'

'You were lucky the littl'un didn't fall out and crack 'is skull open.'

Reassured that Joe had come to no harm, she turned her attention to the pram. The axle holding the front wheels had rusted through and broken in half. It was too much, she thought, bursting into tears. She needed the pram to take Joe out and about, but she couldn't afford to have it repaired. She'd been so strong, so determined to flourish, let alone survive, and it had all gone wrong. Now this one little thing, the loss of a wheel, was the end of the world.

On seeing his mother's tears, Joe began to cry as well, making her feel even worse.

'What's going on here?' A kindly looking gentleman in a bowler hat pushed through the small crowd which had surrounded her. 'Can I help you, missus?'

'No,' she cried. There was nothing anyone could do.

'Let me take the pram along to a smith to see what can be done with it.'

'It's a kind offer, but I can't afford to pay for it.'

'There must be someone – family or a friend you can borrer the money from,' he said.

She was reminded of her father. The phrase 'neither a borrower nor a lender be' came into her head. Once you borrowed, all was lost. You never got to pay it back.

'Violet? What a coincidence.' If her heart could have sunk any further, it would. Why did William always have to turn up like a bad penny? She felt underdressed – the hem of her dress was ragged and her shoes second-hand. Her coat was dirty, while William looked every inch the gentleman in his dark wool greatcoat, with a starched collar on his shirt, and shiny black shoes.

She hugged Joe tight, wrapping her shawl around his shoulders to keep him warm, as William walked up to stand beside her. 'I was coming to see you.'

'How would you have found me?' she said, unsure if she believed him.

'You told me you had a workshop in Oxenden Street – I would have knocked on doors until I came across the right address. But it doesn't matter now. Oh, I hate to see you in distress. It is only a wheel. As the gentleman here says, it can be fixed.'

'No,' she sobbed. 'It's the least of my troubles.'

'Here's my handkerchief. It is clean.' He handed it over, and she wiped her nose.

'Thank you. No, Joe,' she said, as he tried to grab at it, but he began to protest, and she gave in for the sake of peace and quiet.

'Let me walk you to the Mitre Hotel – I'll buy you tea, then have this fixed by one of the smiths at the Packet Yard while you wait.'

'I don't think it can be repaired.'

'I'll ask them to make up a new axle. They're used to working on the moving parts on a steamship.' William smiled briefly. 'I don't think they'll have any problem with a pram.'

'It will be expensive?'

'They won't charge – they owe me a favour.'

'Then I'd be very grateful,' she decided.

Within a quarter of an hour, she was in the ladies' lounge at the hotel, with Joe on her lap. William took a seat opposite and leaned towards her as they waited for the waiter to deliver her order of tea and toast, and a biscuit for Joe.

'Violet, I have an inkling as to why you're so upset,' William began in a low voice. 'This is about Mr Brooke – I was coming to tell you, but you've already heard the news?'

'What is it?'

'A fisherman has found a body washed up in one of the coves.'

'They think it's him? Arvin?' she said after a pause.

William nodded. 'They say that his body will be returned to France at the Frenchwoman's expense. I'm very sorry.'

'Don't be. I want to make it clear that this information leaves me quite cold. I grieved for Mr Brooke – the man I thought he was – a long time ago. I realise there were some who surmised that he might have survived the night of the *Samphire* incident to tell the tale, that he staged this miraculous disappearance, so he could return with the Rayfields' gold and live a life of luxury, but you and I both know that he drowned.

'It was kind of you to let me know. I don't regret marrying him – if I hadn't gone through with it, I wouldn't have my son.'

'He looks like a fine boy,' William said.

'I wish I hadn't brought him out now – I thought the sea air would do him good.'

'Ah, here's your tea. I'll leave you to enjoy it while I take the pram to the yard. I don't know how long it will take.'

'Should I come and pick it up?'

'Wait for me to return. You don't want to be hanging about on the quay – it's too cold and there are some unsavoury characters lurking about.' He left her to sip at her tea and eat toast and strawberry jam.

There was a newspaper on the tray the waiter had brought to her. She perused the headlines.

Constable Disciplined for Falling into the Dour Drunk Man Fined for Leaving His Horse and Cart Unattended Recovery of the Body of the Bigamous Mr Brooke. The Mystery of his Disappearance Solved.

Arvin had been found as naked as the day he was born, apart from a ring from which he was identified by the information left at the police station by his wife, Madame Brooke.

She became aware that the waiter was looking over her shoulder.

'May I pour you more tea, madam?'

For a moment, she wondered if he'd recognised her, but he continued, 'He got his just deserts, that one, if you ask me. Serves him right. He ruined some poor girl – it caused a terrible scandal. I'm sorry, did you wish me to …?'

'Yes, please.' She watched him place the tea strainer on top of the china cup and pour from the pot. She let him add the milk for her, enjoying being treated for once.

A little while later, the waiter returned.

'Mr Noble says to let you know he's waiting outside,' he said with a smile.

'Thank you. My bill, please.'

'Oh no. It's been paid.'

'I must leave you a tip then.' She began to fumble in her purse, and the waiter, an honest man, told her not to worry because Mr Noble had already given him something for his trouble. Picking Joe up, she carried him outside to find William standing on the pavement with the pram.

'All done.' He smiled, pushing it back and forth. 'Look at that.'

'It's as good as new,' she exclaimed.

'You seem surprised.'

'I am, a little.'

'You shouldn't be,' he said softly. 'Anything can be fixed as long as you pour your heart and soul into it.'

Was he saying that their situation could be resolved if they both wanted it enough? Her knees trembled as she gazed into the blue depths of his eyes. It was the sweetest of sentiments, but just that. They could never be together – her fall from grace would hold him back.

William went on, 'I don't want payment. As I said, the smiths owed me a favour.' He took a card from the inside

341

pocket of his coat and handed it over to her. Joe reached out for it, making William chuckle. At the sound of the deep rumble in his throat, Joe started and stared, then broke into a slow smile.

'Hello.' William grinned back, then turned to Violet. 'If the new axle fails or you need anything else, then you know where I am.'

She read the address.

'I'm going up in the world,' he said.

'I'm pleased for you. You deserve it.' She put Joe back in the pram and covered him with the blanket.

'How's the embroidery business?' William asked.

'It's ... Oh, I could pretend and tell you how well we're doing, but really ... we're struggling against fierce competition from other workshops. The demand's there, but the prices keep falling. I'm sorry – I have to get back.'

'Before you go, here's a gift for the boy.' He slipped a coin into the foot of the pram. 'Spend it as you see fit, Violet.'

'Thank you,' she said simply, before hurrying away.

May and Eleanor had been waiting for her to return to the workshop.

'Where have you been?' Eleanor asked, letting her in. 'Our landlord has had us under siege, wanting his rent.'

'Where is he now?' Violet pushed the pram up against the window, leaving Joe to sleep.

'In there.' Eleanor nodded towards the kitchen door. 'He insisted on coming in and making himself comfortable. He said he'd wait until one o'clock and then we'd have to leave. He'd pack our bags for us, if he had to.'

'You 'ave got the money?' May said.

'Yes, I have.' She opened her purse and counted out the necessary sum. 'Please give this to him.'

May took the money through to the kitchen while Violet sat down.

'We were about to send out a search party,' Eleanor said.

'It's a long story.' Violet untied the ribbons on her bonnet and put it on the table. 'I went to see "uncle", and then as I was walking along, the pram broke. Mr Noble had one of the smiths at the Packet Yard make a new axle for it.'

'How come he was there? He always seems to be there when you're in trouble.'

'He's like a guardian angel,' Violet said wistfully. 'He gave Joe a gift as well. Look in the foot of the pram – but don't wake him up!'

'That's very generous of him.' Eleanor came back with a silver crown and dropped it into Violet's outstretched palm. 'Dear William – he goes beyond the call of duty.'

'He said he was on his way to call on us to give me some news.' As she put the coin in her pocket, she found his handkerchief – she had forgotten to give it back. 'Arvin ...' Her voice faltered. 'He's been found.'

'Alive?' Eleanor said.

Violet shook her head when her sister continued, 'You know, I always had an idea that he'd turn up still living, dressed in one of his hideous frock coats. I can't believe he's dead. Oh, Violet—'

'I don't care about Mr Brooke. I'm glad that there's a proper end to it, but that's all. I'll be able to tell Joe the truth when he's older: that his father died before he was born. I won't need to keep looking over my shoulder, wondering if he might return to rake up trouble between me and my son. It's possible that he would have found a way to take him away from me.'

'Do you think that's what he would have done?'

'Who knows? At least I have confirmation of his fate. My mind is at ease on that score.'

'Are you going to see William again? I mean, is he sweet on you?'

343

'Eleanor! What would he see in me? Look at how our circumstances have changed. I have one half-decent black dress, cheaply made and it shows, and my stockings have all been darned to the nth degree. My hands are rough with needle scratches and I have dark circles around my eyes.'

'I've told you this before – appearances don't matter,' her sister said sternly.

'I would argue that it does. Society judges us on how we look. Are we wearing the right clothes, the latest fashions and fabrics? Do we live in a house that suits our status? Are our reputations beyond reproach? You see, that's where we're at a disadvantage, thanks to Mr Brooke. He was found without his clothes, and I'm glad that he was seen naked and lacking in dignity. It's what he deserved.' Violet raised her hand to silence Eleanor as she opened her mouth to speak. 'I'm not bitter – I let go of my feelings of anger a long time ago. We have more important things to do than waste another moment talking about that man.' She stood up again. 'Let's go and restock the larder for a start.'

The larder, unlike the walk-in cupboard at Camden Crescent, was a small cabinet in the kitchen to keep the flies and vermin off their food, not that they had many mice or rats because Dickens had become adept at getting rid of them.

Having bought food for the next day or two, Eleanor set about preparing dinner, boiling up tripe then simmering it with milk and onions, while May worked on an anti-macassar set and arm caps, embroidering them with sprays of pink flowers. Violet washed William's handkerchief with hot water and lye soap, rinsed it and hung it over the firescreen in the workshop.

'That don't belong to you. I've never seen it before,' May said.

'It's William's.' Violet was trying not to blush, but the more she thought about it, the hotter her face became. 'I'd like to return it – out of politeness, that's all.'

'You could put his initials in one corner,' May suggested.

'I could ... I'd like to thank him in some way, but is that too little to express my gratitude for what he did? Would it offend him?'

'You could embroider a whole set of handkerchiefs, one for every day of the week.'

'That might be too much when he expressly said that he didn't want any payment. May, do you think a gift of any kind might be misconstrued?'

'Just sew 'is initials on and go and return it to him.' May chuckled. 'Really, Violet. It isn't that 'ard. You're makin' a mountain out of a molehill.'

Later that afternoon when she was fretting over what colour silks to use for the W, and Joe was lying on his blanket, holding a piece of linen in front of his eyes, transfixed by the pattern of threads, a woman, wearing an exquisite navy velvet coat and hat which shaded much of her face, came into the workshop unannounced.

'Miss Whiteway,' Eleanor exclaimed. 'It is you! How marvellous.'

Violet couldn't believe her eyes. A ring glinted from Miss Whiteway's finger as she removed her fine kid gloves.

'My dears, I never expected our paths to cross. You are well?'

'We are all well,' Violet said. 'How and why did you find us?'

'I've seen some of your workmanship on a dress. I have a friend who was showing me her wardrobe of gowns the other day, and one caught my eye. I recognised your signature – I suppose that's what you'd call it – the characteristics of the embroidery that say it's yours. I could tell from the neatness and regularity of the stitches, the shading in the butterflies' wings, and the way they seemed to come to life on the material.

'Violet, you can't imagine how delighted I was when I realised that the embroidery had to be yours. My friend told me that she'd had the dress made by a Mrs Kinnaird. I called on her, she gave me your address and here I am. It took me a while to find you.'

'I'm pleased that you did. It's lovely to see you after all this time, but you find us in straitened circumstances.' Violet wished that they hadn't chosen tripe for dinner – the smell was decidedly unpleasant.

'I'm hoping that I'll be able to help – I have a proposition for our mutual benefit. I'd like you to embroider something very special for me. You will do it?'

'Well, yes. Of course. Eleanor, would you make some tea?' They had exchanged rank – Violet was in trade and Miss Whiteway was her customer. 'Take a seat, Miss Whiteway.'

Their old governess took off her hat and coat and sat down.

'Let me take the child,' May said, leaning down. 'We don't want 'im disturbin' you.'

'Don't worry about him,' Miss Whiteway said. 'What a handsome little boy. Look how he smiles. He takes after his mama, doesn't he? How old is he?'

'He's four months old,' Violet said.

'Time flies. So much has happened since we last met.'

'You have heard of the Rayfields' misfortunes?' Violet pulled up a chair and sat next to Miss Whiteway, who nodded. 'I hope you can forgive me and Eleanor for what our parents did to you – they treated you very badly.'

'They weren't kind to you either, marrying you off to Mr Brooke. I always thought he was too good to be true.

Anyway, it makes no difference to me. Thanks to your intervention – the letter you wrote – I found another place.'

'What letter?' Violet said.

'It's no use trying to bluff your way out of it. I recognise your handwriting as well as your stitches.'

'Did I hear that right?' Eleanor came back with two cups of tea. 'I hope this isn't too weak for you, Miss Whiteway.'

'It's perfect, thank you. And yes, in answer to your question, your sister did write me a character reference in your mother's name.'

'Violet! I'm ashamed to be your sister,' Eleanor exclaimed, but she was smiling.

'I have to confess that I was grateful for it – there was a moment when I feared that the fakery was going to be discovered, but I managed to convince my new employer not to check with your mother, knowing how ill she was. I'm sorry, by the way, for your loss. I learned of it from your Aunt Felicity – I met her at a soiree given by some mutual friends in Canterbury.'

'You are still employed as a governess?' Violet asked, frowning.

'My life has changed for the better.' Miss Whiteway sounded different, her voice lighter and her speech less formal, and she looked much prettier, and younger, in her beautiful clothes.

'I was engaged to care for a gentleman's ward, a young lady, and now I am to marry my master. There is a certain amount of irony in that, don't you think? I have been caught up in a situation that I once eschewed, trapped into marriage by the love of a very dear man.

'One day, women like you will break us out of our chains – those of duty above desire,' Miss Whiteway continued as Joe gurgled and chewed on his fist. 'I thought

I would be the one to make a difference, but those days are gone. I've been beguiled into matrimony and I'm here to ask if you would accept a commission for a wedding dress. Mrs Kinnaird's seamstresses would put the gown together and you would customise it.'

'Are you sure? I'm – we'd be honoured,' Violet said.

'I don't want anyone else to do it. I want everyone talking about my gown – having been used to fading into the background as a governess, I would find it gratifying to be the centre of attention, even if it's only for one day.'

She paused before continuing, 'I heard that Ottilie's marriage caused a bit of a rumpus. I was told that Mr Chittenden has cut his son off – he's written him out of his will and refused to have anything more to do with him, while poor Mrs Chittenden is distraught. I believe she would have forgiven her only son for marrying ... Oh, what am I saying?'

'You were saying that she would have forgiven John for marrying one of the Rayfield daughters,' Violet finished for her, realising that the situation between Mr Chittenden and John would prevent Ottilie coming back to Dover to look for her sisters.

'I'm afraid there's a lot more work to do before society changes its opinions. Have you heard from Ottilie?'

'We've had several letters from her, saying she and John are happy and settled in Woolwich.' Violet kept the fact that Ottilie had said in her last letter that she was with child to herself.

'I would love to see her again – give her my kind regards. I'm very glad that I've spoken to you. I've often wondered how you were and what you were doing. I know we had our differences – especially you, Violet – but I missed you. It's one of the sorrows of being a governess, growing to look on your charges with great affection, and then grieving when you move on.'

'But you aren't a governess any more,' Violet said, feeling more cheerful. 'You are getting married. What is your fiancé like?'

'You're still as impertinent as ever, I see.'

'I mean, do we know of him?'

Smiling, Miss Whiteway named a Mr Fullagar who owned a modest country house near Chillenden. 'When I marry Mr Fullagar, I shall be taking on his ward as my stepdaughter, and I hope that one day I shall have a boy just like your Joe, and a girl, and if it turns out that we aren't blessed with children between us, it won't matter. Not too much anyway,' she went on. 'Now, I mustn't take up any more of your time. How shall we proceed? Shall I arrange a meeting with Mrs Kinnaird so we can discuss the designs for the gown? Perhaps you could bring some sketches of the patterns you might use. In the meantime, I'll leave you a small deposit in advance. I insist,' she said before Violet could protest.

Miss Whiteway drank her tea and took her leave.

As the door clicked shut, Violet, May and Eleanor stared at each other.

'Did that really happen?' Violet said after a long silence. 'Was I dreaming?'

'No, Miss Whiteway was here in our workshop,' Eleanor said. 'She placed an order for the embroidery on her wedding dress.'

'Hurrah! We are saved by the skin of our teeth,' May cheered. 'Our prospects are lookin' up.'

Violet chose an ombre silk of shades of blue for William's handkerchief.

May was right. Miss Whiteway had given them a lifeline and it was up to her to make it work.

Chapter Twenty-Four

Looking on the Bright Side

The tide was beginning to turn. The next day one of Mrs Kinnaird's girls delivered a note with the date and time of the meeting with the dressmaker and Miss Whiteway for the first of December the following week.

Violet washed the better of her two remaining dresses and hung it out to dry in the yard, but the sea mist came rolling in, adorning it with silver beads of moisture, so she brought it in again and draped it in front of the fire. She made new cuffs from offcuts from the haberdasher and trimmed the frayed hem, edging it with a strip of lilac ribbon to add colour and show that she was no longer in deep mourning for her parents.

'Do you think that's presentable?' She showed Eleanor the finished article the next day.

'It looks much better, but is this for the meeting with the dressmaker, or does it have more to do with calling on William? You *are* going to call on him after all that time and effort you put into embroidering his handkerchief?' Eleanor's eyes twinkled with amusement. 'I'm sorry. I mustn't keep teasing you. I know nothing will come of it – not in that way.'

Her sister had taken the wind out of her sails. Should she bother with taking it back to him, or should she just forget it?

'Don't listen to me,' Eleanor said. 'Take it. I'll mind Joe.'

Having changed into her clean dress, and taken some time to put up her hair, Violet hurried along the seafront, keeping her eyes averted when she passed Camden Crescent, not wanting to be reminded of the past. She found William's house in Athol Terrace overlooking the sea with the backdrop of the white cliffs and Dover Castle behind it. It was a pretty house with bay windows, a slate roof and painted render. There were railings at the front and a path which led to a dark blue door with a brass letter box.

She rang the bell and waited. Had she made a mistake in coming here? She glanced towards the sea which seemed to merge with the grey November sky. There was still time to change her mind.

Too late, William answered the door, raising his eyebrows in surprise at seeing her.

'Good afternoon,' she said.

'It's a pleasure to see you, Violet. Do come in.'

'No, thank you. I've just come to return this.' She handed him the package she'd wrapped earlier that day in tissue paper secured with a ribbon.

'Thank you, but what is it?'

'You may open it,' she said.

He unfastened the ribbon and opened the paper. He picked up the corner of the handkerchief with his finger and thumb, and let it unfurl.

'You needn't have … I have plenty of others. Oh, you've embellished it. How wonderful.' He held it up to the light. He couldn't have looked more delighted if she'd given him one hundred pounds, she thought happily. 'Can I pay you for your trouble?'

'No,' she said firmly. 'It's yours.'

'Are you sure?'

'Just accept it for what it is, a gesture. Listen to us. If neither backs down gracefully, we will be here till Christmas, not this one coming up, but the one after.'

'You're quite right.' William laughed, and she joined in. 'I should know better than to argue with a member of the fairer sex. I couldn't do what you do. I did once pick up a needle and try to darn a pair of socks, but Ma lost patience with me. Are you sure you won't come in? My housekeeper baked a cake this morning.'

'No, thank you. Eleanor is minding Joe for me, and I have work to do.' And it would be wrong of her to be alone with him in his house, whether or not his housekeeper was there. 'We've just been commissioned to embroider a wedding dress which has to be ready by March.'

'That's a long time ahead.'

'There's a lot to do. It appears that the lady who ordered the dress has recommended us to some of her friends – there's a good chance that we're going to be very busy.'

'Perhaps one day, you'll be by royal appointment.'

'That would be something to shout about. In the meantime, though, I want to make sure that everything we do comes out flawless.'

'I believe flaws add to a subject's charm,' William said lightly, and she wondered what or whom he was referring to. 'Perfection is predictable and rather dull, in my opinion.'

'What about the boilers you build for the ships?' she asked. 'Don't you demand perfection for those?'

'You're right. I do. I'm talking about people, not stitches or boats.' He changed the subject. 'Let me change into my shoes and find my coat and I'll walk you home. Look, it's started to rain, and you haven't brought an umbrella.'

Violet took pleasure in strolling along with him as he carried the umbrella above their heads along the seafront and back towards Oxenden Street.

'I wonder if you'd be interested in working on a small project for me,' he said.

'What is it?'

'I'd like you to embroider a waistcoat that I can wear for smart occasions.'

'You're trying to impress someone ... a young lady, perhaps?' Her heart missed a beat and another, waiting for his reply.

'Oh no, nothing like that,' he said, relieving her of her anxiety. 'I'm often invited out to dine, and I'd like to wear something bespoke that sets me apart from the other gentlemen.'

'You must come and see us at the workshop sometime – we can look at creating a design,' Violet said.

'What you just said about impressing a young lady ... there is some truth in that. Violet, I hope you don't mind me speaking frankly. There are times when I've felt that we are kindred spirits. Am I presuming too much?'

'No. I've always' – she remembered seeing him clamber out of the boat at the regatta, and raise his arms in victory – 'felt drawn to you, but I was very young, only eighteen when we met—'

'You aren't much older now.' He smiled.

'Yes, but I didn't know anything of the world back then. I didn't understand.'

'I knew my place. You were set above me, so I didn't pursue my natural inclination, and I thought I'd put those feelings behind me until I saw you on the *Samphire* that night, looking like a mermaid, your beauty beyond compare.'

'I looked at my worst – I was sick.' It had been nothing to do with finding her sea legs – she had been carrying Mr Brooke's child.

'And then you reminded me you were married, and I couldn't understand why your husband wasn't there to protect you. You looked so sad and delicate as if you were about to break, and all I wanted to do was put my arms around you and hold you together in one piece.'

'But now I have fallen far below you,' she said gently, to control the waver in her voice.

'I don't see it like that. You are exactly the same as you were before – just up to my shoulder in height.' He glanced towards her, his mischievous expression putting her at ease.

'You deliberately misunderstand me.'

'I try not to take on the mantel of my father's puritanical values about how we should act. As far as I'm concerned, everyone should be treated the same – from the lowly apprentice to the Lord Warden of Dover – with respect. It makes me bitter when I read the newspapers – I'm sorry, you don't want to go over this again.' He looked wounded on her behalf.

'I prefer it to be acknowledged between us. People of my acquaintance either dismiss the episode for the sake of my feelings, as if it never happened, or they are suddenly reminded. I've seen them crossing the road or turning away in the pretence of searching their pockets so that they don't have to give me the time of day. The shame still follows me. I can't escape it, no matter how much I try. It occurred to me to move away, but Dover is my home. I belong here.'

'You have every right to live here. It makes my blood boil to think of anyone hurting you. Mr Brooke was unimaginably dreadful and your father—' He stopped abruptly. 'No, I will bite my tongue. My mother brought me up to treat people as I would be done by, to do no harm to anyone with words or actions.'

'I wish I could have met her,' Violet said. 'Anyway, I refuse to be cowed by anyone. I'm not a victim – I chose to do my duty to my father and Ottilie when I married Mr Brooke. I had no idea then how it would work out.' She paused before continuing. 'We are nearly there – you can turn back now if you like.'

He cleared his throat. 'I wonder if you'd like to accompany me to an evening at the museum next week. I don't know if it's something you have any interest in, but there's a lecture about the chemistry of the breakfast table. I have a subscription and can take a guest. We can have a look at the exhibits and take refreshment there. There'll be wine and a light supper. What do you think?'

She stopped and gazed into his eyes. 'I'd like it very much, thank you.'

'I'll call for you at half past six, a week on Friday. Let me walk you the rest of the way so I know where to find you.'

She wished him goodbye outside the workshop on Oxenden Street. He doffed his hat and smiled. 'I'll see you again soon.'

Violet returned indoors to greet Joe, who was delighted to see her as she picked him up.

'How did it go?' Eleanor asked.

'It was fine. I don't know why I got into such a stew about it. He's asked me to embroider a waistcoat for him. How about that?'

'It's only to be expected – he favours you, Violet.'

'Let me do supper,' she said, changing the subject. 'I think it must be my turn.'

'I'd like that – I have a fancy for taking up my writing again. I haven't had the enthusiasm for it recently, but I have an idea for a romantic novel, a simple tale of love between two people who realise after a long time apart that they've always been destined for each other.'

'Oh, Eleanor. You are teasing me again.'

'I'm not. I'm going upstairs to write. I can't concentrate with Joe making noise all the time, much as I love him.'

Violet prepared a meal of cold meats, pickles and bread with a bottle of ale to toast their improving prospects. They ate together with Joe, then set up a game of draughts that May had acquired on one of her expeditions. The board was scruffy, and they had to use buttons to replace the few missing counters, but it would do.

'You've bin all of a flutter ever since you came back from seein' Mr Noble,' May said when they had finished clearing up and Joe was tucked up in his crib.

'You've not said much about it,' Eleanor said. 'Did he make an arrangement to see you again?'

'As a matter of fact, he did.'

'Why didn't you say so?' May said.

'Because I wanted to keep it to myself for a while. Anyway, to satisfy your curiosity, let me tell you that he's asked me to a lecture at the museum.'

'Oh my goodness,' May said. 'How dull. Where is the fun in that?'

'I think it could be very interesting.' Violet blushed.

'Each to their own. I suppose you're goin' to want one of us to look after Joe?'

'If you wouldn't mind.'

'We do lead very busy lives – look at all our invitations lined up on the mantelpiece.' Eleanor waved towards the fireplace. 'Of course we'll sit with Joe, won't we, May?'

'That depends on when it is. I 'ave an interesting engagement of my own.'

'What is it?' Violet asked.

'Tom Ward – our landlord – 'as asked me to walk out with 'im, and I said yes.'

'The squeeze-crab?' Violet laughed. 'I thought you didn't like him.'

'Let's say 'e's changed my mind. He isn't so bad when you get to know 'im, and although 'e looks old and bent almost in two, 'e's got a twinkle in 'is eye and a bit of money in his pocket.'

'I'm feeling a little left out here. It looks as if it will be just me and Joe,' Eleanor said, walking over to him and picking him up.

'Joe, be nimble. Joe, be quick.' She carried him in her arms. 'Joe jumps over the candlestick. Joe jumps high, Joe jumps low, Joe jumps ooooover ...' she made him soar then dip '... and burns his toe.'

Joe couldn't stop chuckling.

'It's good luck to jump over a candlestick without puttin' out the flame,' May said.

'And highly dangerous,' Violet observed. 'Let's not try it. I don't think our landlord—'

'May's fancy man,' Eleanor interrupted with a giggle.

'I don't think he'd be too happy to see us burn the place down,' Violet went on. 'We need this workshop – we'll be starting on Miss Whiteway's dress very soon.'

At the meeting a few days later, Mrs Kinnaird and Miss Whiteway welcomed her ideas for a pattern of spring motifs in whitework for a March wedding. The amount of sewing was daunting, but Violet looked forward to the challenge. This was what she had been born to do.

She planned their schedule, allocating some of the embroidery to May and enlisting Eleanor in the preparation and finishing. Violet took responsibility for much of the sewing and for checking the quality of every section before it was delivered to Mrs Kinnaird.

As she sewed, her mind often drifted. The date of the soiree at the museum was approaching rapidly and she was growing increasingly nervous. What if she made a fool of herself? She didn't know the first thing about the subject of the lecture, but what did it matter? He'd asked her because he wanted her there. With William, everything was clear-cut. He didn't try to trick her or wheedle his way around her with false words and charm. And he was handsome too. Her needle slipped and stabbed her finger. Ruefully, she sucked the blood from her skin, regretting her lapse in concentration. It wouldn't do to spoil Miss Whiteway's dress.

When the evening came, Violet worked as late as she could, struggling to make out the pattern of stitches in the light of the oil lamps in the workshop, until Eleanor insisted that she put her work down and get ready to go out.

'Gone are the days when we had a choice of outfit to wear,' Violet said, having changed into the dress she'd repaired.

'You can borrow one of mine,' Eleanor offered. 'It's black faded to a dark brown, and shorter at the front than the back, as is the fashion.'

'And it's very similar to this one.' Violet smiled.

'Looking on the bright side, our clothes take up very little room and hardly require laundering, saving on soap and hot water. We aren't compelled like other ladies to spend hours agonising over what to wear.'

'Perhaps I shouldn't go. I don't want to let him down.'

'You look beautiful whatever you wear – I envy you. You turn heads.'

'For the wrong reasons. You're the pretty one.' Her sister was growing from a cygnet into an elegant swan, but she didn't know it. 'One day, you'll have young men falling at your feet.'

'Stop it.' Eleanor giggled. 'Let me do your hair.'

She brushed some oil through Violet's blonde locks, braided them and put them up, leaving a few ringlets loose at the side of her face. Violet looked in the mirror, pinched her cheeks and bit her lip to add colour.

'There, you look perfect,' Eleanor said. 'I hope you have a wonderful evening.'

'If he turns up – he might have thought better of it.'

'Of course he'll turn up. Have faith.'

Within the half-hour, Violet found herself walking at William's side along the streets towards the museum in Market Square. It had been built above the market, and a sign outside read, 'The Dover Museum and Philosophical Institute: Founded 1836 for the Promotion of Literary and Scientific Knowledge'.

'I'm not sure if this is the kind of entertainment you'd normally choose,' William said as they moved towards the entrance where other people were gathering. 'Perhaps you would have preferred to go dancing or to the theatre?'

'Not at all. We can go dancing on another occasion. I've never been to hear a lecture before, and to my regret, I haven't visited the museum even though it's on our doorstep. This will be a new experience and I'm looking forward to it.'

He smiled, apparently reassured.

'To be honest, Violet, I don't mind where we go or what we do. All I want is to spend time with you. I hope I haven't overstepped the mark in saying so.'

'You have made me blush.' She smiled back. 'But, William, I feel the same.'

'Let's go inside,' he said, offering his arm.

Putting etiquette aside, she took it gracefully and he guided her through the door and up the stairs where a member of the museum staff took their coats. He showed them through to a room that was at least three times the size of the drawing room at Camden Crescent, with venetian blinds across the windows. Violet looked along the shelves and cabinets which lined the walls and encroached towards the central space, where someone had placed rows of chairs ready for the lecture. It was overwhelming, the gaslights reflected in the rippled glazing which protected the exhibits: minerals, strange fossils, boxes and boxes of taxidermy. All the eyes seemed to stare fixedly towards the visitors in an accusatory way, making Violet shudder. There were owls, gulls, hares and even some kittens which reminded her of Dickens, but they weren't the only creatures looking at her.

'Mr Noble, good— Oh!' Uncle Edward stopped, his jaw dropping open when he saw Violet. 'This is an—'

'An unexpected pleasure, I know,' William finished for him. 'You remember Miss Rayfield.'

Violet read the consternation on Mr and Mrs Chittenden's faces. Would they turn their backs on William for his choice of companion, or would they stay to make polite conversation, exposing themselves to gossip? Mrs Chittenden took a firm grip on her husband's arm as though to steer him away, but Uncle Edward went against her.

'I'm glad to see some younger members making use of their subscription to the museum,' he said. 'It's gratifying to see how popular these events are. I don't know if you've heard, Mr Noble, but I put forward your name the other day as a speaker if you'd be interested. We are all keen to find out more about the latest developments in steam propulsion.' He turned to his wife. 'Aren't we, my dear?'

Mrs Chittenden nodded, but she looked unconvinced.

'Let me have a quiet word with this young gentleman about possible dates,' he went on.

'I don't know how you've managed that,' Mrs Chittenden said in an aside to Violet.

'What exactly?' she said sweetly. 'I have no idea what you mean.'

'Oh, I think you do. In fact, I know you do. After all the scandal that's tarnished the Rayfield name, you've managed to come up smelling of roses. I don't understand how you've managed to snag someone like Mr Noble. I mean, what are you wearing? The cheapest-looking mourning dress I've ever seen, and no adornment whatsoever.'

'Mr Noble is an honourable man who doesn't hold my past against me. You should look at yourself, Mrs Chittenden. You cut off your only child for going against you and marrying my loving and blameless sister. I expect it was just as painful for you as it was for John.' Violet watched Mrs Chittenden's expression change from one of superiority to doubt. She had touched a raw nerve, she realised. 'I don't expect us to become bosom friends, or fond acquaintances, but I shall be staying in Dover and will continue to associate with Mr Noble, whether you like it or not.'

'I understand, Miss Rayfield.' Mrs Chittenden's eyes glinted with what Violet suspected was a tear. 'Please, tell me. Have you heard anything of John?'

'I've had word from my sister. They are both well and living in Woolwich. If you wish, I can ask them if they would consider writing to you.'

'Oh, that's ... I'm glad they are well. Yes, if you will.' Mrs Chittenden lowered her voice. 'I'm sorry for what happened to you, Violet. Shall we sit down? The lecture is about to begin.'

Violet took a seat between William and Mrs Chittenden. The speaker was a professor with a lively manner, but within a quarter of an hour, Mrs Chittenden was asleep, nodding now and again. Violet glanced towards William, who smiled.

'Thank goodness for that,' Mrs Chittenden said, having woken up for the end. 'I'm glad we dined before we came out.'

'Did you enjoy the talk?' William asked after the Chittendens had taken their leave.

'It was ... food for thought,' she said, making him chuckle. 'I'll think of what the professor said when I next poach an egg – I'll add vinegar to stop it falling apart. Otherwise, much of it went over the top of my head.'

William invited her to see some of the exhibits before supper, and soon she was absorbed looking through a large collection of butterflies from all over the world, their colours and shapes beyond her imagination.

'I remember the butterflies on your gown,' William said. 'Did you embroider those yourself?'

She smiled at the memory. 'They're my favourite subject. I can't wait to do some more, taking inspiration from some of these. They're wonderful.'

Having eaten and drunk a small glass of wine, they signed the visitors' book and left the museum.

'Shall we walk back along the promenade, or do you need to get back for Joe?' William asked.

'I hope he will be asleep by now,' she said.

'So, your answer is yes?'

She nodded and they headed via Fishmongers Lane and New Bridge to Waterloo Crescent where they strolled along the front. It was a chilly November evening, but Violet hardly noticed the cold.

'May I take your arm?' she ventured as they stopped to watch the sea wash across the shore, the waves topped with white horses which gleamed in the light from the streetlamps.

'It's coming up for the first anniversary of the accident,' she said. 'That time has flown.'

'It'll soon be Christmas. I'm going to find it ... well, it will be different without Ma.'

'It will be hard for all of us, I think.' Recalling poor Mama, she stared out towards the horizon where she could just make out the lights on a steam packet. 'Our mother would have wanted us to enjoy it – I'm determined to put on a small celebration. Do you ... Would you like to come to us for dinner on Christmas Day? Oh, what am I saying? I'm sure you have better things to do. You move in different circles – I mean, you're going to give a lecture at the museum.'

William smiled. 'Actually, I've already received an invitation to spend Christmas at Walmer Castle, the Lord Warden's residence.'

'Oh, then you can't possibly accept,' Violet said, disappointed.

'No, I can't. The Lord Warden will have to do without me. I'm very grateful for your offer – I'd love to join you. I'll send a joint of meat – as my contribution to the day. Shall I come to you straight after the service at St Mary's?'

'Yes, that will suit us very well.' She felt a little guilty that she wouldn't be going to church – she preferred to stay at home with Joe.

Proud to be on the arm of the man she admired more than anyone, Violet walked on again.

'I hope I don't offend you by asking if you think you will remarry?' William began.

'I won't, but that's because I was never married. I'm not offended by your question, by the way, just a little surprised.'

'Then I think it would be even harder for you to contemplate the idea of marriage,' he went on. 'You are a person in your own right, beholden to no one and free to make decisions as to how you bring up your son and run your business.'

'If I choose not to marry, then I would be sacrificing the opportunity of companionship and love.'

'And Joe's chance of having a loving pa in his life.'

'It would be good for him to have a father figure, I agree, but I'd have to have more reason than that to commit to a husband.' She wondered what Arvin would have made of Joe. She thought he would have been proud of the child they had made together. She hoped the Lord had forgiven him for what he'd done, and that he'd found peace.

'What about children? Wouldn't you like to be blessed with more?'

'That would definitely be a consideration.'

William squeezed her arm, sending the hairs on her neck up on end. Her love for him surged through her like the waves that washed across the shingle. She wished she could walk at his side for ever.

'Violet, if you did marry, would you wish to continue running the workshop?'

'Of course. I prefer that to overseeing a household, and I'd hate to give up embroidery for a husband. It's my life.'

'Are you saying that you don't want a husband? That you would resent him for being your jailer?'

'I didn't say that. It's marriage that's the imprisoning element, not the husband himself,' she said. 'Matrimony is a way of controlling and subjugating women – oh dear, you think me an activist, but it's what our governess, Miss Whiteway, used to say. Men and women, husbands and wives should allow each other the freedom to do as they wish, not confine them to their separate spheres in society.'

'I understand.'

'I'm not against marriage. I'm afraid of losing my independence again after having fought so hard for it. William, I'm very fond of you.'

'I respect your opinions. I love you for who you are – there, I've said it. I love you, Violet. I wouldn't want you to change.'

'I'm not saying that I'll never marry,' she pointed out gently. 'It's just that I wouldn't want anyone to offer to marry me out of pity, or a sense of duty, no matter how honourable that is.'

'Then I may hope?'

She nodded.

'In that case, I'm a happy man.'

He walked her the rest of the way back to Oxenden Street and wished her goodnight.

May and Eleanor had retired to bed and the candles were out, so she made her way upstairs in the dark. She crept into the room she shared with her sister, checked on Joe who was fast asleep in his crib, undressed and slid under the covers.

William had said he loved her. The more she mulled over their conversation, the more convinced she was that he was planning to propose. She had laid out her views on marriage, the benefits and disadvantages, and how she felt about it. Her initial joy and anticipation began to fade. Had she put her views across too forcefully? In the cold light of day, would he change his mind?

Chapter Twenty-Five

The Turn of the Tide

Three weeks later, on the afternoon of Christmas Eve, there was great excitement and anticipation at the house in Oxenden Street. Violet and May were occupied with embroidering what would become the train for Miss Whiteway's wedding dress, while Eleanor kept Joe occupied, and Dickens away as much as she could, shutting the cat in the kitchen when he yowled plaintively to come back.

May looked up and blinked. 'Oh, this is beginning to hurt my eyes.'

'And mine.' White thread on white fabric wasn't the easiest to work with, but the effect was beautiful, like the subtle shades in a cloud on a summer's day. Violet heard the sleet clattering against the window outside, and the knock on the door.

'Oh, who is that?' she sighed. They had already been disturbed twice that day – by Tom Ward wanting his rent, and by Mrs Kinnaird bringing an order for decorating the bodice of a ballgown for an acquaintance of Miss Whiteway's. It hadn't been the first time that their old governess had put a good word in for them. 'I'll get it.'

She opened the door to find the butcher's boy standing bedraggled on the step, with his trolley covered with an oilcloth.

'This is for a Miss Rayfield,' he said, lifting the cloth and picking up a great fat goose, plucked and ready to be cooked.

'I haven't ordered this,' Violet said, but the boy read the label that was tied around its neck, confirming that it belonged to her, and then she remembered that William had offered to contribute to dinner the next day. She thanked the boy, took the goose and gave him a penny for his trouble.

'Look what I've got.' She carried the goose through the workshop in both arms. Eleanor opened the kitchen door at the sound of the disturbance.

'A goose,' she shrieked. 'Oh my goodness! It's huge. What are we going to do with that? It won't fit in the oven.'

'We'll have to force it in. How long do you think it will take to cook?'

'Hours,' Eleanor said.

'William sent it.'

''E must have an enormous appetite if 'e thinks we're going to eat all that,' May said over her shoulder.

'Is Tom alone for Christmas?' Violet asked. 'Perhaps you'd like to invite him over to help us get through the goose.'

'Would you mind?' May's eyes lit up. 'I thought you were none too keen on 'im.'

'Only because of him being our landlord. We haven't really had the chance to get to know him.'

'She wants to make sure he's good enough for you, May,' Eleanor said lightly.

'Ask him,' Violet repeated.

'I'll do that then,' May said. 'I'm glad I went out to buy some mistletoe.'

'You didn't!'

'Oh, I did. I'll put it up later. You don't mind, do you, Violet?' May gave her a sly smile, her eyes bright with humour.

Violet blushed. She looked down quickly to where Dickens was prowling around her ankles, twitching his whiskers and licking his lips.

'Where are we going to put this bird, so the cat doesn't get it?' she said. 'The range is already warm – it can't go in there.'

'You'll have to leave it upstairs in the bedroom and make sure the door is closed.' Eleanor gave her a meat plate to stand it on. 'It's freezing up there, so it'll keep all right until tomorrow.'

Violet took it upstairs and left it on the dressing table before returning to the embroidery, working with May until dusk fell and they couldn't see well enough to continue. Sometimes they worked by oil lamp into the night, but today Violet decided that they deserved a rest and time to prepare for the following day.

She lit the oil lamps and they cleared the workshop, packing everything away in boxes, and wrapping the pieces they were working on in clean sheets. Eleanor laid the table in advance while Violet arranged the chairs. May pinned the mistletoe above the kitchen door.

'It can't go there. It's in the way,' Eleanor said, looking up from where she'd started preparing the potatoes. 'Really, May, I can't have you and Tom all entangled with each other while I'm trying to get past with the gravy. I know that's what you do – you think I don't notice when you're kissing him out in the yard.'

'It don't matter – we'll soon be man and wife,' May said. 'We're goin' to see the vicar in the New Year. I want to do it properly.'

'Congratulations,' Violet said, hugging her. 'We'll have to make you a gown. Oh, but that means you'll be leaving us?'

'I'll only be moving next door. Don't worry – I'll still 'ave to work because Tom can't afford to keep me in the manner to which I'm becoming accustomed. I'll be 'appy to mind Joe as well. One day, I'll 'ave littl'uns of my own.'

'I think May is going to be disappointed. Isn't Tom too old to have children?' Eleanor asked Violet later when they had retired to bed, all their gifts wrapped and ready for Christmas, and the goose still on the dressing table.

'I don't think so.' Violet smiled. 'He isn't that ancient – forty, maybe.'

'He's at least fifty – May said so. It would be lovely for Joe to have company nearer his own age.'

'Well, we'll have to wait and see what happens. Now go to sleep. You're keeping me awake with all your fidgeting.' It was all very well, Violet thought, but she couldn't sleep either for looking forward to Christmas Day.

On hearing a cry, Violet opened her eyes.

'Hush, Joe. It's still dark,' she whispered, but he cried out again.

With a sigh of regret at having to leave the warmth of her bed, Violet got up, put on her slippers and a thick shawl over her gown, and went to pick him out of his crib.

'Come on, my darling. I'll take you downstairs.' She carried him into the kitchen where Dickens was lying curled up beside the range, making the most of the vestiges of its heat from the day before. 'The fire should be lit by now, or that goose will never be cooked. Eleanor,' she called.

Her sister appeared with a candle, looking bleary-eyed, and with her hair like a rat's nest.

'I'm sorry. I overslept. Leave this to me, Violet. I expect you couldn't sleep for thinking about our guest.'

'He hasn't crossed my mind,' Violet fibbed.

Later, when the kettle had boiled, she fed Joe on porridge and warm milk before dressing him in his best clothes.

She carried him down to the workshop and smiled as the aroma of oranges, cinnamon and hot grease filled her nostrils. May had laid holly with bright red berries across the mantelpiece above the fire which was alight in the grate, the cutlery was gleaming on the table and their gifts were piled up in the centre of the cloth.

'Let's go and see how Auntie Eleanor is getting on in the kitchen,' she said.

'Everything is under control – at least, I think so.' Eleanor was boiling the giblets in a pan and steaming the plum pudding in its muslin cloth. Everything was bubbling so fiercely that there was water trickling down the walls.

'Where's May?'

'Guess.'

'Oh, I see.'

'Did I 'ear someone takin' my name in vain?'

Violet turned to find May behind her, holding Tom Ward's hand and dragging him towards the mistletoe. Tom, looking rather sheepish, pecked at his beloved's cheek.

'Oh Tom, that isn't right. You 'ave to do it like this.' May grabbed him and planted a kiss on his lips, then, triumphant, she reached up, plucked one fat white berry from the mistletoe and put it aside. 'That's one kiss down, but there are plenty of berries to go.'

Violet thought that they should take it down, but she kept this to herself, guessing that she'd be teased to death if she mentioned it.

She went to answer a knock at the door.

'William, welcome!' she exclaimed.

'For you.' He handed her a small bouquet of holly and ivy.

Blushing, she thanked him. 'And thank you for the goose as well.'

'I hope it's big enough,' he said anxiously. 'The butcher deemed it would be.'

'There's enough there for two Christmases. Come in. I'll introduce you to Tom.' She took his coat and hat, and the two men shook hands before May offered them ale.

'You'll take us as you find us. I'm afraid it isn't what you're used to,' Violet said.

'It's delightful.' William smiled and her heart turned over. 'It reminds me of home.'

'I'm going to leave the goose to roast,' Eleanor said, joining them from the kitchen. 'Shall we play games or have a singsong while we wait?'

They sat around the fire. Joe sat on Violet's lap, facing her and holding her hands for balance.

'Christmas is coming, the goose is getting fat,' she began. 'Please put a penny in the old man's hat.' Eleanor and May took up the rhyme, 'If you haven't got a penny, a ha'penny will do. If you haven't got a ha'penny, God bless you.'

Joe grinned from ear to ear.

'How about "I Saw Three Ships"? Would Joe like that one?' William asked.

'We'll see,' Violet said, and the two of them started to sing.

'I saw three ships come sailing by on Christmas Day, on Christmas Day ...'

The others joined in, Tom revealing a surprisingly fine baritone voice.

After a few more songs and a game of charades, Eleanor went to check on the food.

'Oh dear,' she called out. 'The day's going to be all topsy turvy – the meat is nowhere nearly ready, but the potatoes are crisp and the carrots soggy.'

'Never mind,' Violet called back. 'We can have a vegetable course, then the goose.'

'I fear that we'll have to have pudding before the main.'

'We can wait,' William said. 'It will taste all the better for it. I have brought a gift for Joe – can I give it to him before dinner?'

Everyone was in agreement, and they moved to the table for sherry and ginger beer, and Violet handed out the gifts she'd put out earlier, while William fetched his from where he'd left his shoes on the mat just inside the door. They exchanged oranges, crisp Kent apples which had been stored since the autumn harvest, and handfuls of nuts. Violet put the knitted sweater that she'd bought for Joe over his head and slipped his arms through the sleeves.

'There, you look like a little sailor.' She smiled.

Violet gave Eleanor a length of red ribbon which she'd had her eye on at the haberdasher's, and May a strip of fancy buttons. She handed Tom a handkerchief on which she'd embroidered his initials the night before, not wanting him to feel left out. As for William, she hadn't known what to get him. What did you give a man who appeared to have everything he needed? A pipe or a smoking cap? As far as she knew, he didn't indulge in tobacco. If she gave him something expensive, it would seem vulgar, and anything cheap would appear insulting. She hoped she hadn't offended him by deciding not to give him more than an apple and some walnuts.

He handed her a box to give to Joe, but Joe didn't know what to do with it, seeming just as delighted with the box as whatever might be inside it.

'Look,' Violet said, lifting the corner of the lid. 'This is what you do with it.'

He pulled the lid off and looked inside and Violet helped him extract a wooden boat, a simple version of a steam packet, painted red and blue with a black funnel, from the tissue paper inside the box.

Joe took it and put it in his mouth. Violet gently exchanged it for a crust of dry bread and put the boat on the table.

'Chug, chug, chug.' She slid it across the cloth, and Joe grinned and bounced up and down on her knee. 'Thank you, William. That's the best thing you could have chosen for him.'

'I guessed he'd like it.' He smiled. 'I mean, he's probably too young to recognise that it's a boat, but my ma used to say that babies like bright colours.'

Joe looked on while the others played cards and draughts until half past four when the sun had set and the goose was finally ready. Eleanor carried the bird to the table, Tom carved and William handed out the plates.

'That's the best meat I've ever tasted,' May said, sounding a littled soused. 'It would make me very 'appy if I could have the parson's nose.'

'Of course you can,' Violet said, and Tom carved it off for her.

Eventually, they had had their fill, and Tom suggested that it was time he went home.

'It's been a monsterful day,' he said, 'but my back's beginning to give me gyp. I need a little lie-down.'

'I have one more surprise before the day is out.' William fetched a handful of Christmas crackers from his coat pocket, each one a twist of red paper tied at each end with gold thread. 'I'd heard that these were the latest fashion.' He handed them out – one each. 'I've put your names on them. I'm sorry, I didn't bring one for you, Tom. If I'd known in advance ...'

'Don't worry about it.' Tom grinned. 'I'll 'elp May with 'ers.' He and May pulled the first one – it popped, spilling sweets across the table.

'Oh, sugared almonds,' May said. 'My favourite.'

'I filled Joe's with raisins,' William said aside to Violet. 'I reckoned the nuts would be too hard for him to chew on.' Joe, sitting propped up in a box at the table, waved his cracker. William made a great show of puffing and heaving at it, but it wouldn't snap, and in the end he pulled it for him.

Joe started picking up the raisins and shoving them into his mouth.

'Your turn, Violet,' William said.

'You pull it with me.' The cracker snapped and the sugared almonds flew out, along with a piece of folded paper. 'For me?' She picked it up. 'This isn't some kind of game?'

'You'll have to read it to find out.' William's cheeks were pink and his eyes alight with expectation mixed with ... she wasn't sure. Was it fear?

She unfolded the paper and began to read the tiny handwriting.

Dear Violet,

When we spoke the other day, you gave me reason to hope. I love you with all my heart. Will you marry me?
There is no way of letting me down gently, so a simple yes or no will do.

Your affectionate friend,
William

'Oh!' She touched her throat as hot tears sprang to her eyes.

'Well?' he said softly.

'My answer is yes ...' She got up and he leaned across the table in an awkward embrace.

'You've made me the happiest man alive. Oh, let me come to you – I want to hold you in my arms, my darling.' He walked round to her and she flung her hands around his neck.

'You're getting married!' Eleanor squealed. 'Let me be the first to congratulate you.' She jumped up and hugged them, followed by May, who was determined to be the second to give them her best wishes.

Tom leapt like a mountain goat on to the table, making Violet wonder if he really had anything wrong with his back.

'A toast,' he shouted. 'There must be a toast. Everyone raise a glass to the happy couple. To Violet and William.'

'To you, my love,' William whispered in her ear, as May and Eleanor moved away to refresh their glasses. She reached up and stroked his cheek.

'The mistletoe's over there,' she heard May say. 'It would be a shame to waste it.'

As the hubbub went on around them, Violet took her fiancé's hand and led him to the kitchen doorway where she turned to face him. He placed his hands on her waist and, oblivious to anyone else – forgetting the past and not thinking about the future – Violet leaned up to receive his kiss. She was aware of the warmth in his eyes, the heat of his body and the sweet scent of his breath as he pressed his mouth to her cheek, then her lips.

'Ignore them,' he murmured at the sound of applause. He raised his eyes briefly. 'There are five berries left.'

'I'm not counting,' Violet giggled. 'When shall we get married?'

'As soon as we can,' he said. 'I feel as if I've waited for ever – I don't want to waste another minute without you at my side.'

Chapter Twenty-Six

Myrtle: A Symbol of Love

During the next few weeks, Violet, May and Eleanor were occupied with extra sewing, making new dresses for the weddings as well as keeping up with their orders. Eleanor wrote to Ottilie inviting her to Dover for the end of January when Violet would become Mrs William Noble on the same day as May wed Tom. Violet wrote separately to Miss Whiteway, asking her if she would consider acting as Joe's sponsor at his christening as well as attending her wedding. She wasn't sure if she would accept. She knew that she wouldn't decline out of prejudice, but she wasn't sure if her fiancé, Mr Fullagar, would be able to see past her reputation as a fallen woman with a child born out of wedlock.

William made the arrangements for the ceremonies to be held at St Paul's on Minnis Lane, sensitive to Violet's preference that she should marry anywhere but St Mary's.

On the morning of the chosen day, there was a knock on the workshop door.

'Can you go, Eleanor?' Violet said. 'I'm not quite ready.'

Eleanor was already hurrying down the stairs. She heard doors banging and the cat yowl – her sister must have tripped over him in her rush, Violet thought with a rueful smile. Poor Dickens.

'Ottilie! John! They are here! Violet, come down quickly!'

Violet checked her appearance in the mirror on the dressing table, picked Joe up from the cot she'd bought for him, and went to greet their guests, her heart tripping with excitement.

Ottilie was in the middle of the workshop, hugging Eleanor who was laughing and crying with joy. Violet joined them, throwing one arm around her sisters while Joe stared.

'It's wonderful to see you,' she cried. 'Be careful, Eleanor. She is with child.'

'Don't fuss – I'm fine,' Ottilie said. 'I have at least another month or two to go. Who is this darling little lad?'

'It's Joe, of course,' Eleanor said.

'Meet Auntie Ottilie,' Violet said to him as Ottilie reached out and touched the dimple in his chin, making him grin.

'Oh, he's adorable,' she said.

'We'll be looking after him today,' Eleanor said. 'You are still in your coat. Let me take it. Go through to the kitchen – there's a fire lit in there. We have tea or chocolate to warm you up.'

Violet turned to John who was standing aside, waiting for their exclamations to die down before he greeted them.

'Thank you for joining us,' she said. He looked very well with his hair cut short and his beard neatly trimmed, and wearing a black dress coat, white shirt and black doeskin trousers.

'It's a pleasure, sister-in-law.' He took her hand and pressed it to his lips. 'You make a beautiful bride, almost as beautiful as your sister,' he added with a wink at Ottilie. 'We will take tea, but we shouldn't dwell for too long. I believe I am giving you away in less than an hour.'

There was another knock at the door.

That can't be William or Tom – they know it's bad luck to see their brides before the wedding,' Eleanor said, frowning.

'I'll get it,' May said, bustling through the workshop and smoothing the lace on her gown at the same time. She pulled the door open. 'Who is it callin' at this time of day? Don't you know we're getting ready for not one but two weddin's and a christenin'?'

'Your carriages await, ma'am,' said the caller, a short, elderly man in green livery.

'We 'aven't ordered no carriages.' May frowned. 'We're walkin' up to St Paul's.'

'They've been 'ired by Mr Noble to carry the brides and their families to the church. I was told to be here at nine o'clock sharp. The 'orses will fidget and fret if you 'ang about for too long.'

'Carriages. How wonderful,' Violet said, touched by William's gesture. He'd thought of everything. 'Thank you, sir. We'll be with you in a few minutes.'

'Joe isn't dressed yet,' Eleanor said, panicking.

'His clothes are in a box, ready. We can take it with us and change him on the way,' Violet said.

'Our flowers,' May said. 'Where are they?'

'In the kitchen in a bucket,' Violet replied. Eleanor fetched Joe's christening robe and May collected the bouquets – Violet had a simple posy of myrtle sprigs tied with a ribbon of duck-egg blue to match her gown, while May had chosen rosemary, evergreens and pale pink silk roses.

'What about food for Joe and a toy to keep him occupied?' Eleanor said. 'And our coats – we need our coats today.'

Violet glanced through the window – the sky above the houses opposite was grey and dark, threatening rain or snow. 'Umbrellas too,' she added.

John sighed good-humouredly. 'I'll go and tell the coachman that we're nearly ready.'

The party arrived at the church as the bell tolled the hour. John and the footmen helped the ladies from the carriages before Violet and May were ushered into the church where they waited for the people who had joined them – Miss Whiteway and her fiancé, Mr Fullagar, Ottilie, Eleanor and Joe, William's cousin Mr Robert Lane, other relatives and his rowing crew, some of May's friends and distant family – to settle in the pews.

John offered Violet his arm as the organist began to play a joyful tune, Handel's 'Arrival of the Queen of Sheba'.

'I didn't realise there would be so many people,' she whispered.

'It's delightful, isn't it?' John said. 'Ours was much quieter.'

'But just as special, if not more so.'

He patted her hand. 'Let's walk. Your groom is waiting.'

When they reached the altar, she released his arm, turned to William and gazed at him through her veil. He smiled, the sight of him taking her breath away. How long had they waited for this day? As the vicar guided them through the ceremony and they said their vows, her mind went back to the regatta, how she had seen him wading from the boat towards the beach, his hands up in triumph. If she was being honest with herself, she had fallen in love with him then. With trembling hands, he slipped the ring on to her finger and they were, at last, man and wife.

They stood aside for the vicar to marry May and Tom before both couples went to the registry to sign the register, then returned to the church for the final part of the morning.

The vicar said a few words before inviting Eleanor to bring Joe to the font, followed by Miss Whiteway and

Mr Lane, then Violet and William. The guests gathered around the font as the sponsors took their places, Joe's godmother to the right and his godfather to the left. Violet's heart was in her mouth when Eleanor handed Joe over, worried that he would cry at seeing a stranger or that the vicar would drop him.

'Who is the sponsor for this child?' the vicar said as Joe tried to grab at his spectacles, and the two godparents inclined their heads.

They made their promises to guide and support Joe throughout his life before the vicar made the sign of the cross on his forehead then poured water from the font over his head, at which, after a moment of confusion, Joe smiled.

'I baptise you, Joseph Noble, in the name of the Father, and of the Son and of the Holy Spirit. Amen.'

'Amen,' Violet murmured. It was done. She felt William's hand rest lightly against her back and a tear trickle down her cheek. Not only had she married the love of her life, she had gained respectabilty for her precious son. Their son, she corrected herself, because William had taken him on as his own without question.

After the ceremonies, they met their guests – and May's – at the Shakespeare Hotel for the wedding breakfast and christening celebration, William having decided that the house at Athol Terrace was too small for comfort. Violet couldn't tear herself away from her new husband's side for any longer than to congratulate Mrs Ward on her marriage, and check that Joe was happy with Eleanor and Ottilie.

'Where is Eleanor?' she asked when she realised that John had taken Eleanor's place, saying that it was useful for him and Ottilie to practise caring for a little one. 'I asked her not to impose on you—'

'Be kind to her, Violet,' Ottilie scolded lightly. 'She's over there – I believe she's taken a fancy to Mr Lane, who's being most solicitous in swapping his piece of cake for hers. She has a sudden aching-tooth for marzipan.'

'And William's cousin. Oh dear.'

'What's wrong with that? He seems like a pleasant enough young man.'

'There's nothing wrong – it's just that it hadn't crossed my mind that Eleanor would start courting so soon.'

'She's seventeen.'

'I know, but I still think of her as our little sister. I'll be keeping a close eye on them.'

'I'm sure you will. I'm so proud of you, Violet. I don't know how you've managed it, but you've done well. Who would have dreamed that you would have ended up as a wife and mother, and running a workshop, after all you've been through?'

'It took luck, determination and' – she glanced towards William, who was helping one of his elderly aunts find her coat in readiness for leaving – ' the love of a good man.'

After the weddings and christening, they took one day off for Violet to move her belongings into the house at Athol Terrace and to settle Joe in the brand-new nursery on the top floor with its glorious views across the sea towards France. Eleanor came with them, but Dickens stayed at Oxenden Street to keep the place clear of vermin. May set up residence with her husband in the house next door to the workshop.

As Violet wished, she and May continued to work on their embroidery while Eleanor minded Joe and ran errands. Within a week, Violet realised that they couldn't manage the workload without taking on another needle-woman. She advertised for an experienced embroideress, and among the applicants, she found a suitable candidate by the name of Miss Devlin, who turned out to be the maid who had repaired her dress when Mr Brooke had stepped on it at the regatta ball.

Although she hadn't done much in the way of white-work before, she picked it up quickly, her needle flying in and out of the fabric with great speed and accuracy. The orders came rolling in, along with the money to pay the rent, wages and other costs, and it wasn't long before Violet had the satisfaction of changing her mind and returning to Mr Cove to redeem the Rayfields' jewellery, except for Arvin's ring. She left that behind.

Miss Whiteway's wedding dress was ready in time for March, and the three sisters and May had the pleasure of attending the ceremony and wedding breakfast. Mrs Fullagar then visited them after her honeymoon to thank them and order some embroidered linens, and most of all, see her godson. Violet felt rushed off her feet, and so was William, who was setting up a workshop of his own, developing prototype boilers, next to Sawyers Velocipede Manufactory in St James Street.

'It's a great success,' Eleanor said one day when she was pushing Joe's pram along by the sea on their way home from a long day's work. 'But don't you think – well, I don't like to ask this, but I wonder if you're trying to do too much. I mean, you see less of your husband than I expected. He's often home before us, and I can't help noticing that you're usually nodding off by nine in the evening. Is it any way to live?'

'I've been thinking much the same,' Violet said. 'It's all very well what Miss Whiteway used to say, about women having the freedom to work and bring up a family and be affectionate with their husbands, but there aren't enough hours in the day ... Something has to give, and I've made a decision – I'm going to take on two more ladies, which will leave me with time to manage the workshop.'

'Won't you miss the sewing?'

'I'll do some.' Violet smiled ruefully. 'I miss William – I should be with him when he's at home – and I should be making the most of the years I have with our son. I've been so preoccupied with making a success of the business, that I've forgotten what's important.'

'Like Pa did,' Eleanor said quietly.

'That's right. Although he loved us, he forgot to put his family first.'

That evening, after she had kissed Joe goodnight and Eleanor had retired to bed, Violet sat down on the chaise beside her husband. She leaned back and surveyed the parlour, newly decorated in creams and pale blues. There wasn't a splash of green in sight – she wouldn't have it in the house.

'William, I have something I'd like to discuss,' she said, and she began to explain her plan.

'Are you sure you want to do this?'

'I've been neglecting you and our marriage.' She felt the weight of his arm around her shoulders as he pulled her close and kissed her cheek.

'You've been doing your utmost to keep the workshop going. I don't blame you. You said you wanted to keep working and I respect you for that, but it's wearing you out.' He turned slightly and pressed his forehead against hers. She looked into his eyes.

'I can see right into your soul,' he murmured. 'I love you, my dear wife. You must do what makes you happy.'

From then on, she made more time for her family, ensuring that she spent the evenings and Saturdays and Sundays in William's company. By the middle of June, she had found a new routine.

'We should invite Ottilie to visit us again,' she suggested one evening. 'The sea air would do her good. What do you think?'

'I'm hardly going to refuse, am I?' William smiled. 'I know how much you're looking forward to seeing our new niece. Ottilie is well enough to travel now?'

Ottilie and her daughter had taken a chill soon after the birth and the doctor had said that it would be unwise for them to travel or receive visitors in case it was contagious. Violet and Eleanor had been disappointed and anxious, reassured only by Ottilie's regular correspondence. 'I'll write to her.'

William yawned.

'Oh dear, the passion is wearing off. You find me dull, I think.'

'Not at all,' he said with a grin. 'I was thinking of retiring.'

'So early,' she said archly, glancing at the clock. 'I wonder why you're so keen?'

'I'll tell you when we get to bed, my love.' He stood up and reached for her hand.

Two weeks later, on a hot summer's afternoon, they went for a walk in Connaught Park, strolling along the terraced lawns before heading down the hill away from the castle.

Violet spread a blanket out beneath one of the trees beside the artificial lake at the bottom. Ottilie sat down with her daughter, Patience, in her arms. She was three months old and a bonny child with blonde ringlets and blue eyes. Violet settled beside her older sister, brushing a beetle from her skirt.

'Thank you for putting us back in touch with John's mother,' Ottilie said, looking towards the water where her husband was standing with William, their attention focused on a model steamship that William had built – as much for himself as for Joe, Violet thought, amused. He'd taken great care over it, even making a wind-up propeller with an India rubber band. 'We've accepted her invitation to call on her and Uncle Edward – they're keen to mend fences so they can meet their granddaughter.'

'That's generous of you and John after what they did.'

'I want Patience to know her family.' Ottilie smiled. 'And if I'm honest, I want to show them how well my husband has done without his father's help and influence. I couldn't be more proud of him.'

'He couldn't have done it without you,' Violet pointed out.

'That's true. I hope that Eleanor will be as lucky as we are. Is she walking out with Robert Lane? She turned bright crimson when I asked her about him.'

'They're courting now, but I won't let them sit up together yet.'

'You sound just like Mama. You're right, though – Eleanor is very young.'

'I have to remind myself that she's only a year younger than I was when I met Mr Brooke.' Violet found that she could talk of him now without regret. 'Our little sister has barely written a word recently – she's finding romance more fascinating in real life than on the page.'

'Which is how it should be, don't you think?' Ottilie giggled. 'Look at our handsome husbands.'

John and William lifted the boat out of the water while Joe looked on with Eleanor, who was holding both his hands to help him walk.

'Pa,' Joe called. ''Oat.'

'He means his father's boat,' Violet said, recalling William's joy the first time Joe had called him Pa.

Joe bounced up and down and screamed, the frustration showing on his face because he wanted the boat put back on the water.

'Hush, have some decorum,' Violet said, worrying about what passers-by would think about her son making a scene.

'You sound like Mama again,' Ottilie said, laughter bubbling up in her throat.

'I do, don't I? Oh dear.'

'I do the same. I wish she was here to see her grandchildren. She'd be very proud.'

'Duck!' Joe pointed towards the lake.

Eleanor walked him down the sloping bank to the water where she handed him a piece of stale bread from the paper bag she'd brought with them. Joe put it straight into his mouth and chewed it.

'That was for the mother duck,' Eleanor said with a chuckle. 'Watch.' She threw a piece and the mother duck and one other rushed towards it, quacking and scrapping over it. Joe laughed, and Eleanor gave him another piece of bread. This time, he held it aloft and made a great effort to launch the bread towards the mother duck and her ducklings, but somehow managed to throw himself in with it.

Violet leapt up, hitched up her skirts and ran straight towards where her son was splashing about, coughing and crying in the water, but William got there first. He paddled across to Joe in his shoes and socks, scooped him up and carried him back to safety while the ducklings swam hurriedly away in a row behind their mother.

'Eleanor, what were you thinking, letting go of his hand?' Violet held out her arms.

'I'm sorry,' she said anxiously. 'Is he all right?'

'No harm done, although he's very soggy,' William grimaced and handed him over.

'Poor Joe.' Violet comforted him. 'Oh, William, look at your shoes.'

'They'll dry out – I'll stuff them with some newspaper when we get home. I think he's learned his lesson – he won't do it again.'

'His brother – or sister – might, though,' Violet said softly, so nobody else could hear.

William's eyebrows shot up behind his curls.

'Are you saying what I think you're saying?'

She nodded. 'I'm certain now. The baby quickened – I'm about four months gone. You're going to be a father twice over.'

He smiled. 'I can't wait.'

'It will be a while.'

'How long?'

'I've worked out that the baby will be born in November. William, don't you have any idea about these things?'

'No, but it doesn't matter because I have you to guide me.'

It felt right, she thought. They were equals as she'd hoped they would be, each supporting the other. She carried Joe back to the blanket and rejoined Ottilie. Eleanor sat down with them, a little upset that she and Joe had inadvertently frightened the ducks away. Violet used a handkerchief to wipe the dirt and weed from Joe's face and hands. She took off his sodden clothes and wrapped her shawl around him, making him look like a shepherd in a woollen tunic. He plonked himself down beside his cousin and stared at her.

'She's very pretty, isn't she?' Violet said as Patience reached out to pull his hair.

'No, darling,' Ottilie said, taking hold of her chubby wrist.

'Let's make a daisy chain,' Eleanor suggested to distract them. Ottilie handed Patience over to her and she took the two children on to the lawn to pick daisies.

'You are happy with William?' Ottilie said.

'He's everything I could wish for in a husband. What about you and John? You have no regrets?'

'None at all. John's doing very well – he has some regular clients and we're able to put money aside for a rainy day.'

'Would you consider returning to live in Dover?'

Ottilie shook her head. 'I consider Woolwich our home now, but we'll visit as often as we can, and you must come and stay with us.'

Violet gazed at their children, smiling in the sunshine with crowns of daisies on their heads, and she cast her mind back to the time when she had been at her lowest ebb, an unmarried mother with no money and mouths to feed. Miss Whiteway's order for her wedding dress had given Violet that tiny thimbleful of hope that their fortunes would take a turn for the better, and they had.

Life was better than ever, but she was realistic. There were bound to be times of struggle and darkness, but in the meantime, she would hold on to what she had: a loving husband, happy family and friends on whom she could rely.

Acknowledgements

I should like to thank Laura and everyone at MBA Literary Agents, and Cass and the team at Penguin Random House UK for their continuing enthusiasm and support.

Welcome to

Penny Street

where your favourite authors and stories live.

Meet casts of characters you'll never forget,
create memories you'll treasure forever,
and discover places that will stay with
you long after the last page.

Turn the page to step into the home of

EVIE GRACE

and discover more about

A Thimbleful of Hope...

Dear Reader,

I feel a little guilty for putting poor Violet and her sisters through hard times in *A Thimbleful of Hope*, but I did enjoy writing about them, and researching Dover's maritime heritage along the way.

I have fond memories of Kent – I was born in Whitstable on the coast, and I spent many happy times with my grandparents in Canterbury. One of my grandad's favourite pastimes was a drive to Dover to look out across the channel to France. We would watch the boats coming in and out of port before being treated to an ice-cream with a flake.

I also remember the thrill of spotting the iconic White Cliffs on the ferry on our way back from family holidays in Europe, knowing that we would soon be home – although on one particularly memorable journey, the ferry crashed into the dock with a huge bump which buckled the doors, so the cars couldn't be driven off. I'll never forget watching our bright yellow campervan dangling from a crane above the deck as it was lifted onto dry land.

The White Cliffs would have been a landmark for Victorian travellers too, and this inspired me to choose Dover as the setting for Violet's story. The town supported many different trades from shoemaking to shipbuilding, and there was quite a demand for embroidery for uniforms, gowns and household linens.

Influenced by the beautifully embroidered antimacassars and tablecloths that my grandmothers kept around their homes, and an exhibition of samplers that I saw last summer, I decided to include an embroidery theme, hoping that Violet would be able to stitch her life back together after it fell apart.

I hope you enjoyed reading Violet's story and came to love her as much as I did.

The research behind
A Thimbleful of Hope; discovering fatal Victorian fashions

A FATAL FASHION

I loved researching how Violet and her family would have lived in mid-nineteenth century Dover. It really helped me set the scene and describe their home and how they would have decorated accurately.

As I delved deeper into their world, I was intrigued by a snippet of information I found about the dangers of the colour green in Victorian times. As I investigated further, I discovered quite a story behind how industry put its interests before public health.

The Victorians were keen on using arsenic for various purposes – medicine, beauty, dyes for clothing and interior decoration, not to mention rat poison. It was also a handy agent for murder; a fatal dose of white arsenic – also known as the inheritor's powder – was almost impossible to detect in food and drink, and the symptoms were easily mistaken for those of common diseases.

Ladies pursued the ideal of feminine beauty of the time, which was described as the 'consumptive look' – that of a pale complexion. To this end, they ate wafers made from white arsenic mixed with chalk and vinegar. They received a double dose of arsenic if they chose to wear brilliant green dresses, and a triple whammy if they had their homes decorated with fashionable Scheele's green, which was first used in wallpapers back in 1778. The gentlemen were not immune to excesses of arsenic either – there are reports of men being poisoned by their green socks!

Arsenic is a horrible poison; its effects dependent on the dose and how long the person is exposed for. Over a short period, it can cause headaches, vomiting and diarrhoea, and at a high dose: convulsions, coma and death. If the person is exposed over longer periods of time, the signs can include Mees' lines – white lines across the fingernails – along with garlic breath and what is known as glove and stocking distribution of tingling and numbness. Eventually, it causes brain damage, heart disease and death.

Although physicians suspected a link between green wallpaper and illness, it wasn't easy to prove despite there being plenty of circumstantial evidence. For example, a dignitary visiting Buckingham Palace in 1879 complained of being unwell and suggested that it might be caused by arsenic in his room. Having left his quarters for a while, his symptoms improved, and Queen Victoria had all the green wallpaper removed, setting an example to her subjects.

Backed by physicians and the public, the National Board of Health raised the issue in Parliament in the 1880s, calling for a ban on products containing arsenic, but no action was taken. Industrialists, such as William Morris, renowned designer of patterned wallpapers – many of them green – refused to acknowledge that there was a problem, accusing the physicians of hysteria. There was speculation that this was because he had shares in his family's mining company, which coincidentally produced arsenic. There were others who also put commerce above the medical profession's concern for public health and thus, the poisoning continued.

In the late nineteenth century though, it was discovered that not only did people accidentally take in flakes of arsenic by mouth, they also inhaled them, as green wallpaper released a toxic arsenical gas. The public, now convinced of the dangers, started buying 'arsenic-free' products, and green dyes manufactured from pigments were developed.

Having found out about this story, I decided that Violet's family would have wanted to show off their wealth and status by going along with the fashion for Scheele's green, although I did feel a little mean inflicting the consequences of this on some of the poor long-suffering characters in *A Thimbleful of Hope*!

If you enjoyed *A Thimbleful of Hope*
and you're looking for a new book to read,
why not try my Maids of Kent trilogy?

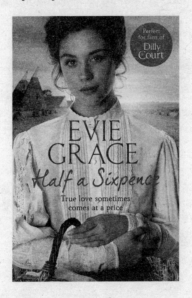

Turn the page to read an extract from
Half a Sixpence, the first book in the series...

Overshill, East Kent 1837

'Matty told me something terrible,' Catherine said, unable to keep her secret from her friend. She lowered her voice. 'I thought it was a dirty lie, but it's true. Promise me you won't say anything.'

'You know me – I'm no tell-tale,' Emily said quietly.

'Ma and Pa are not my true mother and father.'

'Oh, I see.'

'You don't seem surprised.'

'There's always bin rumours, but nobody takes any notice of them. Don't fret. It will all come out in the wash.' Emily smiled. 'Whatever that means.'

'Thank you.' Reassured that Matty hadn't told anyone else and thereby made her the talk of the village, Catherine caught his eye. He nodded, an unspoken understanding passing between them. She walked back in the direction of the farm and he followed, keeping a few paces behind until they reached the crossroads when he caught up with her.

'I'm sorry you had to see that. I don't know what's got into my brother. He's usually the calmest, most gentle person in the world.'

'He thought you were bothering me. He was only trying to do the right thing.'

'I suppose so.' Matty tried to smile.

'You look terrible.'

He pinched the bridge of his nose and looked down at the front of his shirt. When he spoke his voice was thick with blood.

'I look like I've killed a pig.'

'Come back to the farm – you can wash your face and borrow one of John's shirts. If your ma sees you like this it will make her ill. You can wait in the granary so no one sees you.'

'Are you sure?' He hesitated. 'I thought you hated me.'

'I did at first after what you said.' She softened. She had wronged Matty with her scorn. She had made him cry. 'I'm truly sorry for how I treated you. I hope you can forgive me.'

'It was my fault. I upset you. There's nothing to forgive,' he said. 'I should have kept my mouth shut.'

'In a way it's a relief to find out because it explains so many things that I've wondered about. Now I know why I'm the odd one out, why I have dark hair not blonde, like Young Thomas, John and Ivy.'

'It doesn't matter. You are beautiful,' he said quietly as they entered the farmyard.

She couldn't bring herself to look at him. What did he mean? What was he trying to say?

'Go and hide yourself. I'll fetch a shirt.'

It was dark inside the house, since everyone had retired to bed ready for another early start in the hop garden the next morning. She slipped in through the back and filled a dish with lukewarm water from the copper kettle. She sneaked out through the hall and up the stairs, avoiding the fifth step which would creak and give her away if she placed her foot on it. In the spare room, she opened the linen cupboard where she found a piece of soft muslin. She listened on the landing to check that she hadn't been discovered, but all she could hear was Ma snoring.

On her way out, she took one of John's crumpled but clean shirts from the scullery.

Matty was waiting for her in the granary, sitting in the heap of straw that had been left from when the men had laid down their flails to harvest the hops.

Catherine sat down beside him with the shirt and muslin over her arm and the bowl in her lap. She dabbed the end of the cloth in the water.

'This might hurt,' she said softly, turning to face him, her heart aflutter.

'It's all right. You make me brave.'

She touched the damp cloth to his lips. Slowly, she dabbed at the blood and wiped it away. She rinsed the cloth, squeezed it out and started again, cleaning the smears from his cheeks. She could hear his breathing quicken as she took his hands and dipped his fingers into the bowl, entangling them with hers as she washed the blood away. She wrung out the cloth again and dried his hands as best she could.

'There,' she said. 'Now you must change your shirt. You can leave yours here and I'll have a go at getting those stains out.'

'I don't want to get you into any kind of trouble.'

He was smiling. She could tell just from the tone of his voice.

She watched him unfasten the two buttons that held his shirt together.

'I'll mend that at the same time,' she said, pointing towards a rip in the sleeve.

Her breath caught in her throat as his hand rose and trapped hers. She could feel his roughened skin against her fingers and smell his musky scent.

'I haven't anything, any way of thanking you, apart from this,' he whispered. He leaned in close and planted the briefest of kisses on her lips. Trembling, she gazed into his eyes.

'Is that all?' she whispered. 'I reckon you owe me one more at least.'

'Really?' He pressed his mouth to hers. The contact sent her head spinning with joy and desire. She giggled. She'd never felt such happiness.

Eventually, he pulled away.

'Would you do me the honour of walking out with me?' He blundered on. 'If you aren't already spoken for. And Mr and Mrs Rook don't object.'

She held her fingers up to her lips.

'Hush, Matty. I'm not spoken for. Stephen has no claim on me. I'm sure Ma will have her say, but Pa favours your father so I don't think he'll have any objection.'

'You mustn't feel obliged. I don't want to ruin your life.'

'Why on earth would you do that?'

'I don't know. Sometimes when things are bad, I get this feeling of dread. I get this sense that I'm doomed.'

'Don't be silly. There's no reason why anything terrible should happen.'

'I know,' he sighed. 'So you will walk out with me?'

'Yes. Yes, of course.' She'd been caught off guard when Matty had asked her the day before, but with all the drama and tangled feelings since, she had realised how she needed him, and how the strength of her feelings weren't only friendship. She kissed him again. 'I have to go indoors now before anyone misses me. John sometimes wanders and it's my duty to send him back to bed. The last thing I need is for Ma to discover that I'm not in my room.'

'I could sit up all night with you.'

'I'll see you in the morning,' she said firmly, standing up and straightening her skirts. She picked up the dish, cloth and shirt.

'Thank you for everything. Remember that I would do anything for you in return.'

'You can show that by leaving when I ask,' she teased. She waved him away as he began to put on John's shirt, shooing him like she did with the hens, but he looked so sorrowful that she walked up to him, threw her arms around his neck and kissed him again.

'Be careful,' he said, 'more of that and I won't be able to tear myself away. When shall we meet again?'

'Tomorrow, but we must keep it from Ma and Pa for now.'

'I think that's very wise.' He grinned. 'Goodnight, Catherine.'

She wondered how long they would be able to keep their courtship secret and, when it did come out, whether Ma and Pa would approve. Did it matter? she thought as she retired to bed. Why was she worried about their opinion? They didn't have any right to say whom she could or couldn't walk out with when she wasn't their daughter, but she was still dependent on them and she had a conscience. It riled her that they'd kept the truth from her, but they had brought her up when they could have given her away. She had that, and more, to thank them for.

READ THE MAIDS
OF KENT TRILOGY

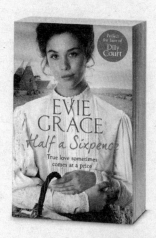

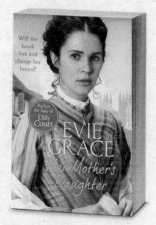

Hear more from

EVIE GRACE